EVEN GREATER MISTAKES

ALSO BY CHARLIE JANE ANDERS

All the Birds in the Sky
The City in the Middle of the Night
Six Months, Three Days, Five Others
Victories Greater Than Death
Never Say You Can't Survive

EVEN GREATER MISTAKES

CHARLIE JANE ANDERS

TOR

A TOM DOHERTY
ASSOCIATES BOOK
NEW YORK

EVEN GREATER MISTAKES

Copyright © 2021 by Charlie Jane Anders

A Tor Book
Published by Tom Doherty Associates
120 Broadway
New York, NY 10271

www.tor-forge.com

Tor® is a registered trademark of Macmillan Publishing Group, LLC.

Library of Congress Cataloging-in-Publication Data

Names: Anders, Charlie Jane, author.
Title: Even greater mistakes / Charlie Jane Anders.
Description: First Edition. | New York : Tor, Tom Doherty Associates Book, 2021. |
Identifiers: LCCN 2021033046 (print) | LCCN 2021033047 (ebook) |
    ISBN 9781250766502 (hardcover) | ISBN 9781250766519 (ebook)
Subjects: LCGFT: Short stories.
Classification: LCC PS3601.N428 E84 2021 (print) | LCC PS3601.N428
    (ebook) | DDC 813/.6—dc23
LC record available at https://lccn.loc.gov/2021033046
LC ebook record available at https://lccn.loc.gov/2021033047

Our books may be purchased in bulk for promotional, educational, or business use. Please contact your local bookseller or the Macmillan Corporate and Premium Sales Department at 1-800-221-7945, extension 5442, or by email at MacmillanSpecialMarkets@macmillan.com.

First Edition: November 2021

Printed in the United States of America

0 9 8 7 6 5 4 3 2 1

COPYRIGHT ACKNOWLEDGMENTS

"As Good as New" appeared on *Tor.com*, September 10, 2014.

"Rat Catcher's Yellows" appeared in *Press Start to Play*, edited by John Joseph Adams and Daniel H. Wilson, 2015.

"If You Take My Meaning" appeared on *Tor.com*, February 11, 2020.

"The Time Travel Club" appeared in *Asimov's Science Fiction*, October–November 2013.

"Six Months, Three Days" appeared on *Tor.com*, June 8, 2011.

"Love Might Be Too Strong a Word" appeared in *Lady Churchill's Rosebud Wristlet* no. 22, June 2008.

"Fairy Werewolf vs. Vampire Zombie" appeared in *Flurb* no. 11, Spring–Summer 2011.

"Ghost Champagne" appeared in *Uncanny Magazine*, July–August 2015.

"My Breath Is a Rudder" appeared in shorter form in *Instant City* no. 6, 2008.

"Power Couple" appeared in substantially different form in *Paraspheres: New Wave Fabulist Fiction*, edited by Ken E. Keegan and Rusty Morrison, 2006.

"Rock Manning Goes for Broke" was serialized in the Apocalypse Triptych of three anthologies edited by John Joseph Adams and Hugh Howey (*The End Is Nigh*, 2014; *The End Is Now*, 2014; and *The End Has Come*, 2015), and was subsequently published as a standalone book by Subterranean Press in 2018.

"Because Change Was the Ocean and We Lived by Her Mercy" appeared in *Drowned Worlds*, edited by Jonathan Strahan, 2015.

"Captain Roger in Heaven" appeared in *Catamaran Literary Reader* no. 14, 2016.

"Clover" appeared on *Tor.com*, October 25, 2016.

"This Is Why We Can't Have Nasty Things" appeared in ZYZZYVA no. 117, the "Bay Area Issue," Winter 2019.

"A Temporary Embarrassment in Spacetime" appeared in *Cosmic Powers*, edited by John Joseph Adams, 2017.

"Don't Press Charges and I Won't Sue" appeared in *Boston Review, Forum IV: Global Dystopias*, Fall 2017.

"The Bookstore at the End of America" appeared in *A People's Future of the United States*, edited by John Joseph Adams and Victor LaValle, 2019.

"The Visitmothers" appeared in *Trans-Galactic Bike Ride: Feminist Bicycle Science Fiction Stories of Transgender and Nonbinary Adventurers*, edited by Lydia Rogue, 2020.

For D. G. K. Goldberg—
the Queen of the Country Where They Sleep Till Noon

CONTENTS

INTRODUCTION

I swore I would never write a novel.

My first allegiance, my deepest loyalty, was to short fiction—the only species of confabulation that grants you total freedom to mess around. I was a natural short story writer who loved to explore a concept to the fullest in a few thousand words and then flit to the next tiny epic. Novels felt like such a serious commitment that I would never dare to try such headlong flights of fancy in them, and I had way more fun soaring (and occasionally crashing) through world after world, one story at a time.

After all, writing short fiction was the reason I'd bailed out of my first journalism career.

Years ago, I was working a soul-crushing job at a local newspaper, where I spent most of my time in a cubicle, freaking out into a telephone. My boss was an easygoing sadist who encouraged me to tell potential sources that I would lose my job if I didn't get a decent scoop soon. (He assured me I wouldn't be lying if I said that.)

I got home from work feeling both drained and freaked out, with no mental energy left for my own writing projects.

Every day at lunchtime, I haunted a newsstand with shelves full of science fiction digests, literary magazines, and other fiction mags. I read every kind of yarn there was and reveled in all the changes a skilled writer could take me through in just a few pages, and I daydreamed about seeing my name on one of those covers.

Then I discovered something that changed my life: a thudding great hardcover that listed every market that published science fiction and fantasy short stories, along with advice on how to break in. I sat in my cubicle, when I was supposed to be calling people and telling them about my precarious employment situation, and pored furtively over the introduction, which promised, "You can get rich writing science fiction and fantasy these days." I immediately quit the newspaper, took a much lower-stress day job, and started cranking out strange yarns with stars in my eyes.

In my first decade of writing short fiction, I racked up over six hundred rejections and published ninety-three stories, mostly in small markets that no longer exist. Not to mention, a few dozen of my stories never found a home. Every day, when I finished work in my lower-stress day job, I walked to the nearest Caribou Coffee, where I guzzled turtle mocha (the drink of champions!) and wrote the sickest fever-dreams I could imagine, full of space theologians, lesbian dung beetles, and disposable genitalia.

I toiled alone on those first ninety-three short stories, but I was always surrounded by friends and fellow travelers. I talked pretty much every day to my best friend and mentor, the late horror writer D. G. K. Goldberg: comparing notes, trading critiques, and commiserating over the latest form letter. I also joined a ton of writers' groups, read at open mics, haunted convention bars, and lurked on forums like SFF.net. The whole process of writing and selling short fiction became a shared experience, and whenever I made it into print, I got to bond with everyone else whose name appeared in the same TOC, or table of contents—we were "TOC-mates."

My rejections were a badge of honor. I kept a document with a careful record of where every story had already gone and which markets I hadn't tried lately, and I also noted which editors had written a personal response. At the bottom of that document, I wrote, "Rejections should be welcomed. There is nothing more joyful and optimistic than the act of putting a story in the mail, especially if that story has already come back once or twice." (Or, more often, a dozen times.)

Online, a bunch of us parsed rejection letters like the entrails of a freshly slaughtered goose. One magazine allegedly used various shades of paper stock, depending on how good your story was. Another editor was rumored to use different Word macros, and you could tell how much he'd liked your story by whether his response employed the word "sadly."

I made all kinds of bargains in my head with the universe: I would give up turtle mochas, I would stop jaywalking, if I could just get one story into a pro market—let alone one of the "year's best" anthologies. And my ultimate dream? Was that I would have a honking big book like the one you're looking at right now, made up of nothing but my own stories.

Writing short stories gave me tons of practice with beginnings and endings, not to mention world-building and character creation—but they also let me work with scores of editors, who collectively mentored and shaped me. I owe a huge debt to the crew at *Strange Horizons*, who published two of those ninety-three stories but also gave me feedback on countless others. Sometimes an editor would take the time to talk through why a story wasn't working, or offered me advice on how to remove some of my inevitable clutter and deadweight.

Not all of these interactions were fantastic, for sure. One lit-mag editor spent an hour on the phone giving me genuinely helpful thoughts about my story—mixed with transphobic observations about my main character.

Another lit-mag editor responded to a submission by saying that he only liked one sentence of my story. Would I take that one sentence, which was about a minor supporting character, and build a whole new story around it? I elected to think of this as a fun challenge, so eventually I produced a whole new story that contained that one sentence. The editor wrote back and said that he now liked two sentences: the one he'd originally liked, plus a new one. He asked me to write a third story from scratch, using those two sentences. After some hesitation, I went ahead and did so, and luckily, the third time was the charm.

At some point, I started reading slush for a few different magazines, and that was also invaluable training in how to think like the editors I was sending my work to. I found out the hard way that when you have hundreds of submissions to get through, you make a lot of snap judgments after the first couple pages, and it's on the writer to give the editor (and reader) a reason to keep reading. In one case, I volunteered for a magazine that had several crates full of unread subs, and I dug out a story that I had sent them a few years earlier. I reread my own piece, saw that it was completely wrong for the magazine, and had the dubious pleasure of sending myself a rejection letter.

Short stories are dangerous: tiny sparks of pure narrative fire that burn hotter because they snuff out sooner. Small, self-contained adventures gave me the freedom to fail—to push my limits, to experiment with styles and ideas that I wasn't sure I could pull off. And fail I did, over and over. I wrote scores of short pieces before I managed to turn out one that fired on all cylinders. The wonderful thing is, if you blow it with something short, you've only wasted a week or three of writing time. And if someone reads your story in a magazine and hates it, there'll be another story, by another author, on the next page.

That's the other thing I love: the flexibility. My stories have been published in a variety of genres, ranging from extremely highfalutin to the very lowest of the falutins. Plus, shorts can worm their way in anywhere. I've published fiction in:

- indie culture magazines that mostly published essays and articles;
- zines that were piled up in coffee shops and record stores;
- an Arizona adult newspaper (the kind that's mostly sex worker ads), which published non-smutty science fiction on its inside back page;
- humor magazines and books that mostly ran essays, cartoons and spoofs;
- small-press anthologies of horror, erotica, queer lit, and political rants;
- an anthology edited by my friend Daphne Gottlieb, entitled *Fucking Daphne*—full of metafictions about people having sex with a fictional character named Daphne Gottlieb;
- glossy food magazines that were mostly recipes and articles about cuisine trends; and
- journalistic outlets like *Slate*, *Technology Review*, and *Wired*.

Many of my stories were written, in part, so I'd have something to read aloud at spoken-word events, music festivals, beauty salons, and Pride stages. Also, some people were printing fiction on bags of fancy mail-order coffee beans, but I'm afraid they never accepted one of my microfictions.

It's one thing to pick up a fiction digest and read a bunch of short stories, but I always loved the idea that someone could be reading potty humor or kitchen advice or a serious article about politics and then turn the page and stumble on a little dollop of unreal writing. Fiction shines even brighter in mixed company.

Journalism taught me to be punchy and concise, and to turn a jumble of facts and self-serving statements into a true story. Erotica showed me how to establish characters quickly and find the emotional "hook" of a particular moment as soon as possible, because the sex wouldn't be fun if we didn't care about the characters. Literary fiction made me pay more attention to my use of language and to the small moments that make the big moments work. A hummingbird fickleness when it came to genre kept me growing as a short story writer.

These days, most of my stories start with "What if?" and end up with a different question: "Who am I to you?" My usual way into a story is to think of a zany scenario that I've never seen before, like "What if the world ended, and the last surviving person found a genie in a bottle?" I keep poking until this becomes a story about people, and then I strive to figure out who those people are, but also what they mean to each other. And how that meaning can shift from the first page to the last.

As you might have figured, I broke my vow and wrote some novels. But my early loyalty to shorter forms paid off, because the practice of producing a couple hundred tales increased my control and helped me get better at sticking the landing. Conversely, when I did write a bunch of novels, they strengthened my world-building muscles and forced me to spend more time developing the inner life of my characters.

The stories in this book reflect that whole journey: the rejections, the slush reading, the genre hopping—though only a handful of them were among my first ninety-three published works. In terms of style and genre, they're all over the place, ranging from gonzo comedy to quiet introspection. They all share that commitment I mentioned, to try to entertain from the very first sentence and give you a reason to keep reading past the first page. A whole book of short stories can be overwhelming, like imaginative speed dating. You have to keep starting over and meeting a new set of characters each time, and what if they just want to talk about stewed eggplant for the whole five minutes? So my fervent hope is that my long apprenticeship gave me the ability to serve up some reasonably fun dates.

After all, I never want to go back to cold-calling strangers and begging them to save me from unemployment.

EVEN GREATER MISTAKES

I sat in a darkened theater and listened to LeVar Burton—LeVar Burton!—reading "As Good as New" to a rapt audience, and I nearly melted into a fondue of imposter syndrome. Every one of my words seemed too feeble, too unworthy, to be spoken in Burton's honeyed voice, but the more I listened, the more I got swept up in his recitation and felt my story taking on a whole new life. I consider it a legit miracle I didn't split into two people.

"As Good as New" started with a neat idea about a genie who survives the apocalypse, but the whole shebang only clicked when I added another layer: Marisol's dilemma about medicine versus theatre, and her creative growth as a playwright. I love stories where people untangle a personal dilemma in the middle of struggling with bigger questions, because the contrasts of scale make the huge stuff feel even huger. This story's theme of clichés helping to destroy the world feels even more relevant now than it did several years ago.

AS GOOD AS NEW

Marisol got into an intense relationship with the people on *The Facts of Life*, to the point where Tootie and Mrs. Garrett became her imaginary best friends and she shared every last thought with them. She told Tootie about the rash she got from wearing the same bra every day for two years, and she had a long talk with Mrs. Garrett about her regrets that she hadn't said a proper good-bye to her best friend, Julie, and her on-again, off-again boyfriend, Rod, before they died along with everybody else.

The panic room had pretty much every TV show ever made on its massive hard drive, with multiple backup systems and a failproof generator, so there was nothing stopping Marisol from marathoning *The Facts of Life* for sixteen hours a day, starting over again with season one when she got to the end of the bedraggled final season. She also watched *Mad Men* and *The West Wing*. The media server also had tons of video of live theatre, but Marisol didn't watch that because it made her feel guilty. Not survivor guilt, failed playwright guilt.

Her last proper conversation with a living human had been an argument with Julie about Marisol's decision to go to medical school instead of trying to write more plays. ("Fuck doctors, man," Julie had spat. "People are going to die no matter what you do. Theatre is *important*.") Marisol had hung up on Julie and gone back to the pre-med books, staring at the exposed musculature and blood vessels as if they were costume designs for a skeleton theatre troupe.

The quakes always happened at the worst moment, just when Jo or Blair was about to reveal something heartfelt and serious. The whole panic room would shake, throwing Marisol against the padded walls or ceiling over and over again. A reminder that the rest of the world was probably dead. At first, these quakes were constant, then they happened a few times a day. Then once a day, then a few times a week. Then a few times a month. Marisol knew that once a month or two passed without the world going sideways, she would have to go out and investigate. She would have to leave her friends at the Eastland School and venture into a bleak world.

Sometimes Marisol thought she had a duty to stay in the panic room, since she was personally keeping the human race alive. But then she thought: What if there was someone else living, and they needed help? Marisol was pre-med, she might be able to do something. What if there was a reproductively viable person, and Marisol could help them repopulate the species?

The panic room had nice blue leather walls and a carpeted floor that felt nice to walk on, and enough gourmet frozen dinners to last Marisol a few lifetimes. She only had the pair of shoes she'd brought in there with her, and it would seem weird to wear shoes after two barefoot years. The real world was in here, in the panic room—out there was nothing but an afterimage of a bad trip.

Marisol was an award-winning playwright, but that hadn't saved her from the end of the world. She was taking pre-med classes and trying to get a scholarship to med school so she could give cancer screenings to poor women in her native Taos, but that didn't save her either. Nor did the fact that she believed in God every other day.

What actually saved Marisol from the end of the world was the fact that she took a job cleaning Burton Henstridge's mansion to help her through school, and she'd happened to be scrubbing his fancy Japanese toilet when the quakes had started—within easy reach of Burton's state-of-the-art panic room. (She had found the hidden opening mechanism some weeks earlier, while cleaning the porcelain cat figurines.) Burton himself was in Bulgaria, scouting a new location for a nanofabrication facility, and had died instantly.

When Marisol let herself think about all the people she could never talk to again, she got so choked up she wanted to punch someone in the eye until they saw stars forever. She experienced grief in the form of freak-outs that left her unable to breathe or think, and then she popped in another *Facts of Life*. As she watched, she chewed her nails until she was in danger of gnawing off her fingertips.

The door to the panic room wouldn't actually open, when Marisol finally decided it had been a couple months since the last quake and it was time to go the hell out there. She had to kick the door a few dozen times, until she dislodged enough of the debris blocking it to stagger out into the wasteland. The cold slapped her in the face and extremities, extra bitter after two years at room temperature. Burton's house was gone. The panic room was just a cube half-buried in the ruins, covered in some yellowy insulation that looked like it would burn your fingers.

Everything out there was white, like snow or paper, except powdery and brittle, ashen. She had a Geiger counter from the panic room, which read zero. She couldn't figure out what the hell had happened to the world, for a long time, until it hit her—this was fungus. Some kind of newly made, highly corrosive fungus that had rushed over everything like a tidal wave and consumed every last bit of organic material, then died. It had come in wave after wave, with incredible violence, until it had exhausted the last of its food supply and crushed everything to dust. She gleaned this from the consistency of the crud that had coated every bit of rubble, but also from the putrid sweet-and-sour smell that she could not stop smelling once she noticed it. She kept imagining that she saw the white powder starting to move, out of the corner of her eye, advancing toward her, but when she turned around there was nothing.

"The fungus would have all died out when there was nothing left for it to feed on," Marisol said aloud. "There's no way it could still be active." She tried to pretend some other person, an expert or something, had said that, and thus it was authoritative. The fungus was dead. It couldn't hurt her now.

Because if the fungus wasn't dead, then she was screwed—even if it didn't kill her, it would destroy the panic room and its contents. She hadn't been able to seal the room properly behind her without locking herself out.

"Hello?" Marisol kept yelling, out of practice at even trying to project her voice. "Anybody there? Anybody?"

She couldn't even make sense of the landscape. It was just blinding white, as far as she could see, with bits of blanched stonework jutting out. No way to discern streets or houses or cars or anything, because it had all been corroded or devoured.

She was about to go back to the panic room and hope it was still untouched, so she could eat another frozen lamb vindaloo and watch season three of *Mad Men*. Then she spotted something, a dot of color, a long way off in the pale ruins.

The bottle was a deep oaky green, like smoked glass, with a cork in it. About twenty yards away, perched in one of the endless piles of white debris. Somehow, it had avoided being consumed or rusted or broken in the endless waves of fungal devastation. This green bottle looked as though someone had just put it down a second ago—in fact, Marisol's first response was to yell "Hello?" even louder than before.

When there was no answer, she picked up the bottle. In her hands, it felt bumpy, like an embossed label had been worn away, and there didn't seem to be any liquid inside. She couldn't see its contents, if any. She removed the cork.

A *whoosh* broke the dead silence. A sparkly mist streamed out of the bottle's narrow mouth—glittering like the cheap glitter at the arts and crafts table at summer camp when Marisol was a little girl, misty like a smoke machine at a divey nightclub—and slowly resolved into a shape in front of Marisol. A man, a little taller than her and much bigger.

Marisol was so startled and grateful at no longer being alone, she almost didn't pause to wonder how this man had appeared out of nowhere after she opened a bottle. A bottle that had survived when everything else was crushed. Then she did start to wonder, but the only explanations seemed too ludicrous to believe.

"Hello and congratulations," the man said in a pleasant tone. He wore a cheap suit in a style that reminded Marisol somewhat of the *Mad Men* episodes she'd just been watching. His dark hair fell onto his high forehead in lank strands, and he had a heavy beard shadow. "Thank you for opening my bottle. I am pleased to offer you three wishes." Then he looked around, and his already dour expression worsened. "Oh, fuck," he said. "Not *again*."

"Wait," Marisol said. "You're a—you're a genie?"

"I hate that term," the man said. "I prefer 'wish facilitator.' And for your information, I used to be just a regular person. I was the theatre critic at *The New York Times* for six months in 1958, which I still think defines me much more than my current engagement does. I tried to bamboozle the wrong individual, so I got stuck in a bottle and forced to grant wishes to anyone who opens it."

"You were a theatre critic?" Marisol said. "I'm a playwright. I won a contest and had a play produced off-Broadway. Well, actually, I'm a pre-med student and I clean houses for money. But in my off-off-hours I'm a playwright, I guess."

"Oh," the man said. "Well, if you want me to tell you your plays are very good, then that will count as one of your three wishes. And honestly, I don't think you're going to benefit from good publicity very much in the current climate." He gestured around at the bleak white landscape around them. "My name was Richard Wolf, by the way."

"Marisol," she said. "Marisol Guzmán."

"Nice to meet you." He extended his hand but didn't actually try to shake hers. She wondered if she would go right through him. She was standing in a world of stinky chalk talking to a self-loathing genie. After two years alone in a box, that didn't even seem weird, really.

So this was it. Right? She could fix everything. She could make a wish and everything would be back the way it was. She could talk to Julie again and apologize for hanging up on her. She could see Rod and maybe figure out what they were to each other. She just had to say the words: "I wish." She started to speak, and then something Richard Wolf had said a moment earlier registered in her brain.

"Wait a minute," she said. "What did you mean, 'Not again'?"

"Oh, that." Richard Wolf swatted around his head with big hands, like he was trying to swat nonexistent insects. "I couldn't say. I mean, I can answer any question you want, but that counts as one of your wishes. There are rules."

"Oh," Marisol said. "Well, I don't want to waste a wish on a question. Not when I can figure this out on my own. You said 'Not again' the moment you saw all this. So this isn't the first time this has happened. Your bottle can probably survive anything. Right? Because it's magic."

The dark green bottle still had a heft to it, even after she'd released its contents. She threw it at a nearby rock a few times. Not a scratch.

"So," she said. "The world ends, your bottle doesn't get damaged. If even one person survives, they find your bottle. And the first thing they wish for? Is for the world not to have ended."

Richard Wolf shrugged, but he also sort of nodded at the same time, like he was confirming her hunch. His feet were see-through, she noticed. He was wearing wingtip shoes that looked scuffed to the point of being scarred.

"The first time was in 1962," he said. "The Cuban Missile Crisis, they called it afterward."

"This is *not* counting as one of my wishes, because I didn't ask a question," Marisol said.

"Fine, fine," Richard Wolf rolled his eyes. "I grew tired of listening to your harangue. When I was reviewing for the *Times*, I always tore into plays that had too many endless speeches. Your plays don't have a lot of monologues, do they? Fucking Brecht made everybody think three-page speeches were clever. Fucking Brecht."

"I didn't go in for too many monologues," Marisol said. "So. Someone finds your bottle, they wish for the apocalypse not to have happened, and then they probably make a second wish, to try and make sure it doesn't happen again. Except here we are, so it obviously didn't work the last time."

"I could not possibly comment," Richard Wolf said. "Although I should say that people get the wrong idea about people in my line of work—meaning wish facilitators, not theatre critics. People had the wrong idea when I was a theatre critic, too. They thought it was my job to promote the theatre, to put buns in seats, even for terrible plays. That was *not* my job at all."

"The theatre has been an endangered species for a long time," Marisol said, not without sympathy. She looked around the pasty white, yeast-scented deathscape. A world of Wonder Bread. "I mean, I get why people want criticism that is essentially cheerleading, even if that doesn't push anybody to do their best work."

"Well, if you think of theatre as some sort of *delicate flower* that needs to be kept protected in some sort of *hothouse*"—and at this point, Wolf was clearly reprising arguments he'd had over and over again when he was alive—"then you're going to end up with something that only the *faithful few* will appreciate, and you'll end up worsening the very marginalization that you're seeking to prevent."

Marisol was being very careful to avoid asking anything resembling a question, because she was probably going to need all three of her wishes. "I would guess that the job of a theatre critic is misunderstood in sort of the opposite way from the job of a genie," she said. "Everybody is afraid a theatre critic will be too brutally honest. But a genie . . ."

"Everybody thinks I'm out to swindle them!" Richard Wolf threw his hands in the air, thinking of all the tsuris he had endured. "When in fact it's always the client who can't express a wish in clear and straightforward terms. They always leave out crucial information. I do my best. It's like stage directions without any stage left or stage right. I interpret as best I can."

"Of course you do," Marisol said. This was all starting to creep her out, and her gratitude at having another person to talk to (who wasn't Mrs. Garrett) was getting driven out by her discomfort at standing in the bleach-white ruins of the world, kibbutzing about theatre criticism. She picked up the bottle from where it lay undamaged after hitting the rock, and found the cork.

"Wait a minute," Richard Wolf said. "You don't want to—"

He was sucked back inside the bottle before she finished putting the cork back in.

She reopened the bottle once she was back inside the panic room, with the door sealed from the inside, so nothing or nobody could get in. She watched three episodes of *The Facts of Life*, trying to get her equilibrium back, before she microwaved some sukiyaki and let Richard Wolf out again. He started the spiel over again about how he had to give her three wishes, then stopped and looked around.

"Huh." He sat and sort of floated an inch above the sofa. "Nice digs. Real calfskin on this sofa. Is this like a bunker?"

"I can't answer any of your questions," Marisol said, "or that counts as a wish you owe me."

"Don't be like that." Richard Wolf ruffled his two-tone lapels. "I'm just trying not to create any loopholes, because once there are loopholes it brings everybody grief in the end. Trust me, you wouldn't want the rules to be messy here." He rifled through the media collection until he found a copy of *Cat on a Hot Tin Roof*, which he made a big show of studying, until Marisol finally loaded it for him.

"This is better than I'd remembered," Richard Wolf said an hour later.

"Good to know," Marisol said. "I never got around to watching that one."

"I met Tennessee Williams, you know," Richard said. "He wasn't nearly as drunk as you might have thought."

"So here's what I figure. You do your level best to implement the wishes that people give you, to the letter," Marisol said. "So if someone says they want to make sure that a nuclear war never happens again, you do your best to make a nuclear war impossible. Maybe that change leads to some other catastrophe, and then the next person tries to make some wishes that prevent that thing from happening again. And on, and on. Until this."

"This is actually the longest conversation I've had since I became a wish facilitator." Richard crossed his leg, ankle over thigh. "Usually, it's just *whomp-bomp-a-lula*, three wishes, and I'm back in the bottle. So tell me about your prize-winning play. If you want. I mean, it's up to you."

Marisol told Richard about her play, which seemed like something an acquaintance of hers had written many lifetimes ago. "It was a one-act," she said, "about a man who is trying to break up with his girlfriend, but every time he's about to dump her she does something to remind him why he used to love her. So he hires a male escort to seduce her, instead, so she'll cheat on him and he can have a reason to break up with her."

Richard was giving her a blank expression, as though he couldn't trust himself to show a reaction.

"It's a comedy," Marisol explained.

"Sorry," Richard said. "It sounds awful. He hires a male prostitute to sleep with his girlfriend. It sounds . . . I just don't know what to say."

"Well, you were a theatre critic in the 1950s, right? I guess it was a different era."

"I don't think that's the problem," Richard said. "It just sounds sort of . . . misanthropic. Or actually woman-hating. With a slight veneer of irony. I don't know. Maybe that's the sort of thing everybody is into these days—or was into, before the world ended yet again. This is something like the fifth or sixth time the world has ended. I am losing count, to be quite honest."

Marisol was put out that this fossil was casting aspersions on her play— her *contest-winning* play, in fact. But the longer she kept him talking, the more clues he dropped, without costing her any wishes. So she bit her lip.

"So. There were half a dozen apocalypses," Marisol said. "And I guess each of them was caused by people trying to prevent the last one from happening again, by making wishes. So that white stuff out there. Some kind of bioengineered corrosive fungus, I thought—but maybe it was created to prevent some kind of climate-related disaster. It does seem awfully reflective of sunlight."

"Oh, yes, it reflects sunlight just wonderfully," Richard said. "The temperature of the planet is going to be dropping a lot in the next decade. No danger of global warming now."

"Ha," Marisol said. "And you claim you're just doing the most straightforward job possible. You're addicted to irony. You sat through too many Brecht plays, even though you claim to hate him. You probably loved Beckett as well."

"All right-thinking people love Beckett," said Richard. "So you had some *small* success as a playwright, and yet you're studying to be a doctor. Or you were, before this unfortunate business. Why not stick with the theatre?"

"Is that a question?" Marisol said. Richard started to backpedal, but then she answered him anyway. "I wanted to help people, really help people. Live theatre reaches fewer and fewer people all the time, especially brand-new plays by brand-new playwrights. It's getting to be like poetry, nobody reads poetry anymore. Meanwhile, poor people are dying of preventable cancers every day, back home in Taos. I couldn't fool myself that writing a play that twenty people saw would do as much good as screening a hundred people for cervical cancer."

Richard paused and looked her over. "You're a good person," he said. "I almost never get picked up by anyone who's actually not a terrible human being."

"It's all relative. My protagonist who hires a male escort to seduce his girlfriend considers himself a good person, too."

"Does it work? The male prostitute thing? Does she sleep with him?"

"Are you asking me a question?"

Wolf shrugged and rolled his eyes in that operatic way he did, which he'd probably practiced in the mirror. "I will owe you an extra wish. Sure. Why not. Does it work, with the gigolo?"

Marisol had to search her memory for a second, she had written that play in such a different frame of mind. "No. The boyfriend keeps feeding his accomplice lines to seduce his girlfriend via a Bluetooth earpiece—it's meant to be a postmodern *Cyrano de Bergerac*—and she figures it out and starts using the escort to screw with her boyfriend. In the end, the boyfriend and the sex worker get together because the boyfriend and the sex worker have seduced each other while flirting with the girlfriend."

Richard cringed on top of the sofa, with his face in his insubstantial hands. "That's terrible," he said. "I can't believe I gave you an extra wish, just to find that out."

"Wow, thanks. I can see why people hated you when you were a theatre critic."

"Sorry! I mean, maybe it was better on the stage, I bet you have a flair for dialogue. It just sounds so . . . hackneyed. I mean, postmodern *Cyrano de Bergerac*? I heard all about postmodernism from this one graduate student who opened my bottle in the early 1990s, and it sounded dreadful. If I wasn't already sort of dead, I would be slitting my wrists. You really did make a wise choice, becoming a doctor."

"Screw you." Marisol decided to raid the relatively tiny liquor cabinet in the panic room and pour herself a generous vodka. "You're the one who's been living in a bottle. So. All of this is your fault." She waved her hand, indicating the devastation outside the panic room. "You caused it all, with some excessively ironic wish granting."

"That's a very skewed construction of events. If the white sludge *was* caused by a wish that somebody made—and I'm not saying it was—then it's not my fault. It's the fault of the wisher."

"Okay," Marisol said. Richard drew to attention, thinking she was finally ready to make her first wish. Instead, she said, "I need to think," and put the cork back in the bottle.

Marisol watched a season and a half of *I Dream of Jeannie*, which did not help at all. She ate some delicious beef stroganoff and drank more vodka. She slept and watched TV and slept and drank coffee and ate an omelet. She had no circadian rhythm to speak of, anymore.

She had four wishes, and the overwhelming likelihood was that she would foul them up, and maybe next time there wouldn't be one person left alive to find the bottle and fix her mistake.

This was pretty much exactly like trying to cure a patient, Marisol realized. You give someone a medicine, which fixes their disease but causes deadly side effects. Or reduces the patient's resistance to other infections. You didn't just want to get rid of one pathogen, you wanted to help the patient reach homeostasis again. Except that the world was an infinitely more complex system than a single human being. Then again, making a big wish was like writing a play, with the entire human race as players. Bleh.

She could wish that the bioengineered fungus had never dissolved the world, but then she would be faced with whatever climate disaster the fungus had prevented. She could make a blanket wish that the world would be safe from global disasters for the next thousand years—and maybe unleash a millennium of stagnation. Or worse, depending on the slippery definition of "safe."

She guessed that wishing for a thousand wishes wouldn't work—in fact, that kind of shenanigans might be how Richard Wolf wound up where he was now.

The media server in the panic room had a bazillion movies and TV episodes about the monkey paw, the wishing ring, the magic fountain, the Faustian bargain, the djinn, the vengeance demon, and so on. So she had plenty of time to soak up the accumulated wisdom of the human race on the topic of making wishes, which amounted to a pile of clichés. Maybe she would have done more good as a playwright than as a doctor, after all—clichés were like plaque in the arteries of the imagination, they clogged our sense of what was possible. Maybe if enough people had worked to demolish clichés, the world wouldn't have ended.

Marisol and Richard sat and watched *The Facts of Life* together. Richard kept complaining and saying things like "This is worse than being trapped inside a bottle." But he also seemed to enjoy complaining about it.

"This show kept me marginally sane when I was the only person on earth," Marisol said. "I still can't wrap my mind around what happened to everyone else. So, you *are* conscious of the passage of time when you're inside the bottle." She was very careful to avoid phrasing anything as a question.

"It's very strange," Richard said. "When I'm in the bottle, it's like I'm in a sensory deprivation tank, except not particularly warm. I float, with no sense of who or where I am, but meanwhile another part of me is getting flashes of awareness of the world. I can't control them. I might be hyperaware of one ant carrying a single crumb up a stem of grass, for an eternity, or I might just have a vague sense of clouds over the ocean, or some old woman's aches and pains. It's like lucid dreaming, sort of."

"Shush," said Marisol. "This is the good part—Jo is about to lay some Brooklyn wisdom on these spoiled rich girls."

The episode ended, and another episode started right away. You take the good, you take the bad. Richard groaned loudly. "So what's your plan, if I may ask? You're just going to sit here and watch television for another few years." He snorted.

"I have no reason to hurry," Marisol said. "I can spend a decade coming up with the perfect wishes. I have tons of frozen dinners."

At last, she took pity on Richard and found a stash of PBS *American Playhouse* episodes on the media server, plus other random theatre stuff. Richard really liked Caryl Churchill but didn't care for Alan Ayckbourn. He hated Wendy Wasserstein. Eventually, Marisol put him back in his bottle again.

She started writing down possible draft wishes in one of the three blank journals that she'd found in a drawer. (Burton had probably expected to record his thoughts, if any, for posterity.) And then she started writing a brandnew play, instead. The first time she'd even tried, in a few years.

Her play was about a man—her protagonists were always men—who moves to the big city to become a librarian and winds up working for a strange old lady, tending her collection of dried-out leaves from every kind of tree in the world. Pedro is so shy, he can't even speak to more than two people, but so beautiful that everybody wants him to be a fashion model. He pays an optometrist to put drops in his eyes so he won't see the people photographing and lighting him when he models. Marisol had no clue how this play was going to end, but she felt a responsibility to finish it. That's what Mrs. Garrett would expect.

She was still stung by the idea that her prize-winning play was dumb, or worse yet, kind of misogynistic. She wished she had an actual copy of that play, so she could show it to Richard and he would realize her true genius. But she didn't wish that out loud, of course. Maybe this was the kick in the ass she needed to write a better play. A play that made sense of some of this mess.

"I've figured it out," she told Richard the next time she opened his bottle. "I've figured out what happened those other times. Someone finds your bottle after the apocalypse, and they get three wishes. So the first wish is to bring the world back and reverse the destruction. The second wish is to make sure it doesn't happen again. But then they still have one wish left. And that's the one where they do something stupid and selfish, like wishing for irresistible sex appeal."

"Or perfect hair," said Richard Wolf, doing his patented eye roll and air swat.

"Or unlimited wealth. Or fame."

"Or everlasting youth and beauty. Or the perfect lasagna recipe."

"They probably figured they deserved it." Marisol stared at the pages of scribbles in her hands. One set of diagrams mapping out her new, as-yet-unnamed play. A second set of diagrams trying to plan out the wish-making process, act by act. Her own scent clung to every surface in the panic room, the recirculated and purified air smelled like the inside of her own mouth. "I mean, they saved the world, right? So they've earned fame or sex or parties. Except that I bet that's where it all goes wrong."

"That's an interesting theory," said Wolf, arms folded and head tilted to one side, like he was physically restraining himself from expressing an opinion.

Marisol threw out almost every part of her play, except the part about her main character needing to be temporarily vision-impaired so he can model. That part seemed to speak to her, once she cleared away the clutter about the old woman and the leaves and stuff. Pedro stands, nearly nude, in a room full of people doing makeup and lighting and photography and catering and they're all blurs to him. He falls in love with one woman, but he only knows her voice, not her face. And he's afraid to ruin it by learning her name or seeing what she looks like.

By now, Marisol had confused the two processes in her mind. She kept thinking she would know what to wish for as soon as she finished writing her play. She labored over the first scene for a week before she had the nerve to show it to Richard, and he kept narrowing his eyes and breathing loudly through his nose as he read it. Then he said it was actually a promising start, actually not terrible at all.

The mystery woman phones Pedro up, and he recognizes her voice instantly. So now he has her phone number, and he agonizes about calling her. What's he afraid of, anyway? He decides his biggest fear is that he'll go out on a date with the woman and people will stare at the two of them. If the woman is as beautiful as Pedro, they'll stare because it's two beautiful people together. If she's plain-looking, they'll stare because they'll wonder what he sees in her. When Pedro eats out alone, he has a way of shrinking in on himself so nobody notices him, but he can't do that on a date.

At last Pedro calls her and they talk for hours. On stage, she is partially hidden from the audience, so they, too, can't see what the woman looks like.

"It's a theme in your work, hmmm?" Richard Wolf sniffed. "The hidden person, the flirting through a veil. The self-loathing narcissistic love affair."

"I guess so," Marisol said. "I'm interested in people who are seen, and people who see, and the female gaze, and whatever."

She finished the play, and then it occurred to her that if she made a wish that none of this stuff had happened, her new play could be unwritten as a result. When the time came to make her wishes, she rolled up the notebook and tucked it into the waistband of her sweatpants, hoping against hope that anything on her immediate person would be preserved when the world was rewritten.

In the end, Pedro agrees to meet the woman, Susanna, for a drink, but he gets some of the eye-dilating drops from his optometrist friend. He can't decide whether to put the drops in his eyes before the date—he's in the men's room at the bar where they're meeting, with the bottle in his hand, dithering—and then someone disturbs him and he accidentally drops the bottle in the toilet.

Susanna turns out to be pretty, not like a model but more distinctive. She has a memorable face, full of life, and she laughs a lot. Pedro stops feeling shy around her, and he discovers that if he looks into Susanna's eyes when he's doing his semi-nude modeling, he no longer needs the eyedrops to shut out the rest of the world.

"It's a corny ending," Marisol admitted. "But I like it."

Richard Wolf shrugged. "Anything is better than unearned ambivalence." Marisol decided that was a good review, coming from him.

Here's what Marisol wished:

1) I wish this apocalypse and all previous apocalypses had never happened, and that all previous wishes relating to the apocalypse had never been wished.

2) I wish that there was a slight alteration in the laws of probability as relating to apocalyptic scenarios, so that if, for example, an event threatening the survival of the human race has a 10 percent chance of happening, that 10 percent chance just never comes up, and yet this does not change anything else in the material world.

3) I wish that I, and my designated heirs, would keep possession of this

bottle, and would receive ample warning before any apocalyptic scenario comes up, so that we would have a chance to make the final wish.

She had all three wishes written neatly on a sheet of paper torn out of
the notebook, and Richard Wolf scrutinized it a couple times, scratching
his ear.

"That's it?" he said at last. "You do realize that I can make anything real.
Right? You could create a world of giant snails and tiny people. You could
make *The Facts of Life* the most popular TV show in the world for the next
thousand years—which would, incidentally, ensure the survival of the human race, since there would have to be somebody to keep watching *The
Facts of Life*. You could do anything."

Marisol shook her head. "The only way to make sure we don't end up
back here again is to keep it simple." And then, before she lost her nerve,
she picked up the sheet of paper where she'd written down her three wishes
and she read them aloud.

Everything went cheaply glittery around Marisol, and the panic room re-
shaped into the Infinite Ristretto, a trendy café that just happened to be
roughly the same size and shape as the panic room. The blue leather walls
turned to brown brick, with brass fixtures and posters for the legendary all-
nude productions of Mamet's *Oleanna* and Marsha Norman's *'night, Mother*.

All around Marisol, friends whose names she'd forgotten were hunched
over their laptops, publicly toiling over their confrontational one-woman
shows and chamber pieces. Her best friend Julia was in the middle of yelling at her, freckles almost washed out by her reddening face.

"Fuck doctors," Julia was shouting, loud enough to disrupt the whole room.
"Theatre is a direct intervention. It's like a cultural ambulance. Actors are
like paramedics. Playwrights are *surgeons*, man."

Marisol was still wearing Burton's stained business shirt and sweatpants,
but somehow she'd gotten a pair of flip-flops. The green bottle sat on the
rickety white table nearby. Queen was playing on the stereo, the scent of overpriced coffee was like the armpit of God.

Julia's harangue choked off in the middle, because Marisol was giving
her the biggest stage hug in the universe, crying into Julia's green-streaked
hair and thanking all her stars that they were here together. By now, everyone was staring at them, but Marisol didn't care. Something fluttery and
heavy fell out of the waistband of her sweatpants. A notebook.

"I have something amazing to tell you, Jools," Marisol breathed in Julia's ear. She wanted to ask if Biden was still president and the Cold War was still over and stuff, but she would find out soon enough, and this was more important. "Jools, I wrote a new play. It's all done, and it's going to change *everything*." Hyperbole was how Marisol and Julia and all their friends communicated. "Do you want to read it?"

"Are you seriously high?" Julia pulled away, and then saw the notebook on the floor between their feet. Curiosity took over, and she picked it up and started to read.

Marisol borrowed five bucks and got herself a pour-over while Julia sat, knees in her face, reading the play. Every few minutes, Julia glanced up and said, "Well, okay," in a grudging tone, as if Marisol might not be past saving after all.

aniel H. Wilson and John Joseph Adams asked me to contribute to an anthology of video game stories called *Press Start to Play*, and I spent several weeks working on a tale about the last surviving video game designers, trying to create a game in a dystopian hellworld. I had to keep excusing myself from the bar at World Fantasy because I had an overdue story to finish. At last I turned in "The Deliverables"—and realized that I loathed it. "The Deliverables" was everything I didn't want my writing to be anymore: superficially funny, smugly dull. Worst of all, that story wasn't *about* anything, and you could tell I'd forced myself to finish it.

I begged Daniel and John to allow me a mulligan, even though the deadline was long past. This time, I wrote about dementia, something that's afflicted too many of my loved ones, and the horror of watching someone lose themself right in front of you. "Rat Catcher's Yellows" just spilled out of me—taking a fraction of the time I had spent struggling to make "The Deliverables" happen. I learned an important lesson: sometimes it's best to admit something isn't working and take a step back.

RAT CATCHER'S YELLOWS

1

The plastic cat head is wearing an elaborate puffy crown, covered with bling. The cat's mouth opens to reveal a touch screen, but there's also a jack to plug in an elaborate mask that gives you a visor, along with nose plugs and earbuds for added sensory input. Holding this self-contained game system in my palms, I hate it and want to throw it out the open window of our beautiful faux Colonial row house, to be buried under the autumn mulch. I also feel a surge of hope, that maybe this really will make a difference. The cat is winking up at me.

Shary crouches in her favorite chair, the straight-backed Regency made of red-stained wood and lumpy blue upholstery. She's wearing jeans and a stained sweatshirt, one leg tucked under the other, and there's a kinetic promise in her taut leg that I know to be a lie. She looks as if she's about to spring out of that chair and ask me about the device in my hands, talk a mile a minute the way she used to. But she doesn't notice my brand-new purchase, and it's a crapshoot whether she even knows who I am today.

I poke the royal cat's tongue, and it gives a *yawp* through tiny speakers, then the screen lights up and asks for our Wi-Fi password. I give the cat what it wants and it starts updating and loading various firmware things. A picture of a fairy-tale castle appears with the logo: THE DIVINE RIGHT OF CATS. Then begins the hard work of customizing absolutely everything, which I want to do myself before I hand the thing off to Shary.

The whole time I'm inputting Shary's name and other info, I feel like a backstabbing bitch. Giving this childish game to my life partner, it's like I'm declaring that she's lost the right to be considered an adult. No matter that all the hip teens and twentysomethings are playing *Divine Right of Cats* right now. Or that everybody agrees this game is the absolute best thing for helping dementia patients hold on to some level of cognition, and it's especially good for people suffering from leptospirosis X, in particular. I'm doing this for Shary's good, because I believe she's still in there somewhere.

I make Shary's character as close to Shary as I can possibly make a cat wizard, who is the main adviser to the throne of the cat kingdom. (I decide that if Shary was a cat, she'd be an Abyssinian, because she's got that sandy-brown-haired sleekness, pointy face, and wiry energy.) Shary's monarch is a queen, not a king, and she's a proud tortoiseshell cat named Arabella IV. I get some input into the realm's makeup, including what the nobles on the Queen's Council are like. Some stuff is decided at random—like, Arabella's realm of Greater Felinia has a huge stretch of vineyards and some copper mines, neither of which I would have come up with.

Every detail I input into the game, I pack with relationship shout-outs and little details that only Shary would recognize, so the whole thing turns into a kind of bizarre love letter. For example, the tavern near the royal stables is the Puzzler's Retreat, which was the gray-walled dyke bar where Shary and I used to go dancing when we were both in grad school. The royal guards are Grace's Army of Stompification. And so on.

"Shary?" I say. She doesn't respond.

Before it mutated and started eating people's brain stems, before it became antibiotic resistant, the disease afflicting Shary used to be known as Rat Catcher's Yellows. It mostly affected animals, and in rare cases, humans. It's a close cousin of syphilis and Lyme, one that few people had even heard of ten years ago. In some people, it causes liver failure and agonizing joint pain, but Shary is one of the "lucky" ones who only have severe neurological problems, plus intermittent fatigue. She's only thirty-five years old.

"Shary?" I hold the cat head out to her, because it's ready to start accepting her commands, now that all the tricky setup is over with. Queen Arabella has a lot of issues that require her Royal Wizard's input. Already some of the other noble cats are plotting against the throne—especially those treacherous tuxedo cats!—and the vintners are threatening to go on strike. I put the cat head right in front of Shary's face and she shrugs.

Then she looks up, all at once lucid. "Grace? What the fuck is this shit? This looks like it's for a five-year-old."

"It's a game," I stammer. "It's supposed to be good for people with your . . . It's fun. You'll like it."

"What the fucking fuck?"

She throws it across the room. Lucidity is often accompanied by hostility, which is the kind of trade-off you start to accept at a certain point. I go and fetch it without a word, and luckily, the cat head is very durable.

"I thought we could do it together." I play the guilt card back at her. "I thought maybe this could be something we could actually share. You and me. Together. You know? Like a real couple."

"Okay, fine." She takes the cat head from me and squints at Queen Arabella's questions about the trade crisis with the neighboring duchy of meerkats. Queen Arabella asks what she should do, and Shary painstakingly types out, "why don't you go fuck yourself." But she erases it without hitting Send, and then instead picks an emissary from among the options already on the screen. Soon, Shary is sending trade representatives and labor negotiators to the four corners of Greater Felinia, and beyond.

2

After a few days, Shary stops complaining about how stupid *Divine Right of Cats* is and starts spending every moment poking at the plastic cat's face in her lap. I get her the optional add-on mask, which is (not surprisingly) the upper three-quarters of a cat face, and plug it in for her, then show her how to insert the nose plugs and earbuds.

Within a week after she starts playing, Shary's realm is already starting to crawl up the list of the one thousand most successful kingdoms—that is, she's already doing a better job of helping to run the realm of Felinia than the vast majority of people who are playing this game anywhere, according to god knows what metric.

More than that, Shary is forming relationships with these cats in their puffy-sleeve court outfits and lacy ruffs. In the real world, she can't remember where she lives, what year it is, who the president is, or how long she and I have been married. But she sits in her blue chair and mutters at the screen. "No you don't, Lord Hairballington. You try that shit, I will cut your fucking tail off."

She probably doesn't remember from day to day what's happened in the game, but that's why she's the adviser rather than the monarch—she just has to react, and the game remembers everything for her. And yet she fixates on weird details, and I've started hearing her talk in her sleep, in the middle of the night, about those fucking copper miners and how they better not try any shit because anybody can be replaced.

One morning I wake up and cold is leaking into the bed from where Shary pulled the covers back without bothering to tuck me back in. I walk out into the front room and don't see her at first, and worry she's just wandered off into the street by herself, which has been my nightmare for months now and the reason I got her RFIDed. But no, she's in the kitchen, shoving a toaster waffle in her mouth in between poking the cat face and cursing at Count Meesh, whom I named after the friend who introduced Shary and me in the first place. Apparently Count Meesh, who's a big fluffy Siberian cat, is hatching some schemes and needs to be taught a lesson.

After that, I start getting used to waking up alone, and going to bed alone. As long as Shary sleeps at least six hours a night, which she does, I figure it's probably okay. Her neurologist, Dr. Takamori, was the one who recommended the game in the first place, and she tells me it's healthy for Shary to be focused on something.

I should be happy this has worked as well as it has. Shary has that look on her face—what I can see of her face, under the cat mask—that I used to love watching when she was working on her diss. The lip chewing, the half-smile, when she was outsmarting the best minds in Melville studies. So what if Shary's main relationship is with these digital cats instead of me? She's relating to something, she's not just staring into space all day anymore.

I always thought she and I would take care of each other forever. I feel selfish for even feeling jealous of a stupid plastic cat face, with its quivery antennae for whiskers.

One day, after Shary has already been playing *Divine Right of Cats* for four or five hours, she looks up and points at me. "You," she says. "You there. Bring me tea."

"My name is Grace," I say. "I'm your wife."

"Whatever. Just bring me tea." Her face is unreadable, half terrifying cat smile, half frowning human mouth. "I'm busy. There's a crisis. We built a railroad, they broke it. Everything's going to shit." Then Shary looks down again at the cat screen, poking and cursing.

I bring her tea, with a little honey, the way she used to like it. She actually thanks me, although without looking up.

3

Shary gets an email. She gave me her email password around the same time I got power of attorney, and I promised to field any questions and consult her as much as I could. For a while, the emails were coming every day, from her former students and colleagues, and I would answer them to the best of my ability. Now it's been weeks since the last email that wasn't spam.

This one is from the Divine Righters, a group of *Divine Right of Cats* enthusiasts. They've noticed that Shary's realm is one of the most successful, and they want to invite Shary to some kind of tournament. Or convention. It's really not clear. Some kind of event where people will bring their king-doms and queendoms together and form alliances or go to war. The little plastic cat heads will interface somehow, in proximity to each other, instead of being more or less self-contained.

The plastic cat head already came with some kind of multiplayer mode, where you could connect via the internet, but I disabled it because the whole reason we were doing this was Shary's inability to communicate with other humans.

I delete the email without bothering to respond to it, but then another email appears the next day. They start coming every few hours, with subject lines like "Shary Please Join Us" and "Shary, we can't do it without you." I don't know whether to be pissed off or freaked out that someone is cyber-stalking my wife.

Then my phone rings. Mine, not hers. "Is this Grace?" a man asks.

"Who is this?" I say without answering his question first.

"My name is George Henderson. I'm from the Divine Righters. I'm really sorry to take up your time today, but we have been trying to reach your partner, Shary, on email and she hasn't answered, and we really want to get her to come to our convention."

"I'm afraid that won't be possible. Please leave us alone."

"This tournament has sponsorship from"—he names a bunch of companies I've never heard of—"and there are prizes. Plus, this is a chance to interface with other people who love the game as much as she obviously does."

I take a deep breath. Time to just come clean and end this pointless fucking conversation. We're standing in the kitchen, within earshot of where Shary is sitting on a duct-taped beanbag with her cat mask and her cat-face device, but she shows no sign of hearing me. I realize Shary is naked from the waist down and the windows are uncovered and the neighbors could easily see, and this is my fault.

"My wife can't go to your event," I say. "She is in no condition to 'interface' with anybody."

"We have facilities," says George. "And trained staff. We can handle—" Like he was expecting this to be the case. His voice is intended to sound reassuring, but it squicks me instead.

"Where the fuck do you get off harassing a sick woman?" I blurt into the phone, loudly enough that Shary looks up for a moment and regards me with her impassive cat eyes.

"Your wife isn't sick," George Henderson says. "She's . . . she's amazing. Could a sick person create one of the top one hundred kingdoms in the entire world? Could a sick woman get past the Great Temptation without breaking a sweat? Grace, your wife is just, just amazing."

The Great Temptation is what they call it when the nobles come to you, the Royal Wizard, and offer to support you in overthrowing the monarch. Because you've done such a good job of advising the monarch on running Greater Felinia, you might as well sit on the throne yourself, instead of that weak figurehead. This moment comes at different times for different players, and there's no right or wrong answer—you can continue to ace the game whether you sit on the throne or not, depending on other circumstances. Still, how you handle this moment is a huge test of your steadiness. Shary chose not to take the throne, but managed to make those scheming nobles feel good about her decision.

Neither George nor I have talked for a minute or so. I'm staring at my wife, whom nobody has called "amazing" in a long time. She's sitting there wearing a tank top and absolutely nothing else, and her legs twitch in a way that makes the whole thing even more obscene. Her tank top has a panoply of stains on it. I realize it's been a week since Shary has gotten my name right.

"Your wife is an intuitive genius," George says in my ear after the pause gets too agonizing on his end. "She makes connections that nobody else could make. She's utterly focused, and processing the game at a much deeper level than a normal brain ever could. It's not like Shary will be the only sufferer from Rat Catcher's Yellows at this convention, you know. There will be lots of others."

I cannot take this. I blurt something, whatever, and hang up on George Henderson. I brace myself for him to call back, but he doesn't. So I go find my wife some pants.

4

Shary hasn't spoken aloud in a couple of weeks now, not even anything about her game. She has less control over her bodily functions and is having bathroom "accidents" more often. I'm making her wear diapers. But her realm is massive, thriving, it's annexed the neighboring duchies.

When I look over her shoulder, the little cats in their Renaissance Europe outfits are no longer asking her simple questions about how to tax the copper mine—instead, they're saying things like, "But if the fundamental basis of governance is derived from external symbols of legitimacy, what gives those symbols their power in the first place?"

She doesn't tap on the screen at all, but still her answer appears somehow, as if through the power of her eyeblinks: "This is why we go on quests."

According to one of the readouts I see whisk by, Shary has forty-seven knights and assorted nobles out on quests right now, for various magical and religious objects as well as for rare minerals—and also a possible passage to the West, which would allow her trading vessels to avoid sailing past the Isle of Dogs.

She just hunches in her chair, frowning with her mouth while the big cat eyes and tiny nose look playful or fierce, depending on how the light hits them. I've started thinking of this as her face.

I drag her away from her chair and make her take a bath, because it's been a couple days, and while she's in there (she can still bathe herself, thank goodness) I examine the cat mask. I realize that I have no idea what is coming out of these nose plugs, even though I've had to refill the little reservoirs on the sides a couple times, from the bottles they sent. Neurotransmitters? Pheromones? Stimulants that keep her concentrating? I really have no clue. The chemicals don't smell of anything much.

I open my tablet and search for "divine right of cats," plus words like "sentience," "becoming self-aware," or "artificial intelligence." Soon I'm reading message boards in which people geek out about the idea that these cats are just too frickin smart for their own good, and they seem to be drawing something from the people they're interfacing with. The digital cats are learning a lot, in particular, about politics and about how human societies function.

On top of which, I find a slew of economics papers—because the cats have been solving problems, inside the various iterations of Greater Felinia, that economists have struggled with in the real world. Issues of scarcity and resource allocation, questions of how to make markets more frictionless. Things I barely grasp the intricacies of, with my doctorate in art history.

And all of the really mind-blowing breakthroughs in economics have come from cat kingdoms that were being managed by people who were afflicted with Rat Catcher's Yellows.

I guess I shouldn't be surprised that Shary is a prodigy, she was always the brilliant one of the two of us. Her nervous energy, her ability to get angry at dead scholars at three in the morning, the random scattering of notecards and papers all over the floor of our tiny grad student apartment—as if the floor were an extension of her overcharged brain.

It's been two weeks since she's spoken my name, and meanwhile my emergency sabbatical is running out. I can't really afford to blow off teaching, since I'm not tenure track or anything. I'll have to hire someone to look after Shary, or get her into day care or a group home. She won't know the difference between me or someone else looking after her at this point, anyway.

A couple days after my conversation with George Henderson, I look over Shary's shoulder and things jump out at me. All the relationship touchstones that I embedded in the game when I customized it for her are still in there, but they've gotten weirdly emphasized by her gameplay, like her cats spend an inordinate amount of time at the Puzzler's Retreat. But also, she's added new stuff. Incidents I had forgotten are coming up as geological features of her Greater Felinia, hillocks and cliffs.

Shary is reliving all of the moments we spent together, through the prism of these cats and their stupid politics. The time we rode bikes across Europe. The time we took up Lindy-Hopping and I broke my ankle. The time I cheated on Shary and thought I got away with it, until now. The necklace she never told me she wanted, that I tracked down for her. It's all in there, woven throughout this game.

I call George Henderson back. "Okay, fine," I say without saying hello first. "We'll go to your convention, tournament, whatever. Just tell us where and when."

5

I sort of expected that a lot of people at the "convention" would have RCY, after the way George Henderson talked about the disease. But in fact it seems as though *every* player here has it. Either because you can't become a power player of Divine Right without the unique mind state of people with Rat Catcher's Yellows or because that's whom they were able to strong-arm into signing up.

"Here" is a tiny convention hotel in Orlando, with fuzzy bulletin boards that mention recent meetings of insurance adjusters and auto parts distributors. We're a few miles from Disney World, but near us is nothing but strip malls and strip clubs, and one sad-looking Arby's. We get served continental breakfast, clammy individually wrapped sandwiches, and steamer trays full of stroganoff every day.

The first day, we all mill around for an hour, with me trying to stick close to Shary on her first trip out of New Hampshire in ages. Then George Henderson (a chunky white guy with graying curly hair and an 8-bit T-shirt) stands up at the front and announces that all the players are going into the adjoining ballroom, and the "friends and loved ones" will stay in here. We can see our partners and friends through an opening in the temporary wall bisecting the hotel ballroom, but they're in their own world, sitting at long rows of tables with their cat faces on.

Those of us left in the "friends and family" room are all sorts of people, but the one thing uniting all of us is a pall of weariness. At least half the spouses or friends immediately announce they're going out shopping, or to Disney World. The other half mostly just sit there, watching their loved ones play, as if they're worried someone's going to get kidnapped.

This half-ballroom has a sickly sweet milk smell clinging to the ornate cheap carpet and the vinyl walls. I get used to it, and then it hits me again whenever I've just stepped outside or gone to the bathroom.

After an hour, I risk wandering over to the "players" room and look over Shary's shoulder. Queen Arabella is furiously negotiating trade agreements and sending threats of force to the other cat kingdoms that have become her neighbors.

Because all of the realms in this game are called Greater Felinia by default, Shary needed to come up with a new name for Arabella's country. She's renamed it Graceland. I stare at the name, then at Shary, who shows no sign of being aware of my presence.

"I will defend the territorial integrity of Graceland to the last cat," Shary writes.

Judy is a young graphic designer from Toronto, with long black hair braided in the back and an eager, narrow face. She's sitting alone in the "friends and loved ones" room, until I ask if I can sit at her little table. Turns out Judy is here with her boyfriend of two years, Stefan, who got infected with Rat Catcher's Yellows when they'd only been together a year. Stefan is a superstar in the Divine Right community.

"I have this theory that it's all one compound organism," says Judy. "The leptospirosis X, the people, the digital cats. Or at least, it's one system. Sort of like real-life cats that infect their owners with *Toxoplasma gondii*, which turns the owners into bigger cat lovers."

"Huh." I stare out through the gap in the ballroom wall, at the rows of people in cat masks, all tapping away on their separate devices, like a soft rain. All genders, all ages, all sizes, wearing tracksuits or business casual white-collar outfits. The masks bob up and down, almost in unison. Unblinking and wide-eyed, governing machines.

At first, Judy and I just bond over our stories of taking care of someone who barely recognizes us but keeps obsessively nation-building at all hours. We turn out to have a lot else in common, including an interest in pre-Raphaelite art and a lot of the same books.

The third day rolls around, and our flight back up to New Hampshire is that afternoon. I watch Shary hunched over her cat head, with Judy's boyfriend sitting a few seats away, and my heart begins to sink. I imagine bundling Shary out of here, getting her to the airport and onto the plane, and then unpacking her stuff back at the house while she goes right back to her game. Days and days of cat-faced blankness ahead, forever. This trip has been some kind of turning point for Shary and the others, but for me, nothing will have changed.

I'm starting to feel sorry for myself with a whole new intensity, when Judy pokes me. "Hey. We need to stay in touch, you know."

I make a big show of adding her number to my phone, and then without even thinking, say: "Do you want to come stay with us? We have a whole spare bedroom with its own bathroom and stuff."

Judy doesn't say anything for a few moments. She stares at her boyfriend (who's sitting a few seats away from Shary) and takes slow, controlled breaths through closed teeth. Then she slumps a little, in an abortive shrug. "Yes. Yes, please. That would be great. Thank you."

I sit with Judy and watch dozens of people in cat masks, sitting shoulder to shoulder without looking at each other. I have a pang of wishing I could just go live in Graceland, a place of which I am already a vassal in every way that matters. But also I feel weirdly proud, and terrified out of my mind. I have no choice but to believe this game matters, the cat politics is important, keeping Lord Hairballington in his place is a vital concern to everyone, or else I will just go straight-up out of my head.

For a moment, I think Shary looks up from the cat head in her hands and gives me a wicked smile of recognition, behind her opaque plastic gaze. I feel so much love in that moment, it's almost unbearable.

Alyssa wouldn't quit my head. I had handed in my second genre novel, *The City in the Middle of the Night*, which ends with a smuggler named Alyssa getting her first glimpse of the eponymous metropolis. (Here's a good place to tell you that if you don't want spoilers for *City in the Middle*, you'd best flip to the next story now. Though I'm sure you could read "If You Take My Meaning" first and then treat the book as an extended prequel, and that would be just fine.) The final image of Alyssa's shining eyes felt like the perfect place to leave things in the book, but I kept wondering what would happen next. What would that vision drive Alyssa to do? "If You Take My Meaning" tied up a few other loose ends, but also raised some brand-new questions which were fun to explore.

IF YOU TAKE MY MEANING

They woke up stuck together again, still halfway in a shared dream, as the city blared to life around them. The warm air tasted of yeast, from their bodies and from the bakery downstairs.

Mouth lay on one side of Sophie, with Alyssa on the other, sprawled on top of a pile of blankets and quilted pads. Alyssa couldn't get used to sleeping in a bedpile out in the open, after spending half her life in a nook—but Sophie insisted that's how everybody did things here. Sophie herself hadn't slept in a bedpile for ages, since she went away to school, but it was how she'd been raised.

"I guess it's almost time to go," Sophie whispered, with a reluctance that Alyssa could feel in her own core.

"Yeah," Alyssa muttered. "Can't keep putting it off."

Sophie peeled her tendrils off Mouth and Alyssa carefully, so Alyssa felt as if she was waking up a second time. One moment, Alyssa had a second heart inside her heart, an extra stream of chatter running under the surface of her thoughts. Then it was gone, and Alyssa was just one person again. Like the room got colder, even though the shutters were opening to let in the half-light.

Alyssa let out a low involuntary groan. Her bones creaked, and her right arm had gone half numb from being slept on.

"You don't have to," Sophie whispered. "If you don't . . . if you'd rather hold off."

Alyssa didn't answer, because she didn't know what to say.

Mouth laughed. "You know Alyssa. Her mind don't change." Mouth's voice was light, but with a faint growl, like she wished Alyssa *would* change her mind, and stay.

The tendrils grew out of the flat of Sophie's rib cage, above her breasts, and they were surrounded by an oval of slightly darker skin, with a reddish tint, like a burn that hadn't healed all the way (just a few inches upward and to the left, Sophie's shoulder had an actual burn scar). Someone might mistake the tendrils for strange ornaments, or a family of separate creatures nesting on Sophie's flesh, until they saw how the tendrils grew out of her, and the way she controlled their motion.

Whenever Alyssa's bare skin made contact with that part of Sophie's body, she could experience Sophie's thoughts, or her memories. Whatever Sophie wanted to lay open to her. But when the three of them slept in this pile, Sophie didn't share anything in particular. Just dream slices, or half-thoughts. Mouth still couldn't open herself up to the full communication with Sophie most of the time, but she'd taken to the sleep sharing.

All three of them had their own brand of terrifying dreams, but they'd gotten better at soothing each other through the worst.

"So that's it." Mouth was already pulling on her linen shift and coarse muslin pants, and groping for her poncho. "You're going up that mountain, and the next time we see you, you'll . . . you'll be like Sophie. The two of you will be able to carry on whole conversations without once making a sound."

Mouth looked away, but not before Alyssa caught sight of the anxiety on her face. Alyssa could remember when she used to have to guess at what the fuck Mouth was thinking, but that was a long time ago.

Sophie noticed, too, and she sat up, still in her nightclothes. "You don't ever have to worry about a thing." Sophie's voice was so quiet, Alyssa had to lean closer to hear. "No matter what happens, after all we've been through, the three of us are in this together."

"Yeah," Alyssa said, punching Mouth's arm with only a couple knuckles. "No amount of alien grafts are going to mess up our situation."

"Yeah, I know, I know, it's just . . ." Mouth laughed and shook her head, like this was a silly thing to worry about. "It's just, the two of you will have this whole other language. I'll be able to listen but not talk. I wish I could go through that whole transformation, but that's not *me*. I need to keep what's in my head inside my head. I just . . . I want you both to fulfill your potential. I don't want to be holding the two of you back."

Alyssa leaned her head on Mouth's left shoulder, and Sophie's head rested on the right. "You speak to us in all the ways that matter," Sophie said.

"It's true," Alyssa said. "You already tell us everything we ever need to know."

Alyssa had grown up with romances, all about princes, duels, secret meetings, courtships, first kisses, and last trysts. She'd have said that real life could never be half as romantic as all those doomed lovers and secret vows . . . except now, those stories seemed cheap and flimsy compared to the love she'd found, here in this tiny room.

For a moment, Alyssa wanted to call the whole thing off. Climb the Old Mother later, maybe just go back to bed. Then she shook it off and pulled on her boots.

"It's time."

Alyssa had handled all kinds of rough terrain in her smuggler days. She'd even gone into the night without any protective gear one time. So she figured the Old Mother would be nothing. But by the time she got halfway up, her hamstrings started to throb and her thighs were spasming. Next to her, Mouth spat out little grunts of exhaustion. Only Sophie seemed to enjoy pulling herself up from handhold to handhold.

"Shit shit shit. How the fuck did you ever get used to climbing this beast?" Alyssa wheezed.

Sophie just rolled her shoulders. And mumbled, "It wasn't a choice at first."

Behind them, Xiosphant had gone dark and still, just a valley of craggy shapes without highlights. Except for one light blaring from the top of the Palace, where the Vice Regent could never bring herself to obey the same shutters-up rule that all of her people lived by. Alyssa didn't want to risk falling, so she only half turned, for an instant, to see the storm damage, still unrepaired. And the piles of debris, where the fighting between the Vice Regent's forces and the new Uprising had briefly escalated to heavy cannon fire.

Everyone knew Bianca couldn't last as Vice Regent, but they had no notion whether she would hold on for a few more sleeps, or half a lifetime. Alyssa tried to avoid mentioning her name, even though her face was impossible to avoid, because Sophie still nursed some complicated regrets and Mouth still felt guilty for helping to lead Bianca down a thorny path. Alyssa was the only one in their little family with clear-cut feelings about the Vice Regent: pure, invigorating hatred.

Alyssa wanted to stop and rest midclimb, but the cruel slope of the Old Mother included no convenient resting places, especially for three people. It would be a shitty irony if they almost reached the top but slipped and fell to their deaths because they wanted to take a breather. The air felt colder and thinner, and Alyssa's hard-won aplomb was being severely tested.

"My fingers are bleeding," Mouth groaned. "Why didn't you mention our fingers would bleed?"

Sophie didn't answer.

They reached the top, which also formed the outer boundary of nothing. Ahead of Alyssa were no sights, no smells (because her nose got numb), and no sensations (because her skin was wrapped in every warm thing she could find). No sound but a crashing wind, which turned into subtle, terrible music after a while.

Alyssa's mother and uncles had sent her off to the Absolutists' grammar school back home in Argelo, when she was old enough to walk and read. That was her earliest distinct memory: her mom holding one of her hands and her Uncle Grant holding the other, marching her down around the bend in the gravel back road to the front gate where the school convened at regular intervals. That moment rushed back into her head now, as Sophie and Mouth fussed over her and prepared to send her away to another kind of school.

Mouth was pressing a satchel into Alyssa's hands. "I got as many of those parallelogram cakes as I could fit into a bag. Plus these salt buns, that taste kind of like cactus-pork crisps. There are a few of your favorite romances tucked in, too."

"Thank you." Alyssa wrapped her arms around Mouth's neck. She couldn't tell if her eyes stung due to tears or the wind, or both. "I'll be back soon. Don't let Sophie take any more foolish risks."

"I'll do my best," Mouth said. "Say hi to the Gelet from me. And tell them . . ." She paused. "You know what? Just 'hi' is plenty."

Then Sophie was hugging Alyssa. "I can't get over how brave you are. You're the first person ever to visit this city knowing exactly what's going to happen."

"Oh shut up." Alyssa was definitely starting to cry.

"I mean it. Your example is going to inspire a lot more people to go there. I think Mustache Bob is close to being ready." Sophie choked on the mountain air. "Come back safe. We need you. I love you."

"I love you too. Both of you." Alyssa started to say something else, but a massive, dark shell was rising out of the darkness on the far side of the mountain. "Shit. I need to go."

Alyssa let go of Sophie, clutching the satchel, and gave Mouth one last smile, then turned to face the writhing tentacles of the nearest Gelet. These two slippery ropes of flesh groped the air, reaching out to her.

As soon as they swathed Alyssa in woven moss and lifted her in their tentacles, she freaked out. She couldn't move, couldn't escape, couldn't even breathe. Her inner ear could not truck with this rapid descent down a sheer cliff, and somehow she wasn't ready for this disorientation, even though she'd talked through it with Sophie over and over. Alyssa wanted to yell that she'd changed her mind, this was a mistake, she wanted to go back to her family. But the Gelet would never understand, even if she could make herself heard.

She kept going down and down. Alyssa tried to tell herself this was just like being inside the Resourceful Couriers' sleep nook next to Mouth, except that she was alone, and she couldn't just pop out if she wanted to pee or stretch or anything. She held herself rigid as long as she could, and then she snapped—she thrashed and screamed, twisting her body until her spine wrenched.

A random memory popped up in Alyssa's head: huddling with the other Chancers in the hot gloom of a low-ceilinged basement on the day side of Argelo, after the Widehome job had gone flipside. (Because they'd burned down the wrong part of the building.) Lucas had squatted next to Alyssa, listing chemical formulas in a low voice, his usual anxiety strategy, and Wendy had fidgeted without making any sound. Every bump and croak above their heads instantly became, in Alyssa's mind, the Jamersons coming to murder them for what they'd done. This was the most terrified Alyssa had ever been, or probably ever would be, but also the closest she'd ever felt to anybody. These people were her indivisible comrades, any of them would die for the others, they were safe together in horrible danger.

Alyssa would always look back on that time in her life as the ideal, the best, the moment when she had a hope-to-die crew by her side, even though she could see all the flaws and the tiny betrayals. Honestly, she'd had way better friend groups since then, including the Resourceful Couriers, but that didn't change how she felt.

Alyssa did not do well with helplessness, or chains, or trusting random strangers. But wasn't that the whole point of this leap into darkness? Alyssa would get this mostly untested surgery, and then she would be able to share unfalsifiable information and have massively expanded threat awareness thanks to the alien sensory organs. Sometimes you have to be more vulnerable in the short term, so that you can become more formidable later.

They must've reached the foot of the Old Mother without Alyssa noticing, what with all the turbulence. She had a sensation of moving forward, rather than downward, and her position in the web of tentacles shifted somewhat as well, and then at last they came to a stop and the Gelet unwrapped her tenderly. She landed on her feet inside a dark tunnel that sloped downward. This was almost scarier than the aftermath of the Widehome job, or at least it was scary in a different way.

They led her down the tunnel, patient with all her stumbles. She couldn't see shit, but at least she was moving under her own power.

Alyssa kept reminding herself of what Sophie had said: she was the first human ever to visit the Gelet city, knowing what awaited her there. She was a pioneer.

The air grew warm enough for Alyssa to remove some of the layers of moss, and there were faint glimmers of light up ahead, so she must be entering the Gelet city proper. They needed to find a better name for it than the "midnight city." Something catchy and alluring, something to make this place a destination.

"I'm the first human to come down here with my eyes open, knowing what awaits," Alyssa said, loud enough to echo through the tunnel.

"Actually," a voice replied from the darkness ahead of her. "You're not. You're the second, which is almost as good. Right?"

His name was Jeremy and he had worked with Sophie at that fancy coffee place, the Illyrian Parlour. Ginger hair, fair skin, nervous hands, soft voice.

He'd been in the Gelet city awhile already, maybe a few turns of the Xios-phanti shutters, but they hadn't done anything to alter him yet. "I can show you around, though I don't know the city very well, because large areas of it are totally dark." He sounded as though he must be smiling.

"Thanks," Alyssa said. "Appreciate any and all local knowledge."

Jeremy kept dropping information about himself, as if he didn't care at all about covering his tracks. He'd been part of the ruling elite in Xiosphant, studying at one of those fancy schools, until he'd fallen in love with a person of the wrong gender. Fucking homophobic Xiosphanti.

So he'd gone underground, slinging coffee to stressed-out working people, and that had been his first real encounter with anyone whose feet actually touched the ground instead of walking on a fluffy cloud of privilege.

The Gelet had cleared a room, somewhere in the bowels of their unseeable city, for human visitors, with meager lighting and some packs of food that had come straight from the Mothership. Alyssa and Jeremy opened three food packs and traded back and forth, sharing the weird foods of their distant ancestors: candies, jerky, sandwiches, some kind of sweet viscous liquid.

They bonded over sharing ancient foods, saying things like: "Try this one, it's kind of amazing."

Or: "I'm not sure this stuff has any nutritional value, but at least the after-taste is better than the taste."

Alyssa chewed in silence and half-darkness for a while, then the pieces fell into place. "Oh," she said to Jeremy. "I just figured out who you are. You're the guy who tried to get Sophie to use her new abilities as a propaganda tool against the Vice Regent. She told us about you."

"I know who you are, too." Jeremy leaned forward, so his face took on more substance. "You're one of the foreign interlopers who helped the Vice Regent to take power in Xiosphant. You stood at Bianca's right hand, until she had one of her paranoid episodes. We have you to thank for our latest misery."

Alyssa couldn't believe she'd shared food with this man, just a short time ago.

"I'm going to go for a walk." Once she'd said this out loud, Alyssa was committed, even though it meant getting to her feet and walking out into a dark maze that included the occasional nearly bottomless ravine. At least the Gelet would keep an eye on her.

Probably.

Alyssa tried to walk as if she knew where she was going, as if she felt totally confident that the next step wouldn't take her into a wall or off the edge. She swung her arms and strode forward and tried not to revisit the whole ugly history of regime change in Xiosphant, and her part in it. She had trusted the wrong person, that was all.

What was Alyssa even doing here? All she wanted was to bury her past deeper than the lowest level of this city, but soon she would have the ability to share all her memories with random strangers. She knew from talking to Sophie that it was easy to share way more than you bargained for—especially at first.

Alyssa might just reach out to someone for an innocent conversation, and end up unloading the pristine memory of the moment when she'd pledged her loyalty to a toxic creep. The moment when Alyssa had believed that she'd found the thing she'd searched for since the Chancers fell apart, and that she would never feel hopeless again. Or Alyssa might share an image of the aftermath: herself wading through fresh blood, inside the glitzy walls of the Xiosphanti Palace.

"This was a mistake," Alyssa said to the darkness. "I need to go home. Sophie will understand. Mouth will be relieved. I should never have come here. When they offer to change me, I'll just say no, I'll make them understand. They'll have to send me home."

She almost expected Jeremy to answer, but he was nowhere near. She'd wandered a long way from their quarters, and there was no sound but the grumbling of old machines and the scritching of the Gelet's forelegs as they moved around her.

"I'm not sure I can go through with this," Alyssa told Jeremy, when she'd somehow groped her way back to the living quarters. "I can't stand the idea of inflicting my past on anyone else."

"I'm definitely going ahead with it," Jeremy replied after a while. "When Sophie showed me what she could do, I couldn't even believe what a great organizing tool this could be. This is going to transform the new Uprising, because people will be able to see the truth for themselves, without any doubt or distortion."

Alyssa had wanted to avoid Jeremy, or shut out his self-righteous nattering. But they were the only two humans for thousands of kilometers, and she couldn't go too long without another human voice, as it turned out.

"So you're about to become one of the first members of a whole new species," Alyssa said, "and you're just going to use it as a recruiting tool for another regime change? So you can take power, and then someone else can turn around and overthrow you in turn? Seems like kind of a waste."

"At least I'm not—" Jeremy barked. Then he took a slow breath and shifted. His silhouette looked as if he was hugging himself. "It's not just about unseating your friend Bianca. It's not. It's about building a movement. I spent so much time in that coffeehouse, listening to people who could barely even give voice to all the ways they were struggling. We need a new kind of politics."

"Bianca's not my friend. I hate her too, in ways that you could never understand." Alyssa found more of the rectangular flat candy and ate a chunk. "But if enough people become hybrids, and learn to share the way Sophie shares, we could have something better than just more politics. We could have a new *community*. We could share resources as well as thoughts. We could work with the Gelet."

"Sure, sure," Jeremy said. "Maybe eventually."

"Not eventually," Alyssa said. "Soon."

"What makes you think a lot of people will buy into that vision, if you're not even willing to go through with it yourself?"

Alyssa groaned. "Look. I'm just saying . . . You have to be doing this for the right reasons or it'll end really badly. You'll lose yourself. I saw it again and again, back in Argelo, people burning up everything they were, just for the sake of allegiances or ideology or whatever."

They didn't talk for a while, but then they went back to arguing. There wasn't anything else to do, and besides, by the sound of it, Jeremy had been a good friend to Sophie, back when she'd really needed someone. So Alyssa didn't want him to wreck his psyche, or his heart, or whatever, by turning his memories into propaganda.

"I can be careful." Jeremy sounded as if he was trying to convince himself. "I can share only the memories and thoughts that will make people want to mobilize. I can keep everything else to myself."

"Maybe," was all Alyssa said.

These Xiosphanti believed in the power of repression, way more than was healthy. Or realistic.

"I wish we could ask the Gelet." Jeremy was doing some kind of stretches in the darkness. "It's a terrible paradox: you can only have a conversation with them about the pros and cons of becoming a hybrid, after you've already become a hybrid."

Alyssa went for another walk in the chittering dark—she shrieked with terror, but only inside her own head—and when she got back, Jeremy said, "Maybe you're right. Maybe I'm going to regret this. Maybe I should stick to organizing people the old-fashioned way, winning their trust slowly. I don't know. I'm out of options."

Alyssa was startled to realize that while she'd been trying to talk Jeremy out of becoming a hybrid, she'd talked herself back into it. She needed to believe: in Sophie, in this higher communion. Alyssa kept dwelling on that memory of cowering in a hot basement with the other Chancers, and pictured herself sharing it with Sophie, or Mouth, or anyone. What would happen to that moment when it was no longer hers alone? She wanted to find out.

The Gelet surrounded Alyssa with their chitinous bodies and opened their twin-bladed pincers, until she leaned forward and nuzzled the slick tubes, the slightly larger cousins of the tendrils growing out of Sophie's chest.

An oily, pungent aroma overwhelmed Alyssa for a moment, and then she was experiencing the world as the Gelet saw it. This Gelet showed her a sense-impression of a human, being torn open to make room for a mass of alien flesh that latched onto her heart, her lungs, her bowels. Alyssa couldn't keep from flinching so hard that she broke the connection.

But when they offered her a choice between the operating room and safe passage home, Alyssa didn't even hesitate before peeling off her clothes.

Alyssa had always said that pain was no big thing—like the worst part of pain was just the monotony of a single sensation that overstayed its welcome. But she'd never felt agony like this, not even on all the occasions when she'd been shot or stabbed or shackled inside a dungeon. Sophie had made this operation sound unpleasant, pretty awful, a nasty shock, but Alyssa started screaming curse words in two languages before she was even half awake, after surgery.

The pain didn't get any better, and the Gelet were super cautious with their hoarded sedatives, and Alyssa was sure something had gone wrong, perhaps fatally. All she could do was try her best to shut out the world. But . . . she couldn't.

Because, even with her eyes closed and her ears covered, she could sense the walls of the chamber where the Gelet had brought her to rest, and she could "feel" the Gelet creeping around her, and in the passageways nearby. Her brand-new tentacles insisted on bombarding her with sensations that her mind didn't know how to process. Alyssa had thought of Sophie's small tentacles as providing her with "enhanced threat awareness," but this was just too much world to deal with.

Alyssa screamed until her throat got sore. Even her teeth hurt from gnashing.

She looked down at herself. The top part of her chest was covered with all of these dark wriggling growths coated with fresh slime, like parasites. Like a mutilation. Before Alyssa even knew what she was doing, she had grabbed two handfuls of tendrils, and she was trying to yank them out of her body with all her strength.

Alyssa might as well have tried to cut off her own hand—the pain flared, more than she could endure. Searing, wrenching. Like being on fire and gutshot at the same time. Even though her eyes told her that there were foreign objects attached to her chest, her skin (her mind?) told her these were part of her body and she was attacking herself. She nearly passed out again from the pain of her own self-assault.

The Gelet rushed over, three of them, and now Alyssa could sense their panic even without any physical contact. Her new tentacles could pick up their emotional states, with more accuracy than being able to see facial expressions or body language, and these Gelet were very extremely freaked out. Two of them set about trying to stabilize Alyssa and undo the damage she'd just caused to her delicate grafts, while the third leaned over her.

Alyssa looked up with both her old and her new senses. A big blunt head descended toward her, with a huge claw opening to reveal more of those slimy strips of flesh, and Alyssa felt a mixture of disgust and warmth. She didn't know what she felt anymore, because her reactions were tainted by the sensory input from her tentacles. The Gelet leaning toward her gave off waves of tenderness and concern—but also annoyance and fear—and this was all too much to process.

"I would very much like not to feel any of what I'm feeling," Alyssa said.

Then the Gelet closest to her made contact with her tendrils and Alyssa had the familiar sensation of falling out of herself, which she'd gotten from Sophie so many times now. And then—

Sophie was standing right in front of Alyssa, close enough for Alyssa to look into her eyes.

"What are you doing? How are you here?" Alyssa asked Sophie, before she bit her tongue. Because of course Sophie wasn't present at all. This was a memory or something.

Sophie was looking at herself, with her tendrils as fresh as the ones Alyssa had just tried to rip out of herself, and she was reaching out with her tentacles to "feel" the space around her, and Alyssa was doubly aware of Sophie's happiness, thanks to her facial expression and all the chemicals she was giving off. At last, Sophie seemed to be saying. Thank you, at long last my head can be an estuary instead of just this reservoir.

Alyssa wanted to reach out for Sophie, but Alyssa wasn't even herself in this memory. Alyssa was a Gelet, with a huge lumbering body under a thick shell and woolly fur, with a heart full of relief that this operation might be working better than anyone dared hope—

—Alyssa came back to herself and looked at the Gelet leaning over her. The disgust was gone, and she "saw" every flex of the segmented legs and every twitch of the big, shapeless head, as if they were the tiny habits of a distant family member.

"I'm sorry," Alyssa said, hoping they understood somehow. "I didn't mean to do that, it was just instinct. I hope I didn't ruin everything. I do want to understand all of you, and go home to Sophie as her equal. I really didn't want to, I'm sorry—I didn't want to, it just happened. I'm sorry."

Maybe if her tendrils weren't damaged beyond repair, she'd be able to tell them in a way they understood. As it was, they seemed satisfied that she wasn't going to try and tear herself apart again, and that they'd done everything they could to stabilize her.

Alyssa lay there cursing herself and hoping and worrying and freaking out, until she heard shrieks echoing from the next room. Jeremy. He'd gotten the procedure too, and he'd just woken up, with the same agony and loathing that had struck Alyssa. She wished she could think of something to say to talk him down. Or at least they could be miserable together, if she could talk to him.

This operation was supposed to help Alyssa to form connections, but she was more alone than ever.

The pain ground on and on. Alyssa would never get used to these stabbing, burning, throbbing sensations. She couldn't tell how much of this discomfort was from the operation, and how much was because she'd attacked herself when she was still healing.

Alyssa rested on a hammock of moss and roots until she got bored and the pain had lessened enough for her to move around, and then she started exploring the city again. This time, she could sense the walkways and all the galleries, all the way down into the depths of the city, and she was aware of the Gelet moving all around her. She started to be able to tell them apart, and read their moods, and all their little gestures and twitches and flexing tentacles began to seem more like mannerisms.

One Gelet, in particular, seemed to have been given the task of watching over Alyssa, and she had a loping stride and a friendly, nurturing "scent." (Alyssa couldn't think of the right word to describe the way she could tell the Gelet's emotions from the chemicals they gave off, but "scent" would do for now.) This Gelet stayed close enough to Alyssa to provide any help she needed, and Alyssa found her presence reassuring rather than spooky.

Alyssa's new friend had survived the noxious blight that had killed a lot of her siblings in the weave where all the Gelet babies grew. (But she was still a little smaller than all the older Gelet.) When she was brand-new, the other Gelet had made a wish for her that boiled down to "Find reasons for hope, even in the midst of death."

That thought reminded Alyssa of a nagging regret: she and Sophie still hadn't succeeded in helping Mouth to figure out a new name, mostly because Mouth was impossible to please.

And this Gelet, whom Alyssa started calling Hope, had devoted most of her life so far to studying the high wind currents, the jet streams that moved air from day to night and back again. Hope's mind was full of designs for flying machines, to let people examine the upper atmosphere up close and find a way to keep the toxic clouds away from the Gelet city. But Alyssa's communication with Hope still only went one way. Her new grafts, the tendrils she'd tried to rip out, still hurt worse than daylight. She tried to shield them with her entire body, as if exposure to air would ruin them further.

What if they never worked right?

What if she could never use them to communicate, without feeling as if hot needles were poking in between her first few ribs?

That moment when she'd grabbed with both hands, tearing at her new skin, kept replaying in Alyssa's head, and she wanted to curse herself. Weak, untrustworthy, doomed—she cringed each time.

Hope kept offering her own open pincer and warm tendrils, which always contained some soothing memory of playing a friendly game with some other Gelet or receiving a blessing from the Gelet's long-dead leader, in some dream-gathering. Alyssa kept wishing she could talk back, explain, maybe learn to become more than just a raw mass of anxiety with nothing to say.

At last, Alyssa decided to take the risk.

She raised her still-sore tendrils to meet Hope's, and tried to figure out how to send instead of receive. Alyssa brought the awful memory to the front of her mind: her hands, grasping and pulling. It was so vivid, it was almost happening once again. She felt it flood out of her, but then she wasn't sure if Hope had received it. Until Hope recoiled and sent back an impression of what Alyssa had looked like to everyone else, thrashing around, and the Gelet rushing in to try and fix the damage.

Alyssa "saw" them touching her body, in the same places that still hurt now, and felt their anxiety, their horror, but also their . . . determination? Bloody-mindedness, maybe. She had the weird sensation of "watching" the Gelet surgeons repairing the adhesions on her chest, while she could still feel the ache inside those torn places. And the strangest part: as she watched the Gelet restore her grafts in the past, Alyssa found the wounds hurt less fiercely in the present.

The pain didn't magically fade to bliss or anything like that, but Alyssa found she could bear it, maybe because she could convince herself that they'd repaired the damage. She started thinking of it more like just another stab wound.

And once Alyssa decided she could use her new organs (antennae?) without wrecking something that was barely strung together, she started opening up more. She shared the memory of this caustic rain that had fallen on her in Argelo, which had seemed to come from the same alkali clouds that had doomed some of Hope's siblings. The moment when Sophie had first given Alyssa a glimpse of this city and the Gelet living here, suffused with all of Sophie's love for this place. And finally, the first time Mouth, Sophie, and Alyssa climbed onto the flat shale rooftops of the Warrens while everyone else slept, the three of them holding hands and looking across the whole city, from shadow to flame.

In return, Hope shared her earliest memories as a separate person, which was also the moment she realized that she was surrounded by the dead flesh of her hatchmates, hanging inside this sticky weave. Tiny lifeless bodies nestled against her, all of them connected to the same flow of nutrients that were keeping her alive. The crumbling skin touching hers, the overwhelming chemical stench of decay—with no way to escape, nothing to do but keep sending out distress pheromones until someone arrived to take away the dead. And then later, when Hope had left the web, and all the other Gelet had treated her like a fragile ice blossom.

Alyssa felt sickened in a deep cavity of herself, somewhere underneath her new grafts.

She tried to send back random scraps of her own upbringing, like when her mom and all her uncles died on her, or when she got in her first serious knife fight. But also, cakes, cactus crisps, and dancing. Kissing girls and boys and others in the crook of this alleyway that curled around the hilt of the Knife in Argelo, where you felt the music more than you heard it, and you could get trashed off the fumes from other people's drinks. Always knowing that she could lose herself in this city, and there were more sweet secrets than Alyssa would ever have enough time to find.

Soon, Alyssa and Hope were just sharing back and forth, every furtive joy and every weird moment of being a kid and trying to make sense of the adults around you—and then growing up but still not understanding, most of the time. The intricacies of the Gelet culture still screwed Alyssa's head ten ways at once, but she could understand feeling like a weird kid, looking in.

Alyssa started to feel more comfortable with Hope than with 99 percent of human beings—until a few sleeps later, Hope showed Alyssa something that sent a spike of ice all the way through her. They were sitting together in one of those rooty-webby hammocks, and Alyssa was drowsing, finally no longer in so much pain that she couldn't rest, and Hope let something slip out. A memory of the past?

No—a possible future.

In Hope's vision, hybrid humans were moving in packs through this city, deep under the midnight chill. Dozens of people, all chattering with their human voices, but also reaching out to each other with their Gelet tendrils. This throng seemed joyful, but there was this undercurrent of dread to the whole thing, which made no sense to Alyssa.

Until she realized what was missing. Hope could see a future where the midnight city was filled with human–Gelet hybrids—but the Gelet themselves were gone.

. . .

"I have something I need to show you," Alyssa said to Jeremy.

He jerked his head up and gaped at her, his new tendrils entwined with those of two Gelet that Alyssa hadn't met yet. He blinked, as if he'd forgotten the sound of language, then slowly unthreaded himself from the two Gelet and stumbled to his feet.

"Okay," Jeremy said. "What did you want to show me? Where is it?"

"Right here." Alyssa gestured at her tendrils.

Jeremy pulled away, just a couple centimeters, but enough so Alyssa noticed.

"Oh," he said. "I hadn't . . . I didn't."

"Don't be a baby," Alyssa said. "I know you bear a grudge, you blame me, I get it. You don't want to let me in."

"It's not even that," Jeremy stammered. "I don't even know. This is all so new, and even just sharing with the Gelet is unfamiliar enough. Being connected to another human being, or another hybrid I mean, would be . . . plus I heard that you . . . I heard you *did* something. You tried to damage yourself. They won't show me the details."

Fucking gossip. Alyssa shouldn't be surprised that the Gelet would be even worse than regular humans about telling everyone her business. The look in Jeremy's eyes made her feel even worse than ever, and her scars felt like they were flaring up.

"This isn't anything to do with me," Alyssa said. "I promise, I won't even share anything about myself, if you're so worried about mental contamination."

"I don't mean to be . . ." Jeremy sucked in a deep breath. "Okay. Okay. Sure. Go ahead."

Among the thousand things that the hybrids were going to need, some kind of etiquette would be one of the most important. A way to use their words to negotiate whether, and how, to communicate with each other non-verbally.

Jeremy leaned forward with his tunic open, and Alyssa concentrated, desperate to keep her promise and avoid sharing anything of her own. Of course, the more she worried about sharing the wrong thing, the more her mind filled with the image of herself inside the Xiosphanti Palace, tracking bloody footprints all over the most exquisite marble floor she'd ever seen.

No no no. Not that. Please.

"Wait a moment." Alyssa paused when they were just a few centimeters apart. "Just. Need to clear. My head."

Curating your thoughts, weeding out the ugly, was a literal headache. If only Sophie was here . . . but Alyssa didn't want to open that cask of swamp vodka or she'd never conjure a clean memory.

Breathe. Focus. Alyssa imagined Hope's scary vision, as if it were a clear liquid inside a little ball of glass, cupped in her palms. Separated from all her own thoughts, clean and delicate. She gave that glass ball to Jeremy in her mind as their tendrils made contact, and felt Hope's dream flow out of her.

A few strands of thought, or memory, leaked out of Jeremy in return: a slender boy with pale Calgary features and wiry brown hair, pulling his pants on with a sidelong glance at his forbidden lover. Bianca and her consort Dash, smiling down from a balcony as if the crowd beneath them was shouting tributes, instead of curses. A woman holding a tiny bloody bundle on a cobbled side street, wailing.

"Ugh, sorry," Jeremy said. Then Hope's vision of a possible future sank in, and he gasped.

"That's . . ." Jeremy disconnected from her and staggered like a drunk, leaning into the nearest wall. "That's . . ."

"I know," Alyssa said. "I don't think . . . I don't think I was supposed to see that."

"We can't let that happen." Jeremy turned away from the wall and sobbed, wiping his eyes and nose with his tunic sleeve.

"Our ancestors already invaded their whole planet. This would be worse." Alyssa looked at her knuckles. "Way worse than when I helped those foreigners to invade your city. I'd rather . . . I'd rather die than be a part of another injustice."

The two of them walked around the Gelet city for a while. Watching small groups of children all connected to one teacher, puppeteers putting on a show, musicians filling the tunnels with vibrations, a team of engineers repairing a turbine. A million human–Gelet hybrids would need centuries just to understand all of this culture. Sophie had barely witnessed a tiny sliver of this city's life, and she'd spent way more time here than either Alyssa or Jeremy had so far.

"We can help, though." Alyssa broke a silence that seemed near-endless. "They didn't turn us into hybrids for our own sake. Right? They need us to help repair the damage that our own people did. Hope showed me some designs for new flying machines that could help them figure out how to keep the toxic rain clouds away, but they can't stand even partial sunlight."

Jeremy covered his face with one hand and his tendrils with the other. His new tentacles retreated behind his back, wrapping around like a pair of arms crossed in judgment. He shivered and let out low gasps. Alyssa wasn't sure if he was still crying, or what she ought to do about it. She just stood there and watched him, until he pulled himself together and they went and got some stewed roots together.

"We're not going to make it, are we?" Jeremy said to his hand. "We can't do this. We won't change enough people in time to help them. I know you did something terrible, right after they changed you, and I . . ." He couldn't bring himself to say what came next. "What I did was much worse. I can't. I can't even stand to think about it."

Between her new tentacles and all her ingrained old skills of reading people, Alyssa felt overwhelmed by sympathy for Jeremy. She could feel his emotions, maybe more clearly than her own, almost as if she could get head-spinning drunk on them. That sour intersection between fellowship and nausea. At least now she knew that she wasn't the only one who'd had a nasty reaction after the Gelet surgery.

Jeremy was waiting for Alyssa to say something. She wasn't going to.

After a long time, he said again, "We're not going to make it." Then walked away, still covering his mouth and tendrils, shrouding himself with all of his limbs.

Alyssa didn't see Jeremy for a few sleeps.

Meanwhile, she was busy gleaning everything she could from the Gelet, even though her brain hurt from taking in so many foreign memories, and concepts that couldn't be turned into words. She learned way more than she would ever understand. She kept pushing herself, even when all she wanted to do was to be alone.

Hope kept turning up, but Alyssa also got to know a bunch of other Gelet, most of them older, but not all. Some of them had come from other settlements originally, and she caught some notions of what life was like in a town of just a few hundred or few thousand Gelet, where everybody really knew everyone else by heart. She got to witness just the merest part of what a debate among the Gelet would feel like.

In her coldest moments, Alyssa caught herself thinking, *I need to learn everything I can, in case one day these people are all gone and my descendants are the only ones who can preserve these memories.* That thought never failed to send her into a rage at herself, even angrier than when she thought she had ruined her own tendrils.

She thought of what Mouth had said to her once, about cultural survival. People died, even nations flamed out, but you need somebody left behind to carry the important stuff forward.

"You were right."

Jeremy had caught Alyssa by surprise when she was dozing in a big web with a dozen Gelet, waiting for their dead Magistrate to show up. Jeremy seemed way older than the last time Alyssa had seen him, his shoulders squared against some new weight that was never going to be lifted away. He faced her eye to eye, not trying to cover any part of himself or turn aside.

"Wait. What was I right about?" Alyssa said. "The last time I won an argument, it involved handfuls of blood and a punctured lung. I've stopped craving vindication."

"There's so much more at stake than who sits inside that ugly Palace back home in Xiosphant." Jeremy shook his head. "I came here hoping to find a new way to organize people against the Vice Regent, but we have more important work to do. You were right about all of it: being a hybrid isn't just a means to an end, it's way more important than that."

"Oh."

Alyssa looked at Jeremy's shy, unflinching expression, and a wave of affection caught her off guard. They'd gone through this thing together, that almost nobody else alive could understand. She couldn't help thinking of him almost as a sleepmate—even though they'd only slept near each other, not next to each other.

"We can't just send people here and expect them to handle this change on their own. Anyone who comes here is going to need someone to talk them through every step of the process, someone who understands how to be patient," Jeremy said. "So . . . I've made a decision. I think it would be easier to show than to tell."

Alyssa understood what he meant after a moment, and she let her tendrils relax, slacken, so his own could brush against them.

She was terrified that she would show him the moment when she tried to rip these things out of her body—so of course that's what she did show him. The screaming panic, the feeling of your fingers grasping and tearing, trying to rip out your own heart.

Jeremy stumbled, flinched, and let out a moan . . . and then he accepted Alyssa's memory. He gave back a brief glimpse of his own worst moment: Alyssa was Jeremy, lashing out, with a snarl in his throat, the heel of his hand colliding with the nearest terrified Gelet, a blood-red haze over everything. *I'll kill you all* repeating in his head. *I'll tear you apart, kill you kill you.* The new alien senses flooding into Jeremy's brain, bringing back all the times when he'd needed to look over his shoulder with every step he took.

"It's okay," Alyssa said, wrapping her arms around Jeremy under the roots of his tentacles. "It's really okay."

"It's not okay." Jeremy trembled. "I'm a monster. At least nobody was badly hurt."

"You're not a monster. You were just scared. We both were." Alyssa clutched him tighter, until he clung to her as well. "We prepared ourselves, but we weren't ready. We need to make sure it goes better next time."

"That's what I was going to tell you about." Jeremy relaxed a little. "This is what I decided." He sent Alyssa another vision, this time of a future he'd envisioned.

Jeremy was here, still inside the midnight city, studying everything the Gelet could teach him. When more humans arrived from Xiosphant, Alyssa saw Jeremy greeting them. Guiding them around the city, preparing them, talking them through every step of the way. The Jeremy in the vision grew old, but never went back to the light.

Alyssa had to say it aloud: "You want to stay here? Forever?"

"I . . . I think it's the right thing to do," Jeremy whispered. "I can organize, I can be a leader, all of that. Just down here, rather than back in Xiosphant. Humans are going to keep coming here, and there needs to be someone here to help. Otherwise, more people will . . ."

"More people will react the way you and I did." Alyssa shuddered.

"Yeah."

Alyssa found herself sharing a plan of her own with Jeremy. She imagined herself going back to Xiosphant, back to Sophie and Mouth—but not just helping them to convince more people to come here and become hybrids. She pictured herself carrying on Jeremy's work: finding the people who were being crushed by all the wrong certainties, helping them to form a movement. Maybe opening someplace like that coffee shop where Sophie and Jeremy used to work. Giving people a safe place to escape from all that Xiosphanti shit.

"You were right too," Alyssa told Jeremy. "People in Xiosphant need to come together. If they had somewhere to go in that city, maybe more of them might be open to thinking about coming here."

"Can you take care of Cyrus, though?" Jeremy sent a brief impression of the biggest marmot Alyssa had ever seen, purring and extending blue pseudopods in every direction. "I left him with a friend, but he needs someone reliable to look after him. Sophie already knows him."

"Sure," Alyssa said, hugging Jeremy with their tendrils still intertwined.

Alyssa stayed awhile longer in the midnight city, healing up but also keeping Jeremy company. After she left, he might not hear another voice for a while—and weirdly, the longer Alyssa had these tendrils, the more important verbal communication seemed to her, because words had a different kind of precision, and there were truths that could only be shared in word-form. Alyssa introduced Jeremy to Hope, and explained in a whisper about everything she'd been through, and Jeremy introduced Alyssa to some of his own Gelet friends, too.

Her surgical scars settled down to a dull ache, and then slowly stopped hurting at all, except for when she strained her muscles or slept weird. The new body parts and what remained of the pain both felt like they were just part of Alyssa, the same way the Chancers and the Resourceful Couriers would always be. "I guess it's time," Alyssa said to herself. She walked up toward the exit to the Gelet city with Hope on one side and Jeremy on the other, though Jeremy planned to turn back before they reached the exit.

Almost without thinking, Alyssa extended her tendrils so she was connected to both Jeremy and Hope, and the three of them shared nothing in particular as they walked. Just a swirl of emotions, fragments of memory, and most of all, a set of wishes for the future that were just vague enough to be of comfort. They stayed in this three-way link until the first gusts of freezing air began to filter down from the surface of the night.

have done trigonometry exactly once since high school, and that was when I was writing "The Time Travel Club." I had become obsessed with a weird question: If you could travel in time, wouldn't you also be relocated in space? Since the Earth is constantly in motion, and the universe is expanding, you couldn't jump forward five minutes and still be in the same place as before, right? I contacted Dr. Dave Goldberg (the writer of io9's "Ask a Physicist" column), and he responded by talking about quantum foam and special relativity. Eventually, Dr. Dave helped me figure out a set of rules for my time travel—but then I had to do a ton of math to calculate how far you'd move through space for every second you traveled in time. I was up at two a.m. crunching numbers.

Once I had the mechanism, I had to figure out who the people in this story were. I had a few false starts, including a story about a feminist collective that builds a time machine. Then I hit on a fun notion: What if there was a regular meeting of people who just want to pretend they're time travelers—and then someone shows up and offers them a real time machine? I wrote the resulting story in linear order, and then rearranged it so it starts in the middle and we get the first half in flashbacks, because that seemed more exciting and timey-wimey.

THE TIME TRAVEL CLUB

Nobody could decide what should be the first object to travel through time. Malik offered his car keys. Jerboa held up an action figure. Then Lydia suggested her one-year sobriety coin, and it seemed too perfect to pass up. After all, the coin had a unit of time on it, as if it came from a realm where time really was a denomination of currency. And they were about to break the bank of time forever, if this worked.

Lydia handed over the coin, no longer shiny due to endless thumb-worrying, and then she had a small anxiety attack. "Just as long as I get it back," she said, trying to keep the edge out of her voice.

"You will," said Madame Alberta with a smile. "This coin, we send a mere one minute into the future. It reappears in precisely the same place from which it disappears."

Lydia would have been nervous about the first test of the time machine in Madame Alberta's musty dry laundry room in any case. After all they'd been through to make this happen, the stupid thing *had* to work. Now she felt like a piece of herself—a piece she had fought for—was about to vanish, and she would need to have faith. She sucked at having faith.

Madame Alberta took the coin and placed it in the airtight glass cube, six by six by six, that they'd built where the washer/dryer was supposed to be. The balsa-walled laundry room was so crammed with equipment, there was scarcely room for four people to hunch over together. Once the coin was sitting on the floor of the cube, Madame Alberta walked back toward the main piece of equipment, which looked like a million vacuum cleaner hoses attached to a giant slow cooker.

"I keep thinking about what you were saying before," Lydia said to Malik, trying to distract herself. "About wanting to stand outside history and see the empires rising and falling from a great height, instead of being swept along by the waves. But what if this power to send things, and people, back and forth across history makes us the masters of reality? What if we can make the waves change direction, or turn back entirely? What then?"

"I chose your group with great care," said Madame Alberta said. "As I have said. You have the wisdom to use this technology properly, all of you."

Madame Alberta pulled a big lever. A whoosh of purple neon vapor into the glass cube, followed by a *klorrrrrp* sound, like someone opening a soda can and burping at the same time—in exactly the way that might suggest they'd had enough soda already—and the coin was gone.

"Wow," said Malik. His eyebrows went all the way up so his forehead concertina-ed, and his short dreads did a fractal scatter.

"It just vanished," said Jerboa, bouncing with excitement, floppy hat flopping. "It just . . . It's on its way."

Lydia wanted to hold her breath, but there was so little air in here that she was already light-headed. This whole wood-beamed, staircase-flanked basement area felt like a soup of fumes.

Lydia really needed to pee, but she didn't want to go upstairs and risk missing the sudden reappearance of her coin, which would be newer by a minute than everything else in the world. She held it, swaying and squirming. She looked down at her phone, and there were just about thirty seconds left. She wondered if they should count down. That was probably too tacky. She really couldn't breathe at this point, and she was starting to taste cotton candy, and everything smelled white.

"Just ten seconds left," Malik said. And then they did count down, after all. "Nine . . . eight . . . seven . . . six . . . five! Four! Three! Two! *One!*"

They all stopped and stared at the cube, which remained empty. There was no soda gas noise, no sign of an object breaking back into the physical world from some netherspace.

"Um," said Jerboa. "Did we count down too soon?"

"It is possible my calculations," said Madame Alberta, waving her hands in distress. Her fake accent was slipping even more than usual. "But no. I mean, I quadruple-checked. They cannot be wrong."

"Give it a minute or two longer," said Malik. "I'm sure it'll turn up." As if it was a missing sock in the dryer, instead of a coin in the cube that sat where a dryer ought to be.

They gave it another half an hour, as the knot inside Lydia got bigger and bigger. At one point, Lydia went upstairs to pee in Madame Alberta's tiny bathroom, staring at a calendar of exotic bird paintings. Eventually, Lydia went outside to stand in the front yard, facing the one-lane road, cursing. Why had she volunteered her coin? And now she would never see it again.

Lydia went home and spent an hour on the phone processing with her sponsor, Nate, who kept reassuring her, in a voice thick as pork rinds, that the coin was just a token and she could get another one and it was no big deal. These things have no innate power, they're just symbols. She didn't mention the "time machine" thing but kept imagining her coin waiting to arrive, existing in some moment that hadn't been reached yet.

Even after all of Nate's best talk-downs, Lydia couldn't sleep. At three in the morning, Lydia was still thinking about her one-year coin, floating in a state of indeterminacy—and then it hit her, and she knew the answer. She turned on the light, sat up in bed, and stared at the wall of ring-pull talking-animal toys opposite her bed. Thinking it through again and again, until she was sure.

At last, Lydia couldn't help phoning Jerboa, who answered the phone still half asleep and in a bit of a panic.

"What is it?" Jerboa said. "What's wrong? I can find my pants. I swear I can put on some pants and then I'll fix whatever."

"It's fine, nothing's wrong, no need for pants," Lydia said. "Sorry to wake you. Sorry, I didn't realize how late it was." She was totally lying, but it was too late anyhow. "But I was thinking. Madame Alberta said the coin moved forward in time one minute, but it stayed in the same physical location. Right?"

"That's right," said Jerboa. "Same place, different time. Only moving in one dimension."

"But," said Lydia. "What if the Earth wasn't in the same place when the coin arrived? I mean . . . Doesn't the Earth move around the sun?"

"Yeah, sure. And the Earth rotates. And the sun moves around the galactic disk. And the galaxy is moving too, toward Andromeda and the Great Attractor," said Jerboa. "Space itself is probably moving around. There's no such thing as a fixed point in space. But Madame Alberta covered that, remember? According to Einstein, the other end of the rift in time ought to obey Newton's first law, conservation of momentum. Which means the coin would still follow the Earth's movement, and arrive at the same point. Except . . . Wait a minute!"

Lydia waited a minute. After which, Jerboa still hadn't said anything else. Lydia had to look at her phone to make sure she hadn't gotten hung up on. "Except what?" she finally said.

"Except that . . . the Earth's orbit and rotation are momentum *plus gravity*. We actually accelerate toward the sun as part of our orbit, or else our momentum would just carry us out into space. Madame Alberta said her time machine worked by opting out of the fundamental forces, right? And gravity is one of those. Which would mean . . . Wait a minute, wait a minute." Another long, weird pause, except this time Lydia could hear Jerboa breathing heavily and muttering sotto voce.

Then Jerboa said, "I think I know where your medallion is, Lydia."

"Where?"

"Right where we left it. On the roof of Madame Alberta's neighbor's house."

Lydia had less than ninety days of sobriety under her belt when she first met the Time Travel Club. They met in the same Unitarian basement as Lydia's twelve-step group: a grimy cellar, with a huge steam pipe running along one wall and intermittent gray carpeting that looked like a scale map of plate tectonics. Pictures of purple hands holding a green globe and dancing scribble-children hung askew with strands of peeling Scotch tape. Boiling hot in summer, drafty in winter, it was a room that seemed designed to make you feel desperate and trapped. But all the twelve-steppers laughed a lot, in between crying, and afterward everybody shared cigarettes and sometimes pie. Lydia didn't feel especially close to any of the other twelve-steppers (and she didn't smoke), but she felt a desperate lifeboat solidarity with them.

The Time Travel Club always showed up just as the last people from Lydia's twelve-step meeting were dragging their asses up out of there. Most of the time travelers wore big dark coats and furry boots, which seemed designed to look equally ridiculous in any time period. Lydia wasn't even sure why she stayed behind for one of their meetings, since it was a choice between watching people pretend to be time travelers and eating pie. Nine times out of ten, pie would have won over fake time travel. But Lydia needed to sit quietly by herself and think about the mess she'd made of her life before she tried to drive, and the Time Travel Club was as good a place as any.

Malik was a visitor from the distant past—the Kushite kingdom of roughly 2,700 years ago. The Kushites were a pretty swell people who made an excellent palm wine that tasted sort of like cognac. Now Malik commuted between the Kushite era, the present day, and the thirty-second century, when there was going to be a neo-Kushite revival going on and the dark, well-cheekboned Malik would become a bit of a celebrity.

The non-binary time traveler Jerboa looked tiny and bashful inside a huge brown hat and high coat collar. Jerboa spent a lot of their time in the year 1 million, a time period where the parties were excellent and people were considerably less hung up on gender roles. Jerboa also hung out in the 1920s and the early 1600s, on occasion.

And then there was Normando, a Kenny Rogers–looking dude who was constantly warping back to this one party in 1973 where he'd met this girl, who had left with an older man just as Young Normando was going to ask her to bug out with him. Normando was convinced he could be that older man, if he could just find that one girl again.

Lydia managed to shrink into the background at the first Time Travel Club meeting, without having to say anything. A week later, she decided to stick around for another meeting, because it was better than just going home alone, and nobody was going for pie this time.

This time, the others asked Lydia about her own journeys through time, and she said she didn't have a time machine and if she did, she would just use it to make the itchy insomniac nights end sooner so she could wander alone in the sun rather than hide alone in the dark.

Oh, they said.

Lydia felt guilty about harshing their shared fantasy like that, to the point where she spent the next week obsessing about what a jerk she'd been and even had to call Nate once or twice to report that she was a terrible person and she was struggling with some Dark Thoughts. She vowed not to crash the Time Travel Club meeting again, because she was not going to be a disruptive influence.

Instead, though, when the twelve-step meeting ended and everybody else straggled out, Lydia said the same thing she'd said the previous couple weeks: "Nah, you guys go on. I'm just going to sit for a spell."

When the time travelers arrived and Malik's baby face lit up with his opening spiel about how this was a safe space for people to share their space/time experiences, Lydia stood up in the middle of his intro and blurted, "I'm a pirate. I sail a galleon in the nineteenth century, I'm the first mate. They call me Bad Bessie, even though I'm named Lydia. Also, I do extreme solar sail racing a couple hundred years from now, but that's only on weekends. Sorry I didn't say last week. I was embarrassed because piracy is against the law." Then she sat down, very fast. Everybody applauded and clapped her on the back and thanked her for sharing. This time around, there were a half dozen people in the group, up from the usual four or five.

Lydia wasn't really a pirate, though she did work at a pirate-themed adult bookstore near the interstate called the Lusty Doubloon, with the Os in "Doubloon" forming the absurdly globular breasts of its tricorner-hatted mascot. Lydia got pretty tired of shooting down pickup lines from the type of men who couldn't figure out how to find porn on the internet. Something about Lydia's dishwater blond hair and smattering of monster tattoos apparently did it for those guys. The shower in Lydia's studio apartment was always pretty revolting, because the smell of bleach or Lysol reminded her of the video booths at work.

Anyway, after that, Lydia started sticking around for Time Travel Club every week, as a chaser for her twelve-step meeting. It helped get her back on an even keel so she could drive home without shivering so hard she couldn't see the road. She even started hanging out with Malik and Jerboa socially— Malik was willing to quit talking about palm wine around her, and they all started going out for fancy tea at the place at the mall, the one that put the leaves inside a paper satchel that you had to steep for exactly five minutes or Everything Would Be Ruined. Lydia and Jerboa went to an all-ages concert together and didn't care that they were about ten years older than everybody else there—they'd obviously misaligned the temporal stabilizers and arrived too late, but still just in time. "Just in time" was Jerboa's favorite catchphrase, and they never said it without a glimpse of sharp little teeth, a vigorous nod, and a widening of their brown-green eyes.

For six months, the Time Travelers' meeting slowly became Lydia's favorite thing every week, and these weirdos became her particular gang. Until one day, Madame Alberta showed up and brought the one thing that's guaranteed to ruin any Time Travel Club ever: an actual working time machine.

Lydia's one-year coin was exactly where Jerboa had said it would be: on the roof of the house next door to Madame Alberta's, nestled in some dead leaves in the crook between a brick gable and the upward slope of rooftop. She managed to borrow the neighbor's ladder by sort of explaining. The journey through the space-time continuum didn't seem to have messed up Lydia's coin at all, but it had gotten a layer of grime from sitting overnight. She cleaned it with one of the sanitizing wipes at work before returning it to its usual front pocket.

About a week later, Lydia met up with Malik and Jerboa for bubble tea at this place in the Asian Mall, where they also served peanut honey toast and squid balls and stuff. Lydia liked the feeling of the squidgy tapioca blobs gliding up the fat straw and then falling into her teeth. Alien larvae. Never to hatch. Alien tadpoles squirming to death in her tummy.

None of them had shown up for Time Travel Club the previous night. Normando had called them all in a panic, wanting to know where everybody was. Somehow Malik had thought Jerboa would show up, and Jerboa had figured Lydia would stick around after her other meeting.

"It's just . . ." Malik looked into his mug of regular old coffee, with a tragic expression accentuated by hot steam. "What's the point of sharing our silly make-believe stories about being time travelers when we built an actual real time machine, and it was no good?"

"Well, the machine worked," Jerboa said, looking at the dirty cracked tile floor. "It's just that you can't actually use it to visit the past or the future, in person. Lydia's coin was displaced upward at an angle of about thirty-six degrees by the Earth's rotation and orbit around the sun. The further forward and backward in time you go, the more extreme the spatial displacement, because the distance traveled is the *square* of the time traveled. Send something an hour and a half forward in time and you'd be over four hundred kilometers away from Earth. Or deep underground, depending on the time of day."

"So if we wanted to travel a few years ahead," Lydia said, "we would need to send a spaceship. So it could fly back to Earth from wherever it appeared."

"I doubt you'd be able to transport an object that size," said Jerboa. "From what Madame Alberta explained, anything more than about 216 cubic feet or about 200 pounds and the energy costs go up exponentially." Madame Alberta hadn't answered the door when Lydia went to get her coin back. None of them had heard from Madame Alberta since then, either.

Not only that, but once you were talking about traversing years rather than days, then other factors—such as the sun's acceleration toward the center of the galaxy and the galaxy's acceleration toward the Virgo Supercluster— came more into play. You might not ever find Earth again.

They all sat for a long time, listening to the Cantopop and their own internal monologues about failure. Lydia was thinking that an orbit is a fragile thing, after all. You take centripetal force for granted at your peril. She could see Malik, Jerboa, and herself preparing to drift away from each other once and for all. Free to follow their separate trajectories. Separate futures. She had a clawing certainty that this was the last time the three of them would ever see each other, and she was going to lose the Time Travel Club forever.

And then it hit her, a way to turn this into something good. And keep the group together.

"Wait a minute," said Lydia. "So we don't have a machine that lets a person visit the past or future. But don't people spend kind of a lot of money to launch objects into space? Like, satellites and stuff?"

"Yes," said Jerboa. "It costs tons of money just to lift a pound of material out of our gravity well." And then for the first time that day, Jerboa looked up from the floor and shook off their curtain of black hair so you could actually see the makings of a grin. "Oh. Yeah. I see what you're saying. We don't have a time machine, we have a cheap, simple way to launch things into space. You just send something a few hours into the future and it's in the exosphere. We can probably calculate exact distances and trajectories, with a little practice. The hard part will be achieving a stable orbit."

"So?" Malik said. "I don't see how that helps anything . . . Oh. You're suggesting we turn this into a money-making opportunity."

Lydia couldn't help thinking of the fact that her truck needed an oil change and a new headpipe and four new tires and the ability to start when she turned the key in the ignition. Not to mention, she needed to never go near the Lusty Doubloon again. "It's better than nothing," she said. "Until we figure out what else this machine can do."

"Look at it this way," Jerboa said to Malik. "If we are able to launch a payload into orbit on a regular basis, then that's a repeatable result. A repeatable result is the first step toward being able to do something else. We can use the money to reinvest in the project."

"Well . . ." Malik broke out into a smile, too. Radiant. "If we can talk Madame Alberta into it, then sure."

They phoned Madame Alberta a hundred times and she never picked up. At last, they just went to her house and kept banging on the door until she opened up.

Madame Alberta was drunk. Not just regular drunk, but long-term drunk. Like she had gotten drunk a week ago and never sobered up. Lydia took one look at her, one whiff of the booze fumes, and had to go outside and dry heave. She sat, bent double, on Madame Alberta's tiny lawn, almost within view of the Saint Ignatius College science lab that they'd stolen all that gear from a few months earlier. From inside the house, she heard Malik and Jerboa trying to explain to Madame Alberta that they had figured out what happened to the coin, and how they could turn it into kind of a good thing.

They were having a hard time getting through to her. Madame Alberta's Fauxropean accent was basically gone, and she sounded like a bitter old drunk lady from New Jersey who just wanted to drink herself to death.

Eventually, Malik came out and put one big hand gently on Lydia's shoulder. "You should go home," he said. "Jerboa and I will help her sober up and then we'll talk her through this. I promise we won't make any decisions until you're there to take part."

Lydia nodded and got in her rusty old Ford, which rattled and groaned and finally came to a semblance of life long enough to let her roll back down the highway to her crappy apartment. Good thing it was pretty much downhill all the way.

When Madame Alberta first visited the Time Travel Club, nobody quite knew what to make of her. She had olive skin, black hair, and a black beauty mark on the left side of her face, which tended to change its location every time Lydia saw her. Madame Alberta wore a dark head scarf, or maybe a snood, and a long black dress with a slit up one side.

That first meeting, her Eurasian accent was the thickest and fakest it would ever be: "I have the working theory of the time machine. And the prototype that is, how you say, half built. I need a few more pairs of hands to help me complete the assembly, but also I require the ethical advice."

"Like a steering committee," said Jerboa, perking up with a quick sideways head motion.

"Even so," said Madame Alberta. "Much like the Unitarian church upstairs, the time machine has need of a steering committee."

At first, everybody assumed Madame Alberta was just sharing her own time travel fantasy—albeit one that was a lot more elaborate, and involved a lot more delayed gratification, than everybody else's. Still, the rest of the meeting was sort of muted. Lydia was all set to share her latest experiences with solar sail demolition derby, the most dangerous sport that would ever exist. Malik was having drama with the Babylonians, either in the past or in the future, Lydia wasn't sure which. But Madame Alberta had a quiet certainty that threw the group out of whack.

"I leave you now," said Madame Alberta, bowing and curtseying in a single weird arm-sweeping motion that made her appear to be the master of a particularly esoteric drunken martial arts style. "Take the next week to discuss my proposition. Be aware, though: this will be the most challenging of ventures." She whooshed out of the room, long flowy dress trailing behind her.

Nobody actually spent the week between meetings debating whether they wanted to help Madame Alberta build her time machine—instead, Lydia kept asking the other members whether they could find an excuse to kick her out of the group. "She freaks me out, man," Lydia said on the phone to Malik on Sunday evening.

"I don't know," Malik said. "I mean, we've never kicked anybody out before. There was that one guy who seemed like he had a pretty serious drug problem last year, with his whole astral projection shtick. But he stopped coming on his own, after a couple times."

"I just don't like it," said Lydia. "I have a terrible feeling she's going to ruin everything." She didn't add that she really needed this group to continue the way it was, that these people were becoming her only friends and the only reason she felt like the future might actually really exist for her. She didn't want to get needy or anything.

"Eh," said Malik. "It's a time travel club. If she becomes a problem, we'll just go back in time and change our meeting place last year, so she won't find us."

"Good point."

Jerboa was the one who found the article in the Berkeley *Daily Voice*—a physics professor who lectured at Berkeley and also worked at Lawrence Livermore had gone missing in highly mysterious circumstances, six months earlier. The photo of the vanished Professor Martindale—dark hair, laughing gray eyes, narrow mouth—looked rather a lot like Madame Alberta, except without any beauty mark or giant scarf.

Jerboa emailed the link to the article to Lydia and Malik. "Do you think . . . ?" the email read.

The next meeting came around. Besides the three core members and Madame Alberta, there was Normando, who had finally tracked down that hippie chick in 1973 and was now going on the same first date with her over and over again, arriving five minutes earlier each time to pick her up. Lydia did not think that would actually work in real life.

The others waited until Normando had run out of steam describing his latest interlude with Starshine Ladyswirl and had wandered out to smoke a (vaguely postcoital) cigarette, before they started interrogating Madame Alberta. How did this alleged time machine work? Why was she building it in her laundry room instead of at a proper research institution? Had she absconded from Berkeley with some government-funded research, and if so were they all going to jail if they helped her?

"Let us say, for the sake of the argument"—Madame Alberta played up her weird accent even as her true identity as a college professor from Camden was brought to light—"that I had developed some of the theory of the time travel while on the payroll of the government. Yes? In that hypothetical situation, what would be the ethical thing to do? You are my steering committee, please to tell me."

"Well," Malik said. "I don't know that you want the government to have a time machine."

"Yeah, yeah," Jerboa said. "They already have warrantless wiretaps and indefinite detention. Imagine if they could go back in time and spy on you in the past. Or kill people as little children."

"Well, but," Lydia said. "I mean, wouldn't it still be your responsibility to share your research?" But the others were already on Madame Alberta's side.

"As to how it works . . ." Madame Alberta reached into her big black trench coat and pulled out a big rolled-up set of plans covered in equations and drawings, which meant nothing to anybody. "Shall we say that it was the accidental discovery? One was actually working on a project for the Department of Energy aimed at finding a way to eliminate the atomic waste. Instead, one stumbled on a method of using spent uranium to create an opening two Planck lengths wide, lasting a few fractions of a microsecond, with the other end a few seconds in the future."

"Uh-huh," Lydia said. "So . . . you could create a wormhole too tiny to see, that only allowed you to travel a few seconds forward in time. That's, um . . . useful, I guess."

"But then! One discovers that one might be able to generate a much larger temporal rift, opting out of the fundamental forces, and it would be stable enough to move a person or a moderate-size object either forward or backward in time, anywhere from a few minutes to a few thousand years, in the exact same physical location," said Madame Alberta. "One begins to panic, imagining this power in the hands of the government. This is all the hypothetical situation, of course. In reality, one knows nothing of this Professor Martindale of whom you speaks."

"But," said Lydia. "I mean, why us? I mean, assuming you really do have the makings of a time machine in your laundry room. Why not reach out to some actual scientists?" Then she answered her own question: "Because you would be worried they would tell the government. Okay, but the world is full of smart amateurs and clever geeks. And us? I mean, I work the day shift at a . . ." She tried to think of a way to say "pirate-themed sex shop" that didn't sound quite so depressing. "Malik is a physical therapist. Jerboa has a physics degree, sure, but that was years ago, and more recently they've been working as a case worker for teenagers with sexual abuse issues. Which is totally great, but I'm sure you can find bigger experts out there."

"One has chosen with the greatest of care." Madame Alberta fixed Lydia with an intense gaze, like she could see all the way into Lydia's damaged core. (Or maybe like someone who was used to wearing glasses but had decided to pretend she had 20/20 vision.) "You are all good people, with the strong moral centers. You have given much thought to the time travel, and yet you speak of it without any avarice in your hearts. Not once have I heard any of you talk of using the time travel for wealth or personal advancement."

"Well, except for Normando using it to get in Ladyswirl's pants," said Malik.

"Even as you say, except for Normando." Madame Alberta did another one of her painful-to-watch bow-curtsies. "So. What is your decision? Will you join me in this great and terrible undertaking or not?"

What could they do? They all raised their hands and said that they were in.

Ricky was the Chief Fascination Evangelist for Garbo.com, a web start-up for rich, paranoid people who wanted to be left alone. (They were trying to launch a premium service where you could watch yourself via satellite 24/7, to make sure nobody else was watching you.) Ricky wore denim shirts with the sleeves square-folded to the elbows, and white silk ties with black corduroys, and his neck funneled out of the blue jean collar and led to a round, pale head, shaved except for wispy sideburns. He wore steel-rimmed glasses. He had a habit of swinging his arms back and forth and clapping his hands when he was excited, like when he talked about getting a satellite into orbit.

"Everybody else says it'll take months to get our baby into space," Ricky told Malik and Lydia for the fifth or sixth time. "The Kazakhs don't even know when they can do it. But you say you can get our Garbonaut Five Thousand into orbit . . ."

". . . next week," Malik said yet again. "Maybe ten days from now." He canted his palms in midair, like it was no big deal. Launching satellites, whatever. Just another day, putting stuff into orbit.

"Whoa." Ricky arm-clapped in his chair. "That is just out of control. Seriously. Like, nuts."

"We are a hungry new company." Malik gave the same bright smile that he used to announce the start of every Time Travel Club meeting. They had been lucky to find this guy. "We want to build our customer base from the ground up. All the way from the ground, into space. Because we're a space company. Right? Of course we are. Did I mention we're hungry?"

"Hungry is good." Ricky seemed to be studying Malik, and the giant photo of MJL Aerospace's nonexistent rocket, a retrofitted Soyuz. "The hungry survive, the well-fed starve. Or something. So when do I get to see this rocket of yours?

"You can't, sorry," Malik said. "Our, uh, chief rocket scientist is kind of leery about letting people see our proprietary new fuel system technology up close. Here's a picture of it." He gestured at the massive rocket picture on the fake-mahogany wall behind his desk, which they'd spent hours creating in Photoshop and After Effects. MJL Aerospace was subletting ultracheap office space in an industrial park, just up the highway from the Lusty Doubloon.

Malik, Lydia, and Jerboa had been excited about becoming a fake rocket company, until they'd started considering the practical problems. For one thing, nobody will hire you to launch a satellite unless you've already launched a satellite before—it's like how you can't get an entry-level job unless you've already had work experience.

Plus, they weren't entirely sure that they could get a satellite into a stable orbit, which was one of the dozen reasons Malik was sweating. They could definitely place a satellite at different points in orbit, and different trajectories, by adjusting the time of day, the distance traveled, and the location on Earth they started from. After that, the satellite wouldn't be moving fast enough to stay in orbit on its own. It would need extra boosters to get up to speed. Jerboa thought they could send a satellite way higher—around 42,000 kilometers away from Earth—and then use relatively small rockets to speed it up as it slowly dropped to the correct orbit. But even if that worked, it would require Garbo.com to customize the Garbonaut 5000 quite a bit. And Madame Alberta had severe doubts.

"Sorry, man," said Ricky. "I'm not sure I can get my people to authorize a satellite launch based on just seeing a picture of the rocket. It's a nice picture, though. Good sense of composition. Like, the clouds look really pretty, with that one flock of birds in the distance. Poetic, you know."

"Of course you can see the rocket," Lydia interjected. She was sitting off to one side, taking notes on the meeting, wearing cheap pantyhose in a forty-dollar swivel chair. With puffy sleeves covering her tattoos (one for every country she'd ever visited). "Just maybe not before next week's launch. If you're willing to wait a few months, we can arrange a site visit and stuff. We just can't show you the rocket before our next launch window."

"Right," Malik said. "If you still want to launch next week, though, we can give you a sixty-percent discount."

"Sixty percent?" Ricky said, suddenly seeming interested again.

"Sixty-five percent," Malik said. "We're a young hungry company. We have a lot to prove. Our business model is devouring the weak. We hate to launch with spare capacity."

Maybe going straight to 65 percent was a mistake, or maybe the "devouring the weak" thing had been too much. In any case, Ricky seemed uneasy again. "Huh," he said. "So how many test launches have you guys done? My friend who works for NASA says every rocket launch in the world gets tracked."

"We've done a slew of test launches," Malik said. "Like, a dozen. We have some proprietary stealth technology, so people probably missed them." And then he went way off script. "Our company founder, Augustus Marzipan IV, grew up around rockets. His uncle was Wernher von Braun's wine steward, so rockets are in his blood." Ricky's frown got more and more pinched.

"Well," Ricky said at last, standing up from his cheap metal chair. "I will definitely bring your proposal to our Senior Visionizer, Terry. But I have a feeling the VCs aren't going to want to pay for a launch without kicking the tires. I'm not the one who writes the checks, you know. If I wrote the checks, a lot of things would be different." And then he paused, probably imagining all the things that would happen if he wrote the checks.

"When Augustus Marzipan was only five years old, his pet dalmatian, Henry, was sent into space. Never to return," said Malik, as if inventing more stories would cushion his fall off the cliff he'd already walked over. "That's where our commitment to safety comes from."

"That's great," said Ricky. "I love dogs." He was already halfway out the door.

As soon as Ricky was gone, Malik sagged as though the air had gone out of him. He rubbed his brow with one listless hand. "We're a young hungry company," he said. "We're a hungry young company. Which way sounds better? I can't tell."

"That could have gone worse," Lydia said.

"I can't do this," Malik said. "I just can't. I'm sorry. I am good at pretending for fun. I just can't do it for money. I'm really sorry."

Lydia felt like the worst person in the world, even as she said, "Lots of people start out pretending for fun and then move into pretending for money. That's the American dream." The sun was already going down behind the cement fountain outside, and she realized she was going to be late for her twelve-step group soon. She started pulling her coat and purse and scarf together. "Hey, I gotta run. I'll see you at Time Travel Club, okay?"

"I think I'm going to skip it," Malik said. "I can't. I just . . . I can't."

"What?" Lydia felt like if Malik didn't come to Time Travel Club, it would be the proof that something was seriously wrong and their whole foundation was splitting apart. This would be provably her bad.

"I'm just too exhausted. Sorry."

Lydia came over and sat on the desk so she could see Malik's face behind his hand. "Come on," she pleaded. "Time Travel Club is your baby. We can't just have a meeting without you. That would be weird. Come on. We won't even talk about being a fake aerospace company. We couldn't talk about that in front of Normando, anyway."

Malik sighed, like he was going to argue. Then he lifted the loop of his tie all the way off, now that he was done playing CEO. For a second, his rep-stripe tie was a halo. "Okay, fine," he said. "It'll be good to hang out and not talk business for a while."

"Yeah, exactly. It'll be mellow," Lydia said. She felt the terror receding, but not entirely.

Normando was freaking out because his girlfriend in 1973 had dumped him. (Long story short, his strategy of arriving earlier and earlier for the same first date had backfired.) A couple of other semi-regulars showed up too, including Betty the Cyborg from the Dawn of Time. Madame Alberta showed up too, even though she hadn't ever shown any interest in visiting their aerospace office. She sat in the corner, studying the core members of the group, maybe to judge whether she'd chosen wisely. As if she could somehow go back and change that decision, which of course she couldn't.

Malik tried to talk about his last trip to the thirty-second century, but he kept staring at his CEO shoes and saying things like "The neo-Babylonians were giving us grief. But we were young and hungry." And then trailing off, like his heart just wasn't in it.

Jerboa saw Malik running out of steam, and they jumped in. "I met Christopher Marlowe. He told me that his version of *Faust* originally ended with Dr. Faust and Helen of Troy running away together and teaching geometrically complex hand dances in Shropshire, and they made him change it." Jerboa talked very fast, like an addict trying to stay high. Or a comedian trying not to get booed offstage. "He told me to call him Kit and showed me the difference between a doublet and a singlet. A doublet is not two singlets, did you know that?"

Sitting in the Unitarian basement, under the purple dove hands, Lydia watched Malik starting to say things and then just petering out with a shrug or a shake of the head, and Jerboa rattling on and not giving anybody else a chance to talk. Guilt.

And then, just as Lydia was crawling out of her skin, Madame Alberta stood up. "I have a thing to confess," she said.

Malik and Lydia stared up at her, fearing she was about to blow the whistle on their scam. Jerboa stopped breathing.

"I am from an alternative timeline," Madame Alberta said. "It is the world where the American Revolution did not happen and the British Empire had the conquest of all of South America. The Americas, Africa, Asia—the British ruled all. Until the rest of Europe launched the great world war to stop the British imperialism. Britain discovered the nuclear weapons and Europe burned to ashes. I travel over and over, I travel through time, to try and change history. Instead I find myself here, in this other universe, and I can never return home."

"Uh," Malik said. "Thanks for sharing." He looked relieved and weirded out.

At last, Madame Alberta explained: "It is the warning. Sometimes you have the power to change the world, but power is not an opportunity. It is a choice."

After that, nobody had much to say. Malik and Jerboa didn't look at Lydia or each other as they left, and nobody was surprised when the Time Travel Club's meeting was canceled the following week, or when the club basically ceased to exist some time after that.

Malik, Jerboa, and Lydia sat in the front of Malik's big van on the grassy roadside, waiting for Madame Alberta to come back and tell them where they were going. Madame Alberta supposedly knew where they could dig up some improperly buried spent uranium from the power plant, and the back of the van was full of pretty good safety gear that Madame Alberta had scared up for them. The faceplates of the suits glared up at Lydia from their uncomfortable resting place. The three of them were psyching themselves up to go and possibly irradiate the shit out of themselves.

Worth it, if the thing they were helping to build in Madame Alberta's laundry room was a real time machine and not just another figment.

"You guys never even asked," Lydia said around one in the morning, when they were all starting to wonder if Madame Alberta was going to show up. "I mean, about me, and why I was in that twelve-step group before the Time Travel Club meetings. You don't know anything about me, or what I've done."

"We know all about you," Malik said. "You're a pirate."

"You do extreme solar sail sports in the future," Jerboa added. "What else is there to know?"

"But," Lydia said. "I could be a criminal. I might have killed someone. I could be as bad as that astral projection guy."

"Lydia," Malik put one hand on her shoulder, like super gently. "We know you."

Nobody spoke for a while. Every few minutes, Malik turned on the engine so they could get some heat, and the silence between engine starts was deeper than ordinary silence.

"I had blackouts," Lydia said. "Like, a lot of blackouts. I would lose hours at a time, no clue where I'd been or how I'd gotten there. I would just be in the middle of talking to people, or behind the wheel of a car in the middle of nowhere, with no clue. I worked at this high-powered sales office, we obliterated our targets. Everybody drank all the time. Pitchers of beer, of martinis, of margaritas. The pitcher was like the emblem of our solidarity. You couldn't turn the pitcher away, it would be like spitting on the team. We made so much money. I had this girlfriend, Sara, with this amazing red hair, who I couldn't even talk to when we were sober. We would just lie in bed naked, with a bottle of tequila propped up between us. I knew it was just a matter of time before I did something really unforgivable during one of those blackouts. Especially after Sara decided to move out."

"So what happened?" Jerboa said.

"In the end, it wasn't anything I did during a blackout that caused everything to implode," Lydia said. "It was what I did to keep myself from ever blacking out again. I got to work early one day and I just lit a bonfire in the fancy conference room. I threw all the contents of the company's wet bar into it."

Once again, nobody talked for a while. Malik turned the engine on and off a couple times, which made it about seven minutes of silence. They were parked by the side of the road, and every once in a while a car simmered past.

"I think that's what makes us such good time travelers, actually." Jerboa's voice cracked a little bit, and Lydia was surprised to see the outlines of tears on their small brown face, in the light of a distant highway detour sign. "We are very experienced at being in the wrong place at the wrong time, and at doing whatever it takes to get ourselves to the right place and the right time."

Lydia put her arm around Jerboa, who was sitting in the middle of the front seat, and they leaned into Lydia's shoulder so just a trace of moisture landed on Lydia's neck.

"You wouldn't believe the places I've had to escape from in the middle of the night," Jerboa said. "The people who tried to fix my, my . . . irregularities. You wouldn't believe the methods that have been tried. People can justify almost anything, if their perspective is limited enough."

Malik wrapped his hand on Jerboa's back, so it was like all three of them were embracing. "We've all had our hearts broken, I guess," he said. "I was a teacher, in one of those Teach For America–style programs. I thought we were all in this together, that we had a shared code. I thought we were altruists. Until they threw me under a bus."

It was then that Malik said the thing about wanting to stand outside history and see the gears grinding from a distance, all of the cruelty and all of the edifices that had been built on human remains. The true power wouldn't be changing history, or even seeing how it turned out, but just seeing the shape of the wheel.

They sat for a good long time in silence again. The engine ticked a little. They stayed leaning into each other as the faceplates watched.

Lydia started to say something like "I just want to hold on to this moment. Here, now, with the two of you. I don't care about whatever else, I just want *this* to last." But just as she started to speak, Madame Alberta tapped on the passenger-side window, right next to Lydia's head, and gestured at her car, which was parked in front of theirs. It was time to suit up and go get some nuclear waste.

Lydia didn't see Malik or Jerboa for a month or so, after Madame Alberta told her weird story about Europe getting nuked. MJL Aerospace shuttered its offices, and Lydia saw the rocket picture in a dumpster as she drove to the Lucky Doubloon. She redoubled her commitment to going to a twelve-step meeting every goddamn day. She finally called her mom back, and went to a few bluegrass concerts.

Lydia got the occasional panicked call from Normando, or one of the other semiregulars, wondering what happened to the club, but she just ignored them.

Until one day Lydia was driving to work, on the day shift again, and she saw Jerboa walking on the side of the road. They kicked the shoulder of the road over and over, kicking dirt and rocks, not looking ahead. Hips and knees jerking almost out of their sockets. Inaudible curses spitting at the gravel.

Lydia pulled over next to Jerboa and honked her horn a couple times, then rolled down the window. "Come on, get in." She turned down the bluegrass on her stereo.

Jerboa gave a gesture between a wave and a "go away."

"Listen, I screwed up," Lydia said. "That aerospace thing was a really bad idea. It wasn't about the money, though, you have to believe me about that. I just wanted to give us a new project, so we wouldn't drift apart."

"It's not your fault." Jerboa did not get in the truck. "I don't blame you."

"Well, I blame myself. I was being selfish. I just didn't want you guys to run away. I was scared. But we need to figure out a way to turn the space travel back into time travel. We can't do that unless we work together."

"It's just not possible," Jerboa said. "For any amount of time displacement beyond a few hours, the variables get harder and harder to calculate. The other day, I did some calculations and figured out that if you traveled one hundred years into the future, you'd wind up around one-tenth of a light-year away. That's just a back-of-the-envelope thing, based on our orbit around the sun."

"Okay, so one problem at a time." Lydia stopped her engine, gambling that it would restart. The bluegrass stopped midphrase. "We need to get some accurate measurements of exactly where stuff ends up when we send it forward and backward in time. To do that, first we need to be able to send stuff out and get it back again."

"There's no way," Jerboa said. "It's strictly a one-way trip."

"We'll figure out a way," Lydia said. "Trial and error. We just need to open a second rift close enough to the first rift to bring our stuff back. Yeah? Once we're good enough, we send people. Eventually, we send people, along with enough equipment to build a telescope in deep space, so we can spy on Earth in the distant past or the far future."

"There are so many steps in there, it's ridiculous," Jerboa said. "Every one of those steps might turn out to be just as impossible as the satellite thing turned out to be. We can't do this with just the four of us, we don't have enough pairs of hands. Or enough expertise."

"That's why we recruit," said Lydia. "We need to find a ton more people who can help us make this happen."

"Except," said Jerboa, fists clenched and eyes red and pinched, "we can't trust just any random people with this. Remember? That's why Madame Alberta brought it to us in the first place, because the temptation to abuse this power would be too great. You could destroy a city with this machine. How on Earth do we find a few dozen people who we can trust with this?"

"The same way we found each other," Lydia said. "The same way Madame Alberta found us. The Time Travel Club."

Jerboa finally got into the truck and snapped the seat belt into place. Nodding slowly, like they were thinking it over.

Ricky from Garbo.com showed up at a meeting of the Time Travel Club several months later. He didn't even realize at first that these were the same people from MJL Aerospace—maybe he'd seen the articles about the club on the various nerd blogs, or maybe he'd seen Malik's appearance on the basic cable TV show *GeekUp!* Or maybe he'd listened to one of their podcasts. They were doing lots and lots of things to expand the membership of the club, without giving the slightest hint about what went on in Madame Alberta's laundry room.

Garbo.com had gone under by now, and Ricky was in grad school. He'd shaved off the big sideburns and wore square Elvis Costello glasses now.

"So I heard this is like a LARP, sort of," Ricky said to Lydia as they were getting a cookie from the cookie table before the meeting started—they'd had to move the meetings from the Unitarian basement to a middle school basketball court, now that they had a few dozen members. Scores of folding chairs, in rows, facing a podium. They even had a cookie table. "You make up your time travel stories and everybody pretends they're true. Right?"

"Sort of," Lydia said. "You'll see. Once the meeting starts, you cannot say anything about these stories not being true. Okay? It's the only real rule."

"Sure thing," Ricky said. "I can do that. I worked for a start-up, remember? I'm good at make-believe."

And Ricky turned out to be one of the more promising new recruits, weirdly enough. He spent a lot of time going to the eighteenth century and teaching Capability Brown about feng shui. Which everybody agreed was probably a good thing for the Enlightenment.

Just a few months after that, Lydia, Malik, and Jerboa found themselves already debating whether to show Ricky the laundry room. Lydia was snapping her thirdhand space suit into place in Madame Alberta's sitting room, with its caved-in sofa and big-screen TV askew. Lydia was happy to obsess over something else, to get her mind off the terrifying thing she was about to do.

"I think he's ready," Lydia said of Ricky. "He's committed to the club."

"I would certainly like to see his face when he finds out how we were really going to launch that satellite into orbit," said Malik, grinning.

"It's too soon," Jerboa said. "I think we ought to wait six months, as a rule, before bringing anyone here. Just to make sure someone is really in tune with the group and isn't going to go trying to tell the wrong people about this. This technology has an immense potential to distort your sense of ethics, and your values."

Lydia tried to nod, but it was hard now that the bulky collar was in place. This space suit was half a size too big, with boots that Lydia's feet slid around in. The crotch of the orange suit was almost MC Hammer wide on her, even with the adult diaper they'd insisted she should wear just in case. The puffy white gloves swallowed her fingers. Malik and Jerboa lowered the helmet into place, and Lydia's entire world was compressed to a gray-tinted rectangle. Good-bye, peripheral vision.

She wondered what sort of tattoo she would get to commemorate this trip.

"Ten minutes," Madame Alberta called from the laundry room. Indeed, it was ten to midnight.

"Are you sure you want to do this?" Jerboa said. "It's not too late to call it off."

"I'm the only one this suit sort of fits," Lydia said. "I'm also the most expendable. And yes. I do want to be the first person to travel through time."

After putting so many disposable objects into that cube, thousands of them before they'd managed to get a single one back, Lydia felt strange about clambering inside the cube herself. She had to hunch over a bit. Malik waved and Jerboa gave a tiny thumbs-up. Betty the Cyborg from the Dawn of Time checked the instruments once more for luck. Steampunk Fred gave a thumbs-up on the calculations. Madame Alberta reached for the clunky lever. Even through her helmet, Lydia heard a greedy soda-belch sound.

A thousand years later, Lydia lost her hold on anything. She couldn't get her footing. There was no footing to get. She felt ill immediately. She'd expected the microgravity, but it still made her feel revolting. She felt drunk, actually. Like she didn't know which way was up. She spun head over ass. If she drifted too far, they would never pull her back. The tiny maneuvering thrusters on her suit were useless, because she had no reference point. She couldn't see a damn thing through this foggy helmet, just blackness. She couldn't find the sun, or any stars, for a moment—then she made out stars. And more stars.

She spun and somersaulted. No control at all. Until she tried the maneuvering thrusters, the way Jerboa had explained. She tried to turn a full 360 so she could locate the sun. She had to remember to breathe normally. Every part of her wanted to hyperventilate.

When she'd turned halfway around on her axis, she didn't see the sun, but she saw something else. At first, she couldn't even make sense of it. There were lights blaring at her. And shapes in motion. She took a few photos with the camera Malik had given her. The whole mass was almost spherical, maybe egg-shaped, but there were jagged edges. As Lydia stared, she made out more details. One of the shapes on the outer edge was the hood of a 1958 Buick, license plate and all. There were pieces of a small passenger airplane bolted on as well, along with a canopy made of some kind of shiny blue material that Lydia had never seen before. Someone had welded a huge collection of junk together, protection against cosmic rays and maybe also decoration.

Some of the moving shapes were people. They were jumping up and down and waving at Lydia. They were behind a big observation window at the center of the egg, a slice of see-through material. They gestured at something below the window. Lydia couldn't make it out at first. Then she squinted and saw that it was a big glowy sign with blocky letters made of massive pixels.

At first, Lydia thought the sign read WELCOME TIME TRAVEL CLUB. Like they knew the Time Travel Club was coming and wanted to prepare a reception committee.

Then she squinted again, just as another rift started opening up to pull her back, a purple blaze all around her, and she realized she had missed a word. The sign actually read WELCOME TO TIME TRAVEL CLUB. They were all members of the club, too, and they were having another meeting. They were inviting her to share her story, any way she could.

L ike many of the other stories in this book, "Six Months, Three Days" started out with a concept: What if two people both saw the future, but they saw it very differently? Doug sees only one future, which can't be changed, while Judy sees many different futures and can choose to steer herself toward the one she wants. This premise opened up fun ideas around fate and free will, but I didn't want to write a treatise about abstract concepts. To turn this into a story about relationships and people, I needed to dig deeper and think about the scariness of falling in love—especially when you know a relationship might not last. I also tapped into one of my biggest obsessions: the fact that we all go through life knowing that horrible loss and devastation awaits us in the future, no matter what we do. "Six Months" morphed into a story about two people who love each other despite knowing too much. This was the first story where I felt like I captured real, raw emotion on the page, after years and years of trying.

SIX MONTHS, THREE DAYS

The man who can see the future has a date with the woman who can see many possible futures.

Judy is nervous but excited, keeps looking at things she's spotted out of the corner of her eye. She's wearing a floral Laura Ashley–style dress with an ankh necklace, and her legs are rambunctious, her calves moving under the table. It's distracting because Doug knows that in two and a half weeks, those cucumber-smooth ankles will be hooked on his shoulders, and that curly reddish-brown hair will spill everywhere onto her lemon-floral pillows; this image of their future coitus has been in Doug's head for years, with varying degrees of clarity, and now it's almost here. The knowledge makes Doug almost giggle at the wrong moment, but then it hits him: she's seen this future too—or she may have, anyway.

Doug has his sandy hair cut in a neat fringe that was almost fashionable a couple years ago. You might think he cuts his own hair, but Judy knows he doesn't, because he'll tell her otherwise in a few weeks. He's much, much better looking than she thought he would be, and this comes as a huge relief.

He has rude, pouty lips and an upper lip that darkens no matter how often he shaves it, with Oakley Scavenger glasses. And he's almost a foot taller than her, six foot four. Now that Judy's seen Doug for real, she's reimagining all the conversations they might be having in the coming weeks and months, all of the drama and all of the sweetness. The fact that Judy can be attracted to him, knowing everything that could lie ahead, consoles her tremendously.

Judy is nattering about some Chinese novelist she's been reading in translation, one of those cruel satirists from the days after the May Fourth Movement, from back when writers were so conflicted they had to rename themselves things like "Contra Diction." Doug is just staring at her, not saying anything, until it creeps her out a little.

"What?" Doug says at last, because Judy has stopped talking and they're both just looking at each other.

"You were staring at me," Judy says.

"I was . . ." Doug hesitates, then just comes out and says it. "I was savoring the moment. You know, you can know something's coming from a long way off, you know for years ahead of time the exact day and the very hour when it'll arrive. Then it arrives, and when it arrives, all you can think about is how soon it'll be gone."

"Well, I didn't know the hour and the day when you and I would meet." Judy puts a hand on his. "I saw many different hours and days. In one timeline, we would have met two years ago. In another, we'd meet a few months from now. There are plenty of timelines where we never meet at all."

Doug laughs, then waves a hand to show that he's not laughing at her, although the gesture doesn't really clarify whom or what he's actually laughing at.

Judy is drinking a cocktail called the Coalminer's Daughter, made out of ten kinds of darkness. It overwhelms her senses with sugary pungency and leaves her lips black for a moment. Doug is drinking a wheaty pilsner from a tapered glass, in gulps. After one of them, Doug cuts to the chase. "So this is the part where I ask. I mean, I know what happens next between you and me. But here's where I ask what *you* think happens next."

"Well," Judy says. "There are a million tracks, you know. It's like raindrops falling into a cistern, they're separate until they hit the surface, and then they become the past, all undifferentiated. But there are an awful lot of futures where you and I date for about six months."

"Six months and three days," Doug says. "Not that I've counted or any-thing."

"And it ends badly."

"I break my leg."

"You break your leg ruining my bicycle. I like that bike. It's a noble five-speed in a sea of fixies."

"So you agree with me." Doug has been leaning forward, staring at Judy like a psycho again. He leans back so that the amber light spilling out of the Radish Saloon's tiny lampshades turns him the same color as his beer. "You see the same future I do." Like she's passed some kind of test.

"You didn't know what I was going to say in advance?" Judy says.

"It doesn't work like that—not for me, anyway. Remembering the future is just like remembering the past. I don't have perfect recall, I don't hang on to every detail, the transition from short-term memory to long-term mem-ory is not always graceful."

"I guess it's like memory for me too," Judy says.

Doug feels an unfamiliar sensation, and he realizes after a while it's com-fort. He's never felt this at home with another human being, especially after such a short time. Doug is accustomed to meeting people and knowing bits and pieces of their futures, from stuff he'll learn later. Or if Doug meets you and doesn't know anything about your future, that means he'll never give a crap about you at any point down the line. This makes for awkward social interactions, either way.

They get another round of drinks. Doug gets the same beer again, Judy gets a red concoction called a Bloody Mutiny.

"So there's one thing I don't get," Doug says. "You believe you have a choice among futures—and I think you're wrong, you're seeing one true future and a bunch of false ones."

"You're probably going to spend the next six months trying to convince yourself of that," Judy says.

"So why are you dating me at all, if you get to choose? You know how it'll turn out. For that matter, why aren't you rich and famous? Why not pick a future where you win the lottery, or become a star?"

Doug works in tech support, in a poorly ventilated sub-basement of a tech company in Providence, Rhode Island, that he knows will go out of busi-ness in a couple years. He will work there until the company fails, choking on the fumes from old computers, and then be unemployed a few months.

"Well," Judy says. "It's not really that simple. I mean, the next six months, assuming I don't change my mind, they contain some of the happiest moments of my life, and I see it leading to some good things, later on. And you know, I've seen some tracks where I get rich, I become a public figure, and they never end well. I've got my eye on this one future, this one node way off in the distance, where I die aged ninety-seven, surrounded by lovers and grandchildren and cats. Whenever I have a big decision to make, I try to see the straightest path to that moment."

"So I'm a stepping stone," Doug says, not at all bitterly. He's somehow finished his second beer already, even though Judy's barely made a dent in her Bloody Mutiny.

"You're maybe going to take this journey with me for a spell," Judy says. "People aren't stones."

And then Doug has to catch the last train back to Providence, and Judy has to bike home to Somerville. Marva, her roommate, has made popcorn and hot chocolate, and wants to know the whole story.

"It was nice," Judy says. "He was a lot cuter in person than I'd remembered, which is really nice. He's tall."

"That's it?" Marva said. "Oh come on, details. You finally meet the only other freaking clairvoyant on Earth, your future boyfriend, and all you have to say is 'He's tall.' Uh-uh. You are going to spill like a fucking oil tanker, I will ply you with hot chocolate, I may resort to Jim Beam, even."

Marva's "real" name is Martha, but she changed it years ago. She's a grad student studying eighteenth-century lit, and even Judy can't help her decide whether to finish her PhD. She's slightly chubby, with perfect crimson hair and clothing by Sanrio, Torrid, and Hot Topic. She is fond of calling herself "mallternative."

"I'm drunk enough already. I nearly fell off my bicycle a couple times," Judy says.

The living room is a pigsty, so they sit in Judy's room, which isn't much better. Judy hoards items she might need in one of the futures she's witnessed, and they cover every surface. There's a plastic replica of a Filipino fast-food mascot, Jollibee, which she might give to this one girl Sukey in a couple of years, completing Sukey's collection and making her a friend for life—or Judy and Sukey may never meet at all. A phalanx of stuffed animals crowds Judy and Marva on the big fluffy bed. The room smells like a sachet of whoop-ass (cardamom, cinnamon, lavender) that Judy opened up earlier.

"He's a really sweet guy." Judy cannot stop talking in platitudes, which bothers her. "I mean, he's really lost, but he manages to be brave. I can't imagine what it would be like, to feel like you have no free will at all."

Marva doesn't point out the obvious thing—that Judy only sees choices for herself, not anybody else. Suppose a guy named Rocky asks Marva out on a date, and Judy sees a future in which Marva complains, afterward, that their date was the worst evening of her life. In that case, there are two futures: one in which Judy tells Marva what she sees, and one in which she doesn't. Marva will go on the miserable date with Rocky, unless Judy tells her what she knows.

(On the plus side, in fifteen months, Judy will drag Marva out to a party where she meets the love of her life. So there's that.)

"Doug's right," Marva says. "I mean, if you really have a choice about this, you shouldn't go through with it. You know it's going to be a disaster in the end. You're the one person on Earth who can avoid the pain, and you still go sticking fingers in the socket."

"Yeah, but . . ." Judy decides this will go a lot easier if there are marshmallows in the cocoa, and she runs back to the kitchen alcove. "But going out with this guy leads to good things later on. There's a realization that I come to as a result of getting my heart broken. I come to understand something."

"And what's that?"

Judy finds the bag of marshmallows. They are stale. She decides cocoa will revitalize them, drags them back to her bedroom, along with a glass of water.

"I have no idea, honestly. That's the way with epiphanies: you can't know in advance what they'll be. Even me. I can see them coming, but I can't understand something until I understand it."

"So you're saying that the future that Doug believes is the only possible future just happens to be the best of all worlds. Is this some Leibniz shit? Does Dougie always automatically see the nicest future or something?"

"I don't think so." Judy gets gummed up by popcorn, sticky marshmallows cocoa, and coughs her lungs out. She swigs the glass of water she brought for just this moment. "I mean—" She coughs again, and downs the rest of the water. "I mean, in Doug's version, he's only forty-three when he dies, and he's pretty broken by then. His last few years are dreadful. He tells me all about it in a few weeks."

"Wow," Marva says. "Damn. So are you going to try and save him? Is that what's going on here?"

"I honestly do not know. I'll keep you posted."

Doug, meanwhile, is sitting on his militarily neat bed, with its single hospital-cornered blanket and pillow. His apartment is almost pathologically tidy. Doug stares at his one shelf of books and his handful of carefully chosen items that play a role in his future. He chews his thumb. For the first time in years, Doug desperately wishes he had options.

He almost grabs his phone to call Judy and tell her to get the hell away from him, because he will collapse all of her branching pathways into a dark tunnel, once and for all. But he knows he won't tell her that, and even if he did, she wouldn't listen. He doesn't love her, but he knows he will in a couple weeks, and it already hurts.

"God damn it! Fucking god fucking damn it fuck!" Doug throws his favorite porcelain bust of Wonder Woman on the floor. Wonder Woman's head breaks into two jagged pieces, cleaving her magic tiara in half. This image, of the Amazon's raggedly bisected head, has always been in Doug's mind, whenever he's looked at the intact bust.

Doug sits a minute, dry-sobbing. Then he goes and gets his dustpan and brush.

He phones Judy a few days later. "Hey, so do you want to hang out again on Friday?"

"Sure," Judy says. "I can come down to Providence this time. Where do you want to meet up?"

"Surprise me," says Doug.

"You're a funny man."

Judy will be the second long-term relationship of Doug's life. His first was with Pamela, an artist he met in college, who made headless figurines of people who were recognizable from the neck down. (Headless Superman. Headless Captain Kirk. And yes, headless Wonder Woman, which Doug always found bitterly amusing for reasons he couldn't explain.) They were together nearly five years, and Doug never told her his secret. Which meant a lot of pretending to be surprised at stuff. Doug is used to people thinking he's kind of a weirdo.

Doug and Judy meet for dinner at one of those mom-and-pop Portuguese places in East Providence, sharing grilled squid and seared cod, with fragrant rice, and a bottle of heady vinho verde. Then they walk Judy's bike back across the river toward the kinda-sorta gay bar on Wickenden Street. "The thing I like about Providence," says Doug, "is it's one of the American cities that knows its best days are behind it. So it's automatically decadent, and sort of European."

"Well," says Judy, "it's always a choice between urban decay or growth, right? I mean, cities aren't capable of homeostasis."

"Do you know what I'm thinking?" Doug is thinking he wants to kiss Judy. She leans up and kisses him first, on the bridge in the middle of the East Bay Bike Path. They stand and watch the freeway lights reflected on the water, holding hands. Everything is cold and lovely and the air smells rich.

Doug turns and looks into Judy's face, which the bridge lights have turned yellow. "I've been waiting for this moment all my life." Doug realizes he's inadvertently quoted Phil Collins. First he's mortified, then he starts laughing like a maniac. For the next half hour, Doug and Judy speak only in Phil Collins quotes.

"You can't hurry love," Judy says, which is only technically a Collins line.

Over microbrews on Wickenden, they swap origin stories, even though they already know most of it. Judy's is pretty simple: she was a little kid who overthought choices like which summer camp to go to, until she realized she could see how either decision would turn out. She still flinches when she remembers how she almost gave a valentine in third grade to Dick Petersen, who would have destroyed her. Doug's story is a lot worse: he started seeing the steps ahead, a little at a time, and then he realized his dad would die in about a year. He tried everything he could think of, for a whole year, to save his dad's life. He even buried the car keys two feet deep on the day of his dad's accident. No fucking use.

"Turns out getting to mourn in advance doesn't make the mourning afterward any less hard," Doug says through a beer glass snout.

"Oh man," Judy says. She knew this stuff, but hearing it is different. "I'm so sorry."

"It's okay," Doug says. "It was a long time ago."

Soon it's almost time for Judy to bike back to the train station, near that godawful giant mall and the canal where they light the water on fire sometimes.

"I want you to try and do something for me." Judy takes Doug's hands. "Can you try to break out of the script? Not the big stuff that you think is going to happen, but just little things that you couldn't be sure about in advance if you tried. Try to surprise yourself. And maybe all those little deviations will add up to something bigger."

"I don't think it would make any difference," Doug says.

"You never know," Judy says. "There are things that I remember differently every time I think about them. Things from the past, I mean. When I was in college, I went through a phase of hating my parents, and I remembered all this stuff they did, from my childhood, as borderline abusive. Then a few years ago, I found myself recalling those same incidents again, only now they seemed totally different. Barely the same events."

"The brain is weird," Doug says.

"So you never know," Judy says. "Change the details, you may change the big picture." But she already knows nothing will come of this.

A week later, Doug and Judy lie together in her bed after having sex for the first time. It was even better than the image Doug's carried in his head since puberty. For the first time, Doug understands why people talk about sex as this transcendent thing, chains of selfhood melting away, endless abundance. They looked into each other's eyes the whole time. As for Judy, she's having that oxytocin thing she's always thought was a myth, her forehead resting on Doug's smooth chest—if she moved her head an inch she'd hear his heart beating, but she doesn't need to.

Judy gets up to pee an hour later, and when she comes back and hangs up her robe, Doug is lying there with a look of horror on his face.

"What's wrong?" She doesn't want to ask, but she does anyway.

"I'm sorry." He sits up. "I'm just so happy, and . . . I can count the awesome moments in my life on a hand and a half. And I'm burning through them too fast. This is just so perfect right now. And, you know. I'm trying not to think. About—"

Judy knows that if she brings up the topic they've been avoiding, they will have an unpleasant conversation, but she has to. "You have to stop this. It's obvious you can do what I do, you can see more than one branch. All you have to do is try. I know you were hurt when you were little, your dad died, and you convinced yourself that you were helpless. I'm sorry about that. But now, I feel like you're actually comfortable being trapped. You don't even try anymore."

"I do." Doug is shaking. "I do try. I try every day. How dare you say I don't try."

"You don't really. I don't believe you. I'm sorry, but I don't."

"You know it's true." Doug calms down and looks Judy square in the face.

Without his glasses, his eyes look as gray as the sea on a cloudy day. "The thing you told me about Marva—you always know what she's going to do. Yeah? That's how your power works. The only reason you can predict how your own choices will turn out, is because other people's actions are fixed. If you go up to some random guy on the street and slap him, you can know in advance exactly how he'll react. Right?"

"Well sure," Judy says. "I mean, that doesn't mean Marva doesn't have free will. Or this person I've hypothetically slapped." This is too weird a conversation to be having naked. She goes and puts on a Mountain Goats T-shirt and PJ bottoms. "Their choices are just factored in, in advance."

"Right." Doug's point is already made, but he goes ahead and lunges for the kill. "So how do you know that I can't predict your choices, exactly the same way you can predict Marva's?"

Judy sits down on the edge of the bed. She kneads the edge of her T-shirt and doesn't look at Doug. Now she knows why Doug looked so sick when she came back from the bathroom. He saw more of this conversation than she did. "You could be right," she says after a moment. "If you're right, that makes you the one person I should never be in the same room with. I should stay the hell away from you."

"Yeah. You should," Doug says. He knows it will take forty-seven seconds before she cradles his head and kisses his forehead, and it feels like forever. He holds his breath and counts down.

A couple days later, Judy calls in sick at the arts nonprofit where she works, and wanders Davis Square until she winds up in the back of the Diesel Café, in one of the plush leather booths near the pool tables. She eats one of those mint brownies that's like chocolate-covered toothpaste and drinks a lime rickey, until she feels pleasantly ill. She pulls a battered, Scotch-Taped world atlas out of her satchel.

She's still leafing through it a couple hours later when Marva comes and sits down opposite her.

"How did you know I was here?" Judy asks.

"Because you're utterly predictable. You said you were ditching work, and this is where you come to brood."

Judy's been single-handedly keeping the Blaze Foundation afloat for years, thanks to an uncanny knack for knowing exactly which grants to apply for and when, and what language to use on the grant proposal. She has a nearly one hundred percent success rate in proposal-writing, leavened only by the fact that she occasionally applies for grants she knows she won't get. So maybe she's entitled to a sick day every now and then.

Marva sees that Judy's playing the Travel Game and joins in. She points to a spot near Madrid. "Spain," she says.

Judy's face gets all tight for a moment, like she's trying to remember where she left something. Then she smiles. "Okay, if I get on a plane to Madrid tomorrow, there are a few ways it plays out. That I can see right now. In one, I get drunk and fall off a tower and break both legs. In another, I meet this cute guy named Pedro and we have a torrid three-day affair. Then there's the one where I go to art school and study sculpture. They all end with me running out of money and coming back home."

"Malawi," Marva says. Judy thinks for a moment, then remembers what happens if she goes to Malawi tomorrow.

"This isn't as much fun as usual," Marva says, after they've gone to Vancouver and Paris and São Paolo. "Your heart isn't in it."

"It's not," Judy says. "I just can't see a happy future where I don't date Doug. I mean, I like Doug, I may even be in love with him already, but . . . we're going to break each other's hearts, and more than that: we're maybe going to break each other's *spirits*. There's got to be a detour, a way to avoid this, but I just can't see it right now."

Marva dumps a glass of water on Judy's head.

"Wha? You—Wha?" She splutters like a cartoon duck.

"Didn't see that coming, did you?"

"No, but that doesn't mean . . . I mean, I'm not freaking omniscient, I sometimes miss bits and pieces, you know that."

"I am going to give you the Samuel Johnson / Bishop Berkeley lecture, for like the tenth time," Marva says. "Because sometimes, a girl just needs a little Johnson."

Bishop George Berkeley, of course, was the "if a tree falls in the forest and nobody hears it, does it make a sound" guy, who argued that objects only exist in our perceptions. One day, Boswell asked Samuel Johnson what he thought of Berkeley's ideas. According to Boswell, Johnson's response to this was to kick a big rock "with mighty force," saying, "I refute it thus."

"The point," says Marva, "is that nobody can see everything. Not you, not Doug, not Bishop Berkeley. Stuff exists that your senses can't perceive and your mind can't comprehend. Even if you do have an extra sense the rest of us don't have. Okay? So don't get all doom and gloom on me. Just remember: Would Samuel Johnson have let himself feel trapped in a dead-end relationship?"

"Well, considering he apparently dated a guy named Boswell who went around writing down everything he said . . . I really don't know." Judy runs to the bathroom to put her head under the hot-air dryer.

The next few weeks, Judy and Doug hang out at least every other day and grow accustomed to kissing and holding hands all the time, trading novelty for the delight of positive reinforcement. They're at the point where their cardiovascular systems crank into top gear if one of them sees someone on the street who even looks, for a second, like the other. Doug notices little things about Judy that catch him off guard, like the way she rolls her eyes slightly before she's about to say something solemn. Judy realizes that Doug's joking on some level, most of the time, even when he seems tragic. Maybe especially then.

They fly a big dragon kite with a crimson tail, on Cambridge Common. They go to the Isabella Stewart Gardner and sip tea in the courtyard. Once or twice, Doug is about to turn left, but Judy stops him, because something way cooler will happen if they go right instead. They discuss which kind of skylight Batman prefers to burst through when he breaks into criminals' lairs, and whether Batman ever uses the chimney like Santa Claus. They break down the taxonomy of novels where Emily Dickinson solves murder mysteries.

Marva gets used to eating Doug's spicy omelets, which automatically make him Judy's best-ever boyfriend in Marva's book. Marva walks out of her bedroom in the mornings to see Doug wearing the bathrobe Judy got for him, flipping a perfect yellow slug over and over, and she's like, *What* are *you?* To Marva, the main advantage of making an omelet is that when it falls apart halfway through, you can always claim you planned to make a scramble all along.

Judy and Doug enjoy a couple months of relative bliss, based on not ever discussing the future. In the back of her mind, Judy never stops looking for the break point, the moment where a timeline splits off from the one Doug believes in. It could be just a split second.

They reach their three-month anniversary, roughly the midpoint of their relationship. To celebrate, they take a weekend trip to New York together, and they wander down Broadway and all around the Village and SoHo.

Doug is all excited, showing off for once—he points out the fancy restaurant where the president will be assassinated in 2027, and the courthouse where Lady Gaga gets arrested for civil disobedience right after she wins the Nobel Peace Prize. Judy has to keep shushing him. Then she gives in, and the two of them loudly debate whether the election of 2024 will be rigged, not caring if people stare.

Once they've broken the taboo on talking about the future in general, Doug suddenly feels free to talk about their future, specifically. They're having a romantic dinner at one of those restaurant/bars, with high-end American food and weird pseudo-Soviet iconography everywhere. Doug is on his second beer when he says, "So, I guess in a couple of weeks, you and I have that ginormous fight about whether I should meet your parents. About a week after that, I manage to offend Marva. Honestly, without meaning to. Then again, in a month and a half's time we have that really nice day together on the boat."

"Please don't," Judy says, but she already knows it's too late to stop it.

"And then after that, there's the Conversation. I am not looking forward to the Conversation."

"We both know about this stuff," Judy says. "It'll happen if and when it happens, why worry about it until then?"

"Sorry, it's just part of how I deal with things. It helps me to brace myself."

Judy barely eats her entrée. Doug keeps oversharing about their next few months, like a floodgate has broken. Some of it's stuff Judy either didn't remember, or has blotted out of her mind because it's so dismal. She can tell Doug's been obsessing about every moment of the coming drama, visualizing every incident until it snaps into perfect focus.

By the time Judy gets up and walks away from the table, she sees it all just as clearly as he does. She can't even imagine any future, other than the one he's described. Doug's won.

Judy roams Bleecker and Saint Mark's Place, until she claims a small victory: she realizes that if she goes into this one little subterranean bar, she'll run into a cute guy she hasn't seen since high school, and they'll have a conversation in which he confesses that he always had a crush on her back then. Because Doug's not there, he's not able to tell her whether she goes into that bar or not. She does, and she's late getting back to their hotel, even though she and cute high-school guy don't do anything but talk.

Doug makes an effort to be nice the rest of the weekend, even though he knows it won't do him any good, except that Judy holds hands with him on the train back to Providence and Boston.

And then Doug mentions, in passing, that he'll see Judy around, after they break up—including two meetings a decade from now, and one time a full fifteen years hence, and he knows some stuff. He starts to say more, but Judy runs to the dining car, covering her ears.

When the train reaches Doug's stop and he's gathering up his stuff, Judy touches his shoulder. "Listen, I don't know if you and I actually do meet up in a decade, it's a blur to me right now. But I don't want to hear whatever you think you know. Okay?" Doug nods.

When the fight over whether Doug should meet Judy's parents arrives, it's sort of a meta-fight. Judy doesn't see why Doug should do the big parental visit, since Judy and Doug are scheduled to break up in ten weeks. Doug just wants to meet them because he wants to meet them—maybe because his own parents are dead. And he's curious about these people who are aware that their daughter can see the future(s). They compromise, as expected: Doug meets Judy's parents over lunch when they visit, and he's on his best behavior.

They take a ferry out to sea, toward Block Island. The air is too cold and they feel seasick and the sun blinds them, and it's one of the greatest days of their lives. They huddle together on deck and when they can see past the glare and the sea spray and they're not almost hurling, they see the glimmer of the ocean, streaks of white and blue and yellow in different places, as the light and wind affect it. The ocean feels utterly forgiving, like you can dump almost anything into the ocean's body and it will still love us, and Judy and Doug cling to each other like children in a storm cellar and watch the waves. Then they go to Newport and eat amazing lobster. For a few days before and a few days after this trip, they are all aglow and neither of them can do any wrong.

A week or so after the boat thing, they hold hands in bed, nestling like they could almost start having sex at any moment. Judy looks in Doug's naked eyes (his glasses are on the nightstand) and says, "Let's just jump off the train now, okay? Let's not do any of the rest of it, let's just be good to each other forever. Why not? We could."

"Why would you want that?" Doug drawls like he's half asleep. "You're the one who's going to get the life she wants. I'm the one who'll be left like wreckage." Judy rolls over and pretends to sleep.

The Conversation achieves mythical status long before it arrives. Certain aspects of the Conversation are hazy in advance, for both Doug and Judy, because of that thing where you can't understand something until you understand it.

The day of the Conversation, Judy wakes from a nightmare, shivering with the covers cast aside, and Doug's already out of bed. "It's today," he says, and then he leaves without saying anything else to Judy, or anything at all to Marva, who's still pissed at him. Judy keeps almost going back to bed, but somehow she winds up dressed, with a toaster pop in her hand, marching toward the door. Marva starts to say something, then shrugs.

Doug and Judy meet up for dinner at Punjabi Dhaba in Inman Square, scooping red-hot eggplant and bright chutney off of metal prison trays while Bollywood movies blare overhead and just outside of their line of vision.

The Conversation starts with them talking past each other. Judy says, "Lately I can't remember anything past the next month." Doug says, "I keep trying to see what happens after I die." Judy says, "Normally I can remember years in advance, even decades. But I'm blocked." She shudders. Doug says, "If I could just have an impression, an afterimage, of what happens when I'm gone. It would help a lot."

Judy finally hears what Doug's been saying. "Oh Jesus, not this. Nobody can see past death. It's impossible."

"So's seeing the future." Doug cracks his samosa in half with a fork and offers the chunky side to Judy.

"You can't remember anything past when your brain ceases to exist. Because there are no physical memories to access. Your brain is a storage medium."

"But who knows what we're accessing? It could be something outside our own brains."

Judy tries to clear her head and think of something nice twenty years from now, but she can't. She looks at Doug's thick sideburns, which he didn't have when they started dating. Whenever she's imagined those sideburns, she always associated them with the horror of these days. It's sweltering inside the restaurant. "Why are you scared of me?" she says.

"I'm not," Doug says. "I only want you to be happy. When I see you ten years from now, I—"

Judy covers her ears and jumps out of her seat to turn the Bollywood music all the way up. Standing, she can see the screen, where a triangle of dancing women shake their fingers in unison at a bearded man. The man smiles.

Eventually, someone comes and turns the music back down. "I think part of you is scared that I really am more powerful than you are," Judy says. "And you've done everything you can to take away my power."

"I don't think you're any more or less powerful than me. Our powers are just different," Doug says. "But I think you're a selfish person. I think you're used to the idea that you can cheat on everything, and it's made your soul a little bit rotten. I think you're going to hate me for the next few weeks until you figure out how to cast me out. I think I love you more than my own arms and legs and I would shorten my already short life by a decade to have you stick around one more year. I think you're brave as hell for keeping your head up on our journey together into the mouth of hell. I think you're the most beautiful human being I've ever met, and you have a good heart despite how much you're going to tear me to shreds."

"I don't want to see you anymore," Judy says. Her hair is all in her face, wet and ragged from the restaurant's blast-furnace heat.

A few days later, Judy and Doug are playing foosball at a swanky bar in what used to be the Combat Zone. Judy makes a mean remark about something sexually humiliating that will happen to Doug five years from now, which he told her about in a moment of weakness. A couple days later, she needles him about an incident at work that almost got him fired a while back. She's never been a sadist before now—although it's also masochism, because when she torments him, she already knows how terrible she'll feel in a few minutes.

Another time, Doug and Judy are drunk on the second floor of a Thayer Street frat bar and Doug keeps getting Judy one more weird cocktail, even though she's had more than enough. The retro pinball machine gossips at them. Judy staggers to the bathroom, leaving her purse with Doug—and when she gets back, the purse is gone. They both knew Doug was going to lose Judy's purse, which only makes her madder. She bitches him out in front of a table of beer-pong champions. And then it's too late to get back to Judy's place, so they have to share Doug's cramped, sagging hospital cot. Judy throws up on Doug's favorite outfit: anise and stomach acid, it'll never come out.

Judy loses track of which unbearable things have already happened, and which lie ahead. Has Doug insulted her parents yet, on their second meeting?

Yes, that was yesterday. Has he made Marva cry? No, that's tomorrow. Has she screamed at him that he's a weak mean bastard yet? It's all one moment to her. Judy has finally achieved timelessness.

Doug has already arranged—a year ago—to take two weeks off work, because he knows he won't be able to answer people's dumb tech problems and lose a piece of himself at the same time. He could do his job in his sleep, even if he didn't know what all the callers were going to say before they said it, but his ability to sleepwalk through unpleasantness will shortly be maxed out. He tells his coworker Geoffrey, the closest he has to a friend, that he'll be doing some spring cleaning, even though it's October.

A few days before the breakup, Judy stands in the middle of Central Square, and a homeless guy comes up to her and asks for money. She stares at his face, which is unevenly sunburned in the shape of a wheel. She concentrates on this man, who stands there, his hand out. For a moment, she just forgets to worry about Doug for once—and just like that, she's seeing futures again.

The threads are there: if she buys this homeless man some scones from 1369, they'll talk, and become friends, and maybe she'll run into him once every few weeks and buy him dinner, for the next several years. In five years, she'll help the man, Franklin, find a place to live, and she'll chip in for the deposit. But a couple years later, it'll all have fallen apart, and he'll be back here. She flashes on something Franklin tells her eight years from now, if this whole chain of events comes to pass, about a lost opportunity. And then she knows what to do.

"Franklin," she says to wheel-faced guy, who blinks at the sound of his name. "Listen. Angie's pregnant, with your kid. She's at the yellow house with the broken wheelbarrow, in Sturbridge. If you go to her right now, I think she'll take you back. Here's a hundred bucks." She reaches in her new purse for the entire wad of cash she took out of the bank to hold her until she gets her new ATM card. "Go find Angie." Franklin just looks at her, takes the cash, and disappears.

Judy never knows if Franklin took her advice. But she does know for sure she'll never see him again.

She wanders into the bakery where she would have bought Franklin scones, and sees this guy working there. And she concentrates on him, too, even though it gives her a headache, and she "remembers" a future in which they become friendly and he tells her about the time he wrecked his best friend's car, which hasn't happened yet. She buys a scone and tells the guy, Scott, that he shouldn't borrow Reggie's T-Bird for that regatta thing, or he'll regret it forever. She doesn't even care that Scott is staring as she walks out.

"I'm going to be a vigilante soothsayer," she tells Marva. She's never used her power so recklessly before, but the more she does it, the easier it gets. She goes ahead and mails that Jollibee statue to Sukey.

The day of the big breakup, Marva's like, "Why can't you just dump him via text message? That's what all the kids are doing, it's the new sexting." Judy's best answer is "Because then my bike would still be in one piece." Which isn't a very good argument. Judy dresses warm, because she knows she'll be frozen later.

Doug takes deep breaths, tries to feel acceptance, but he's all wrung out inside. He wants this to be over, but he dreads it being over. If there was any other way . . . Doug takes the train from Providence a couple hours early so he can get lost for a while. But he doesn't get lost enough, and he's still early for their meeting. They're supposed to get dinner at the fancy place, but Doug forgot to make the reservation, so they wind up at John Harvard's Brew House, in the mall, and they each put away three pints of the micro-brews that made John Harvard famous. They make small talk.

Afterward, they're wandering aimlessly toward Mass Ave and getting closer to the place where it happens. Judy blurts out, "It didn't have to be this way. None of it. You made everything fall into place, but it didn't have to."

"I know you don't believe that anymore," Doug says. "There's a lot of stuff you have the right to blame me for, but you can't believe I chose any of this. We're both cursed to see stuff that nobody should be allowed to see, but we're still responsible for our own mistakes. I still don't regret anything. Even if I didn't know today was the last day for you and me, I would want it to be."

They are both going to say some vicious things to each other in the next hour or so. They've already heard it all, in their heads.

On Mass Ave, Judy sees the ice cream place opposite the locked side gates of Harvard, and she stops her bike. During their final blow-out fight, she's not eating ice cream, any of the hundred times she's seen it. "Watch my bike," she tells Doug. She goes in and gets a triple scoop for herself and one for Doug, random flavors—Cambridge is one of the few places you can ask for random flavors and people will just nod—and then she and Doug resume their exit interview.

"It's that you have this myth that you're totally innocent and harmless, even though you also believe you control everything in the universe," Doug is saying.

Judy doesn't taste her ice cream, but she is aware of its texture, the voluptuousness of it, and the way it chills the roof of her mouth. There are lumps of something chewy in one of her random flavors. Her cone smells like candy, with a hint of wet dog.

They wind up down by the banks of the river, near the bridge surrounded by a million geese and their innumerable droppings, and Judy is crying and shouting that Doug is a passive-aggressive asshole.

Doug's weeping into the remains of his cone, and then he goes nuclear. He starts babbling about when he sees Judy ten years hence, and the future he describes is one of the ones that Judy's always considered somewhat unlikely.

Judy tries to flee, but Doug has her wrist and he's babbling at her, describing a scene where a broken-down Doug meets Judy with her two kids—Raina and Jeremy, one of dozens of combinations of kids Judy might have—and Raina, the toddler, has a black eye and a giant stuffed tiger. The future Judy looks tired, makes an effort to be nice to the future Doug, who's a wreck, gripping her cashmere lapel.

Both the future Judy and the present Judy are trying to get away from Doug as fast as possible. Neither Doug will let go.

"And then fifteen years from now, you only have one child," Doug says.

"Let me go!" Judy screams.

But when Judy finally breaks free of Doug's hand, and turns to flee, she's hit with a blinding head rush, like a one-minute migraine. Three scoops of ice cream on top of three beers, or maybe just stress, but it paralyzes her, even as she's trying to run. Doug tries to throw himself in her path, but he overbalances and falls down the riverbank, landing almost in the water.

"Gah!" Doug wails. "Help me up. I'm hurt." He lifts one arm, and Judy puts down her bike, helps him climb back up. Doug's a mess, covered with mud, and he's clutching one arm, heaving with pain.

"Are you okay?" Judy can't help asking.

"Breaking my arm hurt a lot more . . ." Doug winces. "Than I thought it would."

"Your arm." Judy can't believe what she's seeing. "You broke . . . your arm."

"You can see for yourself. At least this means it's over."

"But you were supposed to break your leg."

Doug almost tosses both hands in the air, until he remembers he can't. "This is exactly why I can't deal with you anymore. We both agreed, on our very first date, I break my arm. You're just remembering it wrong, or being difficult on purpose."

Doug wants to go to the hospital by himself, but Judy insists on going with. He curses at the pain, stumbling over every knot and root.

"You broke your arm." Judy's half sobbing, half laughing, it's almost too much to take in. "You broke your arm, and maybe that means that all of this . . . that maybe we could try again. Not right away, I'm feeling pretty raw right now, but in a while. I'd be willing to try."

But she already knows what Doug's going to say: "You don't get to hurt me anymore."

She doesn't leave Doug until he's safely staring at the hospital linoleum, waiting to go into X-ray. Then she pedals home, feeling the cold air smash into her face. She's forgotten her helmet, but it'll be okay. When she gets home, she's going to grab Marva and they're going straight to Logan, where a bored check-in counter person will give them dirt-cheap tickets on the last flight to Miami. They'll have the wildest three days of their lives, with no lasting ill effects. It'll be epic, she's already living every instant of it in her head. She's crying buckets but it's okay, her bike's headwind wipes the slate clean.

WisCon is my favorite convention for many reasons—but a major one is that I always come home from Madison feeling fired up creatively, after so many inspiring conversations, auctions, karaoke sessions, and dance parties. "Love Might Be Too Strong a Word" came out of a bunch of Wis-Con arguments about queerness and gender in science fiction, which kept fizzing in my brain afterward.

I started writing this story at the Dane County Regional Airport—and by the time I had landed in San Francisco, the first draft was about two-thirds finished. I came up with a complex backstory, in which humans had sent a colony ship full of frozen embryos to a new planet and had engineered six different types of beings to work on the ship, each with their own genders and sexualities. Our hero, Mab, is the only person who refuses to conform to this rigid (but romanticized) gender hierarchy.

To bring things full circle, I was at WisCon the following year, when Gavin Grant informed me in person that he and Kelly Link had decided to accept this story for publication in their zine *Lady Churchill's Rosebud Wristlet*. It felt like kismet. When people ask me which of my own stories is my favorite, I always name this one without hesitation.

LOVE MIGHT BE TOO STRONG A WORD

Here's how I remember it:

A touch shocked me. I was reaching for a flash-seared bog-oyster, and then a fingertip, softer than I'd ever felt, brushed my knuckle. The softness startled me so much, it took me a moment to realize the hand had seven fingers, three more than mine.

Be held a striped cloth in ber other hand. I came up with the correct pronoun by instinct, even before my mind took in the fact that a pilot was touching my hand. Holy shit, a pilot!

I turned. Be smiled at me, mouth impossibly small, eyes panoramic and limpid. So beautiful I wanted to choke. "You dropped this," be said. My bandana looked so foreign in ber fingers, I almost didn't recognize it.

And then be tied my bandana around my neck, so gently I couldn't help shivering. Those fingers!

And then, it opened. Just a tiny dilation, but I almost had to lean against the cafeteria table. Everyone in the universe was watching. I knew, without reaching around, that there was a teeny wet spot on the small of my back.

Until that moment, I'd barely ever thought about my harnt, the little hole just above my tailbone. It was just there. It had never opened on its own, much less gotten wet. And nobody had ever touched it, of course. Now, somehow it knew.

My harnt closed again, but it didn't make as tight a seal as before. Or at least, it felt restless. It was going to bother me. Right now, it was all I could think about.

The pilot had finished tying my bandana, but kept looking at me. "You're so lovely," be said to me. "What's your name?

"Mab." I managed to avoid stammering.

"Short for Mabirelle." Be smiled. "I'm Dot." And then be bowed and left me to face the stares of my fellow dailys.

Here's how they tell it:

Ah love, mystery confounding! Oh lovers, your sighs the dark matter that limns our course. Who can understand the ways of love: ever cruel, ever bountiful? Not the boides, not the breeders, not even the spirers with their countless eyes and base-twenty-seven calculations!

Dot lo Manaret, honored third-level pilot of the City, known for ber gallantry and aplomb, was never word-lost. Until the day be wandered down to the daily canteen and ber eyes fell up on the surpassing loveliness of Mabirelle, most radiant of all the dailys. In that instant, Dot's heart fell into Mabirelle's pocket, and Dot's eyes, which had encompassed interstellar space, now had one vista only. Lost was Dot, lost forever, to the love of Mabirelle!

A chasm wider than the Inner Axis separated these two lovers, one from the highest dar, the other from the lowest. Pity poor Dot and Mabirelle, their love against all society's norms, their furtive meetings stolen from the moments between their far-separate undertakings. Theirs must be a fleeting happiness, but how bright the afterimage!

Love, why do you torment us so? Why must we pine, so far from our Cluster and from our new homeworld? Is happiness a mere whisper on the edge of daydreams? Why, love, why? But love, as ever, disdains to answer. Our tears must be question and answer both!

Love! Love is all they ever talk about, and I've avoided it like the unshielded areas where the outringers work. The obnoxious courtship, the crappy poetry, the singing, the dreamliminals . . . they consume our lives when we're not working, and usually even when we are. It's a miracle the City hasn't spun off course into an Oort cloud long ago.

But really, it's true. The City runs on love. It keeps us sane, more or less. Unlike the dark matter that flows into our massive converters, it's an infinitely renewable fuel. As to whether it pollutes, you probably already have your own opinions about that.

Right after the bandana incident, my sibs started treating me differently. "Mab, I heard be kissed you! That darling little mouth!" "Mab, isn't be beautiful? Oh, of course be's beautiful!" Sometimes they teased: "Mab's going to be a pilot's mate! Mab, what's your secret? Did you steal a holo-shield?" I know for a fact that a few of the other dailys have been with pilots, but furtively, in dark song-booths or under laundry decks.

One daily even tried to sneak me a bubble of some noxious substance. I was supposed to squirt it onto my harnt to make it more pleasant to Dot when be manned me. As if I would ever let *that* happen.

Because we clean the entire City, handle the waste units, and supply the food, dailys go everywhere. The lower middle dars, the boides, and the outringers, romance us sometimes. The upper middle dars, occasionally. But no pilot had ever romanced a daily, as far as any of us remembered.

I figured a few days would pass, then the gossip would stop and the other dailys would go back to being my friends and letting me finger them in their bunks when nobody was looking.

Then the poem showed up. Typical courtship crap: Dot tight-beamed it to my handle, but "forgot" to encrypt it. Which means everybody in the City saw it before I did. "No food can I taste, my course corrections go awry. I falter in everything, dreaming of your touch. O Mabirelle! Your Dot will die without you."

In other words: "Woman to me, or I'll send the City a fraction off course, and we'll all die in starless space." And that's supposed to be romantic!

At that point, I was doomed. They all took turns reading it and squealing. My so-called best friend, Idra, kept hugging me and jumping up and down until I wanted to smack ym. "Mab, it's so beautiful! It's like something from a sugar-box holo!"

"Oh yeah, it's great." I didn't even try to sound excited.

It's weird: I would have given anything for the other dailys to stop being ashamed of me. Even when they let me finger all their holes after lights-out, they wouldn't look at me. They were always trying to introduce me to some dashing boide so I could woman like everybody else. Ever since we left the Cluster, they kept trying to fix me. Now, for the first time, they were proud of me, and I wanted to die.

I don't woman. I just don't.

Oh, I have the involuntary responses just like everybody else. When I meet a particularly stout outringer, my ruhr feels a little itchy. I make a habit of wearing a scarf when I clean the outringers' quarters, so they won't see anything. I just don't like the idea.

A couple of days after the poem, Dot turned up again. Oh, be didn't come over and say hi like a normal person. Of course not. Instead, be turned up in the cafeteria where we'd first met, perched on top of the air shaft on ber knees. Be had all fourteen fingers on a big flarinelle and was playing some dirge-y shanty while moaning about how ber heart was imploding for the love of me. Be wore an outfit with a million laces and buckles, maybe just to remind me just how clever ber fingers were.

I wanted to turn and run back to the dailys' hab areas, but my sibs all grabbed me and cried all over my favorite quicksuit. I had to stay and listen to the whole fucking thing. Dot couldn't sing to save ber life. After that, I was the dailys' greatest romantic hero ever. When was I going to send a poem back? When would I acknowledge Dot's suffering?

The next day, I was on my hands and knees scrubbing the boides' segment. They always claim our knees and backs are genetically engineered to make us better scrubbers. They're filthy liars. Or at least, it's not enough. I hate cleaning up after the boides, who track all sorts of crap from the power units. At least I don't have to clean the power units themselves, since I'm not designed to withstand those forces, the way the boides are.

Anyway, I was crawling around trying to clean up some stuff that I didn't even want to think about. I heard some motion behind me, and scuttled around to see a boide staring at where my ass had just been.

At first I thought po wanted to sexually harass me, which is what the boides usually want when I'm working. Dailys, like me, are pretty much the only dar the boides can man. They woman to the pilots, the outringers, and the breeders. I've heard the boides can man the spirers, too, but it probably doesn't happen much.

"I had a great love once," the boide said. "And I let zm slip away, and I've never forgiven myself." Oh great. Romantic advice. All of a sudden, I wished the boide would just try to grope me. I could tell po wanted to, from the matching bulges on either side of por hip bones. But no. "We're in space for countless decades, but in all that time you may only get one chance at a great love," po said.

"Just because you blew off some dumb breeder once, doesn't mean you get to give me advice." I looked por over: a little less squat and greasy than most boides, but still a solid brick of muscle and radiation-resistant hide. But nimble, the way you have to be if you manipulate the City's power grid.

"The breeders and the pilots are different from you and me," po said. "They have higher concerns, loftier thoughts. When they train that light on us, it can feel like we're going to burn up. That's the closest to real meaning, to glory, we can get."

Normally, the boides treat us as if we're way beneath them. It's only in comparison to a pilot that po and I could become "we." Or if po wanted to man me, we might be "we" for an hour or two. And po did want me, those twin bulges don't lie.

"Thanks for the advice." I snorted. "I feel loftier already."

"Don't laugh it off. When love comes, you have to" blah blah blah. Po kept it up for the next hour or so, while I scrubbed and scraped. There are cleaning machines, of course, but they don't do such a great job with the really nasty stains, and the spirers are too busy doing "exalted" things to upgrade them.

It went on like that. People giving me advice. Worse, the other dailys wouldn't let me touch them anymore after lights-out. "Mab, we let you touch us when there's nothing better around," Idra told me while we waited to step into the bathing tubes. "But a pilot! I mean, don't you think you should save yourself?"

"For what?" I asked, but then the tubes opened and we stepped in, to fall through a tunnel where water, and then supercompressed air, sprayed us. I've heard the pilots and spirers have baths.

I could never get tired of seeing Idra naked, even after I've bathed with ym so many times now, and touched ym in yr bunk. Even though Idra drove me to distraction with yr crushes and yr face-pastes and yr romance dream-liminals, y kept me sane. I didn't know what I'd do if I couldn't talk to Idra. Maybe I even loved ym. A little.

We'd met back in the Cluster, when we were both training for this voyage. Idra and I had been grown for this mission, but we still had to train and prove ourselves. Basic safety stuff, mostly, since the City can't replace us if we get ourselves killed out here. Idra was the only other one in our class, besides me, who'd asked about other stuff, like how the City navigated and how the power grid worked (or failed to, sometimes).

I'd started hanging out with Idra all the time between classes, and we'd laugh at the silly questions some of the other dailys asked, about how to get face-paste in the City. I'd thought y and I would always share everything, until the City launched and y fell in love for the first time, with an outringer. Ever since then, it was one crush after another, putting Idra in an elliptical orbit away from me, and then back to me when it fell apart. I'd mostly gotten used to it.

"You know," I told Idra when we were dressing afterward. "There are only two reasons people are so love-crazy around here. Because the only children in the City are the dormant embryos in the breedpods, waiting for planetfall. And because it helps us forget we're stuck at the bottom of the heap forever."

"If you talk to Dot like that, be'll drop you like a used snot-catcher," Idra told me. Y had a warning look in yr eyes and mouth, but yr nose wrinkled the way it always did when I made ym laugh.

"That's a good idea," I said. "Maybe I'll try that."

Actually, here was my problem. I wanted to say no to Dot, but be never gave me a chance. Be never even asked me if I wanted to pair-bond with ber, or go live in the pilot quarter, or whatever. Be just kept sending little crystal cameos, serenading me from a safe distance, paying other dailys to make little delicacies for me. (A pilot wouldn't know how to cook to save ber life.) Be never came close enough for me to respond.

And yet, I was cruel. I was coy. I tormented Dot. Or so Dot claimed, and so the balladeers announced to the whole City. I was killing a pilot, one of only five hundred in the whole City, with my coldness. Had anyone ever been as cruel as me? In the entire history of the City, and the Cluster before that? Speaking of which, I was famous enough now that my sibs back in the Cluster were going to hear about this.

"I don't get it," I told Idra. "What am I supposed to do anyway? When be threw all those bright catsilk bandanas down to me from the upper walkway, I tried to avoid catching them, but you guys grabbed them for me. How am I supposed to respond?"

"Write back!" Idra said. "Write a poem, or if you can't manage that, a regular letter. I'll tight-beam it for you. You don't even have to write it yourself, I'll write it for you."

Oh, Idra. I never wanted to be you, but I always want to be with you. I certainly never wanted you to want to be me.

"Can I write a letter asking ber to leave me alone?"

"It'll just make ber try harder. Or maybe be'll go away permanently, throw berself into the boides' radiation zone. You can't trifle with love, Mab. Love is the most powerful force in the universe. Love is unstoppable, unfathomable."

"Yeah, yeah, yeah. Love. Got it."

I have no idea how long Dot could have gone on courting me, showering me with tears from those massive eyes. I took the initiative. I sent Dot a message telling ber to meet me in one of the song-booths in the dailys' quarter, where my sibs go to have furtive sex with the other dars.

Dot wrote back, a dozen sonnets filled with leaping jubilation that I would hear ber suit in person. Still, couldn't we meet someplace more romantic? Someplace more beautiful? There were some lovely little restaurants in the pilot quarter. (I knew that, since I'd worked in their kitchens.) Or we could sail a skimmer around the edge of the Outring, on dalfur cushions, with a flarinelle trio playing to us.

"Sorry," I wrote back. "You come to me, or no meeting."

I booked a song-booth and paid for it myself. Instead of some schlocky flarinelle music, I ordered up a couple hours of the most raucous slash-and-grab, the stuff they're always threatening to ban. I showed up early, so I'd be sitting with my feet up when Dot got there.

I'll let you pretend you've never been inside a song-booth. Basically they're coffin-shaped, with a bench running lengthwise and a big screen overhead showing patterns or dumb holo-stories. Big speakers at either end. Unless you're really tall, you can just about sit on the bench if you scoot down, but eventually it becomes easier to lie on it lengthwise, which is what it's really there for. Nobody ever goes there to listen to music and watch pretty colors, unless they're really, really bored.

Dot had feathers all over ber slender body. There are no birds in the City, of course, but I've cleaned up feathers and had a chance to examine them. They're synthetic, but intricate, with little strands that catch the light.

I hadn't seen Dot, up close, since our first meeting. I'd forgotten quite how delicate and lovely be was, how elegant those little bones. I wasn't prepared for the sudden awakening of my harnt and the tightness inside my stomach.

"O Mab! O my Mabirelle! You do so much kindness to my poor faltering heart!" Dot had obviously memorized tons of this crap.

"Shut up and listen," I said. "I've figured out why you're doing this."

"There is no reason, other than your beauty, which so dazzles my eyes that all other sights are cataracted to me."

"I said shut up. And sit down, you're making me nervous." I gestured at the greasy cushion next to me. "So here's what I think: you're doing this for attention. You were losing status, or playing some pilot game that the rest of us don't even grasp, and you decided to make yourself the hero in some epic love story: the pilot who fell in love with a daily, against all odds. They'll sing about you forever, if you don't get thrown out of the upper rings for sullying your honor. It's a gamble, but you're a shrewd one. Am I right?"

"Oh, my Mabirelle. Your wisdom is second only to your beauty, which far surpasses the brightest jewels. But no, you're wrong. There's no purpose to my love other than love itself. And no cure for my love other than your love returned to me."

"I was afraid you'd say that. Okay, let's go. I'll do you right here."

"But I—That's not what I—"

"If it'll end this. Come on, get all those feathers off you. I've never seen a pilot naked. I'm curious."

And I *was* curious. It's weird that pilots are the opposite of dailys, but most of us never get to see what they look like under their fancy ruffles. I helped Dot out of ber five layers (!) of clothing, and slowly ber body revealed itself. Be stared at me, terrified, as I ran my hands over ber.

Naked, Dot was even more gorgeous than dressed. I couldn't stop swallowing. Be was all long sinews and soft skin. Ber body was much the same shape as mine, or any other human, but slender where mine was stout. And be had all those extra appendages, where I only had holes.

"What does this one do?" I pointed to a long vine that curled out from Dot's sternum.

"It's uh, it's my zud, for manning a spirer. They have an opening on that part of their bodies just for pilots, called the duz. It takes three days, and there are fifteen required positions." It went on like that. The three bony prongs sticking out just below ber stomach were for manning a breeder, and ber thighs had matching lumps, which could expand to man an outringer. No matter what your dar, Dot had a way to man you. Just like I could woman to all the other dars.

"Don't you want to see my, uh, my tharn?" Dot gestured to ber lower back, where the outie that matched my innie was quivering with excitement. Be started to turn around, but I stopped ber. Just being so close to ber naked body was making my harnt throb, opening and closing spasmodically like a busted air lock.

"Not really," I said. "There's no rush. And I'm curious." I tried stroking some of the tendrils and spokes coming from the front of Dot's body. Dot moaned with pleasure, but they didn't grow any bigger, because I was the wrong dar to excite them. Pheromones.

"Don't you want me to, uh, to man you?" Dot looked from ber naked body to the quicksuit I was still wearing. It kept ber from seeing that my lumbar region was soaked.

"Nope. I don't woman. But I'll man you if you want."

I didn't think it was possible for Dot's eyes to get any bigger, but they did. Ber eyes were as big as my thumbs.

"Pilots always man, dailys always woman. That's just how it is."

"That's not how I play. You have openings. I have tools. And fingers." My pinky was almost too big for Dot's mouth, but I made it fit. Be sucked on it, half moaning and half gulping. I felt like I was going to implode, I was so skin-struck. "Is this okay?" I asked. Be nodded, shivering.

I left Dot naked and flushed, thanking me through bewildered tears. No more poetry, thank god.

I figured after that, Dot would leave me alone. I might have an even worse reputation than before, depending on what people heard. Maybe that could be a good thing, and some of the dailys would respect me a little more when they heard I'd manned a pilot.

I had to giggle to myself when I thought those words. I manned a pilot! Whatever came next would totally be worth it.

"You did what?" Idra hissed. Y dragged me farther away from the other dailys, just in case they had super-hearing. We were in the noisiest canteen, with the crispiest deep-fried bog-oysters. (Don't tell anyone I told you this, but those things aren't oysters. They grow on the coolant ducts, they're a kind of fungus.) The canteen's walls had been bright red when we'd left the Cluster, but by now they were maroon, and the floors were sticky no matter how much we mopped.

"You heard me." I giggled again. Normally, Idra was the giggler and I was the frowner. Oh, this was so worth it.

"How could you? I always knew you were . . . unnatural. But this? You could be killed! You could be killed and nobody would ever say anything. Stop laughing, Mab! I don't know what I'd do. I don't want to lose you. If Dot tells anyone, if be even whispers it, they'll just erase you! I couldn't bear that. Mab, why didn't you think about me, before you went and threw everything away?"

It went on like that, Idra keeping yr voice low enough that none of the other dailys had a clue. It was so weird, I had to go and man a pilot to find out that Idra loved me too. Love might be too strong a word, but whatever. You get the idea.

"Idra, calm down. Be's not going to tell anyone. What's be going to say?"

"Exactly. What *is* be going to say? Think about the position you put ber in. After weeks of public courtship, you agreed to meet ber in private. Everyone is going to want to know what happened. And be is going to say . . . what? That you manned ber? That be manned you? That you rejected ber? What?"

Why did things have to be so complicated? Be wanted me, so I took ber. Why wasn't that the end of it? But even as I was reassuring Idra that everything was fine, I felt another sensation, as unfamiliar as my harnt's opening had been. They could erase me any time they wanted. I felt weak inside.

"O chaste Mabirelle! O cruel, virtuous Mabirelle, that withstood temptation's nearness with yr far-seeing gaze! How can we praise your inviolate harnt, O Mabirelle?"

I was as shocked as anyone else. Apparently, I wasn't a wanton slut, I was a chaste virgin. Who had cruelly denied Dot's advances even while we were in a tiny padded and soundproofed tube. Though Dot importuned me, I preserved my virtue. Dot proved this by showing someone that ber tharn retained its outer membrane, which meant it had never been inside me.

I didn't even know that a pilot's tharn *had* an outer membrane. You learn something new every day.

As the story went, I had arranged the song-booth meeting as an elaborate test to see if Dot could respect my chastity in such close quarters. Now that Dot had passed the test, I had agreed to hear ber pair-bonding proposal.

I was grateful to Dot for coming up with an explanation of the facts that didn't require anyone to toss me into the Inner Axis. But proposals? The way Idra explained it, I wasn't committed to pair-bonding with Dot, just to hearing ber suit.

Nobody even knew how pair-bonding would work between a pilot and a daily. It wasn't very likely that I'd be able to go live with Dot, and the idea of Dot trying to share my bunk in a roomful of twenty dailys made me giggle. With no children and no property, it was mostly a fancy license for Dot and me to do what we'd already done in that song-booth. Except maybe the other way around.

So this time I had to go up to the pilot quarter, where the air is purer and the gravity lighter. Gleaming star charts on all the walls, varvet covering every surface. I had to keep ducking to avoid the little nozzles spraying perfumey crap and aromatherapy at me. I usually wore my bandana around my mouth and nose when I cleaned around here, but I figured Dot might take it as an insult.

"Hey," I said to Dot. "Thanks, for coming up with a good story. You're good at that, huh? Telling stories. I have to kick myself to keep from believing the stuff you say about me, and I know myself pretty well."

Dot started saying it was all true, and then some. Be wore even more layers than last time, if that was possible, and sat cross-legged on the edge of a massive crescent-shaped couch on the edge of a fake gravity well. You could toss things into it and watch them shrink to a singularity, but it was just an illusion. Dot didn't need to wear the extra buckles, since I would hardly try anything with five chaperones watching us from just outside earshot.

"Anyway, I'm grateful to you. Which is why I'm here," I said, sitting a decent distance away from ber on the crescent thingy.

"Mabirelle, because I love you so, I want to be totally honest with you," Dot said. That sounded like a good idea, so I nodded. Be went on: "I told you the truth before, when I said there was no hidden agenda here, but there is something you don't know. Can you keep a secret?"

"You have no idea how many secrets I've kept," I said. "You can trust me, don't worry."

Dot had to pause to offer me chocolates and little cameos, and order up fancy music. Then be went on. "The spirers think they've developed a much more accurate long-range scanning technique by combining stellar resonance and high-spectrum ghosting." Be waited me for murmur my understanding, then went on. "We think it's dead."

"What's dead?" At first I thought be meant the little dove-hen I was holding.

"The planet. Our colony world. Coriolanus, or whatever they're calling it this week. The breedpods won't function there, the breeders won't be able to sustain a new generation."

"So . . . we left the Cluster for nothing. We're sailing toward nothing. This, all of this, is all for nothing." I gestured around, to indicate the whole City.

"Yes."

"Can we turn back?" I already knew the answer before be shook ber head, but it still felt like a crack in my gut. Be started talking about desperate alternatives: slingshot maneuvers, stellar recharges, increased dark matter efficiency, but I was still saying dead world to myself, over and over.

Dead world.

"I can't stand it among the other pilots anymore, or any of the upper dars. The spirers with all those fingers, with their base-twenty-seven cleverness. The breeders, tending those breedpods as if they're going to amount to something. It all makes me feel so hopeless. But when I'm with you, it's different. I feel alive. Like life is worth something after all."

I started to ask why we couldn't tell everyone the truth, but that was a stupid question, and I don't ask stupid questions. If I thought people in this City were out of control now, just imagine if they knew they were trapped and it was pointless.

"Love," I muttered. "Fucking love. It can't save you from shit. It's just anesthetic."

"Maybe," Dot said. "But it's lifesaving. Mabirelle, I meant everything I said before. Your beauty, your wisdom, the longing inside me. It wasn't a pantomime, or a distraction from my existential crisis. It was itself. I love you, and I can't bear to be away from you."

I didn't love Dot, but I liked ber more and more. Even though be had left me in an ugly spot. I could turn ber down, but then what? I could spend the next few decades among the dailys, knowing we were going nowhere. The dailys would never treat me the same after this, once I went from being the romantic heroine to being the fool who spurned a pilot. They might never let me touch them again. I wasn't sure I could go back to being who I'd been, even if they'd let me.

I took a deep breath and looked around this foolish room. I couldn't help laughing, and then I had to reassure Dot that I wasn't laughing at ber. "Sorry, sorry. It's just all this. How can you live like this? It's ridiculous."

"I'm used to it, I guess," Dot said. "You know what they say about pilots, we're not like other people. I know everyone makes fun of us behind our backs."

"Yeah, but not as much as they make fun of the spirers." I got my giggles under control and then looked into Dot's eyes, which looked like they could swallow me whole. "Listen, I can't live here. But I can't go back, either. Can you make me a little love nest, like in those dumb dreamliminals? A little place where I can live and you can visit? Not in the daily quarter, but not here either."

Dot thought about it for a moment, then started rattling off the various lavish apartments in the interstices between the City quarters, where I could live in luxury. Eventually, be came up with something a bit more realistic, but still comfortable. Even if I was going to be a kept daily, I didn't want to be over the top.

"I guess we can give it a try," I said. "Just two more things. I want my friend Idra to come live with me. So I don't go nuts with loneliness when you're not around. Y needs yr own space, so y can entertain whoever y's madly in love with this week. The other thing is, I won't woman to you. I can think of a few other ways to get rid of that pesky membrane on your tharn, don't worry. I just don't like the idea of back-to-back sex, it's too weird. Oh, and my name is Mab, not Mabirelle or anything else. Okay?"

It wasn't the kind of courtship Dot had had in mind. And when the minstrels sang of our pair-bonding and the dreamliminals re-created it, they portrayed it very differently. The quivering Dot, the beautiful unyielding Mabirelle, the hours of ardent supplication before I finally consented to turn my back on ber and become ber mate, all that crap. I had to bite my tongue whenever people started carrying on. I was starting to learn that you had to leave people their romantic illusions.

airy Werewolf vs. Vampire Zombie" is a little bit *Vampire Diaries* fanfic, I'll be honest. I was (and am) obsessed with the CW's soap opera about vampires, witches, and werewolves, and all of its spin-offs. I started thinking about what would happen if someone got turned into a vampire and a zombie at the same time. Which type of undead curse would win out? (This was before the *Buffy the Vampire Slayer* comic introduced zompires.) But also, what if a werewolf bit a fairy? These are the kinds of important questions that serious grown-ups like me spend our time thinking about. This story has many of my favorite things: an obnoxious narrator, karaoke, romance, karaoke, duels to the death, and karaoke. In spite of the aforementioned romance, the central relationship in this story is a friendship between two very different women.

FAIRY WEREWOLF VS. VAMPIRE ZOMBIE

If you're ever in Freeboro, North Carolina, look for the sign of the bull. It hangs off the side of a building with a Vietnamese noodle joint and an auto mechanic, near an alley that's practically a drainage ditch. Don't walk down that alley unless you're brave enough not to look over your shoulder when you hear throaty noises behind you. If you make it to the very end without looking back, hang a left, and watch your footing on the mossy steps. The oak door at the bottom of the stairs will only open if you've got the right kind of mojo.

If it does open, you'll find yourself in Rachel's Bar & Grill, the best watering hole in the Carolinas. My bar. There's only one rule: if there's any trouble, take it outside. (Outside my bar is good, outside of town is better, outside of reality itself is best of all.) I have lots of stories about Rachel's. There are names I could drop—except some of those people might appear. There is one story that illustrates why you shouldn't make trouble in my bar, and how we take care of our own. It's also the story of how the bar got its mascot.

There was this young woman named Antonia, who went from a beautiful absinthe-drinking stranger to one of my regulars inside of a month. She had skin so pale it was almost silver, delicate features, and wrists so fine she could slide her hand into the wine jug behind the bar—although she'd have to be quick pulling it out again or Leroy the Wine Goblin would bite it off. Anyway, she approached me at closing time, asking if I had any work for her. She could clean tables, or maybe play her guitar a few nights a week.

If you've ever been to Rachel's, you'll know it doesn't need any live music, or anything else, to add atmosphere to the place. If there's one thing we got in spades, it's atmosphere. Just sit in any of the plush booths—the carvings on the wooden tables tell you their stories, and the stains on the upholstery squirm to get out of the way of your butt. From the gentle undulation of the ceiling beams to the flickering of the amber-colored lights to the signed pictures of famous dragons and celebrity succubi on the brick walls, the place is atmosphere city.

But then I got to hear Antonia sing and play her guitar and it was like the rain on a midsummer's day right after you just got your first kiss or something. Real lyrical. I let her play at Rachel's one night and I couldn't believe it—the people who usually just guzzled a pitcher of my "special" sangria and then vamoosed were sticking around to listen to her, shedding luminescent tears that slowly floated into the air and then turned into little crystalline wasps. (The sangria will do that.)

So after Antonia got done singing that first night, I came up to her and said I guessed we could work something out, if she was willing to wipe some tables as well as getting her Lilith Fair on. "There's just one thing I don't get," I said. "It's obvious you're Fae, from the effect you have on the lunkheads that come in here. You're a dead ringer for that missing princess from the High Court of Sylvania. Princess Lavinia." (Sylvania being what the Fae call Pennsylvania, the seat of their power.) "It's said His Supreme Highness the Chestnut King weeps every night and would give half the riches of Sylvania to have you back. The Drag Queen—Titania—her eyeliner has been smudgy for months. Not to mention the lovestruck Prince Azaron. So what gives?"

"I cannot ever return home," Antonia (or Lavinia) wept. "I regret the day I decided to venture out and see the world for myself. For on that day, I encountered a curse so monstrous, I cannot ever risk inflicting it on any of my kin. I cannot undo what is done. The only way I can protect my friends and family is to stay far away. I am forever exiled, for my own foolishness. Now please ask no more questions, for I have tasted your sangria and I'm afraid my tears would sting you most viciously."

I said no more, although I was consumed with curiosity about the curse that kept the fairy princess from returning to the Seelie Court in Bucks County. I didn't learn any more—until a few weeks later, when the full moon arrived.

Antonia appeared as usual, wearing a resplendent dress made of the finest samite and lace (I think it was vintage Gunne Sax). She muttered something about how she was going to play a shorter set than usual because she felt unwell. I said that was fine, I would just put the ice hockey match on the big-screen TV. (Did I mention the big-screen TV? Also a big part of the atmosphere. We do karaoke on Fridays.) Anyway, she meant to play for an hour, but she got carried away with this one beautiful dirge about lovers who were separated for life by a cruel wind, and it grew dark outside just as her song reached a peak of emotion.

And something strange happened. Her hands, so teeny, started to grow, and her guitar playing grew more frenzied and discordant. Hairs sprouted all over her skin, and her face was coarsening as well, becoming a muzzle. "No!" she cried—or was it a howl?—as her already pointy ears became pointier and her hair grew thicker and more like fur. "No, I won't have it! Not here, not now. 'Tis too soon! By my fairy blood, I compel you—subside!" And with that last word, the transformation ceased. The hair vanished from her hands, her face returned to normal, and she looked only slightly wolfier than usual. She barely had time to place her guitar in its case, leaving it on the bar, before she fled up the wooden staircase to the door. I heard her ascending into the alley and running away, her panting harsh and guttural.

Antonia did not return for three days, until the moon was on the wane. When next she sang for us, her song was even more mournful than ever before, full of a passion so hot it melted our internal organs into a fondue of longing.

Now around this same time, I was thinking about franchising. (Bear with me here, this is part of the story.) I had gotten a pretty good thing going in Freeboro, and I wanted to open another bar over on the other side of the Triad, in the town of Evening Falls. The main problem was that you don't want to open a bar aimed at mystical and mythological patrons in the same strip mall as a Primitive Baptist church, a nail salon, and a barbecue place, right on Highway 40. Evening Falls only had a few properly secluded locations, all of which were zoned as purely residential, or only for restaurants.

Now, chances are, if you've been to Rachel's, you've already heard my views on the evils of zoning. But just in case you missed it . . . [Editors' note: the next ten paragraphs of this manuscript consist of a tirade about zoning boards and the ways in which they are comparable to giant flesh-eating cane toads or hornetaurs. You can read it online at www.monstersofurbanplanning.org.]

Anyway, where was I? Franchising. So I know some witches and assorted fixers who can make you believe Saturday is Monday, but it's hard to put a whammy on the whole planning board. So I thought to myself, What can I do to win these people over? That's when I remembered I had my very own enchanting fairy singer, with just a spark of the wolf inside her, on the payroll.

Antonia's eyes grew even huger, and her lip trembled, when I asked her to come and play at a party for the scheming elites of Evening Falls. "I cannot," she said. "I would do anything in my power to help you, Rachel, but I fear to travel where I may be recognized. And my song is not for just anyone, it is only for the lost and the despairing. Can't I just stay here, in your bar, playing for your patrons?"

"Now look," I said, plunking her down on my least carnivorous barstool. "I've been pretty nice to you, and a lot of people would have called the number on the side of the thistle-milk carton to collect the reward on you already. Fairy gold! The real kind, not the type that vanishes after an hour. Not to mention, I put up with the constant danger of you biting my patrons and turning them into werewolves. Which, to be fair, might improve their dispositions and make them better tippers. But you know, it's all about one hand washing the other, even if sometimes one of those hands is a tentacle. Or a claw. Although you wouldn't really want one of the Octo-priests of Wilmington to wash any part of you, not unless you want strange squid-ink tattoos sprouting on your skin for years after. Where was I?"

"You were attempting to blackmail me," Antonia said with a brittle dignity. "Very well, Rachel. You have shown me what stuff your friendship is made of. I shall play at your 'shindig.'"

"Good, good. That's all I wanted." I swear, there should be a special fairy edition of *Getting to Yes*, just for dealing with all their Fae drama.

So we put together a pretty nice spread at this Quaker meeting hall in Evening Falls, including some pulled pork barbecue and fried okra. Of course, given that most of these people were involved in local zoning, we should have just let them carve up a virgin instead. I mean, seriously. [The rest of this section is available at www.monstersofurbanplanning.org—The Editors.]

Where was I? Oh, yes. So it was mostly the usual assortment of church ladies, small-time politicians, local businesspeople, and so on. But there were two men who stood out like hornetaurs at a bull fight.

Sebastian Valcourt was tall, with fine cheekbones and a noble brow, under a shock of wavy dark hair that he probably blow-dried for an hour every day. He wore a natty suit, but his shirt was unbuttoned almost to the navel, revealing a hairless chest that was made of money. No kidding, I used to know a male stripper named Velcro who was three-quarters elf, and he would have killed for those pecs.

The other startlingly beautiful man was named Gilbert Longwood, and he was big and solidly built, like a classical statue. His arms were like sea cliffs and his face was big and square-jawed—like a marble bust except that his eyes had pupils, which was probably a good thing for him. When he shook my hand, his grip made me all weak in the knees. But from the start of the evening, both Gilbert and Sebastian could only see one woman.

Once Antonia began to play, it was all over—everybody in that room fell for her, and I could have gotten planning permission to put a bowling alley inside a church. Afterward, I was talking to Gilbert, while Sebastian leapt across the room like a ballet dancer, landing in front of Antonia and kissing her hand with a sweeping bow. He said something and she laughed behind a hand.

"You throw an entertaining party," said Gilbert, trying not to stare at Sebastian's acrobatic courtship over in the corner. "I don't think I've seen half these people show any emotion since the town historian self-immolated a few years ago." His voice was like a gong echoing in a crypt. I never got Gilbert's whole story, but I gathered he was the son of a wealthy sculptor, part of Evening Falls's most prominent family.

At this point, Gilbert had given up all pretense that he wasn't staring at Antonia. "Yeah," I said. "I discovered that girl. I taught her everything she knows. Except I held back a few secrets for myself, if you get my drift and I think you do." I winked.

"Please excuse me, gracious lady," Gilbert said. When he bowed, it was like a drawbridge going down and then up again. He made his way across the room, navigating around all the people who wanted to ask him about zoning (jackals!), on his way to where Sebastian was clinking glasses with Antonia.

I couldn't quite get close enough to hear the conversation that followed, but their faces told me everything I needed to know. Sebastian's mouth smiled, but his amber-green eyes burned with desire for Antonia, even as he made some cutting remark toward Gilbert. Gilbert smiled back and let Sebastian's fancy wit bounce off his granite countenance, even as he kept his longing gaze on Antonia's face. For Antonia's part, she blushed and looked down into the depths of her glass of Cheerwine.

You could witness a love triangle being born, its corners sharp enough to slice you open and expose your trembling insides to all sorts of infections, including drug-resistant staph, which has been freaking me out lately. I always wash my hands twice, with antibacterial soap and holy water. Where was I? Right, love triangle. This was an isosceles of pure burning desire, in which two men both pined for the same impossibly beautiful, permanently heartbroken lady. My first thought was: There's got to be a way to make some money off this.

And sure enough, there was. I made sure Antonia didn't give out her digits, or even so much as her Twitter handle, to either of these men. If they wanted to stalk her, they would have to come to Rachel's Bar & Grill. I managed to drop a hint to both of them that what really impressed Antonia was when a guy had a large, heavy-drinking entourage.

I didn't have to turn on the big-screen TV once, for the whole month that followed. Sebastian and Gilbert, with their feverish courtship of Antonia, provided as much free entertainment as ten *Married . . . with Children* marathons. Maybe even eleven. Sebastian gave Antonia a tiny pewter unicorn, which danced around in the palm of her hand but remained lifeless otherwise. Gilbert brought enough flowers that the bar smelled fresh for the first time since 1987.

This one evening, I watched Gilbert staring at Antonia as she sat on her stool and choked out a ballad. She wore a long canvas skirt and her feet were crossed on the stool's dowel. He looked at her tragic ankles—so slender, with tendons that flexed like heartstrings—and his big brown eyes moistened.

And then Sebastian arrived, flanked by two other weirdly gorgeous, unnaturally spry men with expressive eyes. Every time you would think their eyebrows couldn't get any more expressive, or their gazes more smoldering, they'd kick it up another notch. Their eyebrows had the dramatic range of a thousand Kenneth Branaghs—maybe a thousand Branaghs per eyebrow, even. The other two smiled wan, ironic smiles at each other, while Sebastian kept his gaze fixed on the tiny trembling lips and giant mournful eyes of Antonia.

A few weeks—and a few thou worth of high-end liquor—later, both Sebastian and Gilbert began to speak to Antonia of their passion.

"A heart so grievously wounded as yours requires careful tending, my lady," Gilbert rumbled in his deep voice. "I have strong hands but a gentle touch, to keep you safe." His sideburns were perfect rectangles, framing his perfectly chiseled cheekbones.

"I fear . . ." Antonia turned to put her guitar in its case, so the anguish on her face was hidden from view for a moment. "I fear the only thing for a condition such as mine is solitude, laced with good fellowship here at Rachel's. But I shall cherish your friendship, Gilbert."

Soon after, Sebastian approached Antonia, without his cronies. "My dear," he said. "Your loveliness outshines every one of those neon beer signs. Your singing, your sweet sad tune, bestirs me in a way that nothing else has for decades. You must consent to be mine or I shall have no choice but to become ever more mysterious, until I mystify even myself. Did I say that out loud? I meant, I'll waste away. Look at my eyebrows and you'll see how serious I am."

"Oh, Sebastian." Antonia laughed, then sighed. "Had I even a sliver of a heart to give, I might well give it to you. But you speak to a hollow woman."

Blah blah blah. This went on and on, and I had to reorder several of the single malt whiskeys, not to mention all the midrange cognacs and Southern Comfort.

Who can say how long this would have gone on, if both Sebastian and Gilbert hadn't turned up on an evening when Antonia wasn't there? (You guessed it: the full moon.) The two of them started arguing about which of them deserved Antonia. Gilbert rumbled that Sebastian just wanted to use Antonia, while Sebastian said Gilbert was too much of a big ugly lug for her. Gilbert took a swing at Sebastian and missed, and that's when I told them to take it outside.

Soon afterward, we all tromped outside to watch. Sebastian was dancing around like Justin Timberlake on a hot griddle, while Gilbert kept lashing out with his massive fists and missing. Until finally, Gilbert's forearm caught

Sebastian in the shoulder and he went flying onto his ass. Then things got entertaining: Sebastian's face got all tough and leathery, and fangs sprouted from his mouth. He did a somersault in midair, aiming a no-shadow kick at Gilbert—who raised his boulder-size fist so it collided with Sebastian's face.

After that, the fight consisted of Gilbert punching Sebastian, a lot. "Stupid vampire," Gilbert grunted. "You're not the first bloodsucker I've swatted."

By this point, Sebastian's jaw was looking dislocated. Those expressive eyebrows were twisted with pain. "I'm not . . . your average . . . vampire," he hissed. Gilbert brought his sledgehammer fist down onto Sebastian's skull.

Sebastian fell to the ground in an ungainly pile of bones and *smiled*. "The more beat up I get . . . the harder to kill . . . I become," he rasped, as he stood on jerky legs, his flesh peeling away.

Sebastian's smile turned slack and distended. Instead of his usual witticisms, he said but one word: "Braaainnsss . . ."

Gilbert kept punching at Sebastian, but it did no good. Nothing even slowed him down. Sebastian thrashed back at Gilbert with a hideous force, and finally he hit a weak point, where Gilbert's head met his neck—and Gilbert's head fell, rolling to land at my feet.

Gilbert's severed head looked up at me. "Tell Antonia . . . my love for her was true." His head turned to stone. So did the rest of his body, which fell into several pieces in the middle of the dark walkway.

Sebastian looked at me and at the couple other regulars who were watching. He snarled, with what remained of his mouth, "Braaaaaaainnsss!"

The nearest patron was Jerry Dorfenglock, who'd been coming to Rachel's for twenty years. He had a really nice smooth bald head, which he'd experimented combing over, and then shaving all the way, Kojak-style, before deciding to just let it be what it was, two wings of fluffy gray hair flanking a serene dome. That noble scalp, Sebastian tore open, along with the skull beneath. Sebastian reached with both hands to scoop out poor Jerry's gray matter, then stopped at the last moment. Instead, he leaned farther down and sank his top teeth into Jerry's neck, draining all the blood from his body in one gulp.

A moment later, Sebastian looked away from the husk of Jerry's body, looking more like his normal self already. "If I—" He paused to wipe his mouth. "If I eat the brains, I become more irrevocably the zombie, but if I drink the blood, I return to my magnificent vampiric state. It's always hard to remind myself. Think of it as the blood–brain barrier between handsome rogue . . .

and shambling fiend." The other patron who'd been watching the fight, Lou, tried to make a break for it, but Sebastian was too fast.

I looked at the bloodless husks of my two best customers, plus the chalky pieces of poor Gilbert, then back at Sebastian—who now looked as though nothing had ever happened, except for the stains on his natty suit. I decided being casual was my best hope of coming out of this alive.

"So you're a half vampire, half zombie," I said as if I was discussing a *Seinfeld* rerun. "That's something you don't see every day, I guess."

"It is an amusing story," Sebastian said. "When I was a mortal, I loved a mysterious dark beauty who grew more mysterious with every passing hour. My heart felt close to bursting for the love of her. At last she revealed she was an ancient vampire and offered me the chance to be her consort. She fed me her blood and told me that if I died within twelve hours, I would become a vampire and I could join her. If I did not die, I could return to my mortal life. She left me to decide for myself. I went out to my favorite spot on the edge of Stoneflower Lake to ponder my decision and savor my last day on Earth—for I already knew what choice I would make. Just then, a zombie climbed out of the lake bottom, where it had been terrorizing the bass, and bit me in the face. I died then and there, but as the vampire blood began to transform me into an eternal swain of darkness, so too did the zombie bite work its own magic. Now I remain a vampire only as long as I have a steady diet of restoring blood."

"That's quite a story," I said. I was already trying to figure out what I would do with Lou's and Jerry's bodies, since I had a feeling Sebastian would regard corpse cleanup as woman's work. "You should sell the TV movie rights."

"Thanks for the advice." Sebastian looked into my eyes, and his gaze held me fast. "You will not speak to anyone of what you have seen and heard tonight." As he spoke, the words became an unbreakable law to me. Then Sebastian sauntered away, leaving me—what did I tell you?—to bury the bodies. At least with Gilbert it was just a matter of lugging the pieces to the Ruined Statue Garden a couple of streets away.

By the time I got done, my hands were a mess and I was sweating and shaking and maybe even crying a little. I went back to the bar and poured myself some Wild Turkey, and then some more, and then a bit more after that. I wished I could talk to someone about this, but of course I was under a vampiric mind-spell thingy and could never speak a word.

Good thing I've got a Hotmail account.

I put the whole thing as plain as I could in a long email to Antonia, including the whole confusing "vampire who's also a zombie" thing. I ended by saying, "Here's the thing, sweetie, Sebastian is gonna think you don't know any of this, and with Gilbert out of the way, he'll be making his move. Definitely do NOT marry him, the half-zombie thing is a *deal breaker*, but don't try to fight him either. He's got the thing where the more you hurt him, the more zombie he gets and then you can't win, he's got you beat either way. Not to mention, the full moon is over as of tomorrow morning, so you got no more wolf on your side. Just keep yourself safe, okay, because it would just about ruin me to see anything happen to you—I mean you bring in the paying customers, don't worry, I'm not getting soppy on you. Your boss, Rachel."

She came in the next day, clutching Gilbert's head. Her eyes were puffy and the cords on her neck stood out as she heaved a sob. I handed her a glass of absinthe without saying anything, and she drained it right away. I made her another, with the sugar cube and everything.

I wasn't sure if Sebastian's mind control would keep me from saying I was sorry, but it didn't. Antonia shrugged and collapsed onto my shoulder, weeping into my big flannel shirt, Gilbert's forehead pressing into my stomach.

"Gilbert really loved me," she said when she got her breath back and sat down on her usual music-playing stool. "He loved me more than I deserved. I was . . . I was finally ready to surrender and give my heart away. I made up my mind while I was out running with the wolves."

"You were going to go out with Gilbert?" I had to sit down too.

"No. I was going to let Gilbert down easy and then date Sebastian. Because he made me laugh." She opened her guitar case, revealing a bright sword made of tempered Sylvanian steel with the crest of Thuiron the Resolver on the hilt, instead of a guitar. "Now I have to kill him."

"Hey, hey, hey," I said. "There are some good reasons not to do that, which I cannot speak of, but hang on, let me get a notepad and a pen and I'll be happy to explain—"

"You already explained." She put her left hand on my shoulder. "Thanks for your kindness, Rachel."

"I don't—" What could I say? What was I *allowed* to say? "I don't want you to die."

"I won't." She smiled with at least part of her face.

"Are you starting your set early tonight? I have a request," Sebastian said from the doorway at the top of the short staircase leading into the bar, framed by the ebbing daylight. "I really want to hear some Van Morrison for once, instead of that—"

Antonia threw Gilbert's head at Sebastian. His eyes widened as he realized what it was, and what it meant. He almost ducked, then opted to catch it with one hand instead, to show he was still on top of the situation. While he was distracted, though, Antonia was already running with her sword out, making a *whoosh* as it tore through the air.

Antonia impaled Sebastian but missed his heart. He kicked her in the face and she fell, blood-blinded.

"So this is how it's going to be?" Sebastian tossed the head into the nearest booth, where it landed face-up on the table. "I confess I'm disappointed. I was going to marry you and *then* kill you. More fairy treasure that way."

"You—You—" Antonia coughed blood. "You never loved me."

"Oh, keep up." Sebastian loomed over Antonia, pulled her sword out of his chest, and swung it over his head two-handed, aiming for a nice clean slice. "I'll bring your remains back to Sylvania, and tell them a lovely story of how you and I fell in love and got married before you were killed by a wild boar or an insurance adjuster. Hold still, this'll hurt less."

Antonia kicked him in the reproductive parts, but he shrugged it off. The shining sword whooshed down toward her neck.

"Hey!" I pumped my plus-one Vorpal shotgun from behind the bar. "No. Fighting. In. The. Bar."

"We can take it outside," Sebastian said, not lowering the sword.

"Too late for that," I said. "You're in my bar, you settle it how I choose."

"And how's that?"

I said the first thing that came into my head. "With a karaoke contest."

And because it was my bar and I have certain safeguards in place for this sort of situation, they were both bound by my word. Sebastian grumbled a fair bit, especially what with Antonia being a semiprofessional singer, but he couldn't fight it. It took us a couple hours to organize, including finding a few judges and putting an impartiality whammy on them to keep it a fair competition.

I even broke open my good wine jug and gave out free cups to everybody. Once his nesting place was all emptied out, Leroy the Wine Goblin crawled onto the bar and squinted.

Antonia went first, and she went straight for the jugular—with show tunes.

You've probably never seen a fairy princess do "Don't Tell Mama" from *Cabaret*, complete with hip-twirling burlesque dance moves and a little Betty Boop thing when she winked at the audience. Somehow she poured all her rage and passion, all her righteous Sarah McLachlan-esque anger, into a roar on the final chorus. The judges scribbled nice high numbers and chattered approvingly.

And then Sebastian went up—and he broke out that Red Hot Chili Peppers song about the City of Angels. He'd even put on extra eyeliner. He fixed each of us with that depthless vampire stare, even as he poured out an amazing facsimile of a soul, singing about being lost and lonely and wanting his freakin' happy place. Bastard was going to win this thing.

But there was one thing I knew for sure. I knew that he'd have to shut his eyes, for at least a moment, when he hit those high notes in the bridge about the bridge, after the second chorus.

Sure enough, when Sebastian sang out "Under the bridge downtown," his eyes closed so his voice could float over the sound of Frusciante's guitar transitioning from noodle mode to thrash mode. That's when I shot Sebastian with my plus-one Vorpal shotgun. Once in the face, once in the chest. I reloaded quick as I could and shot him in the chest again, and then in the left kneecap for good measure.

It wasn't enough to slow him down, but it did make him change. All of a sudden, the lyrics went, "Under the bridge downtown, I could not get enough . . . *braiiiiiinssss!*"

He tossed the microphone and lurched into the audience. The three karaoke judges, who were still enchanted to be one hundred percent impartial, sat patiently watching and making notes on their score sheets, until some other patrons hauled them out of the way. Leroy the Wine Goblin covered his face and screamed for the safety of his jug. People fell all over each other to reach the staircase.

"I shall take it from here." Antonia hoisted her sword, twirling it like a Benihana chef, while Frusciante's guitar-gasm reached its peak. She hacked one of Sebastian's arms off, but he barely noticed.

She swung the sword again, to try and take his head off, and he managed to sidestep and headbutt her. His face caught the side of her blade, but he drove the sharp edge into Antonia's stomach with his forehead. Blood gushed out of her as she fell to the ground, and he caught it in his mouth like rain.

A second later, Sebastian was Sebastian again. "Ah, fairy blood," he said.

"There really is nothing like it." Antonia tried to get up again but slumped back down on the floor with a moan, doubled up around her wounded stomach.

I shot at Sebastian again but missed, and he broke the shotgun in half. Then he broke both my arms. "Nobody is going to come to karaoke night if you shoot people in the face while they're singing. Seriously." I tried not to give him the satisfaction of hearing me whimper.

Antonia raised her head and said a fire spell. Wisps of smoke started coming off Sebastian's body, but he just shrugged. "You've already seen what happens if you manage to hurt me." The smoke turned into a solid wall of flame, but Sebastian pushed it away from his body with a tai chi move. "Why even bother?"

"Mostly," Antonia's voice came from the other side of the firewall, "just to distract yoooouu!" Her snarl became a howl, a barbaric call for vengeance.

There may be a sight more awesome than a giant white wolf leaping through a wall of solid fire. If so, I haven't seen it. Antonia—for somehow she had managed to summon enough of her inner wolf to change—bared her jaws as she leapt. Her eyes shone red and her ears pulled back as the flames parted around her and sparks showered from her ivory fur.

Sebastian never saw it coming. Her first bite tore his neck open, and his head lolled off to one side. He started to zombify again, but Antonia was already clawing him.

"Don't—Don't let him bite you!" I shouted from behind the bar.

Sebastian almost got his teeth on Antonia, but she ducked.

"*Braaainnss!*"

She was on top of him, her jaws snapping wildly, but he was biting just as hard. His zombie saliva and his vampire teeth were both inches away from her neck.

I crawled over to the cooler where I kept the pitchers of sangria, and pulled the door open with my teeth. I knocked pitchers and carafes on the floor, trying to get at the surprise I'd stored there the night before, in a big jar covered with cellophane wrap.

I hadn't actually buried *all* of Lou and Jerry.

I tugged the jar out somehow and wedged it between my two upper arms and my chin, then lugged it over to where Antonia and Sebastian were still trying to bite each other. "Hey," I rasped, "I saved you something, you bastard." And I tipped the jar's contents—two guys' brains, in a nice balsamic vinaigrette—into Sebastian's face. Once he started guzzling the brains, he couldn't stop himself. He was getting brain all over his face as he tried to swallow it all as fast as possible. Brains were getting in his eyes and up what was left of his nose. There was no going back for him now.

Antonia broke the glass jar and held a big shard of it in her strong wolf jaws, sawing at Sebastian's neck until his head came all the way off. He was still gulping at the last bits of brains in his mouth and trying to lick brain bits off his face.

It took them an hour to set the bones on my arms, and I had casts the size of beer kegs. We put Sebastian's head into another jar, with a UV light jammed inside, so whenever the Red Hot Chili Peppers come on the stereo, he gets excited and his face glows purple. I never thought the Peppers would be the most requested artist at Rachel's. I never did get permission to open a second bar in Evening Falls, though.

As for Antonia, I think this whole experience toughened her up and made her realize that being a little bit wild animal wasn't a bad thing for a fairy princess. And that Anthony Kiedis really doesn't have the singing range he thinks he has. And that when it comes to love triangles and duels to the death, you should always cheat. And that running away from your problems only works for so long. There were a few other lessons, all of which I printed out and laminated for her. She still sings in the bar, but she's made a couple of trips back to Sylvania during the crescent moon, and they're working on a cure for her. She could probably go back and be a princess if she wanted to, but we've been talking about going into business together and opening some straight-up karaoke bars in Charlotte and Winston-Salem. She's learning to KJ. I think we could rule the world.

Years after I wrote "Love Might Be Too Strong a Word," I was at WisCon again and I ran into Kelly Link. I talked her ear off about this story I was in the middle of writing, a story about a woman who is haunted by her own ghost. (Meaning that in the future, after she's died, her ghost somehow travels back in time and haunts her.) I had about three-quarters of the story but was having a hard time coming up with an ending. Kelly thought for a moment, and then generously made some suggestions that led to the ending you see here. This story's protagonist, Gloria, is one of the angriest characters I've ever written—which is why she's a comedian—and this story turned into an exploration of how depression and anger feed on each other in an endless spiral. (And just a heads up: this story does deal with depression somewhat intensely, though with a lot of humor.) In the pages and pages of notes for this story, I wrote, "There are a lot of things Gloria would do, if she wasn't there watching herself do them."

GHOST CHAMPAGNE

1
Comedy

You know what I wish? I wish I could just reach into someone's chest and pull out their beating heart and show it to them, like a movie villain. (And then I would put it back and their chest would seal up and they would be fine. I'm not a monster!) But imagine how great that would be, whenever the endless string of entitled assclowns start screwing with you—just reach in, and *Zoooooooop! Oh, what's this? It's your heart. In my hand! You wanna say something now, huh? I didn't think so.* I mean, I would only use this power in extreme circumstances, like when one of the developers in my day job starts mansplaining to me, or when I'm super bored in a meeting. Speaking of which, why is it okay to text in a meeting but not to play Candy Crush? That's discrimination.

My comedy set is off to a pretty good start, and then I notice my ghost at a third-row table, right between the canoodling pierced hipsters and the drunken yuppies.

Some days I hardly notice my ghost, but lately she's in my face a whole lot more. Today she's wearing a lacy Loligoth dress that I wish I owned in real life and a little hat over her wavy dark hair, which is a little shorter than mine. She's drinking a sidecar or an old-fashioned, because yeah, even ghosts must obey the two drink minimum rule at Sal's Comedy Cellar, and she watches me go through my set with the usual disaffected look on her face, like *been-there-done-that-and-died*.

I do what I always do: ignore her. Even when she knocks the candle off her table and turns the floor into a minefield of broken glass and hot wax. Fuck her. Remember the toolkit. Keep going, look past her—I try to gaze instead at my boyfriend, Raj, sitting on a stool in the back. The ghost doesn't matter. She had her chance to be alive, she obviously blew it.

We've reached the butt jokes section of my set. (Dick jokes are for lesser intellects, but butt jokes are *sophisticated*.) And then Raj stands and heads for the staircase, right when I'm getting to the part about how my man has a big butt, and why is there no female equivalent of an ass man? (Nobody ever says ass woman, which just sounds like the worst superheroine ever.) Raj just up and walks out on me. I see my ghost out of the corner of my eye, giving me a look like *What can you do?*

I stumble through my set, but the energy is all gone. I don't even get any love for my spiel about how Japanese toilets are so great, with the heated seats and the jets of warm water, it's like being rimmed by pixies—I sat on one and my butt finally forgave me for the horseback riding lessons I took when I was twelve. My ghost gets so bored she knocks over someone's beer glass with the back of her hand, *crash*. The crowd is a goddamn humor sponge. Fuck all of these people, why do they pay fifteen dollars just to zonk out in public when they could stay home and watch the Homophobia Channel for free?

When I get upstairs to the sidewalk after my set, Raj and the other comedians, mostly dudes, are standing out front smoking. Even though Raj doesn't smoke. It's a cool dry night. They nod at me and then start talking about how Raj and I should have kids. You should have kids so you can enter the America's Funniest Mom competition, you would crush that, says Roddy, who's basically just a handlebar mustache in search of a face. You should have kids so you can get some fashion cred, 'cuz you know, kids are the perfect accessories, says the bleach-blond, sunburnt Campbell. We should have kids so I can be a stay-at-home dad instead of just unemployable, says Raj, choking a little on his cig. If you had kids, you could get a sick reality TV show on public access cable, with your wacky family and shit, Roddy says. I realize that Raj put them up to this, he asked them to broach the idea of having kids, and this is the way they've chosen to go about it.

I just roll my eyes and walk away, heading down Bleecker toward the F. I'm not going to sit through the rest of the night waiting for Raj's set, after this shit show. My ghost slouches on the other side of the street, loitering outside the CVS and the fetish boutique. She gives me a friendly wave and I ignore her.

She didn't laugh once during my comedy set, but now my ghost looks at me, sees my angry tears, and laughs. Ruefully, which goes with the territory, I guess.

I forget the toolkit for once, and just stare at her. As if this time there might be some clue. Just like always, my ghost looks exactly like me, except older. And dead. She has the tilde-shaped scar on her chin that I got rock climbing when I was nineteen (and she had it before I did). She's gazing into the fetish shop, through the aluminum shutters.

2
Authority

Why is my own ghost haunting me, anyway? Do I die in the future and decide that instead of going to whatever afterlife a shitty comedian, lapsed Evangelical, and unfulfilled techie goes to, I'd rather go back in time and haunt my own living self? Is this a curse? A punishment for some mistake I don't know I've made, or maybe haven't made yet? Most of all, why is my ghost such a fucking bitch?

I went to every stupid medium and spiritualist, and got a big goose egg. I went into therapy, and my therapist just wanted to give me pills to make me stop seeing the ghost—but as soon as Dr. Jane reached for her prescription pad, my ghost went Full Poltergeist. She started in with the diplomas on the walls, and then got into the dolls and the office computer, and finally the antique furniture. Dr. Jane's classy office turned into a tweaker's love nest. Dr. Jane couldn't stop hyperventilating, until I held her like a colicky baby for like ten minutes.

Whatever. I stopped worrying about the ghost, since she mostly minds her own business, and I've got a life to live. Trust the toolkit. Trust the toolkit.

Raj grovels for three days and I finally sort of forgive his ass. He's the sweetest guy when we're not around other comedians. Which, we're both trying to break into comedy, so.

I get mad all over again when Raj gets invited to be in a fancy comedy showcase the following week and I'm somehow skipped over. Raj gives me a dozen foot rubs and cleans the bathroom and offers to help me shop for a wedding present for my mom. What do you get your mom when she's marrying a woman the exact same age as you? (Seriously, what?)

But. I notice that when I find out about being left out of the big comedy show, which is headlined by a B-list comedian whose set is basically listing *Star Wars* toys he used to own, my ghost seems to get a little less transparent. I can make out the tiny lines on her/my face more clearly. She's perched on the wooden stool by the kitchen counter of the teeny one-bedroom that Raj and I share in Greenpoint, and she's holding a mug of chai that smells of cinnamon and seaweed. I notice she's got her ears double-pierced, whereas mine are just single-pierced.

Raj notices I'm staring into space and asks what's up. He's got big friendly eyes and a wide pouty mouth, and hair like a single blue flame. He touches my left palm with his right index finger and I kind of melt. I tell him nothing's up, I'm just thinking about the big presentation at work, which, since we're both living off my income, is kind of a thing. He kisses me—hot butterflies!—and tells me to knock 'em dead.

My ghost has a seat in the back of the conference room for my presentation, where I yak about some of the challenges in our next code push. I mostly love being a project manager, except my company keeps changing its business model. This month, we're making an app to help people use their Spotify playlists to get laid, I am not even kidding. It's called Remixr. I'm doing a pretty solid job of talking through the workflow issues we've been having. Except one of the coders named Mickey keeps engaging in micro-aggressions: spreading his legs real wide in his chair, throwing paper balls at the trash right next to where I'm standing (his aim sucks), and yawn-laughing while I'm talking. Everyone else is just bored, probably playing Candy Crush under the chrome table.

Over by the window, my ghost is staring out at the Shake Shack across the street, as if she could really go for an extra-large chocolate shake and fries right now. She's wearing sweatpants in a professional office setting. Her expression plainly says that being a ghost has certain perks, and giving zero fucks about product meetings is one of them.

I breathe and look away from the ghost, but I keep snagging her in my peripheral vision. The thought that's always in the back of my mind surges forward: *You're going to lose your mind, it's in the cards.* The corner of my eye has become my whole field of vision, putting my ghost front and center. I start mumbling and repeating myself, until the bun-haired VP of product, Marcia, thanks me for my efforts and says we should move on.

In my dreams, I'm a semi-famous turbo geek who rocks the comedy scene every night. I have this fantasy of going to some city to give a TEDx talk, where I somehow make everybody laugh and rethink their whole way of looking at everything, and then since I'm already in town, I might as well just go perform at the local comedy spot that's been begging me to show up. I actually enjoy the whole process of making things happen, helping code come together, and putting out products that enrich people's lives. (Even when it's something like Remixr.) I like the problem solving, and I feel like I'm good at making smart people pull their heads out of their butts. Usually.

A few hours after the big presentation, I stumble into one of the one hundred company chat rooms and notice a couple of the C-level execs talking about the upcoming workforce reduction—and then they notice that I'm lurking, and they immediately bail and delete their own conversation. I look up from the screen, where the words "possible strategic layoffs" are fading to white, and see my ghost. She's closer to me than ever—just peering over my cubicle wall—and I can hardly see through her at all.

3
Family

My mom and her new bride take me to brunch at a Moroccan diner, and I'm scared Mom is going to ask me to give her away. Cassie, my soon-to-be stepmom, is pale and skinny, with random tufts of platinum hair coming out of her shaved head. Glam Tank Girl. Her skin is amazing, like she must have microdermabrasion all over her entire body once a day or something. My ghost is sitting at the next table in a sundress, drinking a mimosa. My mom is telling me how she and Cassie are going to be married by a gay

Buddhist who turns your sexual guilt into a stuffed animal as part of the ceremony.

I grew up in a really strict religious household, in a plantation house whose dark wood foundations were being slowly devoured by termites. My mom was raised Presbyterian in Mexico City, and she married this WASPy charismatic preacher who is just a grabby pair of callused hands and a red face in my memories. Before he met my mom, I heard my dad might've done snake handling, which I wish I'd gotten to see, because fuck yeah snakes. The one time I made the mistake of telling my dad I thought I saw a ghost, he and a few of his deacons prayed over me for a full twelve hours, not letting me sleep. One of the deacons had breath that smelled like sour milk, and I started to lose my mind. My mom's family might at least have accepted a ghost as normal and just told me to visit some graveyards, pay some respect.

My parents were neo-Calvinists, which means they believed in predestination, kinda sorta, and the idea that your fate after death is sealed while you're still alive. My mother used to tuck me in every night and tell me that she was afraid my soul was already damned. Now Mom's telling me that she and Cassie have written their own vows, and there's a lot of stuff about giving yourself permission to love without expectations. My mom's family is not coming to the wedding, except for Aunt Letitia, who was cut off before I was even born. My mom has kind of a butch haircut that makes her face look a lot squarer, and she's wearing suspenders over a T-shirt. She looks really good. She looks younger than I feel. She keeps laughing, which is a sound I never even heard until a few years ago. Gloria, she tells me, I really want this day to be special for you as well as us, I want you to feel free.

When I was a teenager, sneaking out after curfew, going to smoke in the woods with the other dead-end kids, my ghost egged me on. My parents locked me in, my ghost let me out. My parents yelled at me, my ghost stood in the corner, arms folded, and glared at them. Jesus has a plan for you, you need to surrender, my mother pleaded, while my ghost studied her hands. Back then, I didn't even recognize myself in her—I just thought she was some random ghost, haunting this old South Carolina house. That place was a natural ghost habitat, with so many gloomy corners and moldy back rooms full of barbed rust.

Cassie is saying she wants us to be friends, something she's said before, and holding my mother's hand across the table in front of me. She's got movie star blue eyes and she really seems to be wild about Mom.

They are waiting for me to say something. Something like, I feel super lucky that we have this second chance as a family. Something like, I'm so happy for the two of you. Those are things I absolutely do feel, though I can tell without looking that my ghost is annoyed by all this hippie-dippie nonsense. My ghost is not okay with this midlife reinvention on the part of the woman who spent so many years telling me I had no choices.

I look at the fried eggs and hummus on my plate, breathe, and say the best thing I can think of: I'm glad you finally figured out your deal. Wish you could have found yourself sooner, but maybe you guys can have a new baby with a turkey baster and give it the perfect childhood, with Montessori and organic candy and no judgment, it's never too late, amirite? When I look up, I see that my comments did not land the way I hoped—my mom looks crushed, actually weeping for fuck's sake, and Cassie is comforting her. My ghost, though, has scooted her chair closer and is practically part of our party.

4
Therapy

Dr. Jane can kind of tell from my gaze that my ghost is standing right behind her chair. She keeps twitching, as if her office furnishings will fly through the air any minute. She's a frumpy fiftysomething lady in a giant cat sweater, and I think I respond to her partly because she's so unlike my mother. She smiles in a distant but nurturing way and asks me what the week brought me. As if the week is a hunting dog that drops rabbits at my feet or something.

I'm freaking out, I say. The toolkit broke.

What broke the toolkit? she asks.

Everything. Everything broke the toolkit. My ghost is one hundred percent not ignorable any longer. My ghost is right up in my business. All of the coping mechanisms are kaput, because the ghost jams them up. All that stuff about connecting with Día de los Muertos and remembering that the dead are part of life, it didn't work. You try telling jokes with your own ghost sitting right there with a dead grimace on her face. You try leading a meeting. You try having an honest-to-god processing conversation with your adorable boyfriend, who keeps trying to claim he's a feminist because he's letting you support him financially. Just try it.

Your ghost only has the power you give it, says Dr. Jane. She doesn't believe that any more than I do—she's the one who had to invest in all new office furniture—but she probably thinks that's a good therapisty thing to say. Goddamn positive thinking. She's the only one but me who's ever seen my ghost in action, and the only one I've told, since I was a kid.

You're doing so well, Dr. Jane says. You've gotten a promotion at work. You're in a position of authority over people. You've been getting better comedy bookings, at bigger venues. You've got a boyfriend whom you adore. You've been rebuilding your relationship with your mother. Just think how much better your life is than when you were first coming to see me.

I don't know, I say. I don't know if any of that is true.

That's how it sounds to me, from the outside looking in. It sounds like you're being a successful grown-up, which is pretty much never fun for anybody, says Dr. Jane. And your ghost? Your ghost was really useful when you were a teenager trying to break out of a bad situation, but now she's just in your way.

I glance up at my ghost, who is looking at my therapist's hand puppets on the shelf, apparently not listening to any of this. I can never tell how much language she understands—like, does everything just sound garbled and weird to her? I've asked her yes-or-no questions, point blank, and she never nodded or shook her head or anything.

I don't feel like my ghost is helpful or unhelpful, I say. I feel like she's waiting. I feel like every time I fail at something, she gets stronger. Every setback, I see her more clearly. Like she's getting power from my screwups. Or like I'm getting closer to turning into her.

Maybe—and here Dr. Jane looks nervous, because she's afraid the ghost will start trashing her office again—maybe it's partly just in your mind. Maybe you just think the ghost is getting closer and more solid. I can't see what you see, so I can't tell for myself.

I don't know. I have a strong sense that my ghost is feeding off my self-destruction. I need a new toolkit.

There's no new toolkit. Dr. Jane scrunches her big brow. There's just the coping mechanisms I already taught you. Don't try to figure out what your ghost's agenda is, or what your ghost wants. Try to figure out what you really want. What do *you* actually care about?

Pffft. As if I could possibly know that.

5
Arrowheads

At the karaoke bar, I foolishly put myself down for a Shakira song—some people say I look like Shakira, but nobody ever says I sound like her. My ghost is at one of the spit-catching tables up front, nursing a margarita. Wearing a dress with a million ruffles.

The screen with the lyrics might as well be Swahili writing, beamed into the void. Raj is up front, dancing, cheering me on, and clapping, but all I can see is the ghost's face, which isn't even looking at me at all. (She's never looking at me whenever I look right at her, I realize for the first time.) She stares at Raj, like she remembers loving him, way back when. Sadness, resignation, on her face. Like she remembers this time, when her life was almost good.

I topple forward off the stage and fall on my knees on the grungy floor, at my ghost's feet. I can't breathe, much less sing. The crowd is still not sure if I'm doing a dramatic dance move or having a medical situation. I can't even hear the music with my ears pounding. Raj comes to me and asks if I'm okay, and I say, Like you care. The song is over. I go home.

My ghost stands between me and the whiteboard in a meeting at work. I'm sitting and watching Marcia talk about the drop-dead deadline for the Remixr launch, but I can't even read the words she's pointing to. My ghost keeps shaking her head in syncopation with Marcia's droning. Today my ghost is wearing a bikini, revealing a tattoo on her stomach that I cannot read at any cost to my eyesight.

I hate her so much. She's going to fuck up everything for me, one way or the other. She's fucking smug, is what she is. She's already lived all this shit and she's over it, and she won't let me just live it for myself.

Marcia is asking me a question. I stare past my ghost and say something about security audits that I think is probably relevant to what she was talking about the last time I paid attention. Security is for version 2.0, Marcia says. We need to launch this thing.

Raj and I are at the mall, shopping for a wedding present for Mom, and we're on the escalator behind three kids who are reading an internet tutorial on how to shoplift. Raj is excited: This mall has three different shops for just socks, socks are the best! Did you know that in the 1970s nobody wore socks? It caused this thing called stagflation, what would happen if you actually blew up a stag party? Raj runs off the escalator and nearly gets away from me. My ghost is right there at my elbow, though.

My ghost sits near my bed at night, watching Raj sleep. My ghost watches Raj perform at the comedy showcase—his big break!—and laughs without making a sound. When I sit in the toilet stall, eavesdropping as Marcia and Sandra from Accounting wash their hands and whisper about the upcoming Rationalization, my ghost is out there next to them, washing her hands in ghost water.

It's like arrowheads are embedded in my back, on either side of my neck, so that even raising my head or lifting my arms causes excruciating pain. I chewed through too many mouth guards, until I gave up on guarding my mouth. I feel like a bomb that's lost its detonator, like I will just go critical forever, without ever getting to explode.

At dinner, my ghost sits in Raj's lap as he tries to talk to me about our relationship.

6
Wedding

Hey, Raj says. I know this is a weird thing for you. Your mom, turning into a lesbian cougar. I wanna tell you that I'm here, and I get it, and I'm on your team.

Raj is touching my hand, leaning over, talking in my ear. We're right up front at the wedding, surrounded by young queer people in incredible fashions. I always thought a tux was a tux, but it turns out that tuxedos have personalities. The sound of Raj's voice is making me feel grounded, like I have a core after all, and what he's saying makes a certain amount of sense. This is a weird thing for me, after so many years of defining myself in opposition to my parents. It's like I don't know who I am.

I don't even see my ghost anywhere. I don't, like, scan the entire room looking for her—I just take the win. Maybe she's hanging back and letting me have this day to myself. Or maybe I've been working on having a more positive attitude and that makes it harder for her to intrude her ass in there. I try to set up a virtuous circle, where I feel more centered, which means I don't see the ghost, and that in turn helps me be even more centered. It could work, right?

I ought to recognize how cool this is, I tell Raj. All of this. Getting to be true to yourself, and make your own family, and throw the stupid rules out the window. I don't want to wait until I'm my mom's age before I let myself open up my heart.

Raj squeezes my thumb like he gets it, and he feels that way too, and this feels like the start of a whole conversation that we'll have later.

Then the ceremony starts, and everyone is whooping with joy and the officiant, who has a U-shaped beard and no mustache or hair, pronounces my mom and Cassie wife and wife. My mother looks like some whole other person, unrecognizable even as the butch dyke I had just started getting used to. She's wearing makeup and a puffy white dress with a black bow on the front that looks like a bow tie. My mom holds Cassie with all her considerable arm strength, and then she beckons me to get in there. My mother poses, sandwiched between two women in their mid-twenties, and Mom looks more alive than I can remember. She whispers in my ear that I'm beautiful and she's so proud of me, which feels like something I ought to be telling her instead.

The Veterans Hall is a celebration of walnut, from the recessed-box pattern on the ceiling to the long, tall panels on the walls. Even the plaque about those who gave their lives appears to be walnut. I concentrate on dodging the bouquet, but then Raj catches it. He giggles and we make out, right in front of everyone. More cheers.

I spot my ghost at last, but she's just another face in the crowd, over by the hors d'oeuvres table.

The bouquet has one dead bud in it. In among the posies, morning glories, pink roses, and the obligatory baby's breath, there's this little gnarled fist, clutched around a gray mouth that never opened. Blighted. The inward-facing petals look like an overcooked crepe. I stare into its dark heart, and then Raj is talking in my ear about taking a trip, just the two of us, to Big Sur, California, where every five yards there's a rock that Henry Miller had kinky sex on top of. Yeah, I say, let's be Henry Miller sex tourists. We laugh and kiss, and all the young lesbians are cheering my mom, whom they all love like a den mother.

I'm dancing with Raj to the zydeco band. He's busting out these ridiculous knee-bending moves and he eggs me on to dance as funny as him. I dance even worse, all neck and ankles. People are cheering. A young enby shoots me a thumbs-up, and my mom waves from the cake stand. Cassie has her arm around my mom's waist, and the love is radiating outward from them, suffusing the entire room. I feel warm and exhausted and inexhaustible.

And then my ghost is right there, dancing right next to us. She doesn't *dance*, exactly—more like sways, so her bony wrists wave back and forth. She smiles at Raj in a nostalgic way. These good times were good, her smile says, and then, well, you know. We all died.

I stop dancing. Raj is so startled, he nearly elbows me in the face. I can't even remember why I was happy a moment ago, and I can't imagine why I would ever feel happy again. The ghost is so close I can see the pearly embroidery on her white dress.

Someone comes with a tray of champagne glasses, and Raj and I take them because there's going to be a big toast or something. My ghost has a flute of champagne in her hand too, and she's actually crying—her ghost tears land on her cheeks like the dew that catches the last of the moonlight. She's just watching my mother and Cassie, and I have this moment of *How dare you?* That is not her mother, it's mine, and this is my life, and I want it back. I want to care about things, without my ghost always throwing shade. My too-tight blue scalloped dress constricts my breathing. I glare at my ghost, but she's staring at my mother.

So maybe it's time I took something of hers.

I reach out and seize the glass of champagne from her loose fingers. It's made of some kind of ghost material, ecto-whatever, but the stem is solid in my hand. I raise it to my face and toss it back. It tastes like . . . bitterness, I guess. It tastes a bit like pukey backwash, stomach acid, but also a bit like Cold Duck, that weird "sparkling wine" the grocery store used to sell for two dollars a bottle. It has an aftertaste of fermented dirt, bubbly regret.

Before I even swallow, it hits me: way past drunkenness, something like a head rush mixed with hypoglycemia and extreme sleep deprivation. Everything looks as though I'm seeing it from a great, vast distance, through a pinhole, and maybe that's what ghost vision looks like. The ghost glass is plucked from my hand before I can let it fall on the floor. I can just barely see my ghost looking around in a mad panic, like the worst possible thing has just happened.

Raj rushes over to me as I sway-crash to the walnut floor. I feel like I'm having an aneurmotherfuckingysm. I feel my legs twitching, my hands flailing. Raj is holding my head in a hand and his fingertips are so gentle and my head at least is supported is overloaded with ghost juice is supported, my ghost vanishes like she can't afford to get caught here with me. The music stops, to be replaced by the crowd freaking out, I'm drunk in a way I've never known was even possible.

As I finally zero out, I feel the cold invade my veins, my bones, my lungs. Petrified, and then dead to the world.

7
Drunk

A ghost wedding is a funeral, only with dancing, and a cake instead of a casket. What do you give the newlyweds at a ghost wedding? Bone china. Ghost vows are much the same as the regular kind, except you vow to stay together for as long as death holds you. I can still just barely glimpse the wedding party of the living (Raj and my mother and Cassie, all freaking) but now I'm among the dead wedding guests. These people are skeletons, except as I move around them, their translucent skin comes into focus and they have faces made of gray mist. The whole dead wedding party is swaying and passing around plates of wormy moldy cake, clinking glasses like the one I chugged from. What do you write on the rear bumper of the honeymoon car at a ghost wedding? Just Buried. The band is still playing zydeco, but the beats keep slowing down and speeding up, and the accordion wheezes with rheumatism. There is a buffet full of eyeballs and tongues, still looking around and trying to talk inside their metal trays over cold candles. What kind of wedding crashers go to a ghost wedding? Dig-up artists. I keep laughing, only I am not per se breathing and every *hee* is slowed way down to the slowest pace of the zydeco drummer and I spin my whole body to keep pace with the spinning of the room, if I spin fast enough the room will stand still. I want to vomit but cannot.

The ghosts at the guest wedding, I mean guests at the ghost wedding, are random dead people plus some that I knew when they lived, like my mom's parents and even my great-grandma Julia and my great-aunt Danielle, and that chain-smoking piano-playing raconteur my parents used to have over when I was little, whose name was Ed or Fred. They see me looking at them and raise their glasses to me, and I salute back. What do you call the congregation at a ghost wedding? Deadly beloved.

I've spun halfway across the room from where I drank the champagne. I look back at the spot where I collapsed, and I'm still there, on the ground. Except it's not me, it's my ghost. She has shorter hair and an older face and she's wearing a white dress instead of a blue dress. My ghost is talking to Raj, and he can actually hear her, and whatever she is saying, he is nodding very seriously. I can't hear what she's telling him, and I can only see it through the end of a long, hazy reverse telescope. Drunk tunnel vision. I want to get closer to them, but no matter how I stumble and twist my angle and sweep my arms for balance, I can't get going in the right direction.

As my ghost talks to Raj, he nods and nods and oh shit now he is crying and still nodding, and I have never yet made him cry in all the months we have dated. He's never given me the look he's giving my ghost. What the fuck is she telling him? Now at last I vomit, but it comes out from my eyes instead of my mouth. The ghosts around me are all gossiping too loud for me to hear a damned thing. Raj's glasses frame big brown eyes—which, serious Raj looks like a totally different person, older and more physically present. I try to get Raj's attention by shouting and flailing but he's only looking at ghost me.

The gossiping of the ghosts around me gets louder and more shrill, and it's all: *Look at her in her shiny dress and her pristine flesh and her red lips, she thinks she's all that just because she's alive, look at that blue-haired man over there, he probably thinks he invented breathing.* The ghosts are getting louder and crankier, and I see them more clearly while Raj and my mother and Cassie are like chalk outlines. Zydeco band salutes me and starts a dirge and I am so blitzed that walking is dancing is falling. I gotta sober up right now or I am lost in the land of the dead forever and maybe my ghost takes my place.

The doorway to the Veterans Hall is open and the caterers are coming in through a ribbon of darkness, bearing weird canapés made of pure decay and fake crab, plus oblivion-in-a-blanket. They keep shoving the trays in my face and trying to make me take a bite, as the ghosts grow more and more vivid and everything else fades. The ghosts urge me: *take one, just try it, don't be ungrateful, don't you know what this wedding cost? You think you're too good to eat with us.*

I look over at Raj, still talking to my ghost, and I feel a pure sour anger— why can't he tell that's not me? This proves he never really cared!—and I'm so pissed that I almost want to open my mouth and let the other ghosts push pieces of the dead wedding feast into my throat. Why the fuck not? And then

I stop, and see Raj again, his face just a wall of tears. Whatever is going on with him and my ghost, from his perspective, he sees that I'm hurting and he is desperate to make it right. I look at Raj's face and I see love, like actual honest-to-god, walk-naked-on-broken-glass love, and my mom is there too, weeping over the ghost and squeezing the ghost's bony hand.

And I feel sorry for my ghost, because she doesn't know how to cope with the two of them caring about her that much. She looks flustered and scared. I see my poor ghost, looking from Raj to my mom and back again, like she's trapped with their love. I barely notice the specters from the ghost wedding now, I'm so fixated on the two of them and my ill-equipped ghost. I am overcome by a mixture of pity and gratitude, two emotions I did not know could be mixed up. The feelings are too big to wrap my mind around, the longer I look at the three of them, and I feel like I am going to fly apart in a million pieces. Soul and mind, intermixing like matter and antimatter. Unthinkable, terrible, amazing.

And then, I am vomiting ghost champagne from my eyes, in huge salty gouts.

I look up. Raj and my mother are looking down at me and I am lying on the floor. I laugh but it becomes a cough. Oh shit, I say, I'm back. I think I ate drank something that didn't agree. My mom says an ambulance is coming, and I tell her that I'm sorry I jacked up her special day, but I don't think anything could really ruin what she and Cassie have going. Because you guys are awesome and I'm proud of you, I say. My mom cries harder than ever, on Cassie's shoulder, and Raj is supporting my head. I tell Raj that I love him—words I have never spoken—and I'm glad he's Team Me. He says he loves me, but I get the impression he already told my ghost that.

I don't see my ghost anywhere. She doesn't show up at the hospital at all, where they find a tiny brain infarct thingy. Nor do I see her hanging around, after they finally send my ass home. Maybe she'll come back, maybe she won't. I hope she's okay, wherever she is.

Raj looks at me funny when I try to ask him what my ghost said to him. Not that I phrase it like that—I just demand to know what I said after I collapsed at the wedding. He's kind of embarrassed, like maybe it's bad form to remind me of my drunken brain-attack rambling.

But I beg and cajole and emotionally blackmail, and he finally says, You told me you felt cursed, and that you blamed yourself, and that you were going to keep hating yourself more and more until you died, and then it would be too late to try and make peace with your past, because your past wouldn't let you in. Honestly, it didn't make a lot of sense to me, and the gist of it is that you need to try a different shrink, and maybe no more regression therapy or whatever. But I'm just a layperson, right?

I agree that regression therapy sucks and that Raj is indeed a person that I want to lay. I climb on top of him, even though he protests that my head is still like a Fabergé egg, and I grind into him while telling him that if he's going to be a kept man, he'd better put out the goods. Dry humping, we are alone together for maybe the first time. I laugh between kisses.

I wrote a ton of first-person stories about queer life in San Francisco back in the day—full of trans people, genderqueer artists, pranksters, poly drama, and gentrification. The first of those stories featured a version of the Cacophony Society and starred a genderfluid artist who's in love with their best friend. Another story featured a trans woman who starts dating someone who speaks only in adverbs. For a while, I thought about turning them into a linked story collection, and I wrote "My Breath Is a Rudder" to be one of the final stories of the bunch. Most of those stories take place in the present, but "My Breath Is a Rudder" takes place in the near future, because I wanted the story collection to move forward in time as it went. My original plan was for that story cycle to end in a far-future, drowned San Francisco—and eventually I got to write that story, which appears later in this collection. I abandoned the idea of the linked queer story cycle but decided that "My Breath Is a Rudder" stands just fine on its own.

MY BREATH IS A RUDDER

I'm standing on Ocean Beach, but I can't see the ocean. I hear it, tearing up its own bed. The waves salt the wind. The sea is so close. Breathing down my neck, on the other side of this giant wall.

I stare for a few hours, just trying to visualize, until the pure white surface starts to make my retinas throb. I feel like crying after a while, or maybe that's the sea air.

Roach comes up behind me and asks if I feel inspired. I almost lie, but what the fuck. So I say no, I feel totally out of my depth. Roach puts his hand on my shoulder and says he has uber faith in me.

The wall doesn't look quakeproof, but they say it is. Maybe two or three feet wide, it runs all along the Great Highway, from Golden Gate Park all the way to Sloat, and then down Skyline Boulevard to protect the fancy golf course and the Olympic Club. Just in case El Niño goes even more bug-ass and the ocean tries to swallow the Sunset. Even a few years ago, nobody would have thought it—but then again, nobody predicted the Manhattan tsunami.

"It's not like you owe me anything, you know." I don't take my eyes off the giant white space, even when I talk to Roach. "Or have anything to *atone for.*" I try to will shapes to appear in that towering whiteness, but it resists.

"It's not like that, Julie," Roach says. "We all thought you were a great muralist, just an awesome artist in general. The whole committee agreed. There's no nepotism."

"Okay."

What would it be like to live in one of these Great Highway houses? First the horrendous construction, then this monstrosity steals away your ocean view. Then some flaky artist chick comes along and paints rainbows or something on it. I'm not painting the whole wall, just one section, a half dozen feet or so.

When I first met Roach, he was in his mid-thirties but looked both younger and older. His face looked boyish, yet ravaged by some bad decisions I don't know all the details of. Now, though, he just looks old. Whatever he was fleeing, it's overtaken him, and he seems glad: he's surrendered to life at last, and it's had its way with him.

Roach leads me to a staircase tucked away behind one big bulwark along the wall, over near Noriega. We climb, and soon we're standing on top, looking down at the waves.

"It's like a paradox," Roach says. "All the places people most want to live are built on the water. Because once upon a time, the cool people went to sea. Or traded, or fucked sea travelers. Maybe they craved a taste of danger, maybe they just wanted to get rich. Either way, we all ended up here, in worse peril than anyone ever bargained on."

I tune out Roach's holistic doomsaying and stare at the waves. They're soothing, yet inexorable, bashing against the concrete, over and over. Would people rather see nautical shit, to remind them of the view they lost? Or would that be too painful, especially with the lingering potential for destruction? Would people rather see something escapist? Heroic? Cultural? Probably they just want comfort.

I ditch Roach, head home, and start painting curios. Little one-inch pictures of horse heads in Admiral Nelson hats or ants surfing in space. It's easier to think small for some reason.

Roach's crotch sort of smelled like the ocean, back when I had sex with him. A seafaring adventure scent, like the wind from the last island in a chain. Nothing past that atoll but knots and knots of blue. Nearby, on his inner hip, there was a scar that he claimed he'd gotten in a knife fight in Albuquerque. (I heard later it was from a teledildonics accident.) His pubic hair was brown, but laced with gray.

Roach responded to my Craigslist ad, back when I still did the "casual encounters" thing. He sold himself as a "business dad" type, but in person he was more like an aging hippie crammed into a suit. He'd been doing open relationships before, but now he was married and cheating, which I didn't realize at first.

"I used to practice kind of a deep sharing," he said, running a hand under his receding light brown hair. "I wanted to be right there with my lovers . . . like if I could bring my center of presence to whoever I was loving that moment, it would be almost like teleportation. The more lovers I had, the more places I could be in at once. Dissolving the *here* and the *there* into just the *where*." So, yeah: hippie in a suit.

I didn't see Roach for a few years. The next time, I didn't recognize him at first, because he was fully clothed and I'd forgotten his face. I was on my knees, trying to capture the magnanimity of Papa Smurf in pencils on a plaster wall. I heard a noise and turned to see this middle-aged, nondescript guy wearing pajamas and a barbecue apron.

He looked all startled and greeted me with exaggerated formality, to let me know I should pretend not to know him. Since I really had no clue who he was, that was easy.

"I'm Roach," he said, slowly and with too much emphasis. "Nice to Meet You."

"I'm Julie," I said, copying his loud-casual diction. "Your Wife Hired Me. I'm Painting a Mural for Your Kid's Wall." Roach's child, Jasmine, had green curtains that matched her eyes but clashed with the deep mahogany of the rest of Roach's Edwardian row house.

"Oh yes," Roach said. "Papa Smurf and the Bosozoku Mice. Cool Combination."

"It Was Your Daughter's Idea," I said. This turned into a discussion of whether the Bosozoku Mice, those rebellious bikers, would like Papa Smurf if they actually met. At some point, I had an inkling I might have met Roach before, but I couldn't place him. Then he mentioned his name again and I finally twigged.

I went, "Oh! I Remember You Now!" in the same exaggerated tone, then covered my mouth.

A half dozen years after that, Roach got in touch, because he was on some committee to pick mural artists to paint sections of the giant seawall and he'd convinced the other members that I'd be the ideal person to turn an eyesore into a neighborhood treasure.

Can't sleep. My bedroom wall becomes The Wall and my clock radio's green flicker becomes sea light. In the half-life of my dream state, I wonder if anybody has tried asking the ocean what it wants. Maybe the ocean's demands are reasonable.

It probably wants maidens, I think. That sounds suitably mythic. Plus it's what everybody wants: maidens lashed to a stone, spray soaking their clothes before the tide even rises to swallow them. Do you still have to be a virgin to be a maiden nowadays? What's the upper age limit? Probably I'm too old.

My skin feels hot but I'm cold inside, like I'm coming down with something. I don't want to wake up my girlfriend, Lexa, by thrashing around.

I extricate myself from the bedsheets as gently as I can and walk into the kitchenette part of our little apartment. The canary yellow cabinet doors never shut properly, so they flap like bat wings at face level, over and over again.

I make tea with the whooshing electric kettle. I think about maidens in chains, at the mercy of the rising waves, or of a tentacley sea monster. This is the kind of kinky shit I used to dwell on, back when I was a slut and had a lot of spare mental capacity.

I pull out my laptop and write an email to Roach, explaining that I can't paint the seawall after all. I'm not the person he thinks I am, and there are so many great muralists in the city who deserve the commission way more. I don't have the Eros to go with the Thanatos. Years of painting Mickey Mouse murals have dulled my rawness, as surely as the deskiest desk job.

After writing a dozen rationalizations and then backspacing over each one, I decide not to send the email after all. I'll sleep on it, if I can sleep at all.

I wake up sketching with one finger in midair, seven inches away from my face. Fancy swirls and shapes. Lexa offers me coffee and I wake up the rest of the way, and I can't remember what I was sketching.

"You looked like you were conducting an orchestra." Lexa leans over me with the coffee cup. I lift enough of my torso to hold a saucer without spattering the bed.

Lexa and I have been together two years, and we've lived together for six months. We have an open relationship, in theory, but we're both too busy to fool around with anyone else. We spend all our downtime together, and we only have one bed.

Lexa is shockingly beautiful, with hazel eyes, light brown skin, and bold cheekbones. Lately, her hair is rust. She dresses like a punk rock kindergarten teacher, but she works for a nonprofit battling against violence.

"It's just weird," Lexa says over breakfast. "We're finally turning San Francisco into a walled city. Like a gated community."

Only a few parts, I point out, and only to protect against the sea. It's not like poor people will have to pass through a checkpoint—and yet it does seem like more and more of our friends are being run out of town these days.

Lexa says a bunch of her friends are going to tear shit up this afternoon, make the yuppies feel unwelcome. A protest? No, more like a riot, but with sprinkles of flash mob and rave. Someone sends a text with an exact time and place, and a target. Could be a person, could be a thing. Everybody swoops down at exactly 4:03 and dishevels the target as nonviolently as possible. By 4:06, everyone has dispersed.

Last week, they all converged on a private equity guy who invests in private prisons and detention centers, while he was walking along Natoma Street. They surrounded him in a whirl of natural fabrics and sweet-smelling oils and put noisy punk hop headphones on his head. Then they stole his clothes, painted slogans in body glitter across his thick chest hair, and dressed him in Roxxxie Dent's Folsom Street Fair castoffs. The whole operation took two minutes and thirty-four seconds, the exact length of DJ Smurfette's "It's Big and Thick and Doesn't Exist (So Suck It)."

I'm not sure how I feel about this, it all sounds very nonconsensual. But Lexa says late-late-late-waytoolate-stage capitalism is also very nonconsensual.

"You should come along," Lexa says. "You'll see how low-key it is. People sometimes thank us for glad-mobbing them, like now they finally know they're in San Francisco. It's all fun. Come on."

An hour later, Lexa and I are riding the N Judah, and I'm still wondering why I said yes. Oh yeah—it was because Lexa promised we could go to Lush and Old Navy while we wait for the call to go fuck shit up. It all balances out. "I love how every wedge of soap has the face of the person who made it, like they're our friends who we're paying to make soap for us," I say.

"If I was rich, we'd have sex on a bed made out of all these soaps," Lexa says. This isn't true. If Lexa was rich, she'd endow a foundation or something, and live exactly the same way she lives now. That's one reason I love her.

Old Navy has hotpants that turn into culottes halfway, they're coolpants. I try on three pairs. Lexa fidgets.

The SMS finally comes while I'm in line: everybody will converge on the Love Engine. Corporate-funded, city-approved, the Love Engine makes everybody ill. It's supposed to be like a steampunk apparatus cranking out Love Energy, on the edge of the Financial District. It could have been weird and ironic, but instead it came out kitschy and smarmy, with pink heart bubbles streaming out of the top and a dingy sweatshop look to the murky valves. Plus gross Summer of Love quotes painted on its base.

I hate the Love Engine as much as anybody, but the idea of defacing someone else's art freaks me out. In the end, I wimp out and go home, and Lexa goes with me.

Roach is obsessed with SkinFranzizko, a new cyber world that he plays every second at work and whenever he can escape his wife and kid at home. At first, the Skin just sounds like a virtual version of San Francisco, where you have an avatar and you can zoom around a perfect representation of SoMa or the Mission, constantly updated, thanks to satellites and street cams. But Roach says there's way more to the Skin than that.

The city can wear different skins, hence the name. You can be in Haight-Ashbury circa 1967, and every little detail will be as perfect as the designers can make it, based on photos, films, and reminiscences. If you were around back then and find a mistake in the 1967 skin, then you can flash the developers and they'll scramble to fix it.

But that's not all. The city can also wear future skins, using the current geography but with flying trolleys, wetware buildings, or half-lizard, half-computer people. You can have Nonstop Orgy San Francisco. You can have Bad Acid Trip San Francisco. Gingerbread San Francisco. Dinosaur Jungle San Francisco. Or Alternate History Soviets Won the Cold War San Francisco.

"Sometimes you'll run into someone on the street, but they're using a different city skin than you are, and it gets kind of weird," Roach says. "In a good way. Last week, I was in Middle Earth San Francisco, as an elf, and I ran into my friend Doggo, who was in the Barbary Coast. To me, he looked like a hobbit. To him, I looked like a sheriff. We could hardly communicate. It's like everybody sees their own version of the city. Sort of like a kind of metaphor."

At Roach's fancy job, they keep changing the meaning of "professional presentation." It's okay to wear shorts at work, until suddenly one day it isn't. You can never be sure if other people have the same idea of what's "professional" that you do.

Roach offers to get me a subscription to the Skin for a month or two, just in case it might give me some ideas. At first I say no, but then I figure what the fuck.

Lexa watches over my shoulder as my avatar whizzes around the virtual city. Every now and then an anthropomorphic flower or Slinky comes up to me and tries to talk me into cybersex, but I just ignore them.

I stop in front of our apartment building. I can make out the pattern of our curtains, count the petals on the flowers in Lexa's window box, and even glimpse movement inside the apartment. My avatar is watching the real me through my bedroom window.

"It's not quite real time," I explain. "This is probably from a few days ago, plus it's been 'virtualized.'" The only time you'll see the ghost of a real person in the Skin is when someone's in a window. The software edits out people from the street.

"That means there are no homeless people, no street performers, no drug dealers," Lexa says. I steer my avatar along Haight and around Civic Center, and sure enough, it's true. We do see one guy sitting on the sidewalk, but he's a developer testing the elasticity of the cement.

"They finally got a San Francisco without poor people." Lexa has that smug-progressive thing in her voice.

I press the ESC key and a sliding bar pops up at the top of the screen. At the right side of the bar is today's date. Over on the left, it's 1880. You can slide the bar and watch San Francisco age in reverse. Go to any spot in the city, then inch the bar back and forth. It's 1972. It's 1995. It's 1945. The little details look more accurate for some eras than others, but it's still addictive.

It's 1906 and the city's on fire, or it's 1989 and there's rubble: just so you're reminded that this city gets destroyed every once in a while.

I start playing with the history bar when Lexa goes off to work, and I'm still sliding it when Lexa gets home again. My eyes pixelate, even when I look away from the screen. I'm that lonesome time traveler who can't change the past or interact with anyone.

It's been a week since I promised to get some concept drawings to the committee. I've filled two notebooks with crappy sketches of fluffy bunnies, mermaids, sea horses, narwhals, and amphibious gay bunnies. Something, anything, to reassure people and keep them from thinking about how badly we fucked up this planet (and this city). At some point I realize that I'm approaching this job as if it was another child's bedroom wall, but I don't know what else to do. The reality of our situation is just too extreme to make sense of. Every now and then my cell buzzes and Roach's name flashes, but I don't pick up.

I go out to Baker Beach and wander into the rocky area set aside for nude frolicking. The sun only bleeds a little through the splashes of cloud cover, but that doesn't stop a handful of cis men from strutting around in just running shoes.

Even in a sweater and thick turtleneck, I feel frozen under the skin. Signs everywhere warn that these are not surfing waves, these waves are a backdrop for sunbathing and furtive masturbation. The waves don't look that hardcore at first, sloshing over the rocks like drunken lap dancers. I sit on one of the big jagged rocks, just around the bend from the Golden Gate Bridge. After a few minutes, one huge wave darts up and breaks in my face, and then the sea goes back to little licks against the crags closer to the shoreline. My clothes are all damp. I could take them off—this is a nude beach, after all— but I don't. I just let the weak sun dry me.

There are two naked guys left, but they don't check each other out, maybe because they're both regulars. They do glance over at me from time to time, but what are they hoping I'll do? Take off my clothes too, or leave so they can have a pure gay area? I have no objection to being naked in front of strangers—I've been to plenty of sex parties—but I'm feeling shy, and really, someone else would have to *want* me to get naked.

"I'm going to go have a wild sexual adventure," I tell Lexa that evening. "I'm going to rock the walls. I'm going to drag the rivers."

"Cool." Lexa doesn't look up from painting a teacup.

"Don't wait up, okay?"

"Okay," Lexa says. "Be safe."

And then I'm outside, on the sidewalk, looking at the head shops and buses as if bacchanalia lurks behind every wall. Where am I going to find my heedless abandon? I could go back inside and start surfing FetLife, but that would ruin my big exit, plus maybe Lexa would look over my shoulder and make snarky comments.

I prowl the Mission and SoMa, with my fake-fur coat buttoned all the way up and stark makeup. Shiny boots with zigzag heels. The whole outfit is supposed to look forbidding and exciting. At first I'm not sure I can pull off this sexy bitch look anymore, but I'm surprised how easily it comes together.

I wind up at the new oxygen bar on Divisadero. From the outside it looks all plush and upholstered, and you don't even realize it's clothing optional unless you get to the velvety back room. Because they only sell oxygen, they don't have to worry about losing their liquor license. During fire season, this place is packed, like the 38-Geary Rapid at rush hour, but right now it's mostly empty.

The plastic oxygen tubes snake inside my nostrils. I snort the fragrance of exotic blossoms, my head lighter and lighter. I don't even intend to put my hand down my skirt, it just happens. I close my eyes, breathless, and touch myself through my panties for a moment.

I take a deep heady breath so as to create enough slack in my skirtwaist to pull my hand out again, before I get in trouble. Then I notice a man watching me, with plastic tubes in his nose. His eyes, under thick brows, are dark and staring. He nods, like *Keep going don't stop.* So I keep my hand down there, slowly inching my skirt upward with my other hand. The super-rich air makes my brain fog.

I end up masturbating in front of five yuppies, all of them with perfect rock star hair and sideburns. Soon I'm naked, except for the boots. One guy solemnly folds my coat and skirt on a chair nearby. None of them tries to touch me. When I run out of chrysanthemum-scented oxygen, one of them buys me more. They run a tab. Maybe I'm damaging my brain, I don't really care.

A thought starts to filter in: Danger is awesome! Art should be dangerous! Or else it's just decoration. Whether they know it or not, Roach's people are paying me to paint some image of danger on their safety barrier. They want, they need, a reminder. Of everything they deny. They demand it.

I come. I come like blazes. I really no kidding almost black out. My breaths are a rudder. The men all applaud. When I come the second time, I can hear them clap harder than ever, but it's further and further away. The third time, I'm all naked, even the boots gone, and everything has a halo.

When I finally yank the tubes out of my nose, it hurts to breathe regular air. It feels wrong. I have cramps all over, and my clothes feel corrugated against my skin. One of the yuppies offers to drive me home, but I say I'll take a cab. I'm very grateful, in retrospect, that none of those guys asked to touch me, because I would have let them but felt weird about it after. As it is, I just feel achy and drained, and happy.

Even the hangover the next morning feels warm.

I was worried Lexa would take a dislike to Roach, like she has with some of my other casual hookups, but they get on fine. His eagerness to please meets her optimism about people and forms a big smooshy cloud. Roach wears fatigues from a war that hasn't happened yet, radioactive purple with fake fur trim. He's singing my praises, which automatically scores him points with Lexa.

"Every time I put Jasmine to bed, I think about Julie, because her art is on the wall," he tells Lexa. "Her work is in so many people's houses, she's stealth famous."

"It's just murals to order. I'm not creating my own stuff." I'm making mojitos in our yellow kitchen, crushing lime and stirring ice with a long spoon.

"Just like all those Renaissance painters were just painting Bible shit to order," Roach said. "It's the same thing. Plus, and also, your Steven Universes don't look like regular Steven Universes. You put something into them. Their own personality."

Turns out Lexa and Roach know some of the same Burning Man people, and Roach's ex was in the same dialectical sex coven as Lexa's best friend. It takes them half an hour to sketch out the connections, including all the various people's messy breakups and restraining orders and contested patents.

"So what have you got." Roach finally turns to me. "I've been keeping the committee on hold. Chewing up my ass."

"Well, it's tentative." I plunge into it: a beautiful, fashionable woman, with glowing dark skin and big mysterious eyes, in some kind of Barbary Coast bordello. Ornate loveliness surrounds her, but everything turns out to be deadly at closer inspection. The chandelier over her head is made of tiny razor blades shimmering among the candles. The dark crushed velvet walls are really barbed wire. She sits on a chaise longue with land mine cushions, her fine ankles crossed on one side.

"Here's the old-fashioned telephone, which is really a mortar grenade," I say.

"That's kind of edgy," Roach says.

"I like it," Lexa says, daring him to disagree.

"Most people won't even notice the scary details," I add hastily. "It'll just look like a beautiful woman in her parlor, with a sort of aura of old-timey decadence."

I'm going to have to compromise, of course. Roach and I both know it, and we skip straight to talking about ways it might happen. Maybe the razor blades will be too much; can we make them sharp diamonds instead? Maybe the floor of poisonous toads and spiders could be just toads, toads can be cute. Lexa is scandalized that I don't even make a token stab at preserving my pristine vision. I try to explain that compromise is built into my artistic philosophy: especially with original work, constraints make the creation possible.

In the end, as I expected, Roach agrees to take the design to the committee as is.

The easy part is over, Roach says.

That night, I dream that I'm up a ladder, penciling in the knife-edge lace curtains of my fancy woman's chamber on the big wall. I'm naked, but it's an unusually bright day in the Sunset and I don't mind. I keep changing position, spreading myself out more to bask as much of my skin as possible. People start gathering on the sidewalk across the street, pointing and rabbiting in loud voices. I can't understand what they're saying. They could be excited to have art in their neighborhood, or worried because they can already tell from the pencils that my courtesan's nest is lethal. It doesn't occur to me at first that my public nudity, in their quiet neighborhood, could be a problem. Too thrilling, or possibly too much middle-aged flesh on display. At last I look for my clothes, but they're gone. Not so much as a drop cloth. Now I'm in trouble. I'm going to learn why exhibitionism is as dangerous as any other -ism. A man walks across the street and taps me on the shoulder, and I lean forward on my stool so he can talk to me, and I hope this will be a reasonable conversation.

He bites me on the arm. Not a love bite, hard enough to break the skin, and then he keeps biting until I give juice. He keeps his mouth locked on, even after his lips are smudgy red, like a drunken debutante's. Someone else walks up and bites my foot, so hard I scream. Another mouth on my thigh, and then one on my breast. Everyone comes across the street and they pour all their teeth into me, tearing me and growling through mouthfuls of my flesh, there will be nothing left even if I survive, and it takes me forever to wake up, shrieking and soaked in sweat.

In the morning, I decide that dream was a wonderful omen.

I didn't intend for "Power Couple" to be a science fiction story at first. I wrote the first third of the story thinking of it as a "realist" work of literary fiction, in which the only technology would be stuff that already exists. But the deeper I got into this story of two young people who are torn between their relationship and their careers, the more it became obvious what should happen next, from a character standpoint: they should take turns going into suspended animation.

"Power Couple" is Exhibit A for why speculative fiction helps me explore real-life stuff in more thoughtful ways than a "grounded" approach ever could. As soon as I added a futuristic plot device to the story, its themes and characters sprang into sharper relief. I was able to see that this is really a story about the pressure we put on young adults to commit to professional identities early on, and to know who they want to be right away—and how toxic all that pressure can become.

POWER COUPLE

His name was John, and he was going to change the world. So was I. We met at the start of senior year, at a college debating tournament, where our team barely held its own against Ivy League champs who declaimed that "This House Believes" some proposition, with impromptu conviction. John was both smart and clever, which I always thought was an either/or proposition. He wanted to become an attorney and help all the people who'd fallen for America's promises—who'd believed it actually meant something when a person in expensive clothes said "This House Believes," not realizing that This House made a virtue of believing whatever was convenient in the moment. Both of us were going to turn our educations into constructive action and pay off not just our mountains of student loans but also any faith that anyone had ever put in us.

John had brown hair with blond highlights that he swore grew that way naturally, and a foxy sharp grin. He caught me gazing at his butt, swept up in a reverie about the bottom as signifier, as synecdoche, as an anatomical feature whose muscles extended all the way up to the hips, and down to the femur. "It's cool," John said, "I just took a gender studies class where we talked about the male gaze and the fact that men never get objectified the same way literally everyone else does, so this feels like praxis." Much later, I discovered that his butt fit perfectly inside my cupped hands, the curve of his undercheek resting just right against my crinkled life lines, as if copping a feel was the whole reason I had palms in the first place.

We blew off the rest of the debating tournament—we'd already lost anyway—and then I bailed on a study group and he canceled his dinner plans. We skipped like children down Franklin Street, we chalked pastel hearts on the campus walkways, and we intentionally mangled the lyrics to Broadway musical numbers. The next thing I knew, it was three in the morning, and we were holding hands in the reddish neon light from the package store, and we were making up names for astronaut cats, and this seemed like the most important work either of us had ever done.

"Meow Clawstrong," John said.

"Captain Starfluff," I countered.

"Major Tom would actually be a legit good name for an astronaut cat."

John talked a mile a minute, but then he would come to rest and look at me with a playful stillness. He smelled like brambles and heather, and his ink-smeared hands touched mine with the gentleness of falling maple leaves. By the time the sun came up, and we'd been hanging out for twelve hours, and I felt a pang, a longing, or maybe a realignment. A potential that felt like a presence. All of my senses were so turned up, it felt like the world was touching me in a whole new way.

By winter senior year, John and I were spending every night together and the rest of the world seemed both insignificant and enchanted, a Smurf village at our feet. He was my first love. Spring found us standing on an ancient stone bridge, arms around each other and bodies glued from sternum to ankle, watching algae bloom underwater. We breathed in sync. I leaned into John's shoulder and inhaled slowly. The gathering warmth seemed to well up from the center of the Earth, instead of the returning sun.

Six months later, I looked up from my textbooks and realized I hadn't even talked to John on the phone in a week and a half. We'd barely texted. My first semester at UVA School of Medicine was kicking my ass and I could barely remember when I'd had time for naming astronaut cats, or even for going outside in the daytime. John was at Princeton Law School, a five-hour drive away, and we'd promised to spend every weekend together. Then it became every other weekend, and then it was Christmas and John had become "Hey stranger."

"Fuck, you know I don't like Rieslings. Why would you bring a Riesling when you know I can't stand them?"

"Why won't you give my friends a chance? They're trying really hard to take an interest in you. What the hell is wrong with you?"

"Stop giving me shit for my taste in music, just because I'm not into fucking Japanese noise music doesn't mean I'm garbage all of a sudden."

"Why are we even fighting? I don't know why we're fighting."

"Maybe we're fighting because we need space. I need space. You're suffocating me."

"I haven't even seen you in months, and now I'm fucking suffocating you."

"This isn't working. I can't do this anymore. I hate this."

Somehow it was already spring. Crocuses were wigging out. John and I sat on a bench facing a lake, watching a mother duck misplace her ducklings over and over. Neither of us spoke. We were both on our best behavior, which had come to mean a carefully curated silence. I was visiting John for the weekend, and there was a full schedule of activities with John's friends: law study sessions, tennis matches, and parties where everyone talked about law and tennis.

"Maybe we should see other people," I said to John, as I repacked my weekend bag in his dorm room. He hadn't decorated in here, except for one framed photo of me, looking fizzy and blond.

I turned around and John was half squatting, like he was about to run a hundred-yard dash. "Willa, I—Will you—"

I started to repeat the thing about seeing other people.

He offered up a velvet box in both hands. "Please, just let me finish, I need to say this. I know in the deepest quiet of my soul that we were meant to be together, and you're the best part of my world. I love you and I want to spend the rest of my life with you."

The velvet box contained a twenty-sided die from someone's Dungeons & Dragons campaign—a placeholder, John said.

"You're trying to lock me down." I looked at the die. The number eleven faced upward. Was that like snake eyes? I couldn't remember if snake eyes was lucky or not.

"Yeah. Because otherwise I know I'll look back on this moment as the biggest mistake of my life. We owe it to each other to hold on to this. I wish we'd met later in life, when we'd done all the heavy lifting and career shit, but I know for sure we belong together."

He wept, and so did I, and then we kissed, and soon we were naked on the bed together crying and kissing and I missed my train back to UVA.

I stuck the twenty-sided die in my pocket, and then we were engaged.

We didn't tell anyone about our engagement, since we hadn't nailed down any of the details, like a date and venue. I went back to UVA with a blessing warmth, and felt its heat death over the next few weeks. We went back to texting once a day, and I actively tried to avoid untangling my emotions toward John—like, I couldn't wait to see him again, but I also dreaded the next fight. In my mind, there were two Johns: my current boyfriend, with whom I had almost nothing in common, and my future husband, with whom I would one day share everything.

I kept thinking about what John had said: if only we'd met later in life. If only we could both be finished with law school and med school and internships and residencies and everything and finally be the people we were waiting to become, and then we would have time to take a long look at each other.

I carried the d20 always, got used to its pointy edges jabbing into my thigh through my pants pocket.

One day that spring, I walked around campus in expanding circles, as if I was searching for something. My thoughts were stuck in a loop, trying to reconcile the two Johns into one person, and I had a sick feeling in a part of me that appeared in no anatomy textbooks I'd ever seen.

I ended up walking past the cryonics lab where my friend Maisie worked, in a boxy red brick converted tobacco warehouse. Inside, I tried to see where workers had hefted bales and rolled cigarettes, but there was nothing but plasterboard walls and purring machines.

The next thing I knew, I had talked to Maisie for a few hours. Maisie showed me all the equipment and introduced me to her boss and coworkers. I had already learned in med school that you could slow the body's functions to a standstill using a combination of intravenous drugs and industrial coolants. Maisie spouted phrases like "metabolic coma" and "molasses-slow polymerase," but I was thinking of *Sleeping Beauty* crossed with Ripley from the *Alien* movies.

I called John a few days later. "I found it. I found the answer. Just listen. Wait, don't say anything yet. You said we'd be better if we'd met later in life, and this way we can. Just imagine the story we'll be able to tell our grandchildren, about our weird courtship. No, hear me out. We both work in fields that were designed for single-achiever families, and it'll be at least seven years before we can pay attention to each other. During that time, we each have to be able to relocate to a random location, like the president at DEFCON two. This is how we make it work. Please tell me you can see how perfect this is." I finished my pitch, breathless.

I waited for John to poke a million holes in my idea.

Instead, he considered. Of course, being a law student, he asked about the legalities. I explained the cryo lab wasn't officially part of the university, it was a private company that benefited from the university's talent pool. The FDA had approved stage 3 cryo trials about five years earlier, and maybe a hundred people around the country were in suspension now. We would have to sign a stack of release forms the thickness of a Gideon Bible.

"You're sure this new technique is safe? No side effects?" John asked. I offered reassurance.

"Sooo . . . I slide into this overgrown lipstick tube for seven years. You keep me sitting around in your room all through med school and residency, like some kind of improbably handsome ice sculpture. Then, when you finish residency, we turn the tables. I go out and conquer the universe, while you turn into the world's lowest-maintenance girlfriend. Right? Then, fourteen years from now, we're both just seven years older, and fully qualified to live where we want and pursue our careers. It's . . . an audacious plan. No doubt about that." He laughed.

"Does that mean you'll think about it?"

"I mean, it reminds me of why I fell in love with you in the first place, Willa. Nobody else could have come up with such sensible lunacy. Let me get back to you."

We each talked to our friends and families. Everyone made fun of my plan, but there was an undercurrent of envy. This was the weirdest and most romantic scheme anyone had ever heard of.

"If I say yes, how do I know you'll awaken me?" John asked, a few days later.

"Because I'll miss your conversation," I laughed. "You'll be a boring stiff."

"There's one thing I gotta do first, though. Unfinished business." John dug in his satchel, past law review papers and lecture notes, and pulled out a tiny ring in a Ziploc bag. An opal the size of a pea, surrounded by lacey metal. It fit perfectly.

I buried my face in his neck and savored his body heat, the tremolo of his carotid, the familiar, amazing scents of cheap soap and expensive deodorant.

John ate his favorite meal (fish tacos) and we had raucous, wall-thunking, tender sex. Then he put on a white suit and black tie and we drove to the medical school, where Maisie and her boss, Dr. Abbye, did some last-minute tests on John and then put him on a slab, which slid inside a great silver shell.

And now my apartment had a new decoration: a shiny chrome tube that rested against one wall, with a big window showing John's face. John's expression looked sardonic from some angles, mournful from others, and he cast a bluish-white glow in the middle of the night. I got used to his presence there, only to have it startle me anew when I'd just gotten out of the shower or sat scratching myself in bed. I got used to explaining John to the lovers I brought home, but also I went over to other people's places instead. Once a month, I trimmed John's beard and fingernails. When I went away on vacation, I got a friend to come in once a day and check on John, whose bio monitors stayed evergreen.

As promised, I talked to John every day when I was around. I told him about my day, about my weirdest little fears and minutiae—including things I never could have shared with an alert John. When I got to residency and started working for thirty hours at a stretch, I lost track of when John was actually present, and I started seeing him all the time. I'd be taking a patient's history on the internal medicine floor and I'd glimpse John's frozen, luminous face staring over my shoulder. I muttered to John's specter in the break room, where I bunked on call. His unweary watchfulness followed me everywhere. I sometimes forgot his name at four in the morning, but not his face.

"Boyfriend in a coma. Han Solo in carbonite." My friend-with-benefits Jezzy giggled. "Everyone should have one."

Residency ended. I slept for a week and went to the beach for another week. I got a pedicure and read trashy novels. I caught up with old girlfriends. After a month, the cryo lab started calling to ask when John and I would come in. I didn't call back. Guilt started to nag at me, somewhere deep between the fascial layers of my abdomen.

"It's not like I prefer him this way or anything," I told Maisie in a moment of weakness. "Maybe I do, maybe I don't. I can't remember the old John well enough to know. He's been a Popsicle for way longer than he was an awake person in my life. But . . . once I wake John, I'll have to take my turn. I'm not so sure I want to do that anymore."

Maisie gently pointed out that John was a person who deserved to get on with his life, and in any case I could discuss the options with John, once he could speak for himself.

I stared into John's eyes as he came back to the world. I'd spent an hour practicing my "adoring girlfriend" expression in the mirror, because I wanted his first sight after seven years to be perfect. I did my hair and makeup and tried to look as much like the old Willa as possible. I searched everywhere for this one brand of shimmery eye shadow that he'd always liked seeing on me, but they'd stopped making it long ago.

John stayed expressionless for ages, after he'd already defrosted. Normal, Maisie said. Nothing to worry about. Then a smile took shape on his face, too slow to track.

"I gotta pee" were his first words back among the living.

The doctors warned me that John might be groggy or disoriented for a while, but an hour after he left that tube he was jumping up and down, talking a hot streak. Sparking with energy. We went to dinner, and he wolfed two entrees.

"I had amazing dreams, full of flying shapes and voices. They're fading already, but I remember I had no body in them. Did you ever think, if information is energy, that means information can't really be created or destroyed? Information just *is*. Can't not be." He fucked me three times, then got up and paced. I heard him masturbating in the bathroom at four in the morning, and again at five.

I'd forgotten how much fun John was. He made me laugh until I snorted. He talked nonstop, a stream of ideas and observations and dreams, and I felt like I could just bask in just how *awake* he was, after I'd gotten accustomed to him at rest. He was packing seven years of conversations and sex and meals and TV binges into a few weeks. The only thing he wouldn't do was sleep a full night next to me.

After a few days, I was starting to worry that his extreme hyperactivity was some kind of side effect.

"I feel fine." His new beard wagged. "I've had plenty of nap time. Now I want to have fun." He went out clubbing—first with me, then without, once it was obvious I couldn't keep up. I got used to being woken up by him returning home at four in the morning, and then again a few hours later, as he held a mug of coffee under my nose.

"Listen, it's nothing to worry about," he said. "We're just different ages now. I'm in my early twenties, you're almost thirty. Those are way, way different life stages. Remember how much you used to go out when you were my age? How much energy you had?"

I didn't have the heart to tell John I was having second thoughts about getting frozen. To him, we'd just made that plan a few weeks ago, but I could barely remember the mind-set I'd been in when I'd come up with it. I had low-key exploratory conversations with a few hospitals. I could get a job, right now, I could start treating women with late-stage cancer, there was no need to wait seven years for my work to begin.

John was constantly on the phone with Princeton and all the law firms that had been interested in having him as a summer intern, and he kept asking when I was going to get rid of my apartment. Wasn't like I was going to need a place to live, and he could move back into grad student housing, or maybe get a place in New Jersey.

"You should tell your landlord," he said. And then an hour later, "Have you talked to your landlord yet? I don't want to have to deal with your landlord after you're frozen."

I finally broke down and confessed: "I'm . . . I'm wondering if maybe it's okay if I just don't? If I . . . I could come with you to New Jersey, just not frozen."

"No." John folded his arms and tapped both feet: *pa-dam, pa-dam, pa-dam.*

"I can move anywhere now. I have so much flexibility. I could even work part time as a locum tenens. I could support you in law school. We could get married sooner."

"That's not the point. You know that's not the point. This whole thing was your idea." He didn't raise his voice or freak out or accuse me of trying to renege, he just looked sad. John had the same look on his face that my father had, that time he ran over a neighbor's dog and we all held our breath in unison as he got out of the car and walked around to inspect the furry body, all of us hoping the dog was just injured. My father already knew the truth, he just hadn't verified yet.

"I've been watching you sleep. It's my favorite sight. I want to watch you sleep all the time, for months, for years. I want to wish you sweet dreams every night before I fall into bed, and drift off knowing that you're waiting for me. The same way I waited for you."

"So there's no way we can just move forward—"

"Listen, you can do what you want. But if you don't go through with your side of this, I don't think we can stay together. It'd break my heart, I'd be wrecked, but . . . this whole plan relied on both of us ending up in the same place. The same age, the same level. There's just no way this can work otherwise."

I felt like I was already half in suspended animation after a while, as the same arguments went around and around.

"I can't believe you're giving me an ultimatum," I said.

"I can't believe you're trying to back out of our deal," John said.

That's as close as we got to fighting. I almost wished John would scream, throw a teacup at the wall—call out my total unfairness. Make it easier for me to walk away.

Instead, John seemed to make a decision: he needed to court me all over again. He slowed down and tried to listen and stopped going out every night without me. We drove to the beach and ate caviar naked with the waves painting our ankles with foam. John looked into my eyes and talked about all the dreams we'd hatched seven years earlier: the two of us, doing great things side by side, an unstoppable team. A power couple. Children, grandchildren, a big house full of laughter. "We've come too far to give up now. Willa, please think about this. We could have the most epic romance, if you just hang in there."

I sat in the bathtub and reminded myself that I had planned this role reversal and that John wasn't just turning the tables on me to be mean.

"I guess you'll mellow out by the time I wake up," I mused to John.

"I'll be easygoing by then. You won't even know any time has passed. I feel as though I barely closed my eyes. I went into the deep freeze knowing that I was loved, and came out the exact same way."

John and I started to feel comfortable together again, once he slowed a little and I relaxed around him. I eased into our old rapport, trading jokes and kisses for hours, for the first time since senior year. "You're the fucking love of my life," I told John. "I never want to lose my faith that love can defeat all obstacles." We spent a whole day in bed, making love and talking about our future. Ours.

Then we went back to the cryo lab together. I lay down on the sliding table and stared up at the nicotine-scarred ceiling.

"Hey." John smiled down at me. I could tell he was fighting the urge to look around the room and focus on five things at once. He held one of my hands and Maisie held the other. (She didn't work there anymore, but she'd come back for this.)

They let go of my hands as I rolled into the tube's darkness, and my mind was full of patterns without meaning.

John was staring down at me, except his beard was gone and his face was a different shape. I started to smile, but my face muscles were hard clay. Then I focused again and realized this wasn't John's face at all.

"I'm sorry," Maisie said. "John's not here."

I tried to nod. I felt so tired. I'd just had the longest sleep ever—why was I so tired?

Tried to form questions. Nonsense poured out instead.

"Maybe I should wait until you've gotten yourself back together," Maisie said.

I made a protesting noise, and she sighed.

"Okay. Here's the situation. You've only been under for a few years," Maisie said, checking my vitals. "Nobody can get in touch with John, and we all got worried when he didn't check in. So we went to his last known address and found you there. There was an eviction notice on the door and the fridge was full of spoiled food."

Spoiled food. And me.

"I shudder to think what would have happened if his electricity had got cut off with you still in suspension. Catastrophic shutdown."

Maisie daubed at my face with a tissue. I thought maybe they had applied some kind of fluid to my face to help the revival process. Then I realized I must be crying. I still felt as though everything was happening a long distance away.

"I'm sorry, maybe I should have waited to tell you the truth," Maisie said.

"But I knew this would be disorienting, no matter what. From your perspective, you just saw him a moment ago."

I nodded. I still felt unable to talk.

They let me go a few hours later, but I had no place to go. I ended up getting a room in a Days Inn nearby. My room was full of weird shapes, and the shadows cast by the single lamp kept creeping up on me. The thick plaid curtains undulated, fleshy monsters in the corner of my eye. Everything kept startling me, and all I could do for a few days was order pizza and watch the home improvement channel for twelve hours a day. The bank kept not unfreezing my account, for some reason.

I went outside after a few days and stared at things. That tree on the edge of the cracked parking lot, would it stay in one place if I stared at it for five minutes? I blinked at the cars on the two-lane highway, trying to see if they flickered. I couldn't trust that none of this was an illusion. The air tasted wrong. I smelled bitter, dank fumes. This would all dissolve if I turned my back.

I only wished I could be hyperactive, the way John had been when he woke up.

I hunted John for a month, in between interviews for locum tenens positions. None of his law school buddies had kept up with him, but one of them gave me an address that turned out to be a warehouse where John had slung car parts. Someone there had lived in a group house with John and a group of death rockers. Finally, someone told me John had moved to Maine.

It took a day to drive through dense woods, along single-lane highways lined by pumpkin stands and stores with names like The Brass Button. The roads frosted and snow spattered my windshield.

John's new housemates seemed friendly and crunchy, not at all death rockerish, and they told me where to find the soap factory where John worked. I pictured John, still hyperactive, running five machines at once, possibly juggling at the same time. Instead, he stood in front of a conveyor belt, calmer than I'd ever seen him. His beard had spread out, but otherwise he looked the same. I watched him until his break.

"Remember those lavender and chamomile soaps you liked?" he asked me. "I make those. It's way more socially beneficial than lawyering would have been."

He led me across the street to a sandwich shop. It had the local newspaper and a menu with three choices.

"Are you all right?" I asked.

He nodded. "I was a tad jumpy for a while after I defrosted. Then I returned to normal. If anything, everyone said I was more mature, considering I hadn't aged."

"Then why—"

"I dropped out of law school. I guess you knew." He shrugged and ordered a bacon roll and cocoa. I got some cookies. "It wasn't some weird side effect of the freezing process, though. I just wasn't cut out for law, it turned out. You know, I was just out of college, I didn't really know what I wanted to be. Still don't know. I partly went to law school because everyone expected me to do something big and fancy. Including you. Especially you."

"I didn't care what you did, I just wanted—"

"You liked me because I was smart, right? And I didn't want to disappoint. Remember how we used to talk about our future all the time? We were going to work like beavers and put off everything else, like our relationship and anything else fun, and it was all going to be worth it. We were going to be a doctor and a lawyer. Delayed gratification is a sick joke."

He sat down at a Formica-coated table near the window, and I just kept standing, clutching a wax paper bag.

"Don't try and make this my fault," I said. "This isn't on me."

"It's definitely not your fault, but—"

"I almost died." I stood over him as he ate his sandwich. "If they hadn't found me when they did."

"Georgie didn't take care of you? I sublet my place to him, and he promised—"

"Who the fuck is Georgie?" I waved my hand to stop him answering. "Fuck that. I don't care who Georgie is. Jesus, I'm not a fern. I'm not a pet rock. You can't just hand me off to some random friend to—"

John kept waving for me to sit down. I was shaking and making ugly glottal noises in between words, the wax paper bag of cookies was coming apart, I was in danger of falling or knocking something over, I was making a scene in the one sandwich shop in the tiny town where everyone knew everyone.

"I just—I just—I just—" I stepped on something. The cookies. I didn't cry or scream, but everything still looked blurry and my throat still hurt.

"Please just sit down. I'll tell you whatever you want. You can still despise me from a seated position. Please sit. Please sit."

"Just . . . why? Why didn't you? Why didn't you wake me up? You washed out of law school, you gave up, I don't care. Why didn't you wake me when you realized?"

John looked out the window. Someone saw him and waved at him, a child maybe.

"I couldn't face it. I tried to imagine waking you up and telling you that it was all a waste, and I . . . I just couldn't. I figured seven years is a long time, and maybe I could be a success at *something* before I had to look you in the eye again."

I wanted to burn down the life that John had built for himself here. The soap factory, the fluffy-punky roommates, all of it.

"I'm sorry, sorrier than I can put into English." John hunched over, gazing at his sandwich. "I ruined your life. At least you're still young, it's so much better to have your life ruined when you're young. I feel older than dirt, even though I guess I'm technically younger than you."

John wept. I watched him and felt nothing.

There wasn't much to say after that. On the long drive south, I tried to imagine a dramatic ending to my love story. Like a car crash in a New Hampshire snowdrift. Or maybe an irony-laden moment in which I went back and had myself refrozen until John made good, or someone invented a cure for fatal idealism. But I already knew that my life was just going to carry on, at more or less the same pace as everybody else's, until it one day coasted to a complete stop.

I wrote four novels that never got published, before *All the Birds in the Sky*. There was a comic portal fantasy, there was a coming-of-age story set at the start of Bill Clinton's presidency, and there was an urban fantasy about witch hunters. And there was *Rock Manning*. I started writing a version of *Rock Manning* at the start of the Iraq War—it was a meditation on violence, slapstick comedy, and the relationship between the two. The part of us that lets us laugh at someone else's pratfall might also be what allows us to tolerate horrific violence against people who aren't part of our in-group.

Years later I went back and cut *Rock Manning* down to a novella, which was serialized in three anthologies of apocalyptic fiction and then published as a standalone book by Subterranean Press. *Rock Manning* worked better as a novella than as a novel, because I lost some excess subplots, a ton of extra baggage, and some unnecessary sexual violence. It only took fifteen years, but I finally ended up with a streamlined version of this gonzo epic that I felt accomplished what I'd set out to do back in the day.

Just a heads up: this story is extremely violent, by design.

ROCK MANNING GOES FOR BROKE

1
Break! Break! Break!

Earliest I remember, Daddy threw me off the roof of our split-level house. "Boy's gotta learn to fall sometime," he told my mom just before he slung my pants seat and let go. As I dropped, Dad called out instructions, but they tangled in my ears. I was four or five. My brother caught me one-handed, gave me a spank, and dropped me on the lawn. Then up to the roof for another go round, with my body more slack this time.

From my dad, I learned there were just two kinds of bodies: falling, and falling on fire.

My dad was a stuntman with a left-field resemblance to an actor named Jared Gilmore who'd been in some TV show before I was born, and he'd gotten it in his head Jared was going to be the next big action movie star. My father wanted to be Jared's personal stunt double and "prosthetic acting device," but Jared never responded to the letters, emails, and websites, and Dad got a smidge persistent, which led to some restraining orders and blacklisting. Now he was stuck in the boonies, doing stunts for TV movies about people who survive accidents. My mama did data entry to cover the rest of the rent. My dad was determined that my brother, Holman, and I would know the difference between a real and a fake punch, and how to roll with either kind.

My life was pretty boring until I went to school. School was so great! Slippery just-waxed hallways, dodgeball, sandboxplosions, bullies with big elbows, food fights! Food fights! If I could have gone to school for twenty hours a day, I would have signed up. No, twenty-three! I only ever really needed one hour of sleep per day. I didn't know who I was or why I was here until I went to school. And did I mention authority figures? School had authority figures! It was so great!

I love authority figures. I never get tired of pulling when they push, or pushing when they pull. In school, grown-ups were always telling me to write on the board, and then I'd fall down or drop the eraser down my pants by mistake, or misunderstand and knock over a pile of giant molecules. Erasers are comedy gold! I was kind of a hyper kid. They tried giving me Ritalin Ritalin Ritalin Ritalin Riiiitaliiiiin, but I was one of the kids who only gets more hyper hyper on that stuff. Falling, in the seconds between up and down, you know what's going on. People say something is as easy as falling off a log, but really it's easy to fall off anything. Really, try it. Falling rules!

Bullies learned there was no point in trying to fuck me up, because I would fuck myself up faster than they could keep up with. They tried to trip me up in the hallways, and it was just an excuse for a massive set piece involving mops, stray book bags, audio/video carts, and skateboards. Limbs flailing, up and down trading places, ten fingers of mayhem. Crude stuff. I barely had a sense of composition. Every night until three a.m., I sucked up another stack of Buster Keaton, Harold Lloyd, or Jackie Chan movies on the ancient laptop my parents didn't know I had, under my quilt. Safety Last!

Ricky Artesian took me as a personal challenge. A huge guy with a beach ball jaw—he put a kid in the hospital for a month in fifth grade for saying anybody who didn't ace this one chemistry quiz had to be a dipshit. Sometime after that, Ricky stepped to me with a Sharpie in the locker room and slashed at my arms and rib cage, marking the bones he wanted to break. Then he walked away, leaving the whole school whispering, "Ricky Sharp-ied Rock Manning!" I hid when I didn't have class, and when school ended I ran home three miles to avoid the bus. I figured Ricky would try to get me in an enclosed space where I couldn't duck and weave, so I stayed wide open. If I needed the toilet, I swung into the stall through a ventilator shaft and got out the same way, so nobody saw me enter or leave. The whole time in the air shaft, my heart cascaded. This went on for months, and my whole life became not letting Ricky Artesian mangle me. One day I got careless and went out to the playground with the other kids during recess, because some teacher was looking. I tried to watch for trouble, but a giant hand swooped down from the swing set and hauled me up. I dangled a moment, then the hand let me fall onto the sand. I fell on my back and started to get up, and Ricky told me not to move. For some reason, I did what he said, even though I saw twenty-seven easy ways out of that jungle gym cage, and then Ricky stood over me. He told me again to hold still, then brought one boot down on the long bone of my upper arm, a clean snap, my reward for staying put. "Finally got that kid to quit hopping," I heard him say, as he walked across the playground. Once my arm healed up, I became a bouncy frog again, and Ricky didn't bother me.

Apart from that one stretch, my social life at school was ideal. People cheered for me but never tried to talk to me—it was the best of human interaction without any of the pitfalls. Ostracism, adulation: flip sides! They freed me to orchestrate gang wars and alien invasions in my head, whenever I didn't have so many eyes on me. Years passed, my mom tried to get me into dance classes, my dad struggled to get me to take falling down seriously as a noble struggle with gravity, the way my big brother did. Holman was spending every waking moment prepping for the army, which was his own more socially acceptable way of rebelling against Dad.

Sally Hamster threw a brick at my head. I'd barely noticed the new girl in my class, except she was tall for a seventh grader and had big Popeye arms. I felt the brick coming before I heard it, followed by people shouting. Maybe Sally just wanted to get suspended, maybe she was reaching out. The brick grazed my head, but I was already moving with it, forward into a knot of basketball players, spinning and sliding. Afterward I had a lump on my head but I swore I'd thrown the brick at myself. By then the principal would have believed almost anything of me.

I didn't get the *Krazy Kat* reference until years later, but Sally and I became best friends. We sketched lunch trolley incidents and car pileups in our heads, talking them out during recess, trading text messages in class, instant messaging at home. The two of us snuck out to the Winn-Dixie parking lot and Sally drilled me for hours on that Jackie Chan move where the shopping cart rolls at him and he swings inside it through the flap, then jumps out the top. I didn't know martial arts, but I practiced not being run over by a shopping cart over and over. We went to the big mall off I-40 and got ourselves banned from the sporting goods store and the Walmart, trying to stage the best accidents. Sally shouted instructions: "Duck! Jump! Now do that thing where your top half goes left and your bottom half goes right!" She'd throw dry goods or roll barrels at me and then shout, "Wait, wait, wait, go!" Sally got it in her head I should be able to do the splits, so she bent my legs as far apart as they would go and then sat on my crotch until I screamed, every day for a couple months.

The Hamster family had social aspirations, all about Sally going to Harvard and not hanging out with boys with contrarian extremities. I went over to their house a few times, and it was full of Buddhas and Virgin Marys, and Mrs. Hamster baked us rugelachs and made punch, all the while telling me it must be So Interesting to be the class clown but how Sally needed to laser-beam in on her studies. My own parents weren't too thrilled about all my school trouble, and why couldn't I be more like Holman, training all the time for his military future?

High school freshman year, and Sally got hold of a video cam. One of her jag-tooth techno-hippie uncles. I got used to her being one-eyed, filming all the time, and editing on the fly with her mom's hyperbook. Our first movie went online at Yourstuff a month after she got the camera. It was five minutes long and it was called *The Thighcycle Beef*, which was a joke on some Italian movie Sally had seen. She had a Thighcycle, one of those bikes that go nowhere with a lying odometer. She figured we could light it on fire and then shove it off a cliff with me riding it, which sounded good to me.

I never flashed on the whole plot of *The Thighcycle Beef*, but there were ninja dogs and exploding donuts and things. Like most of our early short films it was a mixture of live action and Zap!mation. Sally figured her mom would never miss the Thighcycle, which had sat in the darkest basement corner for a year or so. We did one big sequence of me pedaling on the Thighcycle with Sally throwing rocks at me, which she would turn into throwing stars in postproduction. I had to pedal and duck, pedal while hanging off the back wheel, pedal sidesaddle, pedal with my hands while hanging off the handlebars, etc. I climbed a tree in the Hamsters' front yard and Sally hoisted the Thighcycle so I could pull it up there with me. Then I climbed on and "rode" the Thighcycle down from the treetop, pedaling frantically the whole way down, as if I could make it fly. (She was going to make it fly in post.) The Thighcycle didn't pedal so good after that, but Sally convinced me I was only sprained, because I could scrunch all my fingers and toes and I didn't lose consciousness for that long. We were going to film the climax at a sea cliff a few miles away, but Sally's ride fell through. In the end, she settled for launching me off the toolshed with the Thighcycle on fire. She provided a big pile of leaves for me to fall onto when I fell off the cycle, since I already had all those sprains. I missed the leaf pile, but the flaming Thighcycle didn't, and things went somewhat amiss, although we were able to salvage some of the toolshed, thanks to Sally having the garden hose ready. She was amazingly safety-minded.

After that, Sally's parents wanted twice as hard for her not to see me. I had to lie and tell my parents I'd sprained my whole body beating up a bunch of people who deserved it. My brother had to carry stuff for me while I was on crutches, which took away from his training time. He kept running ahead of me with my junk, lecturing me about his conspiracy theories about the Pan-Asiatic Ecumen and how they were flooding the United States with drugs to destabilize our country and steal our water, and I couldn't get out of earshot.

But all of my sprains were worth it, because *Thighcycle Beef* blew up the internet. The finished product was half animation, with weird messages like "NUNCHUCK SPITTING TIME!" flashing on the screen in between, but the wacky stunts definitely helped. Sally even turned the toolshed into a cliff, although she also used the footage of the toolshed fire elsewhere. People two or three times our age downloaded it to their phones and watched it at work. Sally showed me the emails, tweets, and Yangars—we were famous!

I found out you can have compound sprains just like fractures, and you have to eat a lot of ice cream and watch television while you recuperate. My mom let me monopolize the living room sofa, knitted blanket over my legs and Formica tray in my lap as I watched cartoons. My mom wanted to watch the news, the water crisis and the debt crisis were freaking her shit. I wanted to catch the Sammo Hung marathon, but she kept changing to CNN, people tearing shopping malls apart with their bare hands in Florida, office windows shattering in Baltimore, buses on fire. And shots of emaciated people in the formerly nice part of Brooklyn, lying in heaps with tubes in their arms, to leave a vein permanently open for the next hit. Did I mention ice cream? I got three flavors, or five if you count Neapolitan as three separate flavors, like all right-thinking people everywhere.

I went back to school after a week off, and the Thighcycle had a posse. Ricky—femur-cracking Ricky Artesian—came up to me and said our movie rocked his freaking head. He also said something about people like me having our value, which I didn't pay much attention to at the time. I saw one older kid in the hallway with a Flaming Thighcycle T-shirt, though I never saw any royalties for it.

Sally snuck out to meet me at the Starbucks near school and we toasted with frosty mochas. Her round face looked sunburned and her hair was a shade less mouse than usual. "That was just the dry run," she said. "Next time, we're going to make a statement. Maybe we can go out to the landfill and get a hundred busted TVs and drop them on you." I vetoed the rain of TVs. I wanted to do a roller disco movie because I'd just watched *Xanadu*. We posted on Yangar.com looking for roller disco extras, and a hundred kids and a few creepy grown-ups hit us back. We had to be super selective, and mostly only took people who had their own skates. But Sally still wanted to have old televisions in there because of her Artistic Vision, so she got hold of a dozen fucked old screens and laid them out for us to skate over while they all showed the same footage of Richard Simmons. We had to jump over beach balls and duck under old power cords and stuff. I envisioned it being the saga of skate-fighters who were trying to bring the last remaining copy of the U.S. Constitution to the federal government in hiding, in a bunker under a Chikken Hut. We filmed a lot of it at an actual Chikken Hut that had closed down, off near the Oceanview Mall. I wanted it to be a love story, but we didn't have a female lead, and also Sally never wanted to do love stories. I showed her Harold Lloyd movies, but it made no difference.

Sally got hooked on Yangar fame. She had a thousand Yangar friends, breathless testimonials, and imitators from Pakistan, and it all went to her head. We had to do what the people on the internet wanted us to do, even when they couldn't agree. They wanted more explosions, more costumes and cute Zap!mation icons, funny catchphrases. At fifteen, Sally breathed market research. I wanted pathos *and* chaos!

Ricky and some other kids found the school metal detectors missed anything plastic, ceramic, wood, or bone, and soon they had weapons strapped all over. Ricky was one of the first to wear the red bandana around his neck, and everyone knew he was on his way. He shattered Mr. MacLennan's jaw, my geography teacher, right in front of our whole grade in the hallway. Slow-time, a careful spectacle, to the point where Ricky let us onlookers arrange ourselves from shortest in front to tallest in back. Mr. MacLennan lying there looking up at Ricky, trying to assert, while we all shouted *Break! Break! Break! Break!* and finally Ricky lifted a baseball bat and I heard a loud *crack.* Mr. MacLennan couldn't say anything about it afterward, even if he could have talked, because of that red bandana.

Sally listened to the police scanner, sometimes even in the classroom, because she wanted to be there right after a looting or a credit riot. Not that these things happened too often in Alvington, our little coastal resort city. One time, Sally got wind a Target near downtown had gone off the rails. The manager had announced layoffs and the staff just started trashing the place, and the customers joined in. Sally came to my math class and told Mr. Pope I'd been called to the principal's, and then told me to grab my bag of filming crap and get on my bike. What if we got there and the looters were still going? Sally said looting was not a time-consuming process, and the crucial thing was to get there between the looting and everything being chained up. So we got there and sneaked past the few cops buddying in the parking lot, so Sally could get a few minutes of me falling under trashed sporting goods and jumping over clothing racks. She'd gotten so good at filming with one hand and throwing with the other! Really, nobody ever realized she was the coordinated one, of the two of us. Then the cops chased us away.

My brother got his draft notice and couldn't imagine such luck. He'd sweated getting into the army for years, and now they weren't even waiting for him to sign up. I knew my own draft notice was probably just a year or two down the line, maybe even sooner. They kept lowering the age.

My mom's talk shows were full of people saying we had to stop the flow of drugs into our country, even if we had to defoliate half the planet. If we could just stop the drugs, then we could fix our other problems, easy. The problem was, the Pan-Asiatic Ecumen or whoever was planting these drugs were too clever for us, and they had gotten hold of genetically engineered opioids that they could grow in vats, like brewer's yeast, and they had nine hundred times the potency of regular junk. We tried using drones to take down all their drug labs, but they just relocated to heavily populated areas, and soon it was block-by-block urban warfare in a dozen slums all around Eurasia. Soldiers were fitted with cheap mass-produced HUDs that made the whole thing look like a first-person shooter from forty years ago. Some people said the Pan-Asiatic Ecumen didn't actually exist, but then how else did you explain the state we were in?

Sally fell in love with a robot guy named Raine, and suddenly he had to be big in every movie. She found him painted silver on Main Street, his arms and legs moving all blocky, and she thought he had the extra touch we needed. In our movies, he played Castle the Pacifist Fighting Droid, but in real life he clutched Sally's heart in his cold unbreakable metal fist. He tried to nice up to me, but I saw through him. He was just using Sally for the Yangar fame. I'd never been in love, because I was waiting for the silent-movie love: big eyes and violins, chattering without sound, pure. Nobody had loved right since 1926.

Ricky Artesian came up to me in the cafeteria early on in eleventh grade. He'd gotten so he could loom over *and* around everybody. I was eating with Sally, Raine, and a few other film geeks, and Ricky told me to come with him. My first thought was, whatever truce we'd made over my arm bone was over and gone and I was going to be fragments of me. But Ricky just wanted to talk in the boys' room. Everyone else cleared out, so it was just the two of us and the wet TP clinging to the tiles. The air was sour. "Your movies, they're cool," he said. I started to explain they were also Sally's, but he hand-slashed. "My people." He gestured at the red bandana. "We're going to take it all down. They've lied to us, you know. It's all fucked, and we're taking it down." I nodded, not so much in agreement but because I'd heard it before. "We want you to make some movies for us. Explaining what we're about."

I told him I'd have to ask Sally, and he whatevered and didn't want to listen to how she was the brains, even though anyone looking at both of us could tell she was the brains. Ricky said if I helped him, he'd help me. We were both almost draft age, and I would be a morning snack to the military exoskeletons. I'd seen *No Time for Sergeants*—seventeen times—so I figured

I knew all about basic training, but Ricky said I'd be toast. Holman had been telling me the same thing, when he wasn't trying to beat me up. So Ricky offered to get me disqualified from the army, or get me under some Protection during training.

When I told Sally about Ricky's offer, the first thing she did was ask Raine what he thought. Raine wasn't a robot that day, which caught me off guard. He was just a sandy-haired flag-eared skinny guy, a year or so older than us. We sat in a seaside gazebo/pagoda where Sally thought she could film some explosions. Raine said propaganda was bad, but also could Ricky get *him* out of the army as well as me? I didn't know. Sally didn't want me to die, but artistic integrity, you know.

The propaganda versus artistic integrity thing, I wasn't sure about. How was making a movie for Ricky worse than pandering to our fans on Yourstuff and Yangar? And look, my dad fed and housed Holman and me by arranging tragic accidents for cable TV movies where people nursed each other back to health and fell in love. Was my dad a propagandist because he fed people sponge cake when the whole world was flying apart?

Sally said fine, shut up, we'll do it if you just stop lecturing us. I asked Ricky and he said yes, neither Raine nor I would have to die if we made him a movie.

This was the first time we ever shot more footage than we used. I hadn't understood how that could happen. You set things up, *boom!* you knocked them over and hoped the camera was running, and then you moved on somewhere else. Life was short, so if you got something on film, you used it! But for the red bandana movie we shot literally hundreds of hours of footage to make one short film. Okay, not literally hundreds of hours. But a few.

Raine didn't want to be the Man, or the Old Order, or the Failure of Democracy, and I said tough shit. Somebody had to, plus he was older and a robot. He and Sally shot a ton of stuff where they humanized his character and explained how he thought he was doing the right thing, but we didn't use any of it in the final version. Meanwhile, I wore the red bandana and break-danced under a rain of buzz saws that were really some field hockey sticks we'd borrowed. I wanted to humanize my character, too, by showing how he only donned the red bandana to impress a beautiful florist, played by Mary from my English class. After a few weeks' filming, we started to wonder if maybe we should have had a script. "We never needed one before,"

Sally grumbled. She was pissed about doing this movie, and I was pissed that she kept humanizing her boyfriend behind my back. You don't humanize a robot! That's why he's a robot instead of a human!

Holman came back from basic training, eager to show us the scar behind his left ear where they'd given him a socket that his HUD would plug into. It looked like the knot of a rotten tree, crusted with dried gunk but with a pulsating wetness at its core. It wasn't as though they would be able to remote control you or anything, Holman said—more like, sometimes in a complicated mixed-target urban environment, you might hesitate to engage for a few crucial split seconds and the people monitoring the situation remotely might need to guide your decision-making. So to speak. Holman seemed happy for the first time ever, almost stoned, as he talked us through all the changes he'd gone through in A.N.V.I.L. training and how he'd learned to breathe mud and spit bullets. Holman was bursting with rumors about all the next-generation weapons that were coming down the pike, like sonic cannons that could shatter everything for miles.

Ricky kept asking to see the rushes of our movie, and Raine got his draft notice, and we didn't know how the movie was supposed to end. I'd never seen any real propaganda before. I wanted it to end with Raine crushing me under his shiny boot, but Sally said it should end with me shooting out of a cannon (which we'd make in Zap!mation) into the Man's stronghold (which was the crumbling Chikken Hut) and then everything would blow up. Raine wanted the movie to end with his character and mine joining forces against the real enemy, the Pan-Asiatic Ecumen, but Sally and I both vetoed that. In the end, we filmed like ten different endings and then mashed them all up. Then we added several Zap!mation-only characters and lots of messages on the screen, like "TONGUE-SAURUS!" and "OUTRAGEOUS BUSTAGE!" My favorite set piece involved me trying to make an ice cream sundae on top of a funeral hearse going a hundred miles per hour while Sally threw rocks at me. (I forget what we turned the rocks into, after.) There was some plot reason I had to make a sundae on top of a hearse, but we borrowed an actual hearse from this guy Raine knew who worked at a funeral home, and it actually drove a hundred miles per hour on the cliffside road, with Sally and Raine driving alongside in Raine's old Prius. I was scooping ice cream with one hand and squirting fudge with the other, and then Sally beaned me in the leg and I nearly fell off the sea cliff, but at the last minute I caught one of the hearse's rails and pulled myself back up, still clutching the full ice cream scoop in the other hand. With ice cream, all things are possible.

The final movie clocked in at twelve minutes, way way longer than any of our previous efforts. It was like an attention-span final exam. We showed it to Ricky in Tanner High's computer room, on a bombed-out old Mac. I kept stabbing his arm, pointing out good parts, like the whole projectile rabies bit and the razor-flower-arranging duel that Raine and I get into toward the end. Ricky seemed to hope that if he spun in his chair and then looked back at the screen, this would be a different movie. Sometimes he would close his eyes, bounce, and reopen them, then frown because it was still the same hot sewage.

By the time the credits rolled, Ricky seemed to have decided something. He stood up and smiled, thanked us for our great support for the movement, and started for the door before we could even show him the blooper reel at the end. I asked him about our draft survival deal, and he acted as if he had no clue what we were talking about. Sally, Raine, and I had voluntarily made this movie because of our fervent support of the red bandana and all it stood for. We could post the movie online, or not, it was up to us, but it had nothing to do with Ricky either way. It was weird, seeing Ricky act so weaselly and calculating, like he'd become a politician all of a sudden. The only time I saw a hint of the old Ricky was when he said he'd use our spines as weed wackers if we gave any hint that he'd told us to make that movie.

The blooper reel fizzed on the screen, unnoticed, while Raine, Sally, and I stared at each other. "So this means I have to die after all?" Raine said in his robotic, stating-the-obvious voice. Sally didn't want to post our movie on the internet, even after all the work we'd put into it, because of the red bandana thing. People would think we'd joined the movement. Raine thought we should post it online and maybe Ricky would still help us. I didn't want to waste all that work—couldn't we use Zap!mation to turn the bandana into, say, a big snake? Or a dog collar? But Sally said you can't separate a work of art from the intentions behind it. I'd never had any artistic intentions in my life, and I didn't want to start having them now, especially not retroactively. First we didn't use all our footage, and then there was talk of scripts, and now we had intentions. Even if Raine hadn't been scheduled to go die soon, it was pretty obvious we were done.

I tried telling Raine that he might be okay, the Pan-Asiatic Ecumen could surrender any time now, and they might call off the draft. Or, and here was an idea that I thought had a lot of promise, Raine could work the whole "robot" thing and pretend the draft didn't apply to him because he wasn't a person, but Sally told me to shut the fuck up. Sally kept jumping up and down, cursing the air and hitting things, and she threatened to kick the shit out of Ricky. Raine just sat there slump-headed, saying it wasn't the end of the world, maybe. We could take Raine's ancient Prius, load it up, and run for Canada, except what would we do there?

We were getting the occasional email from Holman, but then we realized it had been a month since the last one. And then two months. We started wondering if he'd been declared A.U.T.U.—and in that case, if we would ever officially find out what had happened to him.

A few days before Raine was supposed to report for death school, there was going to be a huge antiwar protest in Raleigh. We drove all the way there with crunchy bars and big bottles of grape sprocket juice so we'd be sugared up for peace. We heard all the voices and drums before we saw the crowd, then there was a spicy smell and we saw people of twenty different genders and religions waving signs and pumping the air and chanting old-school style about what we wanted and when we wanted it. A platoon of bored cops in riot gear stood off to the side. We found parking a couple blocks away from the crowd, then tried to find a cranny to slip into with our signs. We were looking around at all the other objectors, not smiling but cheering, and then I spotted Ricky a dozen yards away, in the middle of a lesbian posse. And a few feet away from him, another big neckless angry guy. I started seeing them everywhere, dotted throughout the crowd. They weren't wearing the bandanas, they were blending in until they got some kind of signal. I grabbed Sally's arm. "Hey, we have to get out of here."

"What the fuck are you talking about? We just got here!"

I pulled at her. It was hard to hear each other with all the bullhorns and loudspeakers and the chanting. "Come on! Grab Raine, this is about to go apeshit. I'll make a distraction."

"It's always about you making a distraction! Can't you just stop for a minute? Why don't you just grow the fuck up? I'm so sick of your bullshit. They're going to kill Raine and you don't even care!" I'd never seen Sally's eyes so small, her face so red.

"Sally, look over there, it's Ricky. What's he doing here?"

"What are you talking about?"

I tried to pull both of them at once, but the ground had gotten soddy from so many protester boots and I slipped and fell into the dirt. Sally screamed at me to stop clowning around for once, and then one of the ISO punks stepped on my leg by mistake, then landed on top of me, and the crowd was jostling the punk as well as me, so we couldn't untangle ourselves. Someone else stepped on my hand. I rolled away from the punk and sprang upright just as the first gunshot sounded. I couldn't tell who was firing, or at what, but it sounded nearby. Everyone in the crowd shouted, without slogans this time, and I went down again with boots in my face. I saw a leg that looked like Sally's and I tried to grab for her. More shots, and police bullhorns calling for us to surrender. Forget getting out of here, we had to stay down even if they trampled us. I kept seeing Sally's feet but I couldn't reach her. Then a silver shoe almost stepped on my face. I stared at the bright laces a second, then grabbed at Raine's silvery ankle, but he wouldn't go down because the crowd held him up. I got upright and came face-to-shiny-face with Raine. "Listen to me," I screamed over another rash of gunfire. "We have to get Sally, and then we have to—"

Raine's head exploded. Silver turned red and my mouth was suddenly full of something warm and dark-tasting, and then several people fleeing in opposite directions crashed into me and I swallowed. I swallowed and doubled over as the crowd smashed into me, and I forced myself not to vomit because I needed to be able to breathe. Then the crowd pushed me down again and my last thought was that with this many extras, all we really needed would be a crane and a few dozen skateboards and we could have had a really cool set piece.

2
Vikings vs. Steampunks

Sally's face had gotten rounder and brighter since high school, and her hair was a bright crimson swoosh across her forehead. She wore a big black trench coat, shorts, and hiking boots. Next to her stood a skinny African American woman named Janelle, in a FREE YUSUF T-shirt and hoop skirt. They went to film school together, and they had their own private language about mise-en-scène. They were collaborating on a movie about a woman (played by Janelle) who thinks her cat is talking to her. Sally and Janelle lived with a few other people in a ramble-down house just off the main drag in

Jamaica Plain. Outside, the house looked slanty and weather-beaten, but inside it had clean carpets, oak furniture, and huge film posters in metal frames. Sally walked ahead of us as we moved into her house, so she could move vases and bowls of fruit out of my reach, then she got to work making dinner. I offered to help with the cooking, but she didn't need any. All of a sudden, in her vinyl apron, she reminded me of Mrs. Hamster: smiling with one shoulder hunched and tense lines etched in her arms and waist, stirring and cutting.

I'd come up to Boston with this idea that lightning would strike, Sally would take one look at me and the old chemistry would come back and in her excitement maybe she'd hurl a vending machine at me. We would trash a huge section of Boston and then have a tearful conversation in the rubble where we would hash out all the reasons why we hadn't really talked since Raine died. But Sally had gotten quieter and more serious, like some Hamster family genes had kicked in or something. As for me, I'd gone through a bad year and change. For a while there, I couldn't eat any solid food without imagining Raine's skull bursting open and pieces of his brain going into my mouth. I got so skinny and tweaked out, the army recruiter doctors had taken one look and just laughed at the idea of militarizing me. Then the draft had been suspended for the time being, and I'd started eating food occasionally.

After dinner, we watched some of Sally and Janelle's movie. I started bouncing up and down in my seat when the movie showed Janelle stirring her coffee for two whole minutes. You shouldn't stir something for more than a few seconds unless you're baking, and even then you can usually cut the directions in half. (Gooey is good and lumpy is a sign of love.) Janelle walked down a street, stared at a tree, went to the supermarket, ate corn-flakes, and had a halting conversation with this other woman. Sally must have noticed the look on my face, or the fact that my fidgeting had gotten multidimensional, because she said it would be better with music and after editing. I said it was great and I was just jumping up and down because I liked it so much. Uh-huh, said Janelle with a little skepticism. What I didn't get was why the cat didn't talk more. If you have a movie about a talking cat, shouldn't the cat talk all the time? But Sally explained the talking cat was a metaphor, and we were supposed to see Janelle's trip to the post office through the *lens* of the talking cat.

Sally brought some friends home after her classes on the second day, because some of her classmates were curious to meet me after seeing our web movies and hearing about me from Sally. I got confused. Sally's class-mates were fans of *Thighcycle Beef* and the half dozen other movies we'd posted online, but I also got the impression they would look down on Sally if she made movies like that now. Also, Sally seemed embarrassed that they liked her "early works." One of them was named Zapp Stillman, and he was the great-grandson of a famous director whom I'd never heard of. He had artful tufts of curly brown hair, giant sunglasses, and a big sweatband, over a tunic and shorts. According to him, our high school movies were "kinetic but static," because I was constantly in motion but nothing ever changed, and that was "kinda Zen, really."

"I know the talking-cat movie is kind of ass, but that's why I'm in school," Sally said, when we finally got a moment alone together. "To try lots of dif-ferent things and, yeah, to fuck up at most of them. I need to expand my repertoire." That made total sense to me. I'd already figured out that Sally had outgrown our dumb high school movies, and I admired her for it. Just when I was getting ready to tell Sally that I was heading back to North Car-olina in a couple days, and I'd be out of her hair, she said, "Look, are you sticking around? Maybe we can fuck around on weekends, short films. We can have, like, a video tumble with new shorts going online. I'm just thinking of the ad revenue, people might actually want to buy e-books or some other cyber-poo after watching our movies. Young Urban Survivalists and shit. We appeal to that demo, hey?" I said yeah, I could totally see the Yussies watching our demented movies. So Sally figured she could make serious arty movies during the week and dumb little action comedies with me on weekends.

I got a job at the convenience store across Commonwealth Avenue from Boston University, not too far from where I was crashing. Walking to work, I learned to watch where I stepped, because the sidewalks had drugged-up bodies everywhere and the worst thing about stepping on one of those people wasn't the crunch underfoot or the stains on your pants cuff, it was the way they wouldn't react. Not a peep. Like they were too far gone. (Actually, the worst part was the way their blood-smeared faces reminded me of Raine, his exploding head.) Also, sometimes you would walk by a bank that was in the process of being firebombed and chunks of flaming atrium would fly right at your head. I tried to get an explanation for the debt crisis, but it boiled down to: we owed ourselves too much for too long, until we just couldn't forgive ourselves any longer.

The next weekend, Sally and I met at the foot of one of the zillions of fancy stone bridges across the Charles. A freeway on-ramp swooped up alongside a steep bank with colonies of shivering geese and ducks molting next to the river's edge. Sally had a Viking costume that a friend had created for the *Ring cycle* a few years before, plus a giant halberd-type thing, and there was a skateboard that Sally could transform into a mythical beast in Zap!mation. I would come zooming down the freeway ramp and then go flying across the feeder lane and off the riverbank into the water. I wasn't sure about this plan, because there's a difference between comedy and just stunts. I wasn't sure what made this funny, plus what was my motivation? Sally suggested that I could be a Viking warrior chasing something, but it all sounded sketchy to me. We stood around arguing, me in my horned helmet and fur vest and her in jeans and sweatshirt, for half an hour. "Shit, I get enough of this during the week," Sally said. Finally, we agreed I'd be a Viking riding on the World Serpent and attempting to gather some golden apples from the World Tree. The resulting short film wasn't one of our greatest, but at least I only had a mild concussion and the halberd whatever-it-was missed my eye socket by a good half inch.

The last thing I wanted, the first time back working on a movie with Sally in over a year, was to get all high-concept on her and drive her nuts. I knew we were just making silly, throwaway movies that would glimmer for a moment on the internet. I just wanted to have some reason in my head why I was climbing the Harvard science building with people throwing sex toys at me. I made a list of all the reasons that somebody could be rocking at top speed through a treacherous situation:

1) Love, with some huge and fast-moving obstacle to overcome
2) Economic desperation and the promise of financial reward
3) Politics and electioneering
4) War, social upheaval, urban combat, or refugeeism
5) Supernatural forces, or mental illness, or maybe family troubles

There were probably other reasons, but those were the only ones I could think of.

I was glad not to be going back down South, what with all the urban combat and people in different-colored headgear shooting at each other and that guy who played the sheriff on that sitdram getting himself torn in half just like at a tractor pull. I couldn't tell whether things had gotten way worse just since I'd gone up North, or the news just looked worse from here, or both. Then I saw the footage of Wilmington, the water surging over the rubble, and I had to call my parents to make sure they were okay. Not like we were any safer in Boston.

Sally and I quickly realized the other film students would do almost anything we wanted, as long as we let them make superior-ass remarks about it. Once we acknowledged they were way too eminent in their artist-hood for the crap we were making, they'd work themselves into a coma and back, just for our dumb weekend movies. The first few weeks there were just half a dozen film students, then a dozen, then a couple dozen. We were up to our asses in turtlenecks! Soon we had to devise fancier and fancier set pieces to keep everyone occupied. We built a chunk of Roman coliseum in Boston Common, in an hour and a half, out of Styrofoam blocks and set dressings that people hauled out of storage for us, and then we had to decide what to do with a Roman coliseum. How about some kind of vacuum cleaner salesman versus gladiator riff? Time travel, hand waving, okay, go! With a vacuum cleaner / broadsword duel? Vacuum cleaner salesmen are the natural enemies of gladiators. The snarky film students all posted about our movies when they got home, so all their friends reposted it.

Apparently there's this thing called a filming permit, and the police prefer you to have it. *Oh dear, officer, we had no idea, we're actually just making a home movie here to show to our parents back home, and oh gosh, is that really a firebomb that strange dude is setting up against the wall of that shopping center?* Just mentioning firebombs got the police excited, after the recent incidents, and especially with all the rumors the red bandanas were coming up North. Meanwhile everyone kept talking about how China was secretly the power propping up the Pan-Asian Ecumen and everything was all connected and we were victims of a scheme so complicated, the details changed every time you heard about it. Tensions climbed off the scale, and people talked of cranking up the draft again. It didn't make much sense to me, especially since all of the instability in Central Asia was hurting China worse than anybody, but that's why I leave the geopolitics to other people. I'm just the go-to guy if you want someone to ride a vacuum cleaner off the top of a Styrofoam coliseum into a mosh pit of gladiators, Mormons (real Mormons, not costumes), and a confused cop.

One day when I was over at Sally's place, I saw a leader of the red bandanas being interviewed on television: a beefy guy in his mid-twenties, with a buzz cut and devil-beard named Ward. They kept wanting to ask him about reports that the red bandanas were funded by some paranoid trillionaire, and he kept wanting to change the subject to China and how our government was too soft and we would soon have the tools to deal with the Chinese threat once and for all but we wouldn't have the guts to use them. As soon as Sally saw who was on television, she turned it off, and then broke the remote control against the wall.

This guy came into the half-stocked convenience store where I was working, and he wanted me to empty out the safe. He had a waxy mustache and soul patch, and he wore a poncho over a bulky football sweatshirt and knee-high socks. He was waving a shotgun that looked like someone had shot a grouse with it back in 2009 and it had sat in a closet since then. I thought about angles of escape, up over his head or around behind the Juicy Yoo cooler, then shrugged and put up my hands. The trouble was, he couldn't get at the safe because it was keyed to my vital signs, so if my heart or breathing sped up, then the safe went into total lockdown, and if my heart stopped then every alarm went dog-wild. My boss Ramon couldn't even get any cash for legitimate purposes half the time because I'd be doing jumping jacks and thinking about whether we should stage a trolley accident or a scooter joust this weekend. I had to practice no-mind deep breathing just so my boss could grab petty cash. With this guy waving his gun at me, my heart juddered so damn hard the tumblers in the safe hugged each other for dear life. He almost gave up and left, but then he found some extra-drowsy cough syrup and made me drink some of it along with a ton of Grand Marnier, with that shotgun in my face the whole time I was chugging. My heart stayed ferret-like, and I told the guy he'd have to be patient and wait for the stuff to take effect. He wanted to keep force-feeding me downers but I reminded him that if I died, the safe locked up tight. He and I ended up sitting around the store a couple hours, talking about old movies and video games and stuff. Reginald loved all the cop buddy comedies of the eighties and nineties, and he could recite long sections of *Lethal Weapon* from memory. Before I even knew what I was doing, I was telling Reginald that a bunch of us made our own amateur movies in Boston Common and he should swing by this Saturday and join in. I guess it was the cough syrup, or just the fact that we'd been talking for ages and he'd put down the gun by then. Five minutes after Reginald thanked me and wandered off down the street, I took a deep breath and heard the safe un-jam itself.

"So wait. This guy came in with a shotgun and threatened you, and, and, *drugged* you, and you invited him to come make movies?" my flatmate Carrie said when I got home. Since that was a pretty complete summary of my evening, I didn't have much to say in response, except that I'd been thinking more about my character. Not my real-life character, which I didn't really know much about, but my movie character. Think about it! Harold Lloyd is the same guy in every one of his movies—a small-town innocent, maybe a little eggheaded but not street smart, with his heart on his sleeve but also full of ambition. I could be like that, except maybe more cunning and just a little loopy. Or, okay, a lot loopy. Coming off the super-cold-relief formula and cognac buzz, I felt a swelling urgency that people should root for me, not just laugh at my highjinks.

Janelle, the cute film student with the rainbow dreads, agreed with me. The comic hero has to be lovable or relatable, or at least there has to be a moment of connection with the audience in between all the falling gargoyles, she said. The two of us cornered Sally, who kept trying to get us to talk to her hands. Sally was like, "I make art during the week, this weekend shit is just for fun." But Janelle and I both said it wasn't about art, just making the fun as fun as possible.

I forgot to mention about Reginald the corner store robber, until he showed up on Saturday wearing some kind of bright red wrestling costume, or maybe those were just his regular exercise clothes. We dressed Reginald up as a cop, and a bunch of the film school kids were a motorcycle gang who'd started riding bicycles because gas was twelve dollars a gallon, so they all overcompensated by whooping really loud and blasting heavy metal when they pedaled into town. Someone had renovated a whole section of Boston near the river to look like a little "ye olde" village, except it was really all yuppie boutiques that had been boarded up since the debt crisis. So we turned it into a small town that was trying to keep the bikers out with the help of Reginald the cop, and I got mixed up in the middle of their conflict because I had to deliver a cactus to a sick friend. Once again, my motivation was a little hazy, and it bothered both me and Janelle. Sally had her elbow in the way of us doing any kind of love story, for some reason I could never figure. It wasn't just that she'd gotten her heart pulped with her boyfriend Raine's head. She was just dead set against goo-goo eyes. I always tried to remind her about that old saying, that a woman needs a man like a fish needs a bicycle, because what could be more romantic than a school of fish, perched on bikes at the bottom of the ocean, pedaling like wild with all their fins?

Everybody thought Reginald rocked, especially the sequence where a bunch of the bikers rode up a giant ramp we made out of an old herbal facial spa sign and flew over Reginald's head while he tried to kickbox with their wheels. Except that Reginald somehow managed to break Zapp Stillman's nose, but the other film geeks said it would just add some boxery distinction to his face. Sally asked where I found Reginald and I said I just ran into him. Reginald nearly dropped me off the Longfellow Bridge when he found out this was a volunteer gig, but I convinced him the exposure would help him to get other, paying gigs. He got pretty jazzed thinking about his round-house popping up all over the internet and becoming a cult phenom. He was pretty glad he didn't actually kill me, at least for now.

Carrie kept insisting I should tell Sally the truth about Reginald, but I figured he would probably disappear soon anyway, since he made me look like long-attention-span guy by comparison. I hadn't been able to concentrate much before Raine died, but ever since I ate a piece of Raine's brain, I was a human jitter.

People hit our vumble like bam bam bam. Sally thought soon we'd be more popular than we were in high school, and we even sold some advertisements. People would bring us pieces of meat and shoes in return for an ad on the site sometimes. Sally got that gleam in her eye, the one she used to get when Yangar loved her. But she also kept saying how un-artistic our movies were, compared to the fancy stuff she and Janelle were doing for film school.

So Zapp Stillman was a hyper-mega-rich socialite who didn't really notice a lot of what was going on around him, and I was his overeager man-servant trying to cater to all his whims. Despite what Reginald had done to Zapp's face, he still looked delicate and sheltered, and I got to wear this great houndstooth suit that fit really well except for the arms, shoulders, knees, and crotch. I practiced walking straight and butlery, which only made me more splashmanic, and then Zapp and I were supposed to go on a trip to the seaside, except I had to shelter him from all the violence on the streets. Zapp hadn't read a blog or seen a newscast in years and I kept him unaware of the state of the world. So, for example, we rode our two-seater bicycle past piles of comatose bodies, and I convinced Zapp it was just a group of people camping out for tickets to the Imagine Dragons reunion tour. A bunch of guys on scooters chased us to rip our heads off, and I told Zapp it was a friendly race. (All dialogue was big black captions, like in a proper old-school movie.) It was a cool movie, with good character moments, but a ton of stuff went wrong when we were filming. We staged a fake riot, with a bunch of film students in ripped-up clothes pulling down bricks we'd placed strategically. Some random people wandered by and saw what was going on, and they wanted to join in, and pretty soon they were tossing big chunks of wall around, and they saw Zapp and me on our dorky bicycle built for two and threw rocks at us, so the pedaling-for-dear-life sequences were hella more realistic than we'd bargained on. The camera guys had to run like stoats to keep their equipment from being smashed.

Midsummer Boston was all melty, but people on the street sold home-made ice cream and you could ignore all the rotting smells if you thought about the river ducks. I still felt like I was about to crash everyone around me into the gritty old walls. I would forget for a second, I would bounce down the street, jumping over the people on the sidewalk and swinging on the low oak branches. Then I would have a mental image of myself landing the wrong way, with my foot in someone's stomach, maybe someone I loved or maybe a stranger.

Some nights I couldn't sleep because every time I closed my eyes I saw Raine getting his head exploded, the chunks of skull flying apart, the brains splattering into my open mouth. This image blended together with all the ways I'd injured people by accident, or the times when I *could* have injured people, if things had gone a little different. Raine's head got pulpier and more vivid each time.

Janelle and I got together and wrote a movie script, to Sally's total horror. "Okay, so what is this story about?" Janelle asked me twenty or thirty times. We sat on an abandoned swan boat in the middle of the lake in Boston Common, which kept almost capsizing as water sloshed in and out of its gullet. Once tourists had chugged around in these boats, but now they just bobbed their rotting shells in and out of the algae. I didn't know what our story was about, since I didn't even know what the story was. Couldn't we take one leap at a time? But Janelle was scary patient and kept talking themes: communication, the evils of social Darwinism, the impossibility of really knowing other people because the closer you get to them the harder it is to see the whole person. Janelle had run away from home as a kid and had lived in the attic of a bookstore café for years, reading every book in the stockroom and living off of abandoned scones and salads. Nobody had known she was there until she used the store's address for her BU application and the acceptance letter turned up.

We settled on this O. Henry thing where a man and a woman are each trying to save each other from some horrible fate, but in the process of trying to save each other, they're putting themselves in worse danger than before. So I'm this scrappy DJ who owes money to gangsters, who could maybe be Vikings because we had some helmets and fake fur. Janelle is a dancer who posed for some questionable photos years ago, and now this sleazy guy wants to publish them and her strict family will disown her. So I decide to break in and snag the sleazy guy's hard drive, while Janelle wants to do whatever it takes to raise money to bail me out—even take on a dancer job that turns out to involve dancing on an unstable scaffolding at a construction site. And then the Vikings turn up while I'm trying to break into the sleazy guy's studio, and they want to break my legs, but the sleazy guy has a protection deal with the steampunk mafia (because we had a whole crate full of old steampunk and Dickens Fair paraphernalia). So we have a pitched Viking–steampunk battle in a photography studio, while I'm trying to slip past them and grab the hard drive. And Janelle somehow falls off her scaffolding into the middle of our fracas and I have to run around to catch her. It only took us about five hours to come up with that storyline, and by then the swan was submerged up to its neck and water slopped over the sides of its torso. We had to haul ourselves up onto the bridge without breaking our necks.

Janelle took a day off film school to help me location-scout our movie, called *Photo Finish*. We found this large art/performance space, which people actually used as an art studio. She kept wanting to add more messages to the film, like about the downward spiral toward another pointless high-tech war with the entire continent of Asia, and whether steampunk and Viking mob enforcers might have radically different attitudes to the whole concept of cultural imperialism and this could somehow factor into their epic battle.

Reginald nearly bit her head off, trembling in his charging-bull helmet and Muppet fur cloak, while she coached him on his lines. "No, come on Reggie, try it again, and this time put everything you've got into the word 'maul.' You have to *feel* that word. Jesus, Rock, where did you find this guy?"

She tried to choreograph the big Viking–steampunk throwdown, even down to me throwing the big photographic backdrops in people's faces and Zapp Stillman, the steampunk leader, hurling his brass saber pistol at a Viking and hitting the sought-after hard drive instead.

The fifth time we stopped so Janelle could micromanage, Reginald looked ready to light the set on fire, rip several people's heads off, and then use his broadsword to make a head kebab. I was having seismic levels of fidgetiness, to the point where I had to hug myself. Sally pulled me aside. "Jesus, what the fuck are we going to do about Janelle?" Sally torqued her elbows and claws. "She's driving me fucking bonkers, man." I didn't have many answers, except that I was worried about Reginald's inside-out fuse. Another hour went by and you could have made a milkshake on my head. It was thirty seconds' filming and then wait wait wait, ready, no hang on, wait, wait.

The tenth time we stopped, I jittered myself dizzy and stumbled into Zapp Stillman, and before he could finish saying he begged my pardon I fell and on the way down I kicked Zapp's piston-powered cyborg arm into Reginald's crotch, and Reginald fell on top of three other Vikings, so their swords jabbed into his back. He jumped up and announced that just because he'd failed to kill me the first time didn't mean he couldn't finish the job now. He grabbed a long, razor-sharp-looking hook from the studio corner and ran at me. Out of the corner of my eye, I saw Sally gesture to Janelle to get this on film for godssake. Zapp Stillman tried to get between Reginald and me, and Reginald whacked him in the face. I ducked under a big platform and kicked a cart of A/V stuff at Reginald, but he jumped over the cart without breaking his run. Several of the other steampunks thought this was part of the movie and tried to attack Reginald with their aetheric vaporizers, but he just cracked their heads together, so their pith hats shattered. Meanwhile I slid out the other end of the platform and climbed the curtain rope. The rope was on a pulley, so Reginald started pulling and the rope went down as the curtain went up. I had to climb at top speed to stay at the same altitude. Reginald kept pulling the rope with one hand and threw his spike-hook with the other, but I caught the hook and dug it into the curtain, then let go of the rope and swung on the hook across to the other side of the curtain, which tore as I went, so I landed on the ground across the room. A random Viking swung at my head and I barely ducked in time, then I saw a bucket full of water (which was supposed to be photographic solution) and I dumped it on Reginald's head. His helmet's horns stabbed through the bucket so he couldn't get it off, and he started grabbing anyone who got in his way, even other Vikings, and tossing them.

At first I screened the sirens out, because you heard sirens all the time, but I heard more and more, fire sirens as well as cop. Peal after peal, like church bells. I leaned out the window to see what was going on and then Reginald was at my ear, trying to push me out. He'd gotten the helmet and bucket off, and he had one hand under my armpit and the other on my belt. It was probably twenty feet down. I could see flames in the distance, and tongues of smoke from a few other places. I tried to tell Reginald I hadn't meant to hurt him, but he just pushed harder. The window frame gave way and we both tumbled. I twisted my body so Reginald hit the ground first and I landed on top of him.

I couldn't see anything, but I smelled smoke worse than ever. My crotch felt broken, my feet felt broken. I forced my eyes open, but everything had a double image. Sally had the door to the studio building open nearby and was yelling for me to get my ass inside. I limped to my feet and juddered in, then Sally locked the door behind me. Through the window, I watched Reginald try to raise himself up.

"Example of the sort of human garbage they tolerate up here," a voice said. It sounded sort of like Ricky Artesian, from back home, but wasn't. I found a window with a view of the guy, who was a little smaller than Ricky and had tufty black hair. He dressed like Ricky and had the same red bandana. So did the half dozen or so guys behind him. The guy talked for half an hour about Reginald, who kept trying to get to his feet but couldn't quite manage it. Reginald had the bad luck to be the only guy nearby who looked like a junkie and couldn't run for his life. I wanted to go out and help him, but I could barely move, and Sally half supported, half restrained me. Sally wanted to stop watching when they got into it with the crowbars, but this was my fault, sort of, and I had to see it play out. They didn't torch him until they ran out of bones. I hoped he would black out, but he kept screaming the whole time, on fire. Maybe some people can black out and scream at the same time? I sure hoped so.

So at this point, you're wondering what happened to *Photo Finish*. It was our most popular vumble entry yet, even though we only filmed about half the scenes Janelle had scripted, and what we recorded didn't have that much in common with her and my storyline. Sally and some of the others did a fantastic job tweaking it with Zap!mation, to the point where that studio looked like twenty different places. With the red bandanas turning up all over the country and imposing mob rule, everyone was primed for people in silly costumes whacking each other. It turns out when everything is turning into bloody shit, that's when people need Vikings against steam-punks more than ever. Who knew?

The police tried to stop the red bandanas at first, but then the president went on television and said they were an official militia, like in the Con-stitution, because we were losing our grip as a nation. It was probably the Pan-Asiatic Ecumen's fault, but nobody knew for sure.

Two days later, Sally said I had to get out of the house and breathe, be-cause too many people were staying indoors all the time and we had a duty to show we weren't scared. I crutch-hopped my way down the empty street, as Sally ran rings around me for a change. I was glad I didn't have to step over junkies anymore, even though I worried about what had happened to all of them. Sally said prison camps, or bonfires, or just underground hide-outs.

All of the film students cheered for me! Even the ones who'd high-backed me when I first showed up in town. Maybe because I'd become a casualty of art, or maybe because the new movie had gotten mad hits. Either way, people wanted to carry me around and pour stuff down my throat, and every-one signed my osteogenic body sheath. We were promoting creative anar-chy, and that made us super important radical artists, and hey, we should take it to the next level somehow. I thought if they wanted to promote anar-chy, maybe we could find one of the camps, in Medford or Malden, where the red hanky guys had rounded up the homeless people and undesirables, and set them all free. We could film it. We could put Napoleon hats on all of them and turn them loose. It would look cool, sort of like the final ep-isode of *The Prisoner*. Everybody liked that idea, and they were all up for doing it, but not on a day when they had classes. The film students kept adding more and more layers to the plan. We would dress as farm animals, and there would be a huge round clock which we'd roll downhill to cause a distraction, and maybe we could time the attack to coincide with a joint lunar/solar eclipse so the lack of both moon and sun would sensory-deprive everyone. They jumped up and down with excitement, but I finally realized they were making the plans fancier and fancier because they didn't want to have to follow through. That was fine with me, because I was only half serious about the camp liberation idea too.

"Most of those guys, you just tell them where to stand and what to do and they're happy. Don't make them think too hard," Sally told me afterward. Our movies had built her into a queen bee. She wanted to walk me home, but the sun sagged and I didn't want her caught out after dark. I ran into a couple of red bandana groups on my way home, but I told them I was a friend of Ricky Artesian's and they practically saluted. The second group insisted on escorting me home. Film students and red bandanas, both whooping at me, all in one day!

Soon enough I was healed enough to go back to work at the convenience store, where I kept seeing bone-crushed Reginald on fire whenever I looked at the lighters. Nowadays, I saw both Raine and Reginald in my dreams, unless I watched some Buster Keaton right before bedtime.

Some of Carrie's friends were planning a giant protest against the red bandanas and the economic policies and the move to expand the war, and the bizarre weapon projects, like that sonic cannon that people claimed would make a whole city shake itself to pieces from a distance. I was leery because, duh, the last time I'd gone to a protest I'd wound up covered in slippery bodies, choking on a piece of my friend's brain.

I started hoping my body wouldn't heal too quickly, because once it did they would expect me to create more serious mayhem, and just the thought of it made me start to shamblequake. Sally texted me, saying it was time to do some more mad slapstick, and I texted back that we really needed to talk.

I have a perfect recall of my meeting with Sally, maybe cause it was the last time we ever spoke to each other.

We met in the middle of the Mass Avenue bridge, with faded paintwork measuring the bridge's span in "smoots," the height of some long-ago MIT student whose classmates had rolled him across the bridge. On either side of us, the river swelled with gray bracken and flecks of brown foam, and in front of us, the jagged Boston skyline. The John Hancock Tower's windows had all started falling out and hitting people on the head, so they'd condemned the whole building and only gotten halfway through demolishing it, and now it looked like a shiny blue-green zigzag climbing to a single razor point. We watched the water churn awhile. The wind battered us.

Sally was gushing about my chemistry with Zapp Stillman, and how much people liked seeing the two of us interact, and maybe we could do a few more clips featuring the two of us. Gang boss and lieutenant, an awkwardly married couple, boxer and trainer, rock star and manager, superheroes. The possibilities were endless, almost like having Raine back. For a moment I wondered if Sally had a thing for Zapp's gangly ass.

"That's why I wanted to talk to you," I said once I could break in. "I need to take a break from making movies. I was thinking of going back to North Carolina." I tried to explain how I kept seeing Raine and Reginald whenever I closed my eyes lately, but Sally grabbed my scruff and pushed me halfway over the edge of the bridge. My pants fell down and the wind whipped through my boxer shorts. My ass was in space.

"You asshole," Sally said. "What the fuck is wrong with you? Every time I think I can rely on you. What the fuck? I was going to be a real director. I was doing great in film school, making serious movies, and you turned up and sucked me back into spending all my time making these pointless comedies instead. And now you're just going to leave? What? The? Fuck?" She shook me with each word. My shirt tore around the armpits. I could feel my feet, somewhere far away, trampling my pants.

"I'm sorry. I'm so sorry." I looked up into her bugged-out eyes. "I just can't. I can't deal. Jesus, you're my best friend no matter how long I live, but I'm a poison time bomb, you don't want to be around me, I'll just hurt you, I'm so sorry."

She hauled me off the edge and dumped me on my feet. "What the fuck are you talking about, Rock? I love you, but you're so full of shit. Just listen to me, okay. You're not some kind of destructive engine. You are good for exactly one thing, and one thing only, and that's turning people's brains off for a few minutes. You should stick to that. And another thing, did you ever stop to think about what I'm getting out of doing these movies with you? Did you? I mean, jeez. The world we live in now, the only time things make sense is when I'm coming up with bigger and crazier disasters to put on film. I finally decided, slapstick is the new realism. I can't do it without you. Do you understand what I'm saying?"

"Yeah, but . . ." I took a breath and pulled up my pants. The snap had broken, so I had to hold them together with one hand, and that limited my gesture menu a lot. "I keep feeling like I'm going to hurt somebody. I feel like people keep getting hurt around me, and maybe it's my fault somehow. Like what happened with Reginald. And Raine, before that."

"Jesus, this pisses me off. My boyfriend dies, but it's still all about you. What is up with that?"

The bridge rumbled, and I worried the supports had eroded or some-one had sabotaged them. I tried to get Sally's attention, but she was still talking about how shitplastic I was. I grabbed her arm with my free hand and pulled her toward land. She jerked free and said she didn't want to go with me, she was sick of my crap, let go.

"Listen, listen! Something's wrong," I said. I pulled her the other way, toward Boston. By now the bridge was definitely vibrating in a weird way. I could feel it in my teeth. I ran as fast as I could without letting go of my pants clasp. The bridge felt like it was going to collapse any second. We made it to land, but the sidewalks had the same problem as the bridge. The rum-bling got louder and felt like it was coming from inside me.

"What the fuck is going on?" Sally shouted. I raised my hands. By now I was seeing funny, like there were one and a half of her. My teeth clattered. My stomach cramped up. Most of all my ears were full, they hurt like mur-der. I had earaches like someone had jammed sticks into my ear canals, it hurt all the way down my throat.

The last words Sally ever said to me were, "What the hell, we need to get inside—"

The pressure inside my ears built up and then it spiked, like the sticks in my ears had jammed all the way in and twisted like a corkscrew. I can't really describe the pain. People have written tons of poems about it, but mostly they use it as something to compare any other kind of pain with. Two giant hands smacked me in the head, at the same time as a massive force tried to push its way out from the inside of my skull. I staggered and fell over, nearly blacked out.

Blood burst out of Sally's ears at the same time as I felt something splash on my shirt. I tried to say something like *What the fuck just happened* or *Shit I dropped my pants again*, but nothing came out. No, I was doing all the right things to make a sound, but nothing. I couldn't hear birds or traffic. I couldn't hear anything. Sally was moving her mouth, too, but she had the same panic in her eyes as I felt. I sat down on the ground, impact but no noise, like we were in outer space.

Sally was still trying to talk, tears coming down her cheeks. I gestured that I couldn't hear her. She grabbed her phone and fumbled with the but-tons. A second later, my phone vibrated. A text message: "wtf im deaf." I tex-ted back: "me 2." She wrote: "we need help."

She hauled me to my feet and found a safety pin in her bag, for my stupid pants. Then we rushed down Mass Ave, looking for someone who could call an ambulance. I still felt jumpy crossing the streets without being able to hear cars or other vehicles coming up behind me. Plus I kept turning to look over my shoulder in case someone ran up behind me. We found a guy up near Commonwealth Ave, but we could see from a distance he was clutching his ears and crying. Same with the half dozen young people we saw near the boarded-up Urban Outfitters at Mass Ave and Newbury. They all had blood on their shoulders and were texting each other or using pidgin sign language. They tried to plead for our help with their hands, until they realized we had the same problem.

Everywhere we went, newly deaf people wigged out. Sally texted me that we needed to get off the streets, this was going to get ugly. I knew what she meant. Carrie texted me that she'd gone deaf and I told her to get indoors. Sally and I found bikes and rode back to her house as fast as we could, not stopping for traffic lights or any of the people who tried to flag us down.

Janelle kissed her knees on the sofa, her back heaving. The television showed people, all over the world, with bloody ears. Somewhere an airplane had crashed, and somewhere else a power plant had blown up. There was no newscaster, just words scrolling across the screen.

THE SITUATION IS UNDER CONTROL. STAY TUNED FOR UPDATES. DO NOT GO OUTDOORS. TOTAL HEARING LOSS APPEARS TO BE WORLDWIDE. DO NOT GO OUTDOORS. AUTHORITIES HAVE NO EXPLANATION. STAY INSIDE.

We went on the internet and read everything we could find. If anyone on the planet could still hear, there was no sign. Every Yangar, every group, was full of people freaking out. Only the people who had already been part of the Deaf community stayed calm, and they posted teach-yourself-sign-language videos. I knew right away I would never have the patience to learn sign language.

It only took a few hours for the conspiracy theories to start spinning. The Pan-Asian Ecumen had tested out some weapon. Or the U.S. had. A weapon test had gone wrong, or maybe it had gone right. Maybe something had happened with that sonic cannon we'd kept hearing was going to win the war, or maybe it was a false flag by the antiwar protesters, or maybe both. Why not both? Really, it could be anything.

For now, all you could see on television was swarming crowd scenes that looked identical no matter which city name they stuck at the bottom of the screen. People knocking into each other and everything else, a perpetual motion machine that couldn't move. Close-ups of faces in Shanghai and Cleveland, pushed beyond scowls, into some new facial expression that we had yet to put a name to. We had thought we were getting stronger, cleaner, rejecting every confusing piece of ourselves while we prepared to defeat everyone who had ever tried to undermine our national will, but maybe we had just misdirected ourselves. Most of these big production numbers just reminded me of the protest where Raine's head had exploded in front of me, so I changed the channel or walked away whenever they came on.

Day two or three, I got fed up and decided to go to work. By then, we were running out of stuff at Sally's house, and Janelle and even Sally were starting to get on my nerves. They could feel the vibrations from my fidgeting, and the impact when I broke something of theirs, even when they couldn't see me, and I could feel their grief like a blanket all around me. My thumbs got sore from text messaging Sally when she was sitting right next to me. I could have just as much of a conversation from long distance. Sally didn't want me to go out, because the television was still full of people thrashing each other, but I said I'd be careful.

I didn't know if the convenience store still existed, and nobody had told me to come in to work—but nobody had told me not to, either. This could be my contribution to society's continued existence, selling Spam and condoms to people. I passed plenty of looted stores on my way down Commonwealth, and people were setting fire to all sorts of things that were probably terrible for the environment. When I got to the Store 24, it was still there and in one piece. I opened it up. It occurred to me that people would have a hard time asking me how much things cost. So I got out the pricing gun and went around making sure every single item in the store had an individual price sticker, even down to the thirty-seven-cent instant noodles. After that, I had to learn how to stay alert, because the little new-customer bell was no more use to me. An hour or two went by, more boring than anything I'd ever experienced before.

"thk gd yr here," said the message on the guy's cell phone, waved in my face. I nodded and he pulled it away to thumb some more. "didnt want 2 loot." I nodded. "but no stores open." I nodded. Then he went and filled his basket with canned goods and brought it back. I rung him up, and he shook my hand with both hands. He looked like a college professor, fiftyish, white, wearing plaid and stripes and tweed, so he wasn't a professor of fashion design. He saluted, like I was a colonel, then left.

Word spread, and more people came to the store. The shelves got emptier, and I pulled out stuff from the back room. We were going to run out of goods, and I didn't know if any more was coming. People, mostly middle class, thanked me for saving them from being looters. People are funny. I wish I'd had the URL of our vumble handy. I think a lot of those people would have looked at whatever I wanted to show them.

A TV news crew came to "interview" me. Mostly they filmed me serving customers and clowning around. I wrote our URL on a piece of paper and held it up to the camera. Sally said the news channel showed me twice an hour for a day or two, with a scrolling banner saying "Life Returns to Normal." My boss text messaged me and said he'd stop by to empty the safe and register.

Nobody robbed me, even after I was on television, because there were plenty of abandoned stores to rob.

The non-news channels went back to showing regular stuff, except with closed captions for everybody. All the words at the bottom of the screen made all the old sitcoms look like French movies, so I kept waiting for Jennifer Aniston to smoke or commit incest.

Sally emailed her film geek crew, including Zapp, about our next shoot. Who knew if they were even going to have classes anytime soon? She bopped around a little more, bouncing dumb ideas off me, and once or twice she seemed to laugh. I still caught her staring into space or crying into the can of liverwurst I brought home from the store.

3
It's Actually Funnier Without Laughter

People tossed around words like "collapse of civilization" and "postapocalyptic," but really everything was the same mess as always. Only without any soundtrack, and with a "militia" of guys in red bandanas swarming around killing everyone who got in their way. Civilization, you know, has always been a relative thing. It rises, it falls, who can keep track?

So now, sneaking up on people was suddenly way easier—but so was getting snuck up on. The fear of somebody creeping up behind me and cutting my throat was the only thing that kept me from being bored all the time. I always thought noise was boring, but silence bored me even worse. If you walked up behind someone, especially a member of the red bandana militia who were keeping order on our streets, you had to be very careful how you caught their attention. You did not want a red bandana to think you were creeping up on them. Often, you'd find a whole street of stores that were there yesterday but were just burned-out husks today, or bodies piled in an odd assortment, like corpse origami.

I found myself sniffing the air a lot, for danger or just for amusement. If anyone had still been able to hear, they probably would have been doubled up laughing, because we were all going around sniffing and grunting and mumbling in funny voices, as soon as we had no clue how ridiculous we sounded.

Almost every corner seemed to have red bandanas standing on it, looking bored and desperate for someone to fuck with them.

But meanwhile, I was *Entertainer Explainer*'s New Talent of the Month, because I'd managed to avoid getting murdered in an amusing fashion and the video had gone mega-viral. I was seeing my own face on shirts and on people's phablets more and more often. Sally and I were suddenly kind of famous, and we had to clear out our freezer to make room for all the meat and casseroles and stuff that people kept bringing over. Sally thought our web movies were the ideal thing for people to watch now, because they were a wacky escape from reality and had no dialogue or sound effects for anyone to miss out on. "it's actually funnier without any laughter," Sally texted me from three feet away.

Everybody was bracing themselves for the next thing. We still believed in money, kinda sorta, even after a ton of people had lost their savings and investments in the big default spiral. We didn't *not* believe in money, let's put it that way. We still had electricity and cell phone service and internet, even though many parts of the country were on-again, off-again. The red bandanas and the rump government needed a cellular network as bad as the rest of us, because they needed to be able to organize, the conventional wisdom said, so until they figured out how to have a dedicated network and their own power sources, they would make sure it kept running for everyone. We hoped, anyway.

Sally and I spent hours arguing about what sort of movie we should make next. All of my ideas were too complicated or high-concept for her. I wanted to do a movie about someone who tries to be a gangster but he's too nice, like he runs a protection racket but never collects any money from people. Or he sells drugs but only super harmless ones. So the other gangsters get mad at him and everyone has to help him pretend to be a real gangster. He does such a good job he becomes the head gangster, and then he's in real trouble. Or something. Anyway, Sally said that was too complicated for people right now, we had to shoot for self-explanatory. Some of the film geeks wanted us to make a movie *about* the fact that everyone was deaf, but that seemed like the opposite of escapism to me—which I guess would be trappism, or maybe claustrophilia. More and more often, people had these debates partly in sign language, and I couldn't follow what they were saying.

Sally was all about recapturing the Vikings-and-steampunk glory, like maybe this time we could have Amish cyborgs, with handcrafted wooden implants. I was like, Amish cyborgs aren't high-concept? I was happy to keep debating this stuff forever, because I didn't actually want to make another movie. Whatever part of me that had let me turn calamity into comedy had withered when I fell out of a window on top of Reginald, and watched him die on fire.

Every time I looked, there seemed to be more red bandanas around, and I still saw them beating up subversives and hauling them away to the camps outside the city. All the people on television and my phone looked tooth-spitting angry when they even thought about anyone making trouble for these hardworking young men who were sacrificing *so much* to make us all safer in this dangerous time. I would glance at my phone to see the weather, and there would be a video of someone dressed in an authority-figure costume, looking outraged, and then the words would appear, in block capitals, like HOW DARE YOU HAVE NO SHAME, and then maybe scary video of a blurry figure in dark clothes leering at a group of red bandanas while rose-tinted flames consumed everything in the background. Even with everything I knew about Ricky and his friends, I always wanted to find the nearest red bandana and find some way to apologize for all my hurtful thoughts—like I was always groveling inside my own head for a moment, after looking at my phone, until I snapped back to reality.

Snow fell. Then hail, then sleet, and then snow again. Things felt dark, even during the day, and I felt like my sight, smell, and touch were going the way of my hearing. Only my taste burned as strong as ever. Everything was salty, salty, salty. You could slip and break your leg in a ditch and nobody would know you were there for days and days. This was going to be a long winter.

I had the same dream, night after night, for a week or two. I was in a swan boat with Sally, on Boston Common, and everything smelled gray and brown. The water swooshed and the ducks complained. The air, the few cars, our breathing, all had their own music. Our boat didn't need to go any-where special, but Sally beat the water with an oar anyway. She cursed the useless water, looked over and smiled at me, and then went back to hitting and cursing.

"What did the water do to you?" I asked Sally.

"It's not the water, it's everything. It all needs its ass kicked. Actually, the water pisses me off because it keeps running away from me. If it would just sit still, I would go easy on it."

"Look, Sally, I know you said I shouldn't blame myself. For what hap-pened to Raine and all. But it keeps happening, over and over, and when something happens more than twice, chances are it's my fault, right?"

Sally stopped scaring the ducks and touched my arm. She had amazing lightness sometimes. "There's plenty of blame to go around, scooter. You can have your share, don't worry, and I'll have mine. We'll make a party of div-vying it up."

The sky got dark purple all at once, like it does sometimes. "I just don't want to let you down anymore, and I can see another shitfuck coming, bigger than the others. I just don't know if I can keep being the funny falling-down guy any longer, I feel as though I swallowed a statue and it's statue-fying me from the inside out."

Now the sky was all the way dark.

"Well, if it gets to be too much for you, you know what you can always do, don't you?" Sally took both my shoulders in her hands as things got darker and darker, and said, "What you do is—"

That's where I always woke up.

ROCK MANNING. WE NEED YOU.

I stared up at the giant scrolling light-up banner over Out of Town News in Harvard Square. I blinked the snow away and looked a second time. It still looked like my name up there. Okay, so this was it, the thing my school therapist had warned me about back in fifth grade. I was going narcissisto-phrenic and starting to imagine that toasters and people on the television were talking to me or about me. It was probably way too late to start taking pills now.

But then a guy I had met at one of our movie shoots saw it too, tugging on my sleeve and pointing at the scrolling words. So unless he and I were both hallucinating the same way, it really did say my name up there.

A bus zipped past, now that they'd gotten a few buses running again. The big flashing screen on the front didn't say WARNING. BUS WILL RUN YOU OVER. GET OUT OF THE WAY, as usual. Instead, it said ROCK MANNING, YOU CAN MAKE A CONTRIBUTION TO REBUILDING SOCIETY. I grabbed the guy, whose name was Scottie or Thor or something, and pointed at the bus for more independent confirmation that I wasn't losing it. He poked me back and pointed at a big screen in the display window of Cardullo's, which now read ROCK MANNING, COME JOIN US. I grabbed my cell phone and it had a new text message, much the same as the ones I was seeing everywhere. I almost threw my phone away.

Instead I ran toward the river, trying to outrun the words. Over the past few months since the event everyone was calling the Big Boom, I'd seen the screens going up in more and more places, and now all of a sudden they were all talking to me personally. Computer screens on display at the big business store, the sign that normally announced the specials at the Mongolian buffet place—even the little screen that someone had attached to their golden retriever's collar, which would let you know when the dog was barking. They were calling me out. I got to the river and ran across the big old stone bridge. In the murky river water, the letters floated, projected from somewhere in the depths: WHY ARE YOU RUNNING? WE THOUGHT YOU'D BE FLATTERED.

When I got to the other side of the bridge, Ricky Artesian was waiting for me. He was wearing a suit, and instead of the red bandana, he had a red handkerchief in his breast pocket, but otherwise he was the same old Ricky from high school. He held up a big piece of paper:

Relax, pal. We just need your help, the same way we needed you once before. Except this time we're going to make sure it goes right.

Ricky had a couple other guys in suits behind him, also clearly red bandana honchos. I thought about jumping off the bridge. The river had defrosted but still looked chilly. I looked over the edge of the bridge again, tossed a mental coin, and jumped.

The loose boat was right where I thought it was. It had drifted downriver from the Harvard boathouse, and I landed in the stern without capsizing it all the way. I righted the boat and found the oars. Someone had either forgotten to chain it up, or vandalized the chain. Then I slotted the oars into their nooks and started to row. I'd never sculled before, but how hard could it be?

After half an hour of rowing as hard as I could, and going in the same circle over and over, while Ricky watched from overhead, I wondered if I'd made a mistake, plus this all reminded me way too much of my recurring swan boat dream. I texted Sally that I was in a boat trying to escape and didn't know how to row. She googled rowing. She said I needed to straighten out and row the same amount with both oars, and then maybe I'd stop going in circles. Also, go with the current. Meanwhile, Ricky and his friends were grabbing a big scary-looking hook. I tried to figure out what the current was. It took me way too long to find a drifting leaf and figure I should go the same way as it. So I tried to row that way, but the boat kept veering and swerving. Then I saw a bench right in front of me that looked like someone was supposed to sit facing the other way, and I realized that was probably where the coxswain sat. Which was the rear of the boat, right? So maybe part of the problem was that I was sitting backward. I got myself all turned around, but I lost my grip on one of the oars and it floated away, much faster than my boat had gone so far. At this point, the hook snagged my boat, and a moment later I was a landlubber again.

"Hey Rock," Ricky said. I was up to about 10 percent accuracy with my lip-reading. He held out his hand and I took it out of reflex.

We all went for burgers at this little ancient diner nearby, which had survived everything without changing its greasy ways. I admired that. It even still had the little jukebox at each table, and the red checkered vinyl tablecloth with stray burn marks from when you could still smoke indoors. Ricky smoked, because who was going to tell him not to?

"i think it's great you're still doing the same thing as in high school," Ricky's laptop screen said. He swiveled it around and typed some more, then turned it back. Now it said, "you found something that worked for you, and you stuck with it. that's kool." I nodded. If Ricky had been talking instead of typing, he probably would have made this stuff sound like compliments. He typed some more: "you know i always liked you." The other two guys didn't try to say anything, or even read what Ricky was typing, they just ate their burgers and stared out the window at the handful of students who were crawling back to Harvard.

I didn't try to contribute to the conversation either, I just read whatever Ricky typed at me. He hadn't touched his burger yet. He told me about how he'd moved up in the world since Carolina, and now he was working for some pretty juiced-up people in government, and everything was really under control. You would be surprised, he said, at how under control everything really was.

I nodded and half smiled, to show that I knew what he meant, but really I didn't think I would be that surprised.

I thought about the oar that had gotten away from me, floating downriver toward freedom as fast as it could go. Where would it end up?

Ricky said I shouldn't worry about a repeat of what happened last time. We were both older and more experienced, and he'd gotten smarter since then. The thing was, he said, people were still in shock. Almost like little children, right now. They needed their cartoony entertainment to keep their minds off things. So here was the deal: he would get us resources like you wouldn't imagine, like our wildest dreams were this tablecloth and the actuality was up there on the ceiling. In return, we would just portray authority in a kind way. Nothing too heavy, like people wearing the bandana or any army uniforms. Just occasionally we see that the militia and army are trustworthy and the people in charge have your best interests, etc. etc. etc. Most of the time, we'd have a free hand.

I had to get up and go wash my hands so I could type on Ricky's laptop. I didn't want to get his keyboard greasy. Then it took me a minute to hunt and peck: "sally wont go for it she thinks you killed her boyfriend which duh you did."

I swiveled it around before I could think twice about what I'd just typed.

Ricky's eyes narrowed. He looked up at me, and for a moment he was the leg breaker again. I thought he was going to lunge across the booth and throttle me. Then he typed: "the robot guy?" I nodded. "that was a situation. its complicated, and many people were to blame."

I tried really really hard not to have any expression on my face, as if it didn't matter to me one way or the other. I ran out of hamburger, so I ate my fries slow, skinning them and then nibbling at the mashed potatoes inside. Everything smelled meaty.

"tell u what, just dont tell sally im involved," Ricky typed. "just tell her the government wants 2 support your work."

It was easy for me to agree to that, because I knew my face was a giant emoji as far as Sally was concerned, and she would know within seconds that I was hiding something.

Ricky didn't threaten to break parts of us if we didn't go along with his plan, but he didn't need to, and he only made some gauzy promises about payment. He did say he could get me some rowing lessons. Then he said he'd be in touch again soon, and he and his goons left me sitting alone in a booth, staring at grease stains on a plate.

Outside, a half dozen people were gathering on stone benches in front of a Deaf woman who was teaching with a mixture of slow, careful sign language and big posters. This group called the Kind Hands had developed some new curriculum and was mass-producing books and posters, with a heavy emphasis on empowerment and self-esteem. Across the street, two rank-and-file red bandanas studied this group, clearly trying to figure out if it was a subversive gathering, which was one of those questions that could easily fall into some pretty deep philosophical quicksand. The red bandanas watched as the woman, who had Asian features and a hat with a red pom-pom, taught people how to say "Are you hungry?" and "It's snowing again" in sign language, and the bandanas looked down at their phones, because this was boring.

But then just as I was half a block away, the woman unveiled a poster-size card for how to sign "I can take care of myself." The two red bandanas looked at each other, and then they walked across the street with their clubs raised.

I searched for two hours without finding Sally. I almost texted her, but I had a bad feeling about my cell phone. When I finally tracked her down, she was bossing a group of film students building a giant ramp that looked as if they were going to roll a mail cart into a snowbank. She saw me and then turned away, to watch her pals slamming boards together. I nudged her, but she just ignored me. I remembered she'd said something about this movie they wanted to make about a guy who works in the mailroom and discovers a hidden doorway that leads to hell's interoffice mail system, and he has to deliver a bunch of letters to demons before he can get out. High-fuckin-concept. Anyway, she was pissed that I'd been blowing her off for weeks, so now I couldn't get her attention.

Finally, I wrote just the name "ricky a" on my cell and shoved it in front of her, without pressing Send. Her eyes widened and she made to text me back, but I stopped her. I grabbed a pad and a pen and wrote down the whole story for her, including the signs in Harvard Square. She shook her head a lot, then bit her lip. She thought I was exaggerating, but the guy who'd seen the signs showed up and confirmed that part, scribbling, but also signing with his hands.

"We're so small-time," she wrote in neat cursive, under my scrawls. "Why would Ricky care?"

Under that, I wrote: "1. He remembers us from hi skool, unfinished biz. 2. He likes us and wants to own us. 3. He hates us and wants to destroy us. 4. those guys are scared of losing their grip & they think we can help."

A cold wind blew, and I'd gotten kind of wet trying to escape in a boat, plus the sun was going down, so I started to shiver out there on the lawn in front of BU. Some students were straggling back in, just like at Harvard, and they stared at the set, abandoned half-finished against one wall. Sally gestured for her gang to get the ramp to hell's mailroom back into storage.

We piled ourselves into the back of the equipment van, with Zapp Stillman driving, and headed for the Pike, because the sooner we got out of town the better. We got about half a mile before we hit the first checkpoint. Soldiers with big dragonfly helmets stood in front of Humvees, blocking off most of the lanes of Storrow Drive, and between the soldiers and the swiveling cameras on stalks, there was no way you would get past their barricades. They were checking everybody coming in and out of the city, and one hundred yards past them stood an exoskeleton thingy, or a mech, with thighs like Buicks and feet like dumpsters. I couldn't really see its top half from my hiding place in the back of the van, but I imagined piston elbows and some kind of skull face. The kind of people who built a mech like this would not be able to resist having a skull face, to save their lives. My brother Holman had probably piloted one of these things in Central Asia or Central Eurasia, someplace Central. The pilots of these things had a high rate of going A.U.T.U., because of all the neural strain. This one wasn't moving, but it was cranked up and operational, because you could see the ground shivering around it and there were fresh kills nearby. Cars still smoking, a few unlucky bodies.

I thought of the smirk on Ricky's face as he'd typed that everything was under control.

Our van turned onto a side street as fast as possible, and we swerved back toward BU. By the time we got back there, Janelle had found some posts on an underground forum, about the cordoning off of several major cities. This was part of a sweep to round up certain radical elements that threatened the shaky order: you had the red bandanas inside the cities and the army outside. We were still in the van, parked on a side street just off Dummer Street, sheltered by a giant sad oak that leaned almost to the ground on one side. You could put a tire swing on that oak and swing underground and maybe there would be mole people. Mole people would be awesome, especially if they had their own dance routine, which I just figured they probably would, because what else would you be doing stuck underground all the time?

I wasn't sure if we should get out of the van or if someone could spot us, but Sally went ahead and climbed out, and Janelle followed. I got out and stood on the sidewalk, shrugging in a sad rag doll way. Sally stomped her foot and gritted her teeth. She tried some sign language on me, and I got the gist that she was saying we were trapped, every way out of the city would be the same thing. I just looked at her, waiting for her to say what we were going to do, and she looked weary but also pissed. This thing of not talking meant you really had to watch people, and maybe you could see people more clearly when you couldn't hear them. Sally had the twitch in her forearms that usually meant she was about to throw something. She had the neck tendon that meant she was ready to yell at someone, if yelling were still a thing that happened. Her mouse brown hair was a beautiful mess, bursting free of her scrunchie, her face so furious it circled back around to calm. Biting her tongue, the better to spit blood.

She wrote on her phone: "the army outside + red bandanas inside. occupation. city is screwed. we r screwed. trapped." She erased it without hitting Send.

I took the phone and wrote: "red bandanas + army = opportunity."

She just stared at me. I didn't even know what I had in mind yet. This was the part of the conversation where I would normally start spitballing and suggesting that we get a hundred people in koala costumes and send them running down the street while someone else dropped hallucinogenic water balloons from a hang glider. Or something. But I couldn't spitball as fast with my thumbs. I paused and thought about Ricky and the other bandanas I'd met, and how they were so desperate to be loved as well as feared that they were even willing to ask someone like me for help with representing. I thought about Holman and how much he looked down on civilians, even before he got the A.N.V.I.L. socket in his skull. I thought about how Ricky and his guys had engineered a clusterfuck at that peace protest, making the cops think the protesters were shooting at them, so the cops shot back. I thought about how the bandanas weren't leaving the city and the army wasn't coming in.

"I think I have a bad idea," I wrote.

All my life, there had been a giant empty space, a huge existential void, that had needed to be filled by something, and I had never realized that that thing was the Oscar Mayer Wienermobile, with its sleek red hot dog battering ram surrounded by a metal bun. It was like the Space Battleship *Yamato* made of bread and pork, made of metal. This MIT student named Matt had been souping up the Wienermobile with a high-performance electric engine and all-terrain wheels, just saving it for the right occasion. Somehow, Janelle had convinced Matt that our little adventure was it. The tires were the perfect mud color to match the lower part of the chassis, which Matt had rescued from a scrap yard in Burlington. The chassis had a tip as red and round as a clown's nose, on either side of the long, sleek body. This baby had crisscrossed the country before I was born, proclaiming the pure love of Ball Park Franks. Just staring at this beauty made me hungry in my soul.

All around us, Sally's film student minions were doing engine checks and sewing parachutes and painting faces onto boomerangs and inflating sex dolls and making pies for the pie-throwing machine. The usual, in other words. I felt an emotion I'd never felt before in my life, lodged down where I always pictured my spine and my colon shaking hands, and I didn't know how to label it at first. Sort of like excitement, sort of like regret—but this feeling wasn't either of those things. I finally realized: I was afraid. People had told me about fear, but I had never quite believed it existed in real life. I watched Zapp Stillman blowing up a blow-up doll, and something wobbled inside me. I had felt guilt and self-loathing, especially after Reginald, but now I felt worry-fear. Zapp saw me looking at him and gave me a cocky little nod. I nodded back.

Sally was busy studying a big road map with Janelle, charting the escape route and where we were all going to rendezvous if we made it out of town. Sally had taken my vague arm-wheeling notion and turned it into an actual plan, which would let us escape to the Concord Turnpike and make for Walden Pond, that place where Henry David Thoreau had built a comedy waterslide two hundred years ago. And then? Maybe head West. Find a secluded place to wait things out. Sally handed her magic marker off to Janelle and came over to stand with me.

"What changed your mind," she wrote in ballpoint on a pad, "about doing more stunts? You were ready to quit, before."

I took the pad and pen. Chewed the cap. Wrote: "Ricky won't leave us
alone. We gotta blow town and this is the only way. Plus this is different than
just making another weird movie. If this works, maybe we ruin the red bandanas' day. Maybe we ruin their whole week, even. PAYBACK." That last
word, I underlined three times. Sally took the pen back from me and drew
little stars and hearts and rainbows and smiley faces, until this was the most
decorated PAYBACK you've ever seen.

One of our lookouts shone a flashlight, and Janelle nodded, and Sally
and I got stuffed into a little cubby under the floorboards, with no light and
almost no air, with all the cameras and filming equipment on top of us. We
were scrunched together, so her knee was in my face and my left arm dug
into her side. Every few moments, the floor over us shuddered, like someone
was knocking things around. Sally shivered and twitched, so I gripped her
tighter. I was starting to freak out from the lack of light and air and entertainment options, but just as I was ready to wobble myself silly, Janelle and
Thor (Scottie?) lifted the lid off and pulled us out.

So. *Ballpark Figure* was the last movie we ever made, and it was probably
one of the last movies anybody ever made. It was a mixture of fiction, reality, and improv, which Zapp Stillman said was pleasingly meta—we were
counting on the bandanas and the army to play themselves in the story,
but I was playing a fictional character, and so were Janelle and Zapp. My
character was Horace Burton, the last baseball fan on Earth, who had been
heartbroken since the MLB shut down and who was driving his giant hot
dog vehicle to try and find the world's greatest baseball players, in a kind of
Field of Dreams-with-lunch-meat thing. Janelle was a former hot dog mascot who had turned vegan but still wanted to keep dressing up as a hot dog,
just a meatless hot dog this time. Zapp was some kind of coach. We filmed a
sequence of the three of us piling into our hot dog car, with some animated
cue card exposition, and posted it online with minimal editing, as a kind of
prequel to the actual movie, which we promised would be posted live and
streaming, right as it happened, on our vumble.

By the time we were ready to leave town, an hour before dawn, the *Ballpark Figure* prologue had been up for a few hours and we had a few thousand
people refreshing our vumble over and over. I had slept a few hours, but Sally
hadn't slept at all and Janelle was guzzling really terrible coffee. Sally wasn't

going to be in the hot dog, she was going to be one of the people filming the action from—I hoped—a safe distance, using Matt's remote-controlled camera drones, which I had insisted on. If nothing else came of this but Sally getting somewhere safe, where she could start over, I could count that the biggest win ever.

As we rolled into the middle of the street and cranked the hot dog up to its maximum speed of fifty miles per hour, I had time as I clambered out onto the outermost front reaches of the metal bun to obsess over the contradiction between Horace Burton and myself. Horace's goal, in this movie, was to take his hot dog out onto the open road and find the lost spirit of baseball. Horace didn't want any trouble—but I, meanwhile, had no goal other than trouble, and (if I were being honest) no plans after today. How was I going to play that, in a way that preserved the integrity of Horace and his innocent love of sportsmanship? In fact, I reflected as I raised a baseball and prepared to hurl it at the shaved head of the red bandana standing on the nearest corner in front of a shuttered florist, that might be the reason why people root for the comic hero after all: the haplessness. This fresh white baseball was emblazoned with a slogan about bringing back the greatest game, and the story called for Horace to toss them out as a promotional thing, and to hit a militia member in the head purely by accident. So it was important for the story that I not look as though I was aiming, but I also couldn't afford to miss. Horace is a good person, who just wants to bring joy to people, and he gets caught up in a bad situation, and the moment you think Horace brought this on himself through meanness or combativeness, that's the moment you stop pulling for him. The baseball hit the teenager in the jaw, over the neatly tied red cloth that looked too big for his skinny neck, and he whipped around and fired off a few shots with his Browning Hi-Power while also texting his comrades with his free hand.

I tried to wear a convincing look of friendly panic, like I hadn't meant to wake a thousand sleeping giants with one stray baseball, and danced around on the front of the hot dog so hard I nearly fell under the wheels. I slipped and landed on my crotch on the very tip of the hot dog, then pulled myself back up, still trying to toss out promotional baseballs and spread goodwill, and it struck me for the first time that I had spent so much time worrying that I was going to hurt someone by accident, I never dreamed that I would finally reach a point where I would decide to cause harm on purpose. Our hot dog had red bandanas chasing us, with two motorcycles and some kind of hybrid electric Jeep. I had no idea if anybody was still shooting at me, because I couldn't see anyone aiming a gun from where I stood on one foot, and I couldn't see any bullets hitting anything. Until a bullet hit me in the thigh just as the hot dog swerved without slowing and we released the blow-up dolls in their makeshift baseball uniforms. The blow-up dolls flew behind us, and I saw one of them hit a motorcyclist right where the red bandana tucked under his round white helmet, so that he lost his grip on his handlebars and went somersaulting, and I felt blood seeping through my pants like maybe it had missed a bone but hit an artery and I was cursing myself for forgetting to bring a giant comedy bottle of ketchup to squirt at people, because ketchup is the most cheerful kind of fake blood, when Ricky Artesian climbed on top of the third car of by now five that were chasing us and held up a big flat-screen TV that read YOU MADE YOUR CHOICE ROCK, TIME TO PAY, and another bullet tore through my side just as the hot dog made another sharp turn and we disappeared into the tunnel from the abandoned Back Bay T extension project.

The hot dog came to a stop in a dark hutch Xed in by fallen rusted steel girders, just as one of our bready tires gave out and the whole vehicle slumped on one side, and our support crew set about camouflaging the Wienermobile with rocks and planks. Janelle climbed out of the cab and came over to show me the vumble, the snickerdoodle number of hits we were getting right now and the footage, playing in an endless loop, of me hurling baseballs at the red bandanas, and then she noticed that I was pissing blood from my leg and my side, and started trying to get me to lie down. Just then a message came through from Sally, who was still masterminding the filming from a remote location: "theyre not taking the bait." The bandanas were staying on their side of the line and not trying to chase us into the army barricades, like we'd hoped.

I slipped out of Janelle's grasp—easy when you're as slick as I was, just then—and leapt onto Zapp's bicycle. Before anybody could try to stop me, I was already pedaling back the way we'd come, up the ramp and out the hidden entryway that we were just in the process of sealing up, leaping through the closing exit from darkness into the light of day. I raced close enough to Ricky Artesian to make eye contact and hurl my second-to-last baseball, absolutely coated at this point with my own blood, at his pinstripe-suited torso. Then I spun and tore off in the direction of Storrow Drive again, not looking back to see if anyone was following me, racing with my head down, on the ramp that led up to the Pike. My phone thrummed with messages but I ignored it. I was already reaching the top of the ramp, all thoughts of Horace Burton, and lovable fall guys in general, forgotten. The checkpoint was a collection of pale blobs at ground level, plus a swarm of men and women with bug heads rushing around tending their one statuesque mecha and a collection of mustard-colored vehicles. My eyesight was going, my concentration going with it, my feet kept sliding off the pedals, but I kept pedaling nonetheless, until I was close enough to yank out my last limited edition promotional baseball, crook my arm back, and then straighten with the hardest throw of my life. Then I wiped out. I fell partway behind a concrete barrier as Ricky and the other bandanas came up the ramp into the line of fire. I saw nothing of what came next, except that I smelled smoke and cordite and glimpsed a man with the red neck gear falling on his hands and rearing back up, before I crawled the rest of the way behind my shelter and passed out.

When I gained consciousness, I was in a prison camp, where I nearly died, first of my wounds and later of a fiendish case of dysentery like you wouldn't believe. I never saw Sally again, but I saw our last movie, once, on a stored file on someone's battered old Stackbook. (This lady named Shari had saved the edited film to her hard drive before the internet went futz, and people had been copying *Ballpark Figure* on pinky drives and passing it around ever since, whenever they had access to electricity.) The final act of *Ballpark Figure* was just soldiers and red bandanas getting drilled by each other's bullets until they did a garishly herky-jerky slam-dance, and I have to say the film had lost any narrative thread regarding Horace Burton, or baseball, or the quest to restore professional sports to America, not to mention the comedy value of all those flailing bodies was minimal at best. The movie ended with a dedication: "To Rock Manning. Who taught me it's not whether you fall, it's how you land. Love, Sally."

After I wrote "My Breath Is a Rudder," I always meant to go back and write another queer first-person story that takes place after San Francisco is claimed by the ocean. Enter Jonathan Strahan, who asked me to contribute to a post–climate change anthology called *Drowned Worlds*. I had a lot of fun imagining the San Francisco archipelago, using a map that Brian Stokle and Burrito Justice had created of the city following two hundred feet of sea level rise.

Still, I had a lot of trouble finding my way into this story, because I was feeling burned out on depressing postapocalyptic tales. Then my partner, Annalee Newitz, asked me why exactly the story had to be depressing or post-apocalyptic. Why not write about people who are rebuilding and bouncing back? Their insight gave me the breakthrough I needed, and this became a hopeful story about young people living their lives and building something new in the wake of catastrophic climate change. Content warning: suicide, abuse.

BECAUSE CHANGE WAS THE OCEAN AND WE LIVED BY HER MERCY

1
This was sacred, this was stolen

We stood naked on the shore of Bernal and watched the candles float across the bay, swept by a lazy current off to the north, in the direction of Potrero Island. A dozen or so candles stayed afloat and alight after half a league, their tiny flames bobbing up and down, casting long yellow reflections on the dark water alongside the streaks of moonlight. At times I fancied the candlelight could filter down onto streets and buildings, the old automobiles and houses full of children's toys, all the waterlogged treasures of long-gone people. We held hands, twenty or thirty of us, and watched the little candle boats we'd made as they floated away. Joconda was humming an old reconstructed song about the wild road, hir beard full of flowers. We all just about held our breath. I felt my bare skin go electric with the intensity of the moment, like this could be the good time we'd all remember in the bad times to come. This was sacred, this was stolen. Someone—probably Miranda—farted, and then we were all laughing, and the grown-up seriousness was gone. We were all busting up and falling over each other on the rocky ground, in a nude heap, scraping our knees and giggling into each other's limbs. When we got our breath back and looked up, the candles were all gone.

2
I felt like I had always been Wrong Headed

I couldn't deal with life in Fairbanks anymore. I grew up at the same time as the town, watched it go from regular city to mega-city as I hit my early twenties. I lived in an old decommissioned solar power station with five other kids, and we tried to make the loudest, most uncomforting music we could, with a beat as relentless and merciless as the tides. We wanted to shake our cinder block walls and make people dance until their feet bled. But we sucked. We were bad at music, and not quite clueless enough not to know it. We all wore big hoods and spiky shoes and tried to make our own drums out of drycloth and cracked wood, and we read our poetry on Friday nights. There were bookhouses, along with stinktanks where you could drink up and listen to awful poetry about extinct animals. People came from all over, because everybody heard that Fairbanks was becoming the most civilized place on Earth, and that's when I decided to leave town. I had this moment of looking around at my musician friends and my restaurant job and our cool little scene and feeling like there had to be more to life than this.

I hitched a ride down south and ended up in Olympia, at a house where they were growing their own food and drugs, and doing a way better job with the drugs than the food. We were all staring upward at the first cloud anybody had seen in weeks, trying to identify what it could mean. When you hardly ever saw them, clouds had to be omens.

We were all complaining about our families, still watching that cloud warp and contort, and I found myself talking about how my parents only liked to listen to that boring boo-pop music with the same three or four major chords and that cruddy AAA/BBB/CDE/CDE rhyme scheme, and how my mother insisted on saving every scrap of organic material we used and collecting every drop of rainwater. "It's fucking pathetic, is what it is. They act like we're still living in the Great Decimation."

"They're just super traumatized," said this skinny genderfreak named Juya, who stood nearby holding the bong. "It's hard to even imagine. I mean, we're the first generation that just takes it for granted we're going to survive, as like a species. Our parents, our grandparents, and their grandparents, they were all living like every day could be the day the planet finally got done with us. They didn't grow up having moisture condensers and myco-protein rinses and skinsus."

"Yeah, whatever," I said. But what Juya said stuck with me, because I had never thought of my parents as traumatized. I'd always thought they were just tightly wound and judgy. Juya had two cones of dark twisty hair on zir head and a red pajamzoot, and zi was only a year or two older than me but seemed a lot wiser.

"I want to find all the music we used to have," I said. "You know, the weird, noisy shit that made people's clothes fall off and their hair light on fire. The rock 'n' roll that just listening to it turned girls into boys, the songs that took away the fear of god. I've read about it, but I've never heard any of it, and I don't even know how to play it."

"Yeah, all the recordings and notations got lost in the Dataclysm," Juya said. "They were in formats that nobody can read, or they got corrupted, or they were printed on disks made from petroleum. Those songs are gone forever."

"I think they're under the ocean," I said. "I think they're down there somewhere."

Something about the way I said that helped Juya reach a decision. "Hey, I'm heading back down to the San Francisco archipelago in the morning. I got room in my car if you wanna come with."

Juya's car was an older solar model that had to stop every couple hours to recharge, and the self-driving module didn't work so great. My legs were resting in a pile of old headmods and biofills, plus those costooms that everybody used a few summers earlier that made your skin turn into snakeskin that you could shed in one piece. So the upshot was, we had a lot of time to talk and hold hands and look at the endless golden landscape stretching off to the east. Juya had these big bright eyes that laughed when the rest of zir face was stone serious, and strong tentative hands to hold me in place as zi tied me to the car seat with fronds of algae. I had never felt as safe and dangerous as when I crossed the wasteland with Juya. We talked for hours about how the world needed new communities, new ways to breathe life back into the ocean, new ways to be people.

By the time we got to Bernal Island and the Wrong Headed community, I was in love with Juya, deeper than I'd ever felt with anyone before.

Juya up and left Bernal a week and a half later, because zi got bored again, and I barely noticed that zi was gone. By then, I was in love with a hundred other people, and they were all in love with me.

Bernal Island was only accessible from one direction, from the big island in the middle, and only at a couple times of day, when they let the bridge down and turned off the moat. After a few days on Bernal, I stopped even noticing the other islands on our horizon, let alone paying attention to my friends on social media talking about all the fancy new restaurants Fairbanks was getting. I was constantly having these intense, heartfelt moments with people in the Wrong Headed crew.

"The ocean is our lover, you can hear it laughing at us." Joconda was sort of the leader here. Sie sometimes had a beard and sometimes a smooth round face covered with perfect bright makeup. Hir eyes were as gray as the sea and just as unpredictable. For decades, San Francisco and other places like it had been abandoned, because the combination of seismic instability and a voracious dead ocean made them too scary and risky. But that city down there, under the waves, had been the place everybody came to, from all over the world, to find freedom. That legacy was ours now.

Those people had brought music from their native countries and their own cultures, and all those sounds had crashed together in those streets, night after night. Joconda's own ancestors had come from China and Peru, and hir great-grandparents had played nine-stringed guitars, melodies and rhythms that Joconda barely recalled now. Listening to hir, I almost fancied I could put my ear to the surface of the ocean and hear all the sounds from generations past, still reverberating. We sat all night, Joconda, some of the others, and myself, and I got to play on an old-school drum made of cowhide or something. I felt like I had always been Wrong Headed and I'd just never had the word for it before.

Juya sent me an email a month or two after zi left Bernal: "The moment

I met you, I knew you needed to be with the rest of those maniacs. I've never been able to resist delivering lost children to their rightful homes. It's almost the only thing I'm good at, other than the things you already knew about." I never saw zir again.

3
"I'm so glad I found a group of people I would risk drowning in dead water for."

Back in the twenty-first century, everybody had theories about how to make the ocean breathe again. Fill her with quicklime, to neutralize the acid. Split the water molecules into hydrogen and oxygen, then bond the hydrogen with the surplus carbon in the water to create a clean-burning hydrocarbon fuel. Release genetically engineered fish with special gills. Grow special algae that was designed to commit suicide after a while. Spray billions of nanotech balls into her. Now, we had to clean up the after-effects of all those failed solutions, while also helping the sea to let go of all that CO_2 from before.

The only way was the slow way. We pumped ocean water through our special enzyme store and then through a series of filters, until what came out the other end was clear and oxygen-rich. The waste, we separated out and disposed of. Some of it became raw materials for shoe soles and roof tiles. Some of it, the pure organic residue, we used as fertilizer or food for our myco-protein.

I got used to staying up all night playing music with some of the other Wrong Headed kids, sometimes on the drum and sometimes on an old stringed instrument that was made of stained wood and had a leering cat face under its fret. Sometimes I thought I could hear something in the way our halting beats and scratchy notes bounced off the walls and the water beyond, like we were really conjuring a lost soundtrack. Sometimes it all just seemed like a waste.

What did it mean to be a real authentic person, in an era when everything great from the past was twenty feet under water? Would you embrace prefab newness or try to copy the images you can see from the handful of docs we'd scrounged from the Dataclysm? When we got tired of playing music, an hour before dawn, we would sit around arguing, and inevitably you got to that moment where you were looking straight into someone else's eyes and arguing about the past and whether the past could ever be on land or the past was doomed to be deep under water forever.

I felt like I was just drunk all the time on that cheap-ass vodka that everybody chugged in Fairbanks, or maybe on nitrous. My head was evaporating, but my heart just got more and more solid. I woke up every day on my bunk, or sometimes tangled up in someone else's arms and legs on the daybed, and felt actually jazzed to get up and go clean the scrubbers or churn the mycoprotein vats.

Every time we put down the bridge to the big island and turned off our moat, I felt everything go sour inside me, and my heart went funnel-shaped. People sometimes just wandered away from the Wrong Headed community without much in the way of good-bye—that was how Juya had gone—but meanwhile, new people showed up and got the exact same welcome that everyone had given to me. I got freaked out thinking of my perfect home being overrun by new selfish loud fuckers. Joconda had to sit me down, at the big table where sie did all the official business, and tell me to get over myself, because change was the ocean and we lived on her mercy. "Seriously, Pris. I ever see that look on your face, I'm going to throw you into the myco vat myself." Joconda stared at me until I started laughing and promised to get with the program.

One day I was sitting at our big table, overlooking the straits between us and the big island. Staring at Sutro Tower, and the taller buildings poking out of the water here and there. This obnoxious skinny bitch sat down next to me, chewing in my ear and talking about the impudence of impermanence or some similar. "Miranda," she introduced herself. "I just came up from Anaheim-Diego. Jeez what a mess. They actually think they can build nanomechs and make it scalable. Whatta bunch of poutines."

"Stop chewing in my ear," I muttered. But then I found myself following her around everywhere she went.

Miranda was the one who convinced me to dive into the chasm of Fillmore Street in search of a souvenir from the old Church of John Coltrane, as a present for Joconda. I strapped on some goggles and a big apparatus that fed me oxygen while also helping me to navigate a little bit, and then we went out in a dinghy that looked old enough that someone had actually used it for fishing. Miranda gave me one of her crooked grins and studied a wrinkled old map. "I thinnnnnk it's right around here." She laughed.

I gave her a murderous look and jumped into the water, letting myself fall into the street at the speed of water resistance. Those sunken buildings turned into doorways and windows facing me, but they stayed blurry as the bilge flowed around them. I could barely find my feet, let alone identify a building on sight. One of these places had been a restaurant, I was pretty sure. Ancient automobiles lurched back and forth, like maybe even their brakes had rusted away. I figured the Church of John Coltrane would have a spire like a saxophone? Maybe? But all of the buildings looked exactly the same. I stumbled down the street, until I saw something that looked like a church, but it was a caved-in old McDonald's restaurant. Then I tripped over something, a downed pole or whatever, and my face mask cracked as I went down. The water was going down my throat, tasting like dirt, and my vision went all pale and wavy.

I almost just went under, but then I thought I could see a light up there, way above the street, and I kicked. I kicked and chopped and made myself float. I churned up there until I broke the surface. My arms were thrashing above the water and then I started to go back down, but Miranda had my neck and one shoulder. She hauled me up and out of the water and threw me into the dinghy. I was gasping and heaving up water, and she just sat and laughed at me.

"You managed to scavenge something after all." She pointed to something I'd clutched at on my way up out of the water: a rusted, barbed old piece of a car. "I'm sure Joconda will love it."

"Ugh," I said. "Fuck Old San Francisco. It's gross and corroded and there's nothing left of whatever used to be cool, but hey. I'm glad I found a group of people I would risk drowning in dead water for."

4
I chose to see that as a special status

Miranda had the kind of long-limbed, snaggle-toothed beauty that made you think she was born to make trouble. She loved to roughhouse, and usually ended up with her elbow on the back of my neck as she pushed me into the dry dirt. She loved to invent cute, insulting nicknames for me, like "Dolly-pris" or "Pris Ridiculous." She never got tired of reminding me that I might be a ninth-level genderfreak but I had all kinds of privilege, because I grew up in Fairbanks and never had to wonder how we were going to eat.

Miranda had this way of making me laugh even when the news got scary, when the government back in Fairbanks was trying to reestablish control over the whole West Coast and extinction rose up like the shadows at the bottom of the sea. I would start to feel that scab inside my stomach, like the whole ugly unforgiving world could come down on us and our tiny island sanctuary at any moment, Miranda would suddenly start making up a weird dance or inventing a motto for a team of superhero mosquitos and I would be laughing so hard it was like I was squeezing the fear out of my insides. Her hands were a mass of scar tissue but they were as gentle as dried-up blades of grass on my thighs.

Miranda had five other lovers, but I was the only one she made fun of. I chose to see that as a special status.

5
"What are you people even about"

Falling in love with a community is always going to be more real than any love for a single human being could ever be. People will let you down, shatter your image of them, or try to melt down the wall between your self-image and theirs. People, one at a time, are too messy. Miranda was my hero and the lover I'd pretty much dreamed of since both puberties, but I also saved pieces of my heart for a bunch of other Wrong Headed people. I loved Joconda's totally random inspirations and perversions, like all of the art projects sie started getting me to build out of scraps from the sunken city after I brought back that car piece from Fillmore Street. Zell was this hyperactive kid with wild half-braids who had this whole theory about digging up buried hard drives full of music files from the digital age so we could reconstruct the actual sounds of Marvin Gaye and the Jenga Priests. Weo used to sit with me and watch the sun going down over the islands, we didn't talk a lot except that Weo would suddenly whisper some weird beautiful notion about what it would be like to live at sea one day when the sea was alive again. But it wasn't any individual, it was the whole group, we had gotten in a rhythm together and we all believed the same stuff. The love of the ocean, and her resilience in the face of whatever we had done to her, and the power of silliness to make you believe in abundance again. Openness, and a kind of generosity that is the opposite of monogamy.

One day I looked up, and some of the faces were different again. A few of my favorite people in the community had bugged out without saying anything, and one or two of the newcomers started seriously getting on my nerves. One person, Mage, just had a nasty temper, going off at anyone who crossed hir path whenever sie was in one of those moods, and you could usually tell from the unruly condition of Mage's bleach-blond hair and the craggy scowl. Mage became one of Miranda's lovers right off the bat, of course.

I was just sitting on my hands and biting my tongue, reminding myself that I always hated change and then I always got used to it after a little while. This would be fine: change was the ocean and she took care of us.

Then we discovered the spoilage. We had been filtering the ocean water, removing toxic waste, filtering out excess gunk, and putting some of the organic byproducts into our myco-protein vats as a feedstock. Until one day we opened the biggest vat and the stench was so powerful we all started to cry and retch, and we kept crying even after the puking stopped. Shit, that was half our food supply. It looked like our whole filtration system was off, there were remnants of buckystructures in the residue that we'd been feeding to our fungus, and the fungus was choking on them. Even the fungus that wasn't spoiled would have minimal protein yield. This also meant that our filtration system wasn't doing anything to help clean the ocean, at all, because it was still letting the dead pieces of buckycrap through.

Joconda just stared at the mess and finally shook hir head and told us to bury it under the big hillside.

We didn't have enough food for the winter after that, so a bunch of us had to make the trip up north to Marin, by boat and on foot, to barter with some gun-obsessed farmers in the hills. They wanted free labor in exchange for food, so we left Weo and a few others behind to work in their fields. Trudging back down the hill, pulling the first batch of produce in a cart, I kept looking over my shoulder to see our friends staring after us as we left them surrounded by old dudes with rifles.

I couldn't look at the community the same way after that. Joconda fell into a depression that made hir unable to speak or look anyone in the eye for days at a time, and we were all staring at the walls of our poorly repaired dormitory buildings, which looked as though a strong wind could bring them down. I kept remembering myself walking away from those farmers, the way I told Weo it would be fine, we'd be back before anyone knew anything, this would be a funny story later. I tried to imagine myself doing something different. Putting my foot down maybe, or saying fuck this, we don't leave our own behind. It didn't seem like something I would ever do, though. I had always been someone who went along with what everybody else wanted. My one big act of rebellion was coming here to Bernal Island, and I wouldn't have ever come if Juya hadn't already been coming.

Miranda saw me coming and walked the other way. That happened a couple of times. She and I were supposed to have a fancy evening together, I was going to give her a bath even if it used up half my water allowance, but she canceled. We were on a tiny island but I kept only seeing her off in the distance, in a group of others, but whenever I got closer she was gone. At last I saw her walking on the big hill and I followed her up there, until we were almost at eye level with the Transamerica Pyramid coming up out of the flat water. She turned and grabbed at the collar of my shirt and part of my collarbone. "You gotta let me have my day," she hissed. "You can't be in my face all the time. Giving me that look. You need to get out of my face."

"You blame me," I said, "for Weo and the others. For what happened."

"I blame you for being a clingy wet blanket. Just leave me alone for a while. Jeez." And then I kept walking behind her, and she turned and either made a gesture that connected with my chest, or else intentionally shoved me. I fell on my butt. I nearly tumbled head over heels down the rocky slope into the water, but then I got a handhold on a dead root.

"Oh fuck. Are you okay?" Miranda reached down to help me up, but I shook her off. I trudged down the hill alone.

I kept replaying that moment in my head, when I wasn't replaying the moment when I walked away with a ton of food and left Weo and the others at gunpoint. I had thought that being here, on this island, meant that the only past that mattered was the grand, mysterious, rebellious history that was down there under the water, in the wreckage of San Francisco. All of the wild music submerged between its walls. I had thought my own personal past no longer mattered at all. Until suddenly, I had no mental energy for anything but replaying those two memories. Uglier each time around.

And then someone came up to me at lunch, as I sat and ate some of the proceeds from Weo's indenture: Kris, or Jamie, I forget which. And whispered, "I'm on your side." A few other people said the same thing later that day. They had my back, Miranda was a bitch, she had assaulted me. I saw other people hanging around Miranda and staring at me, talking in her ear, telling her that I was a problem and they were with her.

I felt like crying, except that I couldn't find enough moisture inside me. I didn't know what to say to the people who were on my side. I was too scared to speak. I wished Joconda would wake up and tell everybody to quit it, to just get back to work and play and stop fomenting.

The next day, I went to the dining area, sitting at the other end of the long table from Miranda and her group of supporters. Miranda stood up so fast she knocked her own food on the floor, and she shouted at Yozni, "Just leave me the fuck alone. I don't want you on 'my side,' or anybody else. There are no sides. This is none of your business. You people. You goddamn people. What are you people even about?" She got up and left, kicking the wall on her way out.

After that, everybody was on my side.

6
The honeymoon was over, but the marriage was just starting

I rediscovered social media. I'd let my friendships with people back in Fairbanks and elsewhere run to seed during all of this weird, but now I reconnected with people I hadn't talked to in a year or so. Everybody kept saying that Olympia had gotten really cool since I left, there was a vibrant music scene now and people were publishing zootbooks and having storytelling slams and stuff. Meanwhile, the government in Fairbanks had decided to cool it on trying to make the coast fall into line, though there was talk about some kind of loose articles of confederation at some point. Meanwhile, we'd even made some serious inroads against the warlords of Nevada.

I started looking around the dormitory buildings and kitchens and communal play spaces of Bernal, and at our ocean reclamation machines, as if I was trying to commit them to memory. One minute I was looking at all of it as if this could be the last time I would see any of it, but then the next minute I was just making peace with it so I could stay forever. I could just imagine how this moment could be the beginning of a new, more mature relationship with the Wrong Headed crew, where I wouldn't have any more illusions, but that would make my commitment even stronger.

I sat with Joconda and a few others, on that same stretch of shore where we'd all stood naked and launched candles, and we held hands after a while. Joconda smiled, and I felt like sie was coming back to us, so it was like the heart of our community was restored. "Decay is part of the process. Decay keeps the ocean warm." Today Joconda had wild hair with some bright colors in it, and a single strand of beard. I nodded.

Instead of the guilt or fear or selfish anxiety that I had been so aware of having inside me, I felt a weird feeling of acceptance. We were strong. We would get through this. We were Wrong Headed.

I went out in a dinghy and sailed around the big island, went up toward the ruins of Telegraph. I sailed right past the Newsom Spire, watching its carbon fiber cladding flake away like shiny confetti. The water looked so opaque, it was like sailing on milk. I sat there in the middle of the city, a few miles from anyone, and felt totally peaceful. I had a kick of guilt at being so selfish, going off on my own when the others could probably use another pair of hands, but then I decided it was okay. I needed this time to myself. It would make me a better member of the community.

When I got back to Bernal, I felt calmer than I had in ages, and I was able to look at all the others—even Mage, who still gave me the murder eye from time to time—with patience and love. They were all my people. I was lucky to be among them.

I had this beautiful moment, that night, standing by a big bonfire with the rest of the crew, half of us some level of naked, and everybody looked radiant and free. I started to hum to myself, and it turned into a song, one of the old songs that Zell had supposedly brought back from digital extinction. It had this chorus about the wild kids and the war dance and a bridge that doubled back on itself, and I had this feeling, like maybe the honeymoon is over, but the marriage is just beginning.

Then I found myself next to Miranda, who kicked at some embers with her boot. "I'm glad things calmed down," I whispered. "I didn't mean for everyone to get so wound up. We were all just on edge, and it was a bad time."

"Huh," Miranda said. "I noticed that you never told your peeps to cool it, even after I told the people defending me to shut their faces."

"Oh," I said. "But I actually," and then I didn't know what to say. I felt the feeling of helplessness, trapped in the grip of the past, coming back again. "I mean, I tried. I'm really sorry."

"Whatever," Miranda said. "I'm leaving soon. Probably going back to Anaheim-Diego. I heard they made some progress with the nanomechs after all."

"Oh." I looked into the fire, until my retinas were all blotchy. "I'll miss you."

"Whatever." Miranda slipped away. I tried to mourn her going, but then I realized I was just relieved. I wasn't going to be able to deal with her hanging around, like a bruise, when I was trying to move forward. With Miranda gone, I could maybe get back to feeling happy here.

Joconda came along when we went back up into Marin to get the rest of the food from those farmers, and collect Weo and the two others we had left there. We climbed up the steep path from the water, and Joconda kept needing to rest. Close to the water, everything was the kind of salty and moist that I'd gotten used to, but after a few miles, everything got dry and dusty. By the time we got to the farm, we were thirsty and we'd used up all our water, and the farmers saw us coming and got their rifles out.

Our friends had run away, the farmers said. Weo and the others. A few weeks earlier, and they didn't know where. They just ran off, left the work half done. So, too bad, we weren't going to get all the food we had been promised. Nothing personal, the lead farmer said. He had sunburnt cheeks, even though he wore a big straw hat. I watched Joconda's face pass through shock, anger, misery, and resignation, without a single word coming out. The farmers had their guns slung over their shoulders, enough of a threat without even needing to aim. We took the cart, half full of food instead of all the way full, back down the hill to our boat.

We never found out what actually happened to Weo and the others.

7
"That's such an inappropriate line of inquiry I don't even know how to deal"

I spent a few weeks pretending I was in it for the long haul on Bernal Island, after we got back from Marin. This was my home, I had formed an identity here that meant the world to me, and these people were my family. Of course I was staying.

Then one day I realized I was just trying to make up my mind whether to go back to Olympia or all the way back to Fairbanks. In Fairbanks, they knew how to make thick-cut toast with egg smeared across it, you could go out dancing in half a dozen different speakeasies that stayed open until dawn. I missed being in a real city, kind of. I realized I'd already decided to leave San Francisco a while ago, without ever consciously making the decision.

Everyone I had ever had a crush on, I had hooked up with already. Some of them, I still hooked up with sometimes, but it was nostalgia sex rather than anything else. I was actually happier sleeping alone, I didn't want anybody else's knees cramping my thighs in the middle of the night. I couldn't forgive the people who sided with Miranda against me, and I was even less able to forgive the people who sided with me against Miranda. I didn't like to dwell on stuff, but there were a lot of people I had obscure, unspoken grudges against, all around me. Occasionally I would stand in a spot where I'd watched Weo sit and build a tiny raft out of sticks and I would feel the anger rise up all over again. At myself, mostly.

I wondered about what Miranda was doing now and whether we would ever be able to face each other again. I had been so happy to see her go, but now I couldn't stop thinking about her.

The only time I even wondered about my decision was when I looked at the ocean and the traces of the dead city underneath it, the amazing heritage that we were carrying on here. Sometimes I stared into the waves for hours, trying to hear the sound waves trapped in them, but then I started to feel like maybe the ocean had told me everything it was ever going to. The ocean always sang the same notes, it always passed over the same streets and came back with the same sad laughter. Staring down at the ocean only reminded me of how we'd thought we could help to heal her, with our enzyme treatments, a little at a time. I couldn't see why I had ever believed in that fairy tale. The ocean was going to heal on her own, sooner or later, but in the meantime we were just giving her meaningless therapy that made us feel better more than it actually helped. I got up every day and did my chores. I helped to repair the walls and tend the gardens and stuff, but I felt like I was just turning wheels to keep a giant machine going so I would be able to keep turning the wheels tomorrow.

I looked down at my own body, at the loose kelp-and-hemp garments I'd started wearing since I'd moved here. My hands and forearms were thicker, callused, and more veiny with all the hard work I'd been doing here—but also, the thousands of rhinestones in my fingernails glittered in the sunlight, and I felt like I moved differently than I used to. Even with every shitty thing that had happened, I'd learned something here, and wherever I went from now on, I would always be Wrong Headed.

I left without saying anything to anybody, the same way everyone else had.

A few years later, I had drinks with Miranda on that new floating platform that hovered over the wasteland of North America. Somehow we floated half a mile above the desert and the mountaintops—don't ask me how, but it was carbon neutral and all that good stuff. From up here, the hundreds of miles of parched earth looked like piles of gold.

"It's funny, right?" Miranda seemed to have guessed what I was thinking. "All that time, we were going on about the ocean and how it was our lover and our history and all that jazz. But look at that desert down there. It's all beautiful, too. It's another wounded environment, sure, but it's also a lovely fragment of the past. People sweated and died for that land, and maybe one day it'll come back. You know?" Miranda was, I guess, in her early thirties, and she looked amazing. She'd gotten the snaggle taken out of her teeth, and her hair was a perfect wave. She wore a crisp suit and she seemed powerful and relaxed. She'd become an important person in the world of nanomechs.

I stopped staring at Miranda and looked over the railing, down at the dunes. We'd made some pretty major progress at rooting out the warlords, but still nobody wanted to live there, in the vast majority of the continent. The desert was beautiful from up here, but maybe not so much up close.

"I heard Joconda killed hirself," Miranda said. "A while ago. Not because of anything in particular that had happened. Just the depression, it caught up with hir." She shook her head. "God. Sie was such an amazing leader. But hey, the Wrong Headed community is twice the size it was when you and I lived there, and they expanded onto the big island. I even heard they got a seat at the table of the confederation talks. Sucks that Joconda won't see what sie built get that recognition."

I was still dressed like a Wrong Headed person, even after a few years. I had the loose flowy garments, the smudgy paint on my face that helped obscure my gender rather than serving as a guide to it, the straight-line thin eyebrows and sparkly earrings and nails. I hadn't lived on Bernal in years, but it was still a huge part of who I was. Miranda looked like this whole other person, and I didn't know whether to feel ashamed that I hadn't moved on or contemptuous of her for selling out, or some combination. I didn't know anybody who dressed the way Miranda was dressed, because I was still in Olympia where we were being radical artists.

I wanted to say something. An apology, or something sentimental about the amazing time we had shared, or I don't even know what. I had no clue what I wanted to say, and I had no words to put it into. So after a while I just raised my glass and we toasted to Wrong Headedness. Miranda laughed, that same old wild laugh, as our glasses touched. Then we went back to staring down at the wasteland, trying to imagine how many generations it would take before something green came out of it.

I wrote the first half of "Captain Roger in Heaven" to read at a spoken word event organized by superstar blogger Greta Christina. The second half turned out to be a lot trickier, and I wrote a bunch of different endings that didn't quite work. I couldn't crack the ending until I figured out what this story was really about: superficially, it's about sex and death, and the inevitability that any community will go from being loosey-goosey to having Rules and Structure. But I realized that the key to the story was the character of Tanya, the cult leader whom I'd been thinking of as a quasi-villain. Once I stopped and thought about Tanya more carefully, and saw her perspective, I groped my way toward the realization that she was a tragic figure who won an empire by throwing away a chance at real love. Content warnings: sexual assault, torture, religious extremism, mental health issues.

CAPTAIN ROGER IN HEAVEN

1
Marith

Marith didn't mean to start a sex cult, she just wanted to feel sexy for once. She had a stiffness in her neck and shoulders, like a harness she could never unbuckle, and recurrent pain between the notches of her elbows, and she couldn't tell occupational pain from psychosomatic pain anymore. Maybe it was all psychosomatic, one way or another. Marith lived near the Silver Spring station, in one of those narrow brick tenements that's an apostrophe in someone else's sentence. She worked in a record store that also sold sports memorabilia and old video games, and after work she went to the bowling alley, where she never bowled or watched anyone bowl. She sat with her back to the lanes, sipping a Bud Lite and listening to the sound of the balls crashing against the pins, which made her feel like she was on a cruise ship.

This one night, a girl was sitting next to Marith at the bowling alley. Tanya was a grad student in psychology who laughed with a skittishness that said she always put all of herself out there. Tanya's pale skin looked like it bruised at the merest touch, so she probably thought all hurt was superficial, and her blond hair flopped in front of her perfect cheekbones. She was so damn beautiful, and she was talking about operant conditioning in a way that made Marith's heart clatter. Any moment now, Tanya would realize that she was talking to a dull person, and then she would bail.

So when Tanya asked Marith about herself, she lied: "Well," she said, "I work in a record store. But actually I'm apprenticed to Timur. He's a sex prophet. He doesn't like the word 'guru' because it's appropriative, and he's not really a sex 'god' or anything. Just a prophet." She found herself talking about Timur for hours: his shrewd teachings, his ability to collect orgasmic energy (or "Argroms") in a kind of flower vase for later use. His ability to make anyone sexually hectic just by inscribing symbols in midair. Tanya wanted to meet this amazing man, of course, so Marith had to improvise.

"He doesn't want to meet any new people," Marith said, keeping her voice down, so Tanya practically had to kiss her to hear. "He's very secluded and reclusive and secretive. People are always trying to steal his secrets or investigate him or exploit him, so he has to be really really careful. He waited a long time before he would take me back to his vellum, which is what he calls his sanctum."

"Wow," said Tanya, her pale blue eyes widening. "I'm really fascinated by the idea of collecting orgasmic energy. I actually did a big research project on Wilhelm Reich and his theories about cosmic life energy, but I always suspected that the orgone was too nebulous and omnipresent to be useful, and I like the idea of focusing on just sexual energy. Plus I think the notion of collecting energy in a vase rather than a box is really clever, because it's less square. I'm very curious about what kind of techniques your friend is using, it sounds like there must be a mixture of NLP and tantra and a few other things. I promise I won't tell anybody anything, but I would just love to meet this man for myself."

"Well," Marith said. "I'm afraid I can't introduce just anyone to Timur. I have to be able to vouch for you first."

"Is there *anything* I can do to earn your trust?" Tanya said, long slender fingers just resting on Marith's tanned forearm.

At the well of Marith's home, in her narrow bed, Tanya shucked her clothes like she was changing into the best costume ever, and then she bounced on the bed, totally naked and completely hairless as well, her toes fanning in midair as she laughed and demanded that Marith show her just a hint of the secrets of Timur the Sex Prophet.

"Well. I'm not supposed to practice them with outsiders." Marith disrobed more slowly, feeling self-conscious about her rounded workaday body. "But, I mean, also it could be too much for a normal person. I don't want to over-whelm you."

"I'm ready," Tanya said.

"Maybe you should smoke this," Marith said, handing Tanya a pipe and a lighter. "Just to help you get in the right frame of mind so it doesn't shock you too much." She made sure Tanya smoked two whole bowls before she tried to do one of the Sacred Runes. "This one is called the Righteous Goat. Let me get the fingers the right way—just watch out, because this is going to send a pure energy surge right into your neocortex. Are you ready?"

Tanya nodded, total solemnity in her dilated eyes.

Marith spent a minute arranging the fingers of both hands into the coolest goat-shaped pretzel she could manage. Then she turned around and pressed her hands into the center of Tanya's collarbone, pushing her back into the bed so she nearly banged her head against the tiny bookcase. "Reformatum figura!" Marith shouted.

"Ooh," Tanya said, wrinkling her nose and smiling. "I definitely felt some-thing. That was cool."

"You did?" Marith said. "I must tell Timur, he'll be so pleased to hear that."

"Do it again!" Tanya said. Marith did it again.

After that, Marith and Tanya hung out twice a week for a month or two, and Marith teased the younger woman with hints of the forbidden knowl-edge of Timur the Sex Prophet. Unfortunately, by the time Tanya proved that she was ready to meet the great Timur, the Sex Prophet had left town for a few months—he was visiting some of his disciples in Lithuania, and Marith wasn't sure when he would be back. "He told me to keep practicing while he's gone, and also to work on perfecting the Orgasmic Energy Vase."

"I think I know someone who might be able to help us with the vase thing," Tanya said. "There's a cute postdoc in the physics department named Leon, who consulted me for a project he was doing in his spare time on parapsychology—you know, the notion that stray psychic energy could be-come trapped in higher levels of reality, or cosmic 'branes. I think he would be very interested to hear about Timur, and to meet you. Plus he's really, really cute."

"Okay," said Marith, feeling nervous about trying to bring another person in on her Sex Prophet hoax, but not sure how to get out of it. "Okay, sure. I'll check with Timur. But I'm sure he'll say it's fine."

2
Carolyn

Carolyn felt like a walking cliché: thirty-five years old, never had an orgasm. She wasn't repressed; she'd had a decent number of lovers, and one and a half husbands. But she just hadn't quite ever "gotten" there, either on her own or with anybody else, and she'd never wanted to make a big deal about it. She enjoyed the act, she felt thrilled and playful and adored in bed, and she hadn't thought it was worth being goal-oriented or whatever. Maybe she'd read too many issues of *Cosmo* and gotten too good at faking. Now she was alone, after a slew of condescendingly gentle practical jokes, and wasn't sure she needed another permanent presence in her bed ever again.

But then she kept seeing those sex fiends, handing out their literature at the farmers market or roller-skating in the park. Holding hands. Laughing too much. Carolyn decided to take a leaflet as a joke, or a conversation starter at the next committee meeting, and the guy with the cloud beard let his hand brush hers when he wished her a frenzy day. (Friendly day? She couldn't tell if it was "frenzy" or "friendly.") The leaflet talked about their Sex Prophet Timur, who had Ascended to another plane of sexuality, but you could bring him back to Earth with the right hand runes and enough stored energy inside an Orgasmic Energy Vase. It was goofy but also kind of sweet, with all its talk about the importance of being Considerate. The Clan of Miasma didn't seem to impose much morality on its twenty-odd members, but the main exhortation seemed to be Consideration.

Carolyn found herself parking a half a mile down the road from the three-story plantation-style house where the Clan of Miasma mostly lived, like she was just going to scope it out. She ventured a little closer, just close enough to stand by the edge of the gravel driveway, when something flew at her. She flinched—but it was a Frisbee. Somehow, she caught it, and threw it back to the thrower, who was the cute cloud-beard boy who'd given her the leaflet. She wound up playing Frisbee with cloud-beard, whose name was Greg, and another guy named Jamil, for an hour without anybody trying to tell her about Timur or his Sex Prophecies, or Argroms, or nth-dimensional orgasms, or any of that stuff.

"It all just sounds kind of ridiculous," she told Greg.

"Oh, it's totally ridiculous," Greg said. "I've seen proof, but I still don't really believe any of it. I'm just waiting for a better explanation to come along for the things I've seen."

She came to their house three more times without taking off any of her clothing or seeing anybody else naked. They did show her the vases, of which they seemed very proud, and demonstrated to her a little bit of the interdimensional palpation techniques they had been developing.

The fourth time she came out to the Clan of Miasma's house, she couldn't get in at first, because *they* were blocking the driveway. A gang of well-dressed people, mostly white, holding signs with Bible verses on them and praying loudly. One baby-faced man yelled about false idols and people being led into temptation and consigned to hellfire. Carolyn hadn't ever been religious, and she still mostly thought the Clan of Miasma was a bunch of goofy weirdos who would make a good story down the line, but she found herself getting offended on the Clan's behalf by the fact that the First Church of Galilee, the megachurch over in Chevy Chase, had bused in a whole gang of protesters.

They pushed against her, shoving their Bibles in her face and shouting with their starchy breath in her face. One of them even spat on her.

"You people," she shouted at the clean-cut prayerful mob, "have too much time on your hands." They just jostled her harder, cried to Jesus and tried to lay hands on her, until she felt herself destabilized, falling to the ground, in danger of being trampled under their nice boots.

Carolyn finally pushed her way through and marched up to the Clan's veranda. She barely made it inside the house before she tore off all of her own clothing, so emphatically she lost a button. "I want you"—she flung her panties—"to harvest all the goddamn orgasmic energy out of me that you possibly can."

Greg and Jamil looked at each other, raising an eyebrow. "I think we can do that," Greg said.

"Challenge accepted," said Jamil.

Carolyn started spending a lot of time at the house after that, whenever she wasn't working in the oncologist's office where she did the billing, or helping out with the homeless shelter where she volunteered one night per week. She found that being around all these freaks made her feel younger than she'd felt in years, and the orgasms were actually pretty splendid after all. She got to experiment with sex with women and assorted others, and also discovered that threesomes were just more Companionable than other kinds of sex—that was another word the Clan liked, along with "Considerate." They liked things that were "Companionable." There was refreshingly little talk about Timur, their departed Sex Prophet, although people made jokes about him sometimes.

So Carolyn was there the day the government delivered the Visualizer. "What the fuck is this?" Tanya, the perky blonde who was sort of in charge around there, demanded of the man in the gray uniform who rolled up the giant cardboard box on a hand truck.

"Government regulations, ma'am," said the man, who had a few tufts of curly hair under his plain gray cap. "Your religion has reached a large enough membership to receive its own Visualizer."

"Visualizing *what*?" Tanya asked.

"The afterlife, ma'am," the man said, giving her papers on a clipboard to sign.

The device was like a big old television set, but with an alphanumeric keyboard along one side instead of a channel tuner. You could type in the complete name of anyone who had died, recently or long ago, and it would show you where they were in the afterlife. After this technology had been developed, the Christians had pushed through a law insisting that every religion over a certain membership threshold had to own one. Then there had been some controversy, because devout Jews went to no afterlife that the device could visualize, nor could it really represent Nirvana or Samsara, or reincarnation. There had been a bit of a political scandal when people discovered just how many U.S. presidents were being flame-broiled in a very Hieronymus Bosch–inspired hell.

So the members of the Clan of Miasma amused themselves for an hour or two plugging in the names of their grandparents and various rock stars, and their old grade-school teachers. This became too depressing after a while, and they rolled the machine into the corner and put a cloth over it.

By the time Carolyn moved out of her tiny apartment and into the Clan of Miasma's house, she didn't even think of it as joining a cult anymore— she just enjoyed hanging out with these people, and the frankly incredible sex was just a tiny part of a very Companionable existence. Apart from the fact that she sometimes had to cross a line of praying maniacs to go home after work, she stopped thinking of it as a big deal or anything.

Until one day, Carolyn was walking from her car to the homeless shelter, hoisting a big box of hamburger buns for the evening meal they were going to be serving, and she didn't see a beer truck coming out of a convenience store driveway until it crushed her.

After the Clan of Miasma buried Carolyn and had a pretty low-key improvised ceremony—she was the first of their members to die on them, and they hadn't come up with anything yet—they resisted the temptation to look at the Visualizer for as long as possible. But at three in the morning on the night after they'd put her in the ground, Greg found himself coming down the stairs in just his boxer shorts and turning the machine on.

And there was Carolyn, submerged naked in a lake of fire, with demons pulling out her eyes and tongue with exquisite slowness. Those fuckers had been right. She'd gone to hell.

3
Leon

"We don't know that this thing even works." Tanya gestured at the hateful box yet again. It was still showing Carolyn in hell. Now they were flaying her skin in a slow spiral, like an orange peel, while she begged someone, anyone, for mercy. "It could be a trick. A hoax. It's showing exactly what they would want us to see."

"If it's a trick," said Greg, who'd been one of Carolyn's lovers and the closest to her of anybody, "they sure did a good job of capturing her likeness. How did they do that?"

They kept turning it off, but then that felt like turning their backs on her. Their friend and lover, being tortured. Brutalized. By the worst atrocities that an ageless imagination could come up with. Things that would be considered war crimes, or the actions of a major sociopath, if anybody did them on Earth. The games never stopped, but they changed every time anyone looked.

Meanwhile, the First Church of Galilee seemed to gain strength and intensity from what had happened to Carolyn. They were there every day, blocking the driveway, shaking their leather-bound volumes, and waving signs about the fire that was waiting for everyone in this house. The Reverend Clark Denson himself seemed energized, licking his lips, like he'd just eaten a steak dinner.

For days, nobody could even talk, and when they talked about their vases and the teachings of Timur and all the rest of that crap, it was with a weariness, like they were all preparing to grow up at last. What choice did they have, now that they knew Pascal's Wager was rigged? They all had a gun to their heads.

Leon couldn't sleep for three days, because he could dream of nothing but Carolyn's face, distorted, as though she was squeezing out tears with her cheek muscles. Endless Promethean mutilation. Leon had barely known Carolyn, and he'd never had sex with her or anything. (He'd never been intimate with anybody here, aside from one fully clothed cuddle session with Marith, the Clan of Miasma's housekeeper and head bottle washer.) Leon was here for the physics.

Leon's postdoc had been going down the tubes when Tanya had shown up one day and told him about this wild orgasmic energy project. The notion of chasing a quasi-Reichian whippoorwill had seemed liberating, since he'd spent months bashing his head against a wall made of superstrings. Soon they were collecting energies that Leon could not name, much less understand, and it had only made sense to start recruiting more subjects. Until suddenly they had a house full of people, and a name, and teachings. Leon couldn't help feeling he'd helped lead Carolyn into damnation.

Microsleep seized Leon, pulling him into tiny slices of dreams, and in them Carolyn always called out for his help, his personally. Leon took comfort in dumb repetition, like brushing his teeth for two straight hours, and that's when he found the answer.

"Wait a minute," he said out loud, to the bathroom mirror. "Carolyn went to *their* afterlife because we don't have one of our own. We just need to make our own afterlife, and then we'll be fine. Maybe we can even rescue Carolyn eventually."

He explained it to Tanya twice before she could understand his sleep-deprived rambling. Then she shook her head. "How do you *make* an afterlife?" she asked. "Isn't it just something that exists? What would you even make one out of?"

"I don't know," Leon said. "I'm guessing we would make it out of orgasmic energy. We have vases and vases, lest you forget. Maybe if you get enough

Argroms focused in one spot, you can open up a pocket reality? And then you just have to set up some kind of conduit so that people go there after they die." Leon started to make one of his trademark weird jokes, but he was too wiped, and this conversation was already weird enough.

"Shit," Tanya said. "You're right, we have to do this. But . . . damn. I mean, if we were supposed to have our own afterlife, wouldn't Timur have said something? I wish Timur was still here. He would know what to do."

"What was he like?" Leon asked. "Timur? I mean, what was it like to be around him?"

Tanya bit her lip and looked down, then looked up again with a practiced expression. "Timur was very, very gentle," she said. "He was a very gentle and kind person. I feel like he still talks to me sometimes."

"Well, if he talks to you any time soon," said Leon, "ask him how to open an nth-dimensional conduit that can capture someone's essence immediately after death. Because I have a feeling the physics are going to be a beast."

Leon looked out at the window at the dozen or so people waving their signs on the driveway. He could just make out what they were chanting, if he listened hard. They seemed to be able to sustain anger and judgment for hours, without needing to refuel. The longer he stared, the more it seemed to Leon that the Christians were generating their afterlife, focusing psychic energy so that they made a stable conduit and created something on the other side of it. They were almost writing lines of code in the fabric of reality.

Leon still didn't have sex with any of the other Clan members, but he watched them more intently than ever. He measured their Argrom levels and tried to build some toolsets to direct the amassed energy to a single point in spacetime until it began to weaken and perturb. Like a lens distorting, or the rainbows that form on a soap bubble. The more people having sex at once, the greater the dimensional flux. "You may want to start recruiting new members more aggressively," Leon told Tanya.

He also noticed something else. One time, Jamil the chubby comic book geek started spanking Donnie the aspiring bluegrass musician with one hand while sticking two fingers of his other hand in Donnie's butthole, and Jamil teased Donnie about his cute squeals. And Leon discovered that the readings were all-of-a-sudden off the frigging chart. There was a localized spacetime event forming in the middle of the room, and it was practically like the pearly gates were opening to their very own private heaven.

"Sexual humiliation," Leon told Tanya that evening. "It seems to increase the concentration and directionality of the energy flow. Also, edgeplay. Bondage, animal masks, clamps, enemas. I would experiment. I think we're very close to a breakthrough. So to speak."

Tanya nodded slowly, like she was processing. "I'll try, but I can't pressure anybody to do anything they're not comfortable with."

"There's something else," Leon said. "Once we have a stable pocket universe, it'll be basically just a blank void. A tabula rasa. It's almost like programming a computer: we need to learn the language of afterlife creation and use it to construct a world that any of us would want to spend eternity in. I'm guessing that's going to require a lot of dogma, or liturgy, or whatever."

"You focus on trying to stabilize the pocket universe," Tanya said. "Leave the rest to me. I think I know who to talk to about making it a proper afterlife."

4
Sophie

The first few months Sophie was living at the Clan of Miasma's house, she barely even noticed Marith, the lady who seemed to be constantly scrubbing and cooking and keeping to herself. Tanya was their leader and frequently the center of attention, and Greg was the fun bouncy one. Jamil told all the silliest jokes and helped them get their sense of purpose back after Carolyn died. But the dark, curvy Marith just faded into the background, and she disappeared when everyone else was making sexy time.

But then one day Sophie noticed Marith standing in the kitchen watching some bread rise or something, wearing puffy oven mitts and a streaked apron over a long cotton dress. She leaned over to open a drawer, and her dress clung to her hips. Marith let out a deep sigh and straightened up, looking out the window with a dreamy look in her brown-green eyes. As if the snowdrifts were fairy dust. Her auburn hair slipped out of its tie and fell along her neck, just grazing her collarbone, and her small mouth was pursing.

Sophie was filled with a sudden, powerful desire.

"I'd like to give you a bath," Sophie told Marith. Who smiled, slowly.

Sophie spent hours trying to come up with the perfect bath scenario. Candles, sure, but what else? Incense? Maybe a bath bomb from that fancy bath-and-body place downtown? What kind of music would make a bath sexier or more luxurious? Sophie wound up playing *Stevie Wonder's Original Musiquarium I,* and she knelt at either end of the tub, kneading first Marith's shoulders and then her wide, expressive feet. Marith let out a slow sigh of pleasure.

Sophie was one of those people who are better at being desired than desiring. She'd had to learn from scratch as an adult how to sit and stand and walk, how to style her black hair, how to dress and do her nails and makeup. A feral creature until her early twenties, when she was doing a comp lit degree at American U., she had taken herself in hand at great expense. She'd had no idea how to respond when men, and some women, started flirting with her and asking her out.

So the Clan of Miasma had come as a huge relief to Sophie. She could have sex with people she liked and admired, without having to go through the whole process of flirting and idealizing the other person, and being idealized, and imagining their sexuality in relation to your own. Just hook up, as long as everything else seemed copacetic. Sophie had pretty much nonstop sex, with all sorts of people, her first few months in the Clan, and they had built a whole Sophie Yang section of orgasmic energy vases. Eventually, though, she'd kind of slowed down, and the sex was no longer such a big thing for her.

Marith was the first person Sophie had ever actually propositioned, in her entire life. It felt thrilling and scary—weird in a different way than learning to accept propositions from other people had been. But worth the plunge.

Sophie leaned in, cupping Marith's face in both hands, and kissed her in a cloud of steam. Marith let out a deep moan, which encouraged Sophie to go further, and soon she had her hands around both of Marith's breasts, kneading and splashing. They ended up on Marith's bed in the back room, where nobody ever went, and Sophie took great precision in laying Marith down and exploring from her instep to her inner thighs with her tongue and her fingers.

Sophie slept in Marith's bed that night and woke up feeling even more definite that she'd found where she belonged. They held each other a long time, curled around each other's knees and elbows, and Marith smiled at Sophie with a drowsy warmth. "We should get up and have breakfast and start on our chores," Marith said, but Sophie said just five minutes more.

Tanya came to see Marith a couple mornings later, while Sophie was still dozing in Marith's bed. "I need to talk to you," Tanya whispered, sounding way less authoritative than Sophie had ever heard. "About Timur. I need to know more about him."

"I already told you everything, twice," Marith whispered back. "You know more than I do, at this point."

"But I don't know anything. How did you meet him? What exactly did he say, the last time you saw him? What does it mean that he transcended to another plane of sexuality?"

"You already know all of the answers," Marith said. "In your heart."

"For fuck's sake. Don't give me that. I am comfortable with a certain amount of bullshit for the sake of group cohesion, but this is me you're talking to. Just tell me the truth for once."

"Okay. Listen, Timur never really . . . Timur was kind of a . . ." Marith took a deep breath, as if she was going to say something difficult. Then she turned and looked over her shoulder at Sophie, who was sitting up in bed listening to this. Tanya couldn't see Sophie, from where she was standing in the doorway, but catching sight of her new lover seemed to help Marith make a decision. "Timur taught me a rune, that I never showed anybody else, that could maybe let us reach that higher sexual plane. It's called the Hair Tsunami. 'Hair' can be spelled either way."

"We need it. So bad," Tanya said. "We think we've managed to create a stable opening in spacetime after all, and we've glimpsed a pocket universe on the other side. But we need to turn it into something that has enough consistency and substance that you could spend eternity there. Marith, this is serious. You know what happened to Carolyn."

"I do," Marith said. "So the thing about Timur ascending to another plane of sexuality, here's what I think it means. I think it has to do with tuning in to the right kind of awareness. Like when you're getting close to an orgasm and you feel like you're leaving not just your body, but all of your *you*. Becoming free of all of the accumulated garbage, the neurosis, all the slowly decaying self-image that makes us who we are. Eventually, you might dissolve into a kind of blissful state of collective awareness, but it could take a couple million years."

"So basically," said Tanya, "a kind of slow shedding of character armor. Okay. That makes sense. But please, you gotta teach me that rune. And tell me every single detail you know about the cosmology and stuff. Where Timur came from, what he said before he went away, what he believed in, everything."

"I will," Marith said. "Come find me after I get done helping with lunch. I'll give you the full download."

Sophie could barely wait until the door closed. "So wait. You were the only one who ever met Timur in real life? Our glorious founder? So you're *the* person who actually knows what we're doing here? You have to tell me everything. I can't believe it."

Marith just smiled and finished putting on her floor-length skirt. "Timur didn't found this community. We all did. It means whatever we decide it means."

"Oh, la-di-da," Sophie said. "That's a lovely sentiment. But Timur was the one who gave us the runes, and, and the vases, and the principles we supposedly live by. And you were his anointed one. Why aren't you in charge, anyway? Why are you hiding out back here and letting Tanya and Greg call all the shots? What is that about?"

"It's my choice," Marith said slowly. She put on one shoe, as if she hadn't yet decided whether to put on the other one. "I never wanted to be in the forefront of any of this. I didn't even expect it to become such a big deal. I didn't choose anything, really. Timur chose me and gave me his teachings, and then Tanya found me. I was just a vessel, I guess."

Sophie kept laughing, until she worried that Marith would think she was being mocked. "You are so much more than that." Sophie came over to where Marith was sitting at the foot of the bed, and touched her shoulders gently. "You're the heart of this community, I saw it even before I knew any of this. Maybe it's time for you to step forward and tell everybody what you know. You can't hide forever."

Marith shrugged. Then she turned and gave Sophie a slow kiss, touching Sophie's face with one palm and then breathing in Sophie's ear. Neither of them got out of bed that morning.

5
Brady

Stars showed through the slats in the porch swing, like skin under fishnet stockings, with just a blade of the young moon coming into view every now and then. Brady felt at peace lying there under the swing, even though he'd taken too much of something, and then gotten frozen out of the orgy inside the big old house. Who gets shot down at an orgy? Brady felt the planks under his fingertips. His mouth tasted like the dry ice machine from every rave in art school, along with that glitter that was half edible and everyone always forgot which half was which. Brady was going to get up and stagger home to the Ex any moment now. Then someone sat on the swing and started talking in a high, melodic voice about the death drive. Her voice was so sweet. Her ass hovered above Brady's face, denim blue, with a gluteal fold that enclosed every possibility in life. "But for people to cathect onto *me* as an alternative to confronting mortality salience is almost like, I don't know, libidinal bankruptcy—" Something in her voice made Brady certain of the rightness of his act, even as he reached one hand through the gap between the swing's two halves, and made a cup.

Brady's hand got trapped. The owner of that incredible butt, the blonde girl who'd hosted the orgy—Tracey? Tanya? Tanya.—had leapt to her feet, and she had Brady's wrist in a crushing grip. Brady's whole body was contorted because his hand was stuck in the swing. Blood flow crimped.

"Do that again and I'm calling the cops, asshole. Get the fuck out of here and never come back."

He tried to explain that it was all fun and he meant nothing by it, and this was an orgy after all, but she flung him off the porch, using his own unsteady weight to send him into the driveway. Gravel all up in his face.

The Ex was awake when Brady got home. She had the television on, some dating game show, and was talking to her friend on the phone while swiping pictures on a tablet screen, and Brady had a pang of remembering when he had adored her lack of attention span. He and the Ex had broken up six months ago, but neither of them could afford to move out, and they were almost better at ignoring each other than they'd been at loving each other. Except as Brady headed for the walk-in closet where he'd set up a bedroll, he heard the Ex say "death drive" to her friend, and then he had to wait for her to get off the phone.

"What does that mean, 'death drive'?"

The Ex shrugged. "Freudian bullshit. We seek out painful experiences on purpose, so we can numb ourselves, because what we actually want is to return to nothingness."

Brady had a mental image of his hand coming up out of a hanging chair, like a horror movie. "People seek out pain because they're stupid, though." That was the thing Brady had left art school understanding: people make complicated pieces of art to explain human behavior, when the real expla-nation is almost always assholishness.

"Like I said: bullshit." And then the Ex had headphones on, blasting Tay-Swif, plus the TV turned up loud, and Brady went into his closet and groped in the dark for earplugs.

Months passed. Brady finally got his own place, miles from DC or Bal-timore, with a couple of roommates who were half his age. A real bedroom meant he could do art again, in theory, and he set aside a few hours per week for cursing himself in front of a pile of unused art supplies.

One day Brady had a stabbing pain in his side, right where he'd hit the ground when Tanya threw him off the porch. Justice, he figured, but when the pain worsened he went to the ER, and they called it hepatitis. Trans-plant list so long, his name was on the elbow of the person holding the paper. Basically screwed. He read on the internet about people getting drugged and waking up in a bathtub full of ice with their liver missing, but Brady had no clue where to get that much ice, or a big enough tub.

Brady sat there in the ER, on the bench with the metal armrests, and tried to process the fact that he was going to die. He clutched at his side, which somehow hurt way worse now, and wondered who would miss him. Who would even pour one out at his wake. Would the Ex even show up? Then he realized: he wasn't just dying, he was going to hell.

Brady hung out at a punk house where they had one of those Visualizers, which they'd just started selling at Walmart. There was this one painter, named Captain Roger, who used to have a show on PBS where he would paint a whole landscape in half an hour, wearing a sailor hat, and Brady had watched it every day in art school, eating Froot Loops from the box. Now Captain Roger was dead, but he'd gone to heaven because he was a devout Episcopalian. He still did a whole painting in half an hour, but he was sur-rounded by angels and seraphim, and he painted waterfalls with sparkles and rainbows coming out of them. The internet was full of gifs of Captain Roger in heaven.

At some point, the punks got tired of watching Captain Roger and some-one suggested switching to the Hell Channel. The Hell Channel was a guy named James Dixon who had been a hot comedian for a minute, under the name of Jammy Dicks. He even got on *The Daily Show* once, as a guest cor-respondent. Now he was being deconstructed—his intestines unrolled, his organs sorted into neat piles, and so on—while he screamed and screamed. The punks recited Jammy Dicks's most emblematic comedy routines in unison, like the one about fat girls and K-Y Jelly, while they watched him get taken apart by leering, fire engine red monsters.

The next thing Brady knew, one of the punks was slapping his mouth while also talking in a very soothing voice. "Hey, man, it's cool, you're safe. We're all cool here." Another slap, which rattled Brady's head. Brady realized that he was shaking and barking, and his face was soaked. He had no memory of the past few minutes. Brady tried to say that it was fine, he was under control, but it came out as yipping. His pants were wetter than his face.

"Shit, we better change the channel," one of the punks said.

They switched to Jiffy, who was an up-and-coming Visualizer star. Jiffy had been a gay rights activist in the seventies, and then a Radical Faerie in the nineties, and now he was a giant purple unicorn, with a dolphin's tail instead of back legs. He trotted/swam across the shimmering Fields of Liberation, under the beneficent smile of Timur the Sex Prophet, until he met a swarm of pixies (which were apparently another dead perv, named Rebekah). Brady got his tongue back in his mouth, started to feel calmer again. Timur seemed to smile directly at Brady, like it was all going to be fine.

The skinny blonde, Tanya, wouldn't even let Brady in the house. Brady was working hard to avoid looking like a crazy person. He controlled his eyes so they didn't bug out. He was not muttering to himself in the middle of a conversation with another human. Even with his eyes open, he kept seeing Jammy Dicks having his body parts alphabetized. A large part of Brady felt like he was already in hell, and it was exhausting to pretend otherwise. "Please," Brady said. "I'm dying, they're going to get me. Please, I need Timur. Please."

Tanya actually rolled her eyes. "I'm sorry," she said through the chain. "I truly am. We have a whole set of teachings now, we came up with seventy-two categories of Consideration, based on Timur's precepts. There's just no way we could accept you. Try the Hare Krishnas, or Eckankar."

Brady lost track of time, and then two large men were restraining him and he had blood in his eyes and mouth. "Not my fault!" he said. The two men gripping his arms were not demons, and they were not tearing his body apart. Important to remember. Blood mask disguised everything as itself.

The porch light was a dark sun. The hands let go of Brady and he immediately lost balance and crashed. He heard a dread wail, coming closer. He lay in a fetal position under the porch swing, and he could see starlight through the slats again.

6
Tanya

Ernest Becker had ruined anal sex for Tanya. Any time she took it up the ass, or penetrated someone else anally with toys or a strap-on, she found herself thinking about Becker's famous dictum, "We are gods with anuses." To Becker, who wrote *The Denial of Death*, this contradiction defined human nature: we are capable of such brilliance, such soaring imagination, but we still have to expel dead matter through our buttholes, reminding us we are going to die. As a grad student, Tanya became consumed with Becker's idea that you would go raving insane if you ever accepted the reality of death, even after her adviser (a Žižek fanatic) insisted that awareness of mortality was a precondition for consciousness. This bitter debate was why Tanya wrote in Sharpie on a classroom whiteboard, a species of textual murder-suicide that ended her academic career.

Now Tanya hunched on the caved-in sofa, listening to Greg insisting that they needed more rules so that people like that Brady asshole never even came near the Clan of Miasma. "There's going to be an army of Bradys at our door. We need a whole set of new rules, to weed out the shitheels." Tanya remembered when Greg used to be easygoing.

Tanya was only half listening to Greg. She couldn't help staring at Marith, who held hands with her new sweetie, Sophie, on a single tiny ottoman. The look of contentment on Marith's face, the faint flush as Sophie's free hand grazed Marith's ear. Marith had emerged all at once from her isolation and started socializing with the rest of the Clan. Tanya couldn't even explain it to herself, but seeing Marith with Sophie felt like an unresolvable contradiction.

At first, Tanya thought she was feeling threatened by Marith's presence because Marith actually had a link to Timur, one that Tanya only pretended to have. But then she realized she didn't give a shit about her authority—she kept hearing that Joni Mitchell song in her head nonstop, the one that goes

"Lately I wonder what I do it for." Tanya's phone had not stopped shivering in weeks. People needed answers: about the 72 Precepts or the meaning of Desire without Self, or how they were going to get a plumber on the Saturday of a three-day weekend because the toilet was barfing again. The look in Brady's eyes, right before he started beating his head against the wall of their house, kept coming back to Tanya in flashes. Tanya used to worry the Clan of Miasma would go completely off the rails, but now she had the opposite fear: that her little family might be the only sanity left in a world of gods with anuses.

Marith didn't even notice Tanya's desperate gaze. Meanwhile, Timur kept staring at Tanya, with depthless eyes that never needed to blink.

The Sex Prophet hovered in the sky over their afterlife, Shimsanpa—blazing with inner light, like the sun in an old *Teletubbies* episode. He never spoke, but sometimes he seemed to see through the screen of the Visualizer, and even maybe react to things people said in his presence. He was a Lithuanian man in his fifties or early sixties, with a high forehead, a neat beard that had one wispy braid hanging down, and a thin-lipped smile.

Timur, as an actual physical presence, had not been in any of the visions or lessons or maps of the afterlife that Tanya had cobbled together from what Marith had told her. But here he was. Tanya had started to see Timur's face as an indictment of her failure to make the Sex Prophet's teachings come alive. She'd left a Timur-shaped hole, and the dozen Clan recruits who had died thus far had filled it, with an actual Timur. Or else this was the real Timur and he had come to join his people. Either way, he creeped Tanya the fuck out.

"We need personality tests," Greg was saying.

"You know who has personality tests?" Leon said. "The fucking Scientologists."

Greg held up a tablet, with that website that ranked religions according to quality of afterlife, plus ease of getting into the nice version for anyone who joined. The Clan of Miasma was right there at the top. "Just wait until we have a few thousand people in Shimsanpa, and they all have friends and relatives who want to join them," he said. "Shimsanpa is clearly a product, at least in part, of the imaginations of the people who go there. Letting even just one douchebag in could be catastrophic."

Tanya tried again to make eye contact with Marith, but she caught Sophie's eye instead. Sophie smiled at her, but it was not a friendly smile.

"I want to hear what Tanya has to say." The challenge in Sophie's voice was unmistakable. "Tanya, you knew Timur better than anybody, right? So what would Timur say?" As Sophie spoke, Timur seemed to wink.

Of *course*. Marith had told Sophie the truth, that Tanya was a fraud. Tanya tried to play it off: "Well, I mean, Timur! He's inside all of us." But this sounded shitty and unconvincing, even to her. What kind of half-assed cult leader was she? She tried for a tone of reassurance, but then she caught Timur's leering eye again and found herself in that kind of downward spiral where the fakery just eats itself. She'd burned out on dreading this moment, but now that it was here, she still couldn't stand it. "I," Tanya said, "I mean . . . You know, I think. I mean. I don't know."

Sophie kept dropping hints as subtle as dildos, and everybody started to wonder what was up. Timur seemed to laugh until his head wagged, like if he had a belly it would be heaving.

Tanya got up and walked out of the living room and onto the porch, where she nearly stepped on three people she didn't recognize who were daisy-chaining naked under that porch swing that Tanya kept wanting to throw in a bonfire. Brady was dead, and Tanya had not been able to summon the aplomb to look him up on the Visualizer. Out on the lawn the Christians waved signs and Tanya marched right up to them. The Reverend Clark Denson shook with rage—no, wait, it was tremors, and the left side of his face appeared immobilized, along with his left leg.

"So you've made your own heaven." The Reverend Clark Denson spat between facial tics. "Do you think that makes you God?"

Tanya shook her head. All she could think of to say was, "I don't believe in heaven."

Tanya walked down the road, past subdivisions where people were shouting in disjointed rhythms, past strip malls where tires and appliances were burning in the parking lot, past a Primitive Baptist church where a hostage crisis was taking place and the police spoke into bullhorns. She kept walking until her knees and hips were sore, under a sun that was strangely distant and faceless.

Somehow Tanya ended up at the bowling alley where she had first met Marith. She stood in the parking lot for a moment, watching the neon pins flicker, and thought about how she had come here with a couple other grad students, right after the Sharpie incident. They'd bowled a couple hours, and Tanya had kept noticing this beautiful girl at the bar, looking at neither the lanes nor the big-screen TV. She was just in her own head, as her hands played off each other, like they might have been fairy tale puppets. Tanya kept looking over at this girl, whose narrow lips always pursed, except when they lifted into a wicked half-smile. A couple days later, Tanya had gone back to bowl alone, and the girl was there again, but none of Tanya's attempts at flirting had even made an impression. When Tanya went a third time to the bowling alley, she'd needed twenty minutes in this parking lot to psych herself up—*you can do this, you are a flirting wizard*—before she'd sat herself down next to the cute girl and just introduced herself.

Now Tanya sat at that same bar, with a plastic cup of MGD, staring at the lines of notifications on her phone until she turned it off. On a weekday afternoon, she had the place to herself, except for one old guy at the bar and a couple of ladies bowling. The carpet underfoot was plastic shag, almost like a miniature golf course.

Sitting here, Tanya saw things more clearly than she had in months. She remembered Marith's smile as she'd spun this whole story about Timur, how shy and playful she'd sounded. Unlike anybody Tanya had ever met. Tanya tried to imagine the life she and Marith could have had. Just the two of them, living in an apartment above an antiquarian bookstore, eating the shitty fake Dan-Dan noodles that Tanya used to make out of instant ramen, soy sauce, Sriracha, and Skippy peanut butter. Every night, Marith could have told Tanya more stories, about Timur or anything else she wanted. They could have fallen asleep watching television together, or reading books on human sexuality and folklore. Maybe she could have taught Marith how to bowl. Tanya was starting to realize that the Clan of Miasma was a consolation prize.

Tanya had this idea, in the back of her head, that Marith would somehow know where she had gone and would come looking for her. The only person who could possibly guess Tanya's location was Marith, and maybe she would show up alone. The two of them could talk in private, and Tanya could apologize, explain herself at last. Marith would beg Tanya to come back to the Clan, because Marith didn't want to be stuck being the voice of Timur herself, but maybe also because Marith still cared for Tanya? Maybe Marith would even say that she understood, and it wasn't Tanya's fault that Marith's private fancy had become this whole production. Tanya had the whole conversation mapped out in her head.

Marith never showed. After a few MGDs, Tanya felt wiped out, and the darkness outside was triggering a kind of primitive shelter instinct. She could probably crash with Joyce, one of her grad school classmates, for a few days. But she kept remembering that she'd left an awful mess back at the Clan house, and it was her responsibility. She had made her choice a long time ago. The power went out at the bowling alley, and Tanya was left staring at the silhouettes of bottles. Someone dropped a bowling ball on their own foot, and their yelps echoed around the room. Tanya's head started to throb and she was seeing migraine blobs, like afterimages of neon, as she sat alone in total darkness.

lover" is another quasi-sequel to one of my novels (just like "If You Take My Meaning"). The good news is there are no spoilers for *All the Birds in the Sky* in "Clover," and you don't need to have read the book to appreciate any of it. After *All the Birds in the Sky* was published, I started hearing from readers that I'd left a loose end: What happened to Berkley the cat? I learned the hard way that you should never leave the fate of an adorable creature unresolved.

Without going too deep into spoiler territory, Patricia the young witch went off to magic school and left her beloved cat behind in the care of her horrible family. So how did Patricia rescue Berkley? I decided the answer was a lot more complicated, and it starts with a couple of characters who don't appear in *All the Birds*: Anwar and Joe.

Heads up: this story contains brief mentions of homophobia and Islamophobia, and a moment of fat-shaming.

CLOVER

The day after Anwar and Joe got married, a man showed up on their doorstep with a cat hunched in the cradle of his arms. The man was short and thin, almost child size, with a pale, weathered face. The cat was black, with a white streak on his stomach and a white slash on his face. The man congratulated them on their nuptials and held out the squirming cat. "This is Berkley," he said. "If you take him into your home, you'll have nine years of good luck."

Before Anwar and Joe had a chance to debate the matter of adoption, Berkley was already hiding in their apartment somewhere. They found themselves googling the closest place to get a cat bed, a litter box, and some grain-free, low-fat organic food for an indoor cat. It was a chilly day, with scattered clouds that turned the sunset into a broken yolk.

Berkley didn't come out of hiding for a month. Food disappeared from his bowl, and his litter box filled up when nobody was looking, but the cat himself was a no-show. Until one night Anwar had a nightmare that the tanks cracked and his precious, life-giving beer sprayed everywhere. He woke to find the cat perched on the side of the bed, eyes lit up, one leg outstretched.

Anwar froze for a moment, then tentatively reached out an arm and touched the cat's back so lightly the fur lifted. Then Berkley scooted in next to Anwar and fell asleep, thrumming slightly. From then on, Berkley slept on their bed at night.

Their luck didn't become miraculous or anything, but things did go well for them. Anwar's microbrews grew popular, especially Nubian Nut and Butch Goddess, and he even managed to open a small brewpub, an "airy cavern," in the trendy warehouse district between NC State and downtown, not far from where that leather bar used to be. Joe documented a couple of major atrocities without becoming a statistic himself and wrote a white paper about genocide that he really felt might could make genocides a bit less likely. Anwar and Joe stayed together, and Joe's hand along Anwar's lower ribs always made him feel safe and amazed. Everyone they knew was suffering—like Marie, whose restaurant went under because she couldn't get half the ingredients she needed due to the drought, and then she went back to Ohio to care for an uncle who'd gotten the antibiotic-resistant meningitis, and wound up getting sick herself. But Anwar and Joe kept being good to each other, and when problems came, they muddled through.

They almost didn't notice the ninth anniversary of Berkley's arrival. By now, the cat was the defining feature of their home, the lodestone. Berkley's moods were their household's moods: his pleasure, their pleasure. They went across town to get him the exact food he wanted, and kept him well supplied with toys and cat grass, not to mention an enormous climbing tree. Anwar's most popular stout was the Black Cat's Tail.

Nine years after Berkley's arrival, to the day, another man showed up at their door, with another cat. A female this time, a fluffy calico with an intense glare in her wide yellow eyes. This cat did not squirm or fidget, but instead had a wary stillness.

"This is Patricia," the big bearded lumbersexual white dude said without introducing himself. "You won't have any extra luck if you take her in, but she'll be a good companion for Berkley." He deposited her on their doorstep and skipped away before Anwar or Joe had a chance to ask any questions.

They decided Patricia was an odd name for a cat, and named her Clover instead, because of the pattern of the spots on her back.

Berkley had worked for years to get Anwar and Joe's apartment under control, and this represented both a creative enterprise and a labor of love. He had carved out cozy beds atop the laundry hamper, inside the old wicker basket that contained extra brewing supplies, and in the hutch where Joe kept his beloved death metal concert shirts. Berkley knew exactly where the sunbeam came through the slanty front windows in the mornings, and the best hiding places for when Anwar brought out the terrifying vacuum cleaner monster, versus when Anwar and Joe started shouting after Joe came home from one of his trips. Berkley had trained both men to sleep in exactly the right positions for him to curl up between their legs.

And now this new cat, this jag-faced maniac, sprinted around the front room, the bedroom, the kitchenette, the bathrooms—even the laundry nook! She trampled everything with her wild feet. She put her scent everywhere. She slept on the sofa, where Joe sat and stroked her shiny fur with both hands. She was just all over everything.

Berkley made no secret of his feelings on the subject of this invasion. His oratorio spanned two octaves and had an infinite number of movements. But his pleas and remonstrations went unheeded, as if his companionship were a faded, shredded old toy that had lost all its scent. Berkley should have known. This was the way of things: you get a sweet deal for a while, but just when you get comfortable, someone always comes and rips it away.

This lesson, Berkley had learned as a kitten. His first proper human had been a young girl, who had sworn to protect him, and Berkley had promised to watch over her in turn. Somehow, they had struck this deal in the language of cats, which made it much larger than the usual declarations that cats and people always make to each other. And then she had disappeared.

Berkley never knew what had happened, only that he'd had a friend and then she was gone. He was left alone in this giant wooden house, where every smell was a doorway. He'd searched for her over and over, his tail down and his head upcast. He had cried much too loud for his own good. There were still people in that house, but they didn't love Berkley, or even wish him well. Their angry shouts and stomping boots had echoed off the ancient walls ever since Berkley's friend disappeared. Every time he emerged from hiding to call out to his lost friend, he risked getting plucked off his feet by grabby hands.

He kept thinking he heard her or smelled her, but no. This always set off the wailing again.

Quick quick quick sleep.

Quick quick quick sleep.

Sometimes the grabby hands caught him, and then his hard-gotten dignity was all undone. His body bent into shapes where it didn't want to go.

They heard Berkley cry, the angry people, and they shouted, they pounded the walls. He didn't have a way to stop crying.

"Friend" didn't mean to Berkley the same thing it would to a dog, or a human. But this girl had been the shoulder he slept on, the hand that scritched his ear, the voice that sang to him. Even the cozy old attic felt colder and darker, and the old wooden house smelled like nothing but mildew.

Berkley was just letting go of the last of his kittenhood when another pair of hands had lifted him, gently, and brought him to this new house, where the scents were different (yeast, flowers, nuts) but the people were kind. Berkley forgot almost everything in life, but he never entirely forgot the girl, his original disappointment.

The same way the girl had been taken away from Berkley with zero warning or good-bye, now this new cat was going to steal from him all his comfort. Clover tried to talk to him a few times, but he was having exactly none of that. Berkley hissed at her like she was made of poison.

The thing is, Anwar really believed, deep down, in the nine years of good luck. He always referred to Berkley as their *maneki-neko*, like one of those Japanese cat statues that waves a paw in the window and brings in good fortune. When the second guy showed up exactly nine years later, with another cat, and he knew so much, that clinched it.

Anwar had a sick feeling: *Our luck just ran out.*

Raleigh was an okay friendly city, mostly, but lately when he found himself downtown at night, he felt like he was going to get jumped any minute. Big scary dudes had followed him out to his truck from the bar once or twice, but Anwar had always gotten away. The mosque in Durham had gotten graffiti-ed, and the gay bar off I-40, bricked. Inside the bar, Anwar was getting more ignorant tipsy people up in his face, asking why he was brewing alcoholic drinks anyway—when hello, the Egyptians *invented* beer, thank you very much. The barback, a large Hungarian named Vinnie, had needed to eject more and more abusive drunks recently. Anwar didn't want to live in fear, so instead he lived in the sweet spot between paranoia and rage.

The one-bedroom apartment, with its scuffed hardwood floors, crimson drapes, and shelves sagging with ancient books, always seemed like a refuge. Locking the door from the inside, Anwar always took a deep breath, like his lungs were expanding to the size of the stucco walls. He felt ten years older outdoors than indoors.

But lately, Joe woke up angry, because of funding cuts, and he was constantly having to haul ass up to DC for crisis strategy meetings. When Joe was home, and not crashing at Roddy's place near Adams-Morgan, he was a piece of driftwood in the bed, rigid and spiky. Joe talked to a point somewhere to the left of Anwar, instead of looking straight at him. The cats had gone to ground, as if sensing a high-pressure front: Berkley in one of his thousand hiding places, Clover under the sofa. Anwar screwed up his hamstring and limped around the apartment, and when he ventured outside it was with a "what now" feeling—maybe this time his truck wouldn't start, or the neighbors would have a campaign sign for that guy who insisted North Carolina would never accept refugees from any of the places where Joe kept track of atrocities.

"You got the right idea, staying home all the time," Anwar told Berkley, who grudgingly offered his white tummy.

One day, Anwar got done showering, and all the real towels were dirty. So he dried off using a hand towel. He emerged from the bathroom, cupping himself in that small cotton square, and saw Joe staring at him, gray eyes wide and unwavering. Anwar felt himself blush, was about to say something flirtatious to his husband, but Joe was turning to close the half-open front curtain, where anybody could see in from the front stoop.

"You might want to do a *lot* more crunches before you pose in front of an open window like that."

Anwar bit his own tongue so hard his mouth filled up with blood. He just backed away—first into the bathroom, but there was nothing to cover him there, so he took a hard left into the bedroom. Still limping, he nearly stepped on Clover, who ran to get out of his way. Joe might as well have broken that window instead of covering it.

"Hey, I didn't mean." Joe came in just as Anwar was pulling on his baggiest pants. "You know I think you're beautiful. I just meant, the neighbors. I was just teasing. That came out all wrong. I didn't mean it like that."

"Don't you have a meeting in DC to get to?"

Once Joe was gone, Anwar fell onto the sofa, wearing just his big sweatpants. He felt gross. All of Joe's previous relationships had ended with some combination of sarcasm and distraction, but Anwar always thought he'd be different. Anwar looked at his forearms, which at least were buff thanks to pouring so much beer. He had to be there in a few hours, unless he called in sick.

Clover had jumped on the sofa when Anwar wasn't looking, and had scrunched next to him with her head resting on his thigh. He scritched her head with one hand and she purred, while Berkley glared from the opposite end of the room. "Hey, it's not your fault our luck went south when you showed up," he told her. "I'm sorry you had to see us like this. We were a lot cooler when everything was going our way."

The cat looked up at him with her eyes perfect yellow spheres, except for tiny black slits, and said, "Oh, shit."

Then she sprang upright. "Shit! I'm a cat. WTF. I didn't mean for this to . . . how long have I been a cat? This is really bad. You have to help me or I'm going to get stuck like this. Listen, do you have a phone? I need you to dial for me, because I have no freaking opposable digits. Listen, it's—"

Then Clover stopped talking, abruptly. She sat down, looked up at him, and let out a long, high chirp, like the sound a cat makes when it's sitting at an open window and trying to communicate with passing birds.

Berkley's life was ruined, and it felt worse than the first time. He was a lot older this time, and, too, he couldn't run and hide from this.

Joe was just gone. As in, just not at home anymore—he had been around less and less lately, but now days had passed without his scent or his voice. Anwar was still there, but he wasn't acting like Anwar. No gentle pats, no tug-of-war with the catnip banana. No silly noises. The only cat that Anwar paid attention to was Clover, and he acted as if Clover had quit in the middle of playing a game that Anwar really wanted to continue.

It was way past time someone sent Clover to The Vet.

Berkley was a fierce, crafty hunter. He found the perfect bookshelf from which to watch for Clover emerging from under the sofa. She usually came out when the mail rained down from the slot in the front door, because that was like a daily miracle: paper from the skies! Berkley had a claw, ready to swipe.

He almost got her. She ducked out of the way, just as the claw came down, and he caught some dust mites instead. She ran back toward the sofa, and he followed.

"New cat!" he hissed at her. "You ruined it all!"

"I didn't mean to!"

As Berkley stalked her, he found himself telling her the story of his original disappointment: how he'd lived in an old wooden house with a cruel girl and a strange girl. Berkley had made the strange girl his own, until she was taken away and he was left worse than before. That "worse than before" was where Berkley was now, and he had nothing left but to share that feeling with Clover.

"But," Clover said from under the sofa. "That was me. *I* was the weird girl. I remember now. I promised to protect you. I kept my promise! That's how you got here. I kept my promise. Now I need you to help me in return."

Just like that, Clover lost her fear of Berkley. She talked her wild talk at him, out in the open, and no amount of claw swipes could scare her off. As mad as she was acting, it was almost like she *wanted* to go to The Vet.

"I was a person. I lived with you," Clover kept saying. "I went away to learn more tricks. I could speak Cat, sometimes, but I wanted to do more. But after I left, I thought about you all the time. I had bad dreams about you. Scary dreams. I imagined you all alone in that old house, with my family, and I had to save you. My teachers wouldn't let me leave the school, so I asked them to save you."

Berkley growled. "So then you just told a man to come and take me away? That was all you did?"

"They said they found you the perfect home, the best family for you. They said I could repay them later. I didn't understand what they meant, but now! I have to turn back into a person soon or I will lose myself. I don't know how. I think this is a test, and I'm failing it. You have to help me. Please!"

Berkley considered this for a moment. "So. You say you are the girl who abandoned me as a kitten, and spoiled my good thing. And now you've come back as a cat, to spoil my good thing a second time. And you want *me* to help *you*?" Berkley let out the most disdainful, vengeful hiss that he possibly could, then turned and walked away without looking back.

Anwar had met Joe at this death metal concert that his friends had dragged him to, in a beer-slick dark club that resembled the inside of a giant van. When he saw Joe in his torn denim and tank top waiting at the bar, his heart had just flipped, and he'd stood next to Joe for ten minutes before he got up the nerve to say hi. Their first three dates, Anwar lied his ass off and pretended to be a death metal fan, to the point where he had to keep sneaking away to text his friends with questions about Finnish musicians. Joe had this mane of red hair and permanent five o'clock shadow flecked with white, and a way of talking about guitar solos that was way better than listening to music.

When Joe found out that Anwar actually loathed metal, he'd nearly wept. "Nobody's ever done anything like that for me. That is so . . . beautiful." He kissed Anwar so hard, Anwar tasted whiskey and felt Joe's stubble on the corners of his mouth. That's when Anwar knew this was the man he wanted to marry.

Joe was Anwar's first real proper love. But Joe was more than a decade older, and had already lived through a string of two-year and three-year relationships. Joe had experienced enough relationship failure to be inured. When they'd first hooked up, Joe had prized Anwar's twenty-something body, his lean golden frame, and seeing that covetous look in the eyes of this slightly grizzled rocker dude had punched a button Anwar didn't even know he had.

Anwar prized Joe's independence, the way he always said "live like the fuckers don't own you," even after they went all domestic together. His gentleness, even when he was pissed off, and the warm sound of his voice when he checked in. Joe had not checked in in ages—they had barely even talked on the phone—because the emergency in DC had given birth to other emergencies, and now there was a whole emergency extended family.

Meanwhile, Anwar's truck kept not starting, there was a weird stain on the bathroom wall, and, well, Anwar was losing his mind and imagining that his cat had talked to him. Clover hadn't spoken since that one time, but she'd been on a tear: chasing Berkley around, making weird noises, knocking things over. Both cats were upset, since Joe was gone and Anwar wasn't himself. Anwar kept trying to pull himself together and at least be there for these two fur balls, but he only stayed together for a minute or two at a time, no matter how hard he tried.

Then another one of those men showed up at his door—this one pale and thin, with elaborate tattoos on his hands and a dark suit with a thin tie. "Don't mind me," the man said. "I just want to talk to your cat." Anwar stepped aside and let the man come in.

"How was the good luck, by the way?" The man peered under various pieces of furniture, looking for Clover. "Were you happy with how it turned out?"

"Um, it was okay, I guess," Anwar said. "I'm still trying to decide, to be honest." He wanted to say more—like maybe he and Joe had never been tested, as a couple, because everything had gone so smoothly for them until now. Maybe they'd have been stronger if they hadn't had training wheels. Maybe they were just fair-weather lovers.

"Okey doke," the man said. "I could get you another dose of luck, but it would cost a lot more this time." He squatted in front of the sofa where Clover eyed him. "Has she talked to you?"

"Um," Anwar said. "I guess so. Yes."

"Don't believe anything she says." The man reached out a hand gently, and Clover let him pet her, fingers under the chin. "She's the worst combination of congenital liar and delusional. Even she doesn't always know if she's telling the truth."

"So she was lying when she told me that she used to be a person?"

"No, that was true. She wanted me to do her a favor, and this was the result." The man snapped his fingers in front of Clover's face. "Come on, then. What do you have to say for yourself?" *Snap, snap.* "How's the food?" *Snap.* "Are you enjoying your accommodations?"

Clover just stared at him and grumbled a little. She twitched whenever he snapped his fingers, but she didn't try to run away.

"Either she's unable to speak, because she just hasn't gotten it under control, or she's just being pissy. Either way, disappointing." The man stood up. "Please let me know if she speaks to you again." He handed Anwar a business card that just had a Meeyu handle. "And if you decide you need another lucky break, just @ me."

"What exactly would I have to do to get more good luck?"

"It really depends. Some of it might be stuff where you wouldn't really be you by the end of it. I tell you what, if you can get that cat speaking English again, that would go a long way."

The man spun on one heel, almost like one of Joe's old dance moves, and walked out the door without saying good-bye or closing the door behind him. Anwar hated when anyone left the door open, even a second, because he never wanted the cats to get any ideas.

Joe called when Anwar was in the middle of trying to coax words out of Clover with cat treats and recitations of Sufi poetry. (No dice.) "Things are impossible, you have no idea. I'm trying to come back to you but every time I think I'm going to get out of here, there's another fucking drama eruption. The auditors are maniacs." In the background, Anwar could hear guitar heroics and laughing voices. "I am going to make it up to you, I swear. I still have to apologize properly for being such an ass before. I gotta go." Joe hung up before Anwar could even say anything.

Anwar had sort of wanted to ask Joe if he felt like they'd been lucky, these past nine years, and whether the luck would be worth going to extremes to get back. But he couldn't think of a way to ask such a thing.

Berkley took a wild skittering run from one end of the apartment to the other, and just as he hit peak speed, he reached the front door, where Clover was sitting, waiting for the mail to rain down. He vaulted over her, paws passing almost within shredding distance, and landed at the front door so hard the mail slot rattled.

Clover just looked at him, eyes partway hooded.

Berkley pulled into a crouch, ready to spring, claws out, ready to tear the new cat apart, but that bored look in her eyes made him stop before he jumped. He was a cunning hunter. He could wait for his moment. She hadn't talked any more nonsense to Berkley since that one time, but she still didn't seem scared of him. He didn't know what he was dealing with.

"New cat," Berkley said in a low voice. "I'm going to send you to The Vet."

Clover didn't reply. The mail fell, but it was just a single envelope with red shapes on it.

Sometime later, Anwar cried into his knees on the couch. He smelled wrong—pungent and kind of rotten instead of like nice soap and hops. He was all shrunk inward, in the opposite of the ready-to-pounce stance that Berkley had pulled his whole body into when he'd been preparing to pounce on Clover. Anwar didn't look coiled or ready to strike, at all. He was making these pitiful sounds, like he couldn't even draw enough breath to sob properly.

Berkley saw the new cat creeping across the floor toward Anwar, and he ran across the room, reaching the sofa first.

"No," he told Clover. "You don't do this. This is mine. You're not even a real cat. Go *away!*"

Berkley climbed up on the sofa without even waiting to see if the new cat went away. He rubbed his forehead against Anwar's hand, which was holding his knee, and licked the web between his fingers a little bit. Anwar let his knees down and made a lap for Berkley. Anwar's hand felt good on Berkley's neck, and he let out a deep satisfied purr—but then he heard Anwar say something in a deep, mournful voice. Hopeless.

The new cat was watching the whole thing from on top of the bookcase. Berkley narrowed his eyes and told her, "I want to hurt you, but I want to bring back the other human more. If I help you, can you bring the humans back together? Yes or no?"

Clover looked down at him and said, "I think so. I'll do what I can."

A few hours later, Anwar had stumbled out of the house and the cats were alone again. "I keep forgetting who I am," Clover said. "It's hard to hold on to. But I remember I begged the teachers to help me save you from my family, and I talked about how you were suffering. They said if I understood cats so much, why didn't I try being one? I was like, 'Fine.' I didn't realize what I had signed up for, until years later."

"So you climbed into a place that you cannot get out of again," Berkley suggested. "Because there is not enough room to turn around."

"Sort of, yeah."

"So," said Berkley, tail curled and ears pointed. "Don't turn around."

Anwar's ankle was kind of swollen and he had no money for a doctor visit and the stain on the bathroom wall had gotten bigger. The Olde Time Pub had gotten a totally bullshit citation from the North Carolina department of Alcohol Law Enforcement, which had the hilarious acronym of ALE. His truck still kept not starting. Anwar longed to rest his head on Joe's shoulder, breathing in that reassuring scent, so Joe could say fuck 'em, it would be all good. On his lonesome, Anwar only knew how to spiral.

Clover came up to him as he sat on the bed getting laboriously dressed. She perched on the edge of the mattress and made noises that usually meant "feed me" or "throw my fuzzy ball." Anwar just shrugged, because he'd wasted three days trying to get her to talk.

Just as Anwar finally got his good shirt buttoned and stood up, Clover said, "Hey."

"Well," Anwar said. "Hey."

"Oh thank god. I finally did it. I'm back," Clover said. "Oh thank goodness. I need your help. One time before, I became a bird, but I needed help to turn back into a human. Now I feel totally stuck in cat form."

Anwar was already reaching for his phone to go on Meeyu and @ that guy, to let him know the cat finally started talking again. He no longer cared if he was being a crazy man. What had sanity done for him lately?

"The longer I go without turning back into a person, the harder it's going to be," Clover said, jumping on the bed. "You look like shit, by the way. Berkley is worried about you. We both are."

"Hey, it's fine. You're okay." Anwar picked her up and looked into her twitchy little face. "I already told those guys, the ones who dropped you off here. They know you're talking again. They're probably on their way. They'll help you out, and maybe they'll give Joe and me some more luck."

Clover squirmed, partly involuntarily. "You really shouldn't take any luck from those guys. It'll come with huge strings attached."

"Well, they told me that you're a liar. And you know, I have nothing to lose." But Anwar had a sudden memory of the man saying, *You wouldn't really be you anymore.*

"Please! You have to help me change back to a person before they get here," Clover said.

"I don't know how to do that."

And anyway, it was too late. The door opened, without a knock or Anwar having to unlock it, and a man entered. He had dark skin pitted with acne scars, long braids, and a purple turtleneck and matching corduroys. "So," the man said, "what does she have to say for herself?"

"You wasted a trip," Clover told him. "I'm still working on changing myself back. I only just got my human voice working. I've got a ways to go before I'm in my own body again."

The man shrugged and picked Clover up with one hand. "You already did what we needed you to do. Just think what we'll be able to do with a cat who talks like a person and knows how to do magic. You'll be way more useful to us in this form." Clover started squirming and shouting, and tried to claw the man, but he had her in a tight grip. He turned to Anwar. "Thanks for whatever you did. We'll consider this a down payment, if you decide you want more luck."

"No!" Clover sounded terrified, on an existential level. "This is messed up. I don't want to be stuck as a cat forever. I have a boyfriend. I have friends. You have to help me!" She looked right at Anwar, her yellow eyes fixed on him, and said, "You can't let them take me."

Anwar thought about how things had been before, with just the one cat, and Joe there, and everything peaceful. He wanted nothing more than to bring back that version of his life. But he looked at Clover, her whole body contorted with terror—claws out, eyes huge and round, mouth full of teeth. He knew what Joe would say if he was here: *Live like the fuckers don't own you.*

The words came out before Anwar had even thought them through. "You can't take my cat."

"I beg your pardon?" the man said. His stare was impossible to meet.

"You can't." Anwar swallowed. "That's my cat. You can't take her."

"Thank you thank you," Clover whispered.

"This isn't a cat. She's a whole other thing. Whatever she told you, she was lying. That's what she does."

Anwar drew courage from the fact that the weird man was arguing with him instead of just taking the cat and leaving. "You gave this cat to me. You didn't say it was a loan. She's mine. I have all the records to prove it."

Now the man *did* turn to leave, but Clover leapt out of his arms. She landed on three feet, nearly tumbled head over tail, and then got her balance fast enough to run back into the apartment. She headed for one of the hundred hiding places that she'd gotten to know, but the man was right behind her. Anwar just stood and watched as the man ran through the apartment, knocking over Joe's guitar. He was right on top of Clover, leaning to scoop her up.

There was another cat between the man and Clover. As he bent down to grab the cat who was still shouting in English, his hand connected instead with Berkley. Who bit his thumb, hard enough to draw blood.

Berkley growled at the man, in a pose Anwar had never seen before. Standing his ground, snarling, bloody teeth bared. Roaring. Like a tiny lion. This would have been the most ridiculous sight ever, if it wasn't so heroic.

Clover stopped and looked at Berkley, defending her. Her jaw dropped open, her ears were all the way up. "Berkley, shit," she said. "You just bit the thumb of the most powerful man on Earth. I can't believe you. Whatever happens now, I want you to know I regret leaving you behind. And no matter what price I end up paying, I'm glad I rescued you. I'm sorry, and I understand what you went through."

That last phrase was like a string breaking, or a knot being undone after hours of pulling and worrying. As soon as Clover said "understand," the cat was gone. A naked woman stood in Anwar's hallway, holding Berkley in her arms. He looked up at her and seemed to recognize her. He put his head on her shoulder and purred.

The woman looked at the man, who was nursing his thumb. "I know you're still pissed about Siberia. I get it. But jeez. This was mean, even for you."

The man rolled his eyes, then turned to look at Anwar. "I hope you enjoy not having any luck ever again." Then he stomped out of the apartment, leaving the door open.

As soon as the man was gone, Anwar fell onto the couch, hands on his face. He felt weird having a naked stranger in his home, and even weirder that this girl had seen so much of him at his worst, and he'd had his hand on her face so many times. The whole thing was weird. He felt a huge letdown in his gut, because he'd convinced himself somehow that they would get more luck and it would be fine.

"So that's it," Anwar muttered mostly to himself. "We're screwed."

"Hey, can I borrow some clothes?"

While the girl—Clover—was getting dressed, she tried to talk him down. "Joe is coming back. He loves you, he just sucks at expressing it sometimes. I've seen how you guys are." Somehow she managed to put clothes on without letting go of Berkley. "So listen. I suck at giving advice. But the absence of good luck is not bad luck. It's just . . . life."

"I guess that sort of makes sense," Anwar said.

"That would be a first for me." Clover looked twitchy, like she was still ready to chase a ball around or eat a treat out of Anwar's hand. Anwar wondered if she was going to be stuck having cat thoughts forever. "I can fix your injured ankle, no problem. Also, I think I know how to get rid of that stain on your bathroom wall. I'll have a look at the truck, I'm pretty good with engines. And I'll leave you my Meeyu info, if you ever have another problem you need help with. I'll be around if you need me, okay?"

Anwar nodded. He was starting to think having this magical girl on speed dial could be better than good luck anyway.

Joe came home an hour later, after Clover had already left. "Hey," Joe said. "I lost my job. But I think we're better off, and I already have a line on something where I'll never have to leave town again. I just wanted to say I'm really sorry about being a jackass and leaving for so long, and I love you. You're the most beautiful thing I've ever seen."

Anwar just stared at his husband for a moment. Joe had a case of highway sunburn on one arm and part of his neck, and his hair was a mess, and he looked like a rock star. Anwar threw his arms around Joe and whispered, "The cats missed you." Then he realized there was only one cat and he was going to have to explain somehow. But he was too busy kissing the man he loved, and there would be time for that later.

Watching the two men from the top of his fuzzy climbing tree, Berkley looked immensely self-satisfied.

The venerable literary magazine ZYZZYVA was one of the first high-profile places to publish my fiction, way back in 2002. So when publisher Oscar Villalon and editor Laura Cogan asked me to contribute to a special Bay Area issue, I was delighted. "This Is Why We Can't Have Nasty Things" isn't really speculative fiction—instead, it's a return to the first-person queer stories about San Francisco that I used to write, one of which had appeared in ZYZZYVA back in the day. All those old themes about queer artists and gentrification felt even bigger in 2019 than they did in the early 2000s, especially with so many queer landmarks shuttering. I didn't have to try too hard to imagine being present at the last night at a local watering hole that's about to be gone forever. Heads up: there's a brief mention of sexual assault.

THIS IS WHY WE CAN'T HAVE NASTY THINGS

"I have something to tell you. I'm leaving. I still love you, but I can't love this city anymore." She gestures around, indicating the remains of San Francisco.

Smoke break. Wanda and I pass a pre-roll back and forth on the sidewalk in a crowd of five people: girls in skimpy clubwear, guys in either track pants or crinkled business suits that they clearly just wore on an airplane. A homeless guy watches us from across the street, the same dude who was just telling us that the city seized all his belongings, after we gave him twenty bucks.

"I can't help loving this town," I say. "I'm one of those weird people who's a slut except when it comes to cities."

"Yeah, but." Wanda blows a hot fragrant invisible cloud. "They killed our bar."

Glamrock isn't actually dead yet, but it's holding its own wake tonight. This sticky-floored, railroad-car-shaped dive bar has nurtured and protected (and sometimes annoyed) generations of trans girls, punk sluts, sex workers, drag performers, strippers, and random queers. It's the sort of place where the bathroom stalls have no doors so nobody can have sex or do drugs inside them, and it's going out of business next week. San Francisco used to have a million pockets and folds in her long flowery skirts, where the strange and barely loved could create their own reality. Lately, not so much.

"This is why we can't have nasty things," Wanda grumbles. The joint burns all the way down to her fingertips, so she tosses it and heads back inside, and I follow.

Random memories overwhelm me when I venture inside Glamrock. Over here, on this tiny stage, I did my first and last performance in the Friday nite drag show (which was mostly trans women), lip-synching to an old Sheena Easton song about walls made of sugar. Over there, some creepy dude grabbed my ass, under my tiny pleather skirt and thong, and demanded to know about the status of my genitalia. The back corner, with the long bench against the mirrored wall, where I used to hide with five or six trans friends from the Brat Army, snarking about everything.

And right here, by the women's room with the busted hand dryer, is where I met Wanda for the first time ever. They were playing an old Destiny's Child song and something shifted inside me when I saw her long dark hair, huge false lashes, and fuck-everything smile. I can't describe the feeling in terms of a physical sensation, except that it was like there was this valve inside me that had rusted shut, maybe never opening fully since the end of adolescence, and suddenly someone grabbed a pair of pliers and yanked it all the way to the left. Something flowed that was warmer than blood and twice as oxygenated. My head floated. I felt Destiny's Child in the soles of my feet.

We danced on and off surfaces, with and without rhythm, eyes open and eyes closed, until our hands became petals for our stamen faces.

I couldn't believe Wanda actually wanted to go home with me, out of all the pervert stars in this place. Mouths glued together, hands on each other's elbows, grunting/giggling as we rolled around my futon. But we also never left this bar at all, or at least we always came back here, every weekend and many weeknights. Dating Wanda meant getting to know every filthy inch of this place, and the names and backstories of a few dozen semiregulars. Our whole relationship centered on this one watering hole.

There are places where you go to get picked up, or to pick someone up— but then, if you spend enough time in them, you find yourself getting adopted instead. Becoming part of a whole scene.

I told this to Wanda, and she laughed. "Sometimes the best communities come out of people just trying to get laid. I love that moment where we

start taking care of each other instead of only wanting to fuck each other."
Wanda works as a graphic designer, and her phone is full of work contacts—
but also, people she had sex with five years ago, who will still drop everything to help her move a refrigerator. "That's how it works."

It's true. Back when I met Wanda, I had so many lovers that I had no more
bandwidth for all their problems, like Gravy was getting evicted and Jeri's
bed frame shattered and Roxie was getting evicted and Susie's water heater
broke down and ZQ was getting evicted and Frankie's truck was making a
noise like one of those truffle-sniffing pigs all the time, and also Frankie was
getting evicted too. I couldn't be there for all of them. So I started just net-
working them with each other, like I got Frankie to replace the bed frame
while Gravy fixed Frankie's truck, and I was also sleeping with a housing
rights attorney named Trini, who helped everyone fight their evictions. I basically became a referral service among the people I was fucking.

Inside Glamrock, everybody mourns, raising dirty shot glasses to catch
the flickering black light and dancing on their stools to the club music. Rikki
hugs two people at a time, Wilmot keeps buying me drinks, Jezz wants to
take selfies in front of the neon sign with anyone who comes near. "I'm
seriously going to have no place to go anymore where I don't feel like an
endangered species," Angela yells over the vintage techno.

We drink and drink, but we don't get drunk, because Glamrock has always watered its drinks like tropical ferns.

The next smoke break, Wanda starts talking about all her lovers who live
in other cities: the cute enby in Portland, the soft-bearded boi in Detroit,
and so on. Maybe it's time to become poly-itinerant, or poly-nomadic. Poly-
peripatetic? Traveling around from lover to lover, living nowhere except for
a dozen sweeties' bedrooms all over the place. Wanda has a job that she can
do anywhere and an apartment she doesn't mind abandoning, unlike me.
Every city a different body.

"You're really just going to up and leave?" I say. The neon sign sputters
and goes off for a moment.

"I'll come back." Wanda looks into the gutter. "You can be one of the
lovers I visit."

I don't want to be a way station. I don't want to have to reconnect and dis-
connect, over and over. I want to be the place where Wanda comes to rest.

As long as we never leave this bar, it'll never be over. I order another round
of drinks and start singing along with Whitney Houston, trying to draw

Wanda deeper into the gloomy back area. Every well-worn dance song that comes on the crackly speakers is my favorite, every tiny occurrence is another excuse for a toast. I point out the spot where Wilmot bonked his head on Trizzie's stiletto heels, and the burn mark on the carpet from the Great Violet Wand Disaster of 2017. The warm darkness closes in around us, the arch corned beef scent could almost be all the nourishment we might ever require.

It's settled. We'll just stay here forever, at the Glamrock.

"We should get going," Wanda says in my ear. "Almost closing time."

The last-call bell clangs, loud enough to echo off the heavy ceiling beams.

"We can't go yet!" I tug at her sleeve. "One more dance, one more drink, I think I figured out how we can give each other mutual lap dances at the same time. Come on, the night is—"

But Wanda is already hustling me out the front door, toward the future. I wish I could take her someplace else that would change her mind, some art event that lasts twenty-four hours and turns your eyes to stained glass if you stay the whole time. Some beer bust where the Sisters pull a brand-new hanky code out of the center of the roast goat carcass and the first person to decode it gets to assign everyone else a new kink. I wish there was an Anon Salon happening now, or an underground dungeon party, or a body-painted literary festival.

"I remember when cities used to be prisms, or warrens," Wanda says. "I don't even know what a city is supposed to be now. Maybe every city is better visited than lived in these days."

Nobody will write a huge tribute to Glamrock, or put up a plaque. This neighborhood will barely notice it's gone. Some other, fancier bar will occupy that space and be objectively better in almost every way, except for drink prices and clientele.

I can't begin to quantify what I'm about to lose. Angela and Jezz file out of the bar, heads bowed and arms folded against the night wind. I don't know when I'll see either of them again, or where I'll be hanging out after next week. Wanda is the one, of the two of us, who would put in the work to identify our new dive bar, someplace to transplant as much of our scene as possible.

The anticipation of loneliness, surrounded by the people who will soon be gone, is maybe worse than actual loneliness. You can't get used to something that hasn't even started yet.

Begging Wanda to stay will do no good, which only makes me more anxious to beg. *We can make our own San Francisco,* I want to say. *We can become the thing this city can't get rid of.*

I'm still trying to think of a way to petition Wanda when she gets there first. "Promise me something," she says.

"Umm . . . okay."

"Promise me you'll go out, a lot. Wear that skirt you used to wear when I first knew you. Lip-sync to 'Sugar Walls' again, or some other embarrassing eighties song about sex. Keep in touch with all these people. Make a terrible scene that people need a whole hashtag to complain about. When I come back in a few months, I want you to give me a tour of all the sites of your disgrace. Okay?"

"Okay."

She holds out her hands and I take them, and we both lean forward until we're kissing. The wind picks up, and the air runs colder, and Wanda and I huddle together. She smells of booze and weed and rose petals, and for a moment we're both completely at rest, wrapped in each other. The neighborhood is quieting down, except for a late-night hipster meatball place and a group of young straight people who just got kicked out of their own bar. We can't stay out here.

"Let me take you home," I mumble, and Wanda nods, and we find a taxi. The driver is playing the same nineties dance music as the DJ at Glamrock, and Wanda starts to dance inside the constraint of her seat belt.

was stoked when John Joseph Adams asked me to contribute to *Cosmic Powers*, a book of fun space opera stories in the vein of *Guardians of the Galaxy*, because I adore silliness in space more than anything. I wasn't sure what to write, until I thought about my deep and enduring love of Harry Harrison's Stainless Steel Rat books, which tell the story of "Slippery" Jim diGriz, interstellar rogue. To give my two con artists, Kango and Sharon, a decent sandbox to play in, I had to whip up a whole universe. My master document, explaining the economics and politics of this galaxy, ended up being pretty long and detailed just to set up some throwaway jokes (and to make sure there were meaningful stakes). Kango and Sharon were created by a culture of amoral libertines who delight in perverse pleasures, and their battle for the right to define their own identities resonated with me. I wrote a second Kango and Sharon story, "Cake Baby," which you can read at *Lightspeed* magazine, and I have notes for a few others. If you'd like to read more about these two rogues and their friend Jara, please let me know!

A TEMPORARY EMBARRASSMENT IN SPACETIME

1

Sharon's head itched from all the fake brain implants, and the massive cybernetic headdress was giving her a cramp in her neck. The worst discomfort of all was having to pretend to be the loyal servant of a giant space blob. Pretending to be a *thing* instead of a person. This was bringing back all sorts of ugly memories from her childhood.

The Vastness was a ball of flesh in space, half the size of a regular solar system, peering out into the void with its billions of slimy eyemouths. It orbited a blue giant sun, Naxos, which used to have a dozen planets before the Vastness ate them all. That ring around the Vastness wasn't actually a ring of ice or dust, like you'd see around a regular planet. Nope—it was tens of thousands of spaceships that were all docked together by scuzzy umbilicals, and they swarmed with humans and other people, who all lived to serve the Vastness.

The Vastness didn't really talk much, except to bellow "I am everything!" into every listening device for a few light-years in any direction, and also directly into the minds of its human acolytes.

After five days, Sharon was getting mighty sick of hearing that voice yelling in her ear. "I am everything!" the Vastness roared. "You are everything!" Sharon shouted back, which was the standard response. Sharon really needed a shower—bathing wasn't a big priority among the devotees of the Vastness—and she was getting creeped out from staring into the eyes of people who hadn't slept in forever. (The Vastness didn't sleep, so why should its servants?)

"We're finally good to go," said Kango's voice in Sharon's earpiece, located under the knobby black cone she was wearing over her cranium.

"Thank Hall and Oates," Sharon subvocalized back.

She was standing in a big orange antechamber aboard one of the large tributary vessels in the ring around the Vastness, and she was surrounded by other people wearing the same kind of headgear. Except that their headgear was real, and they really were getting messages from the Vastness, and they probably would not be thrilled to know that her fake headgear actually contained the ship's hypernautic synchrotrix, which she'd stolen hours earlier.

Sharon and Kango had a client back on Earthhub Seven who would pay enough chits for that synchrotrix to cover six months' worth of supplies. Plus some badly needed upgrades to their ship, the *Spicy Meatball*. If she could only smuggle it out of here without the rest of these yo-yos noticing.

Kango had finally spoofed the Vastness's embarkation catechism, so the *Meatball* could separate from the ring without being instantly blown up. Sharon started edging toward the door.

"I am everything!" the Vastness shouted through every speaker and every telepathic implant on the tributary ship, including Sharon's earpiece.

"You are everything!" Sharon shouted . . . just a split second later than everyone else in the room.

She was halfway to the door, which led to an air lock, which led to a long interstitial passageway, which led to a junction, which led to a set of other ships' antechambers, beyond which was the air lock to the *Meatball*, which they'd disguised to look just like another one of these tributary ships.

Sharon tried to look as though she was just checking the readings on one of the control panels closer to the exit to this tributary ship. The synchrotrix was rattling around inside her big headdress, and she had to be careful not to damage it, since it was some incredibly advanced design that nobody else in the galaxy had. Sharon was so close to the exit. If she could just—

"Sister," a voice behind her said. "What are you doing over there? How do your actions serve the Vastness?"

She turned to see a man with pale skin and a square face that looked ridiculous under his big cybernetic pope hat, staring at her. Behind him, two other acolytes were also staring.

"Brother, I . . ." Sharon groped around on the control table behind her. Her hand landed on a cup of the nutritious gruel that the servants of the Vastness lived on. "I, uh, I was just making sure these neutron actuator readings were aligned with, uh, the—"

"That screen you are looking at is the latrine maintenance schedule," the man said.

"Right. Right! I was concerned that the Vastness wouldn't want us to have a faulty latrine, because, um . . ."

"I am everything!" the Vastness shouted.

"Because, I mean, if we had to wear diapers—you are everything!—then I mean, we wouldn't be able to walk as quickly as the Vastness might require when it summons . . ."

Now everybody was staring at Sharon. She was so damn close to the door.

"Why did you not make your response to the Call of the Vastness immediately?"

"I was just, uh, so overcome with love for the Vastness, I was momentarily speechless." Sharon kept looking at the man, while groping her way to the door.

The man pulled out a gun—a Peacebreaker 5000, a nice model, which would have been worth some chits back on Earthhub Seven—and aimed it at her. "Sister," he said, "I must restrain you and deliver you to the head acolyte for this sector, who will determine whether you—"

Sharon did the only thing she could think of. She shouted, "I am everything!"

The man blinked as she spoke the words reserved only for the Vastness. For a second, his mind couldn't even process what he had just heard—and then the cupful of cold gruel hit him in the face.

The man lowered his gun just long enough for Sharon to make a lunge for it. Her headdress cracked and the synchrotrix fell out. She caught it with her left hand, while she grabbed for the gun with her right hand. The man was trying to aim the gun at her again, and she headbutted him. The gun went off, hitting one of the walls of the ship and causing a tiny crack to appear.

Both of the women had jumped on Sharon and the man, and now there were three acolytes trying to restrain her and pry the gun and synchrotrix from her hands. She bit one of the women, but the other one had a choke hold on her.

"I am everything!" shouted the Vastness.

"You are everything!" responded everyone except Sharon.

By the time they'd finished giving the ritual response, Sharon had a firm grip on the gun and it was aimed at the head of the shorter of the two women. "I'm leaving here," Sharon said. "Don't try to stop me."

"My life means nothing," the woman said, with the gun right against her cone head. "Only the Vastness has meaning."

"I'll shoot the other two after I shoot you," said Sharon. She had reached the door. She shoved the woman into the antechamber, leapt through the doorway, and pushed the button to close the door behind her. The door didn't close.

"Crap," Sharon said.

"The overrides are on already. You won't escape," the woman Sharon had threatened at gunpoint gloated. "Praise the Vastness!"

"Screw the Vastness," said Sharon, aiming at the crack in the ship's hull and pulling the trigger on the Peacebreaker 5000. Then she took off running.

2

"You took your time." Kango was already removing his own fake headdress and all the other ugly adornments that had disguised him as one of the Vastness's followers. "Did anybody see you slip away?"

"You could say that." Sharon ran into the *Spicy Meatball*'s control area and strapped herself into the co-pilot seat. "We have to leave. Now." She felt the usual pang of gladness at seeing Kango again—even if they got blown up, they were going to get blown up together.

Just then, the Vastness howled, "I have been robbed! I am everything, and someone has stolen from Me!"

"I thought you were the stealthy one." Kango punched the ship's thrusters and they pushed away from the Vastness's ring at two times escape velocity. "You're always telling me that I make too much noise, I'm too prone to spontaneous dance numbers, I'm too—what's the word—irrepressible, and you're the one who knows how to just get in and get out. Or did I misinterpret your whole 'I'm a master of stealth, I live in the shadows' speech the other day?"

"Just drive," Sharon hissed.

"You just think you're better than me because I'm a single-celled organism and you're all multicellular," said Kango, who looked to all outside appearances like an incredibly beautiful young human male with golden skin and a wicked smile. "You're a cellist. Wait, is that the word? What do you call someone who discriminates against other people based on the number of cells in their body?"

They were already three-tenths of a light-year away from the Vastness and there was no sign of pursuit. Sharon let out a breath. She looked at the big ugly blob of scar tissue, with all of its eyemouths winking at her one by one, and at the huge metallic ring around its middle. The whole thing looked kind of beautiful in the light of Naxos, especially when you were heading in the opposite direction at top speed.

"You know perfectly well that I don't hold your monocellularity against you," Sharon told Kango in a soothing tone. "And next time, I will be happy to let you be the one to go into the heart of the monster and pull out its tooth, and yes I know that's a mixed metaphor, but . . ."

"Uh, Sharon?"

". . . but I don't care, because I need a shower lasting a week, not to mention some postindustrial-strength solvent to get all this gunk off my head."

"Sharon. I think we have a bit of an issue."

Sharon stopped monologuing and looked at the screen, where she'd just been admiring the beauty of the Vastness and its ring of ships a moment earlier. The ring of ships was peeling ever so slowly away from the Vastness and forming itself into a variation of a standard pursuit formation—the variation was necessary, because the usual pursuit formation didn't include several thousand Joybreaker-class ships and many assorted others.

"Uh, how many ships is that?"

"That is all of the ships. That's how many."

"We're going to be cut into a million pieces and fed to every one of the Vastness's mouths," Sharon said. "And they're going to keep us alive and conscious while they do it."

"Can they do that?" Kango jabbed at the *Meatball*'s controls, desperately trying to get a little more speed out of the ship.

"Whoa, I'm going as fast as I can," said Noreen, the ship's computer, in a petulant tone. "Poking my buttons won't make me go any faster."

"Sorry, Noreen," said Sharon.

"Wait, I have a thought," said Kango. "The device you stole, the hypernautic synchrotrix. It functions by creating a Temporary Embarrassment in spacetime, which lets the Vastness and all its tributary ships transport themselves instantaneously across the universe in search of prey. Right? But what makes it so valuable is the way that it neutralizes all gravity effects. An object the size of the Vastness should throw planets out of their orbits and disrupt entire solar systems whenever it appears, but it doesn't."

"Sure. Yeah." Sharon handed the synchrotrix to Kango, who studied it frantically. "So what?"

"Well, so," Kango said. "If I can hook it into Noreen's drive systems . . ." He was making connections to the device as fast as he could. "I might be able to turn Noreen into a localized spatial Embarrassment generator. That, in turn, means that we can do something super super clever."

Kango pressed five buttons at once, triumphantly, and . . . nothing happened.

Kango stared at the tiny viewscreen. "Which means," he said again, "we can do something super super *super* clever." He jabbed all the buttons again (causing Noreen to go "ow") and then something did happen: a great purple and yellow splotch opened up directly behind the *Spicy Meatball*, and all of the ships chasing them were stopped dead. A large number of the pursuit ships even crashed into one another, because they had been flying in too tight a formation.

"So long, cultists!" Kango shouted. He turned to Sharon, still grinning. "I created a Local Embarrassment, which collided with the Temporary Embarrassment fields that those ships were already generating, and set up a chain reaction in which this region of spacetime became Incredibly Embarrassed. Which means . . ."

". . . none of those ships will be going anywhere for a while," Sharon said.

"See what I mean? I may only have one cell, but it's a *brain* cell." He whooped and did an impromptu dance in his seat. "Like I said: you're the stealthy one, I'm the flashy one."

"I'm the one who needs an epic shower." Sharon pulled at all the crap glued to her head, while also putting the stolen synchrotrix safely into a padded strongbox. She was still tugging at the remains of her headgear when she moved toward the rear of the ship in search of its one bathroom, and noticed something moving in the laundry compartment.

"Hey, Kango?" Sharon whispered, as she came back into the flight deck. "I think we have another problem."

She put her finger to her lips, then led him back to the laundry area, where she pulled the compartment open with a sudden tug, to reveal a slender young woman, curled up in a pile of dirty flight suits, wearing the full headgear of an acolyte of the Vastness. The girl looked up at them.

"Praise the Vastness," she said. "Have we left the ring yet? I yearn to help you spread the good word about the Vastness to the rest of the galaxy! All hail the Vastness!"

Sharon and Kango just looked at each other, as if each trying to figure out how they could make this the other's fault.

3

Sharon and Kango had known each other all their lives, and they were sort of married and sort of united by a shared dream. If a single-celled organism could have a sexual relationship with anybody, Kango would have made it happen with Sharon. And yet, a lot of the time they kind of hated each other. Cooped up with Noreen on the *Spicy Meatball*, when they weren't being chased by literal-minded cyborgs or sprayed with brainjuice from the brainbeasts of Noth, they started going a little spare. Kango would start trying to osmose the seat cushions and Sharon would invent terrible games. They were all they had, but they were kind of bad for each other all the same. Space was lonely, and surprisingly smelly, at least if you were inside a ship with artificial life support.

They'd made a lot of terrible mistakes in their years together, but they'd never picked up a stowaway from a giant-space-testicle cult before. This was a new low. They immediately started doing what they did best: bicker.

"I like my beer lukewarm and my equations ice cold," Kango said. "Just sayin'."

"Hey, don't look at me," Sharon said.

The teenager, whose name was TheVastnessIsAllWonderfulJaramella-

LovesTheVastness, or Jara for short, was tied to the spare seat in the flight deck with thick steelsilk cords. Since Jara had figured out that she'd stowed away on the wrong ship and these people weren't actually fellow servants of the Vastness, she'd stopped talking to them. Because why bother to speak to someone who doesn't share the all-encompassing love of the Vastness?

"We don't have enough food, or life support, or fuel, to carry her where we're going," Kango said.

"We can ration food, or stop off somewhere and sell your Rainbow Cow doll collection to buy more. We can make oxygen by grabbing some ice chunks from the nearest comet and breaking up the water molecules. We can save on fuel by going half-speed, or again, sell your Rainbow Cow dolls to buy fuel."

"Nobody is selling my Rainbow Cow dolls," Kango said. "Those are my legacy. My descendants will treasure them, if I ever manage to reproduce somehow." He made a big show of trying to divide into two cells, which looked like he was just having a hissy fit.

"Point is, we're stuck with her now. Praise the Vastness," Sharon sighed.

"Praise the Vastness!" Jara said automatically, not noticing the sarcasm in Sharon's voice.

"There's also the fact that they can probably track her via the headgear she's wearing. Not to mention she may still be in telepathic contact with the Vastness itself, and we have no way of knowing when she'll be out of range of the Vastness's mental influence."

"Oh, that's easy," Sharon said. "We'll know she's out of range of mental communication with the Vastness, when—"

"You are everything!" Jara shouted, in response to a message from the Vastness.

"—when she stops doing that. Listen, I'm going to work on disabling, and maybe dismantling, her headgear. You work on rationing food and fuel and figuring out a way to get more without sacrificing the Rainbow Cows."

"Do not touch my sacred headpiece," the girl said at the exact same moment that Kango said, "Stay away from my Rainbow Cows."

"Guys," said Noreen. "I have an incoming transmission from Earthhub Seven."

"Can you take a message?" Kango said. "We're a smidge busy here."

"It's from Senior Earthgov Administrator Mandre Lewis. Marked urgent."

"You are everything!" Jara cried, while struggling harder against her bonds.

"Okay, fine." Kango turned to Sharon. "Please keep her quiet. Noreen, put Mandre on."

"You can't silence me!" Jara struggled harder. "I will escape and aid in your recapture. All ten million eyemouths of the Vastness will feast on your still-living flesh! You will—"

Sharon managed to put a sound-dampening field up around Jara's head, cutting off the sound of her voice, just as Mandre appeared on the cruddy low-res screen in the middle of the flight console. Getting a state-of-the-art communications system had not been a priority for Kango and Sharon, since that would only encourage people to try and communicate with them more often, and who wanted that?

"Kango, Sharon," Mandre Lewis said, wearing her full ceremonial uniform—even the animated sash that scrolled with all of her many awards and titles. "I can't believe I'm saying this, but we need your assistance."

"We helped you one time," Kango said. "Okay, three times, but two of those were just by accident, because you had used reverse psychology. Point is, I am not your lackey. Or your henchman. Find another man to hench. Right, Sharon?"

Sharon nodded "No henching. As Hall and Oates are my witness."

"You are everything!" Jara mouthed, soundlessly.

"Listen," said Lewis. "You do this one thing for me, I can expunge your criminal records, even the ones under your other names. And I can push through the permits on that empty space at Earthhub Seven, so you can finally open that weird thing you wanted. That, what was it called?"

"Restaurant," Sharon breathed, like she couldn't believe she was even saying the word aloud.

"Restaurant!" Kango clapped his hands. "That's all we've ever wanted."

"It sounds perverted and sick, this whole thing where you make food for strangers and they give you chits for it. Why don't you just have sex for money, like honest decent people? Never mind, I don't want to know the answer to that. Anyway, if you help me with this one thing, I can get you permission to open your 'restaurant.'"

"Wow." Kango's head was spinning. Literally, it was going around and around, at about one revolution every few seconds. Sharon leaned down and slapped him until his head settled back into place.

"We'll do it," Sharon said. "Do you want us to infiltrate the spacer isolationists of the broken asteroid belt? Or go underground as factory workers in the Special Industrial Solar Systems? You want us to steal from the lizard people of Dallos IV? Whatever you want, we're on it."

"None of those," said Mandre. "We need you to go back to Liberty House and get back inside your former place of, er, employment. We've heard reports that the Courtiers are developing some kind of super-weapon that could ruin everybody's day. We need you to go in there and get the schematics for us."

"Holy shit." Sharon nearly threw something at the tiny viewscreen. "You realize that this is a suicide mission? The Courtiers regard both of us as total abominations. We can't open a restaurant if we're dead!"

Lewis made a "not my problem" face. "Just get it done. Or don't even bother coming back to Earthhub Seven."

Kango's head started spinning in the opposite direction from the one it had been spinning in a moment earlier.

4

They were about halfway to the outer solar systems of Liberty House, and they decided that Jara had probably passed out of range of the Vastness's telepathic communication. Plus they were pretty sure they'd disabled any tracking devices that might have been inside Jara's headdress. So Sharon leaned over the seat that Jara was still tied to.

"I know you can hear me, even though we can't hear you. If I turn off the dampening field, do you promise not to yell about the Vastness?"

Jara just stared at her.

Sharon shrugged, then reached over and disabled the dampening field. Immediately, Jara started yelling, "The Vastness is all! The Vastness sees you. The Vastness sees everybody! The Vastness will feast on your flesh with its countless mouths! The Va—"

Sharon turned the dampening field back on with a sigh. "You've probably never known a life apart from the Vastness, so this is the first time you haven't heard its voice in your head. Right? But you stowed away on our ship for a reason. You can claim it was so you could be a missionary and tell the rest of the galaxy how great the Vastness is, but we both know that you had to have some other reason for wanting to see the galaxy. Even if you can't admit it to yourself right now."

Jara just kept shouting about the Vastness, and its boundless wonderful appetite, without making any sound.

"Fine. Have it your way. Let me know if you need to use the facilities, or if you get hungry. Maybe I'll feed you one of Kango's Rainbow Cows." (This provoked a loud and polysyllabic "noooo" from Kango, who was in the next compartment over.)

When Sharon wandered aft, Kango was waist deep in boxes of supplies, looking for something they could use to disguise themselves long enough to get inside Liberty House.

"Do we have a hope in hell of pulling this off?" she asked.

"If we can get the permits, absolutely," Kango said. "We might have to borrow some chits to get the restaurant up and running, but I know people who won't charge an outrageous rate. I already have ideas of what kind of food we can serve. Did you know restaurants used to have this thing called a Me-N-U? It was a device that automatically chose the perfect food for me, and the perfect food for you."

"I meant, do we have any hope of getting back inside of Liberty House without being clocked as escaped Divertissements and obliterated in a slow, painful fashion?"

"Oh." Kango squinted at the piles of glittery underpants in his hands. "No. That, we don't have the slightest prayer of doing. I was trying to focus on the positive."

"We need a plan," Sharon said. "You and I are on file with the Courtiers, and there are any of a thousand scans that will figure out who we are the moment we show up. But Mandre is right, we know the inner workings of Liberty House better than anybody. We were made there, we lived there. It was our home. There has to be some way to play the Courtiers for fools."

"Here's the problem," said Kango. "Even if you and I were able to disguise ourselves enough to avoid being recognized as the former property of the Excellent Good Time Crew, there's absolutely no way we could hide what we are. None, whatsoever. Anyone in the service of the Courtiers will recognize you as a monster and me as an extra, at a glance."

"I know, I know," Sharon raised her hands.

"We wouldn't get half a light-year inside the House before they would be all over us with the biometrics and the genescans, and there's no way around those."

"I know!" Sharon felt like weeping. They shouldn't have taken this mission. Mandre had dangled a slim chance at achieving their wildest dreams, and they'd lunged for it like rubes. "I know, okay?"

"I mean, you'd need to have a human being, an actual honest-to-Blish human being, who was in on the scam. It's not like we can just pick up one of *those* on the nearest asteroid. So unless you've got some other bright—" Kango stopped.

Kango and Sharon stared at each other for a moment without talking, then looked over at Jara, who was still tied to her chair, shouting soundlessly about the wonders of the Vastness.

"Makeover?" Kango said.

"Makeover." Sharon sighed. She still felt like throwing up.

5

"Greetings and tastefully risqué taunts, O visitors whose sentience will be stipulated for now, pending further appraisal," said the man on the viewscreen, whose face was surrounded by a pink and blue cloud of smart powder. His cheek had a beauty mark that flashed different colors, and his eyes kept changing from skull sockets to neon spirals to cartoon eyeballs. "What is your business with Liberty House, and how may we pervert you?"

Kango and Sharon both looked at Jara, who glared at them both. Then she turned her baleful look toward the viewscreen. "Silence, wretch," she said, speaking the words they'd forced her to memorize. "I do not speak to underthings." Kango and Sharon both gave her looks of total dismay, and she corrected herself: "Underlings. I do not speak to underlings. I am the Resplendent Countess Victoria Algentsia, and these are my playservants. Kindly provide me with an approach vector to the central Pleasure Nexus and instruct me as to how I may speak to someone worthy of my attention."

They turned off the comms before the man with the weird eyes could even react.

"Ugh," Kango said. "That was . . . not good."

"I've never pretended to be a countess before," said Jara. "I don't really approve of pretending to be anything. The Vastness requires total honesty and realness from its acolytes. Also, how do I know you'll keep your end of our bargain?"

"Because we're good honest folk," said Sharon, kicking Kango before he could even think of having a facial expression. "We'll return you to the

Vastness, and you'll be a hero because you'll have helped defeat a weapon that could have been a threat to its, er, magnificence."

"I don't trust either of you," said Jara.

"That's a good start," said Kango. "Where we're going, you shouldn't trust anybody, anybody at all." By some miracle, the man with the cloud of smart powder around his face had given them an approach vector to Salubrious IV, the central world of the Pleasure Nexus, the main solar system of Liberty House. Either the man had actually believed Jara was a countess or he had decided their visit would afford some amusement to somebody. Or both.

"So I'm supposed to be a fancy nobleperson," said Jara, who was still wearing her tattered rags, apart from a splash of colorful makeup and some fake jewels over her headdress. "And yet, I'm flying in this awful old ship, with just the two of you as my servants? What are you two supposed to be, anyway?"

"We were made here," said Kango. "I'm an extra. She's a monster."

"You don't need to know what we were." Sharon shot Kango a look. "All you need to know is, we're perfectly good servants. This ship is an actual pleasure skimmer from Salubrious, and you're going to claim that you decided to go off on a jaunt. We're creating a whole fake hedonic calculus for you. The good thing about Liberty House is, there are a million Courtiers, and the idea of keeping tabs on any of them is repugnant."

"This society is evil and monstrous," said Jara. "The Vastness will come and devour it entire."

"Of course, of course," said Kango with a shrug. "So we have a few hours left to teach you how to hold your painstick, and which skewer to use with which kind of sugarblob, and the right form of address for all five hundred types of Courtiers, so you can pass for a member of the elite. Not to mention, how to walk in scamperpants. Ready to get started?"

Jara just glared at him.

Meanwhile, Sharon went aft to look at the engines, because their "plan," if you wanted to call it that, required them to do some seat-of-their-heads flying inside the inner detector grid of Salubrious IV, to get right up to the computer core, while Kango and Jara provided a distraction.

"Nobody asked me if I wanted to go home," said Noreen, while Sharon was poking around in her guts. "I wouldn't have minded being at least consulted here."

"Sorry," said Sharon. "Neither of us is happy about going back, either. We got too good an offer to refuse."

"I've been in contact with some of the other ships since we got inside Liberty House," Noreen said. "They don't care much one way or the other if we're lying about our identity—ships don't concern themselves with such petty business—but they did mention that the Courtiers have beefed up security rather a lot since we escaped for the first time. Also, some of the ships are taking up a betting pool on how long before we're caught and sent into the Libidorynth."

"I can't believe the Libidorynth is still a thing," Sharon said.

Sharon and Kango spent their scant remaining time making Jara look plausibly like a spoiled countess who had been in deep space much too long, while Kango gave Jara a crash course in acting haughty and imperious. "When in doubt, pretend you've done too many dreamsluices and you're having a hard time remembering things," said Kango.

"Silence, drone," said Jara, in an actually pretty good impersonation of the way a Courtier would speak to someone like Kango.

"We've got landing points," said Noreen, and seconds later the ship was making a jerky descent toward the surface of Salubrious IV. From a distance, the planet looked a hazy shade of brownish gray. Once you broke atmosphere, the main landmass was coated with towers of pure gold studded with purple, and the oceans had a sheen of platinum over them. They lowered the *Spicy Meatball* into the biggest concentration of gilded skyscrapers, and all the little details came into focus: the millions of faces and claws and bodies gazing and squirming from the sides of the buildings, the bejeweled windows, and the shimmering mist of pleasure gas floating around all of the uppermost levels. Gazing at her former home, Sharon felt an unexpected kick of nostalgia, or maybe even joyful recognition, alongside the ever-present terror of *Hall and Oates save me, they're going to put us in the Libidorynth.*

They touched down, and Noreen seemed reluctant to open her hatch, because she was probably having the same terrifying flashbacks that were eating Sharon's brain. Things Sharon hadn't thought of in years—the cage they had kept her in, the "monster training," the giggles of the people as she chased them around the dance floor, which turned to shrieks after she actually caught up with them. The painsticks. Sharon felt the bravado she'd spent years acquiring start to flake away.

As they stepped out of the hatch, a retinue of one hundred Witty Companions and assorted Fixers and Cleansers swarmed to surround them. "How may we pervert you?" they all asked, with an eagerness that made Sharon's stomach twist into knots. They all felt obliged to declare their fealty to this long-lost, newly returned countess right away, and this became deafening. One of the Witty Companions, who introduced himself as Barnadee, started listing all of the Courtiers who were dying to meet their cousin, but Jara gave him a sharp look and said that she was tired after her long journey.

"Of course, of course," said Barnadee, bowing and flashing his multicolored strobe-lit genitalia as a show of respect. "We will show you to your luxurious and resplendent quarters, where any debauchery you may imagine will be available to you."

Jara snorted at all of this nonsense—it was all pointless, because it did nothing to glorify the Vastness—but her disdain sounded enough like the petulance of a jaded hedonist that it only made Barnadee try harder to please her.

6

"Drone, bring me more cognac-and-bacon," said Jara, waving one finger. Sharon and Kango looked at each other, as if each trying to blame the other for turning this girl into their worst nightmare. They'd been on Salubrious IV for a week and a half and you wouldn't recognize Jara anymore. Her skin had been retro-sheened until it glowed, they had put jewels all over her face and neck, and she was wearing the newest, most fashionable clothes. Most of all, Jara had gotten used to having whatever she wanted, at the exact second she decided she wanted it. They were staying in one of the more modest suites of the Pleasure Nexus, with only seventeen rooms and a dozen organic assembly units—so it might take a few whole minutes to build a new plaything for the Countess Victoria or to create whatever meals or clothing she might desire. The walls were coated with living material, sort of like algae, that looked like pure gold (but were actually much more valuable) and had the capacity to feel pain, just in case someone might find it amusing to hear the golden walls howl with agony.

"I grow bored," said Jara, as Sharon rushed over with her cognac-and-bacon. "When will there be more amusement for me?"

Sharon had a horrible feeling that she could not tell if Jara was faking it any longer. She'd had that feeling for a few days.

"Um," said Sharon to Jara, "well, so there are five orgies this evening, including one featuring blood enemas and flesh-melting. Also, there's that big formal evening party."

"Is this the sort of party where you used to be the featured monster?" Jara held her cognac-and-bacon in both hands and gulped it, with just the sort of alacrity you'd expect from someone who'd only ever tasted gruel until two weeks ago.

"Um, yes," Sharon said. "They would turn me loose and I would chase the guests around and try to eat them. I've told you already."

"And how did that make you feel?" Jara asked.

"I don't want to talk about it."

Sharon turned and looked at Kango, who was tending to the countess's assembly units, but also double checking that there were no listening devices in here and they could speak freely. Kango gave her the "all clear" signal.

"Let's talk about you instead," Sharon said to Jara. "Are you ready to go to the big party? It's one thing to playact at bossing Kango and me around in private. At this party you'll see all sorts of weird things—depravities that the Vastness never prepared you for. You can't bat an eye at any of them."

"I'll do whatever I have to," Jara said. "You said there's a weapon here that's a threat to the Vastness, and I'll endure any horrors and monstrosities to protect the Vastness. Praise the Vastness!"

"Do you think she's ready?" Sharon asked Kango, who shrugged.

"She's got the attitude," Kango said. Just a few hours earlier, Jara had made Kango go out and fetch her some still-living mollusk sushi from the market, and meanwhile she'd gotten Sharon to fabricate a tiny legion of pink fluffy shock troopers for her amusement (they goose-stepped around and then all shot each other, because their aim was terrible).

"Thank you," Jara said. "Drone."

"But she's still rusty on the finer points of Courtier behavior," Kango said. "She doesn't know a painstick from a soul fork."

"She's a quick study, and she'll have you to help her," Sharon said. "As long as you don't get all re-traumatized by being back inside the Grand Wilding Center. I can't even imagine."

"You two," Jara said out of nowhere. "You talk as though each of you was the Vastness to the other."

"Yeah," Kango said. "We're a family, that's why."

278 EVEN GREATER MISTAKES

Jara was shaking her head, like this was just another perversion among many that she'd encountered on her journey. "At least the people here in Liberty House care about something bigger than they are, even if it's only a pointless amusement. You two, you are so small, and all you care for is each other. How can you *stand* to have no connection to greatness?"

"We had enough of other people's greatness a long time ago," Sharon said. "You start to realize that 'something bigger than you are' is usually just some kind of stupid mass hallucination. Or a giant scam."

"I feel sorry for you." Jara finished her cognac-and-bacon and gestured for more.

"You can pretend that you're still pure," Sharon said. "But you've been enjoying that cognac-and-bacon way, way too much. What do you think the Vastness would think about that? How can the Vastness be everything when it doesn't have cognac-and-bacon? When it doesn't even know what cognac-and-bacon *is*?"

"Shut up, drone," Jara said, falling back into her "countess" voice as a way out of this conversation.

"Keep an eye on her, okay?" Sharon whispered to Kango. "I really think there's a part of her that wants to be her own person, but she just doesn't know how."

He shrugged and nodded at the same time.

And then they were surrounded by a few dozen other servants and Fixers, who had heard that the Countess Victoria was going to the evening's most exclusive party and were here to help her become as resplendent as possible in hopes of winning some favor. So there was no further chance to talk about their actual plans for stealing the specs on the secret weapon—but lots and lots of chances to obsess over whether the countess should wear the weeping dolphin eyes or the blood pouches.

At last, the countess was ready to go to the party, and Sharon was preparing to peel off and sneak back to the *Spicy Meatball*. "Wish me luck," she whispered to Kango.

"You've got this," he whispered back. "We're going to open our restaurant. We'll serve all the classic food items: handburgers, Ruffalo wings, damplings, carry . . . It'll be great."

"Let's not get ahead of ourselves here," said Sharon, kissing Kango on the cheek.

7

The central computer core of the Pleasure Nexus looked like a big mossy rock floating over the city between two giant esorotic spires of pure silver. But as the *Spicy Meatball* flew closer, the computer core looked less like a rock and more like some kind of ancient sauroid, with thick plates of spiky armor guarding its fleshy access points. They flew into its shadow.

Sharon was concentrating on navigating past the tiny guardbots flying around the computer core, while finding the exact vector that would allow the *Spicy Meatball* to come right up to the exposed patch of underbelly. Then Sharon and Noreen just had to hover there, directly underneath the computer core, where anybody could spot the ship's impact-scarred hull, waiting for Kango's diversion to happen. And obsessing about the thousand things that could go wrong.

"I've been telling the other ships about us," said Noreen. "Our smuggling runs to the Scabby Castles, that time we conned those literal-minded cyborgs into thinking Kango was some kind of cyber king . . . They're pretty jealous of us. The other ships might even give us a slight 'head start' if it comes down to a pursuit. Although it wouldn't make any difference, of course."

"I appreciate the gesture," said Sharon. She stared at the crappy little vidscreen, showing the undulating flesh of the computer core—just sitting there, a few inches away from their hull. She was regretting a lot of her recent life choices. She'd sworn for years that nobody was ever going to make her into an object again, but she'd willingly put herself back into that position—and the fact that she was "just pretending" didn't make as much difference as she wanted. She felt bad that Kango, who'd had a rougher time than she had, was being forced to confront this awfulness again. And she was realizing that she'd projected a lot onto that Jara girl, as if a week or two of pretending to be a countess would break a lifetime of conditioning and psychic linkage to a giant space glob. This was probably going to be a career-ending mistake.

"We got it," Noreen said, just as Sharon was getting sucked into gloom. Their vidscreen was streaming some news reports about the Estimable Lord Vaughn Ticklesnout unexpectedly catching on fire and being chased by his own party monster. Some three hundred terrorist organizations had already claimed responsibility for this incident, most of them with completely silly names like the Persimmon Permission Proclamation, but the party had dissolved into total chaos. They picked up footage of the crowd scattering as a man on fire ran around and around, pursued by a bright blue naked woman who could have been Sharon's twin sister.

"Great," Sharon said. "I'm setting up the uplink. Let's hope the distraction was distracting enough." She started threading through layers of security protection, some of them newly added since she and Kango had escaped from Liberty House, and spoofing all of the certs that the computer demanded. There were riddles and silly questions along with strings of base-ninety-nine code that needed to be unraveled, but Sharon and Noreen worked together, and soon they had total leet-superuser access.

Sharon searched for any data on the new super-weapon, and found it helpfully labeled "Brand-New Excellent Super-Weapon." A few more twists of the computer matrix, and she was instructing the computer to transfer all the data on the weapon.

"Uh," said Noreen. "I think you might have made a mistake."

"What?" said Sharon. "I asked it to send over everything it had on the super-weapon."

"Check the cargo hold," said Noreen. "Right next to the boxes of Rainbow Cows. The main computer just auto-docked with us a second ago."

Sharon took a split second to process what Noreen had said, then took off running down to the cargo hold, where a squat red ovoid device about the size of a human baby had been deposited. The object made a faint grumbling noise, like a drunken old man who was annoyed at being woken up. "Oh shit," Sharon said.

"Please keep it down," said the super-weapon. "Some of us are trying to rest."

"Sorry," Sharon said. "I just didn't expect you to show up in person."

"I go where they send me," groaned the super-weapon. "All I want to do is get some rest until my big day. Which could be any day, since they never give me a timetable. That's the problem with being the ultimate deterrent: people *talk* about using me a lot, but they never actually follow through."

"Just how ultimate a deterrent are you?"

"Well, actually, I'm *very* ultimate. Ultimately ultimate, in fact." The super-weapon seemed to perk up a little bit as it discussed its effectiveness. "If anybody tries to interfere with Liberty House's sacred and innate right to seek amusement in any form they deem amusing, then I send a gravity pulse to the supermassive black hole at the center of the galaxy, causing it to, er, expand. Rather a lot. To the size of a galaxy, in fact."

"That's, er, pretty fucking ultimate." Sharon felt as though she, personally, had swallowed a supermassive black hole. This was getting worse and worse. Added to her own low-single-digit estimation of her chances of survival was the realization that her former owners were much, much worse people than she'd ever fathomed. She was so full of terror and hatred, she saw two different shades of red at once.

"Hate to ruin your moment," said Noreen, "but we've got another problem."

"Don't mind me," said the super-weapon. "I'll just go back to sleep. My name is Horace, by the by."

Sharon rushed back to the flight deck, where the vid-screen showed Kango and Jara in the custody of several uniformed Fixers, along with one of the senior Courtiers, a man named Hazelbeem who'd been famous back in Sharon's day.

"We have captured your accomplices." Hazelbeem's lime green coiffure wobbled as he talked. "And we are coming for you next! Prepare for a wonderfully agonizing death—accompanied by some quite delicious crunketizers, because this party left us with rather a lot of leftovers."

"We have your bomb," said Sharon into the viewscreen. "Your ultimate weapon. We'll set it off unless you release our friends."

"No you won't," said Hazelbeem, who had a purple mustache that kept twirling and untwirling and twisting itself into complex shapes, "because you're not self-destructively vindictive."

"Okay. It's true, we won't. But what does that say about you, creating something like that?"

Hazelbeem's mustache shrugged elaborately, but the man himself had no facial expression.

"Leave us," Kango shouted. "Get out of there! Take their stupid bomb with you. We're not worth you sacrificing your lives to these assholes. Just go!"

"You know I can't do that," said Sharon.

"There are fifty-seven attack ships, approaching us from pretty much every possible direction," said Noreen.

"Can we at least disable their stupid bomb permanently before they capture us?" said Sharon. "I'm guessing not. We'd need weeks to figure out how it works."

"Hey," Jara said, pushing herself forward. "I wanted to say, I guess you were kind of right about why I stowed away. I always wanted to be special, not just another one of a billion servants of the Vastness. When I saw your ship about to disembark, I thought maybe I could help spread the word about the Vastness to the whole galaxy, and then I'd be the best acolyte ever. But it turned out the only way I could be special was as a fake countess."

"You were a great fake countess though," Kango said, squirming next to her.

"Thanks. And thanks for taking me to that party," Jara told her. "I got to see all sorts of things that I'd never even imagined. It started me thinking, maybe I really could find a way to reinvent myself as an individual, the way you two did. In fact, I'm starting to realize that—You are everything!"

"What the hell? You just said—"

"I can't control it," said Jara. "It's like an instinctive response whenever—You are everything!"

And then they lost the signal, because a voice broke in on every single open frequency. The voice was shouting one thing over and over: "I am everything! I am everything! I am everything!"

"Uh," said Sharon.

"So, you probably already guessed this," said Noreen. "But sensors are showing that a Temporary Embarrassment, the size of several planets, has just appeared on the edge of the central Pleasure Nexus of Liberty House. The weather control systems on Salubrious IV are all working overtime."

"You're right, I did actually guess that," said Sharon.

"The good news is, all the ships that were about to attack us have been diverted onto a new heading," said Noreen.

"We gotta go rescue Kango," said Sharon. "And Jara, I guess."

"I have some excellent news," came a plummy male voice from the cargo hold. Horace, the super-weapon. "My activation sequence has been initiated. It's the moment I've been waiting for my whole life!"

8

Hazelbeem, whose full name was Hazelbeem Sternforke Paddleborrow XXVII, was standing in front of the Grand Wilding Suites and Superior Fun Center, where the party had been held. He had a half dozen Fixers with him, and they were holding Kango and Jara in chains as the *Spicy Meatball* landed on the front lawn (which screamed and tried to bite the *Meatball's* landing struts).

"So! Not only did you steal our top secret ultimate weapon," said Hazelbeem, his mustache knotted in anger, "but you brought the wrath of the most revolting giant monster in the galaxy down on us. Were I an existentialist masochist, this would be my happiest day ever. Too bad I am an objectivist sadist, instead."

"Just let my friends go," said Sharon. "We can help. We know what the Vastness wants."

"You are everything!" shouted Jara.

"We are past the point of negotiation," said Hazelbeem. "We have already activated the weapon on board your ship, as soon as we detected a major threat to our way of life. If we cannot continue the absolute pursuit of amusement, with zero limitations, then there's no reason for this galaxy to continue existing. I must say, when we created you and your friend here"—he gestured at Kango—"we did not imagine it could ever lead to so many un-amusing incidents."

"This just proves that amusement is subjective," said Kango, struggling against his chains. "I've been highly amused by many of today's events."

"You are everything!"

"You were made as a brothel extra," said Hazelbeem to Kango. "You weren't even supposed to have a mind of your own. You're a single-celled organism, are you not? Made to appear like a beautiful young man, to stand in the background of the crowd scenes at a brothel. Something must have gone very wrong—perhaps you received too high a dose of neuropeptides in the vat."

"I may only have one cell," said Kango, "but *you've* just been nucleused."

"I don't even know what that means." Hazelbeem's mustache crinkled.

"It was supposed to be a play on the fact that I have a single nucleus, and I'm . . . Oh, just forget I said anything."

"Already forgotten," said Hazelbeem.

"You are everything!"

"Can you stop shouting that?" Hazelbeem said to Jara. "It's giving me a headache."

"We've been trying, believe me," said Sharon.

"It's a reflex," Jara told Hazelbeem. "I belong to the Vastness, no matter what I do. I was foolish to think anything mattered except for the Vastness. I'm probably going to be punished for doubting even a little, in my heart."

"You are a very tiresome little person," Hazelbeem told her.

The sky was churning with angry black swirlies, which reminded Sharon of one of the first parties at which she'd been the designated monster, when the Marquis of Bloopabloopasneak had set off some kind of weather bomb, left over from one of the old galactic wars. Five hundred–odd people had died in the hurricanes and blizzards, before the Pleasure Nexus's weather control systems had regained control, and the Marquis of Bloopabloopasneak had played really loud glam-clash music to drown out the screams and the roaring of the elements.

Hazelbeem was looking at the big fob hanging from his inner jacket (which was made of tiny living people, all of them squirming in a vain attempt to escape from the stitching that stuck them together). "That hypertrophic organism and its fleet of ships have torn through our planetary defenses, in the worst disaster since that all-you-can-eat buffet escaped from its trays and grew until it devoured an entire planet. I blame! I really do. I blame."

"Just let my friends go and we'll deal with the Vastness for you." Sharon shouted to make herself heard over the howling in the sky. "There's no need for any of this."

"This is what happens when playthings try to think for themselves," Hazelbeem snorted. "First they start trying to act like *people*, and before you know it, they—"

Sharon ate Hazelbeem. This happened too quickly for anybody to react. One second, Hazelbeem was working himself up into a tirade about toys that get ideas above their station, and the next, Sharon's mouth expanded to several times its normal size and just gobbled him up. She spat out his boots a second later.

"Ugh," Sharon said. "I promised myself I would never do that again, but there's provocation and then there's *provocation*. I've had a lot of pent-up rage these past few days." She looked at the gaggle of Fixers who were holding her friends prisoner and yelled, "Let my friends go, or you're next!"

"Whatever you say!" the head Fixer stammered as she unlocked Kango and Jara. "We all just want to be with our families—or possibly go to an end-of-the-galaxy blood orgy. One of those. Bye!" The Fixers all took off running in different directions, leaving Sharon, Kango, Jara, and Hazelbeem's boots.

Sharon looked down at the boots. "He just pushed me too far."

"It's fine," Kango said in her ear, as he touched her arm. "Just because you eat the occasional horrible person, doesn't prove you're actually the monster they tried to make you into. I promise."

"You are everything!" Jara said, then added, "That guy was asking for it. As an official countess, I pardon you."

"Thanks," Sharon said, still raising her voice over the awful din. "Now we just gotta save the galaxy. Any ideas?"

They all looked at each other, then at the pair of boots on the ground, as if the boots might suddenly offer a helpful suggestion.

9

The Vastness had somehow taken over the festival speakers all around the Superior Fun Center and was shouting about the fact that someone had dared to steal from its all-encompassing magnificence. Nobody escaped the Vastness! To underscore this, a flotilla of the Vastness's Joybreaker-class ships was swooping down over the surface of Salubrious IV and firing Obliteron missiles at every freestanding structure. The ground shook, the sky churned, and the Superior Fun Center and several other buildings collapsed, as Kango, Sharon, and Jara ran back to the *Spicy Meatball*—stumbling and falling on their faces while the Vastness shrieked at top volume.

"You are everything," said Jara, face in the dirt.

Kango flung himself into his pilot seat aboard the *Spicy Meatball* and tried to lift off, but the entire airspace consisted of pretty much nothing but explosions, dotted with the occasional deadly warship. Barely a few hundred yards off the ground, the *Spicy Meatball* was forced to go into a dive to avoid a huge chunk of burning debris. Kango and Noreen screamed in unison.

"You know," said Horace. "I've heard it said that death is what makes life meaningful. In that case, I am about to create more meaning than all of the artists in history, combined."

Kango was a blur as he tried to steer through the flaming obstacle course.

At last, they reached the upper atmosphere . . . just as some terrible *presence* appeared directly beneath them. It was just a dark shape that blotted out their view of Salubrious IV. Sharon struggled to make out any details for a moment, and then she saw some undulating barbed tentacles, and she *knew*.

"No," said Sharon. "They released the planet-eater."

"Is that Liberty House's last line of defense?" asked Jara, fascinated by the shape on their external viewer.

"No," Kango said. "They made it for a party, years ago. It basically just eats planets, much as its name implies. We're between it and the Vastness. Hold tight!"

"To what?" Sharon demanded.

The planet-eater thrashed around as it forced its way out of the atmosphere of Salubrious IV and tried to swim toward the Vastness. The planet-eater's uncountable limbs lashed out, trying to pull everything in their path into the one enormous maw at its center. One of those huge barbed tentacles swiped within a few feet of the *Spicy Meatball*, which dodged and nearly ran into another flotilla of Joybreaker-class attack ships.

"Hall and Oates!" Sharon cursed.

"You are everything!" Jara cried out.

"Keep it down, you two," Kango growled. "It's hard enough trying to make evasive maneuvers between pretty much everything deadly without also having to listen to a lot of religious mumbo jumbo."

"Oh, as if *you* have it all figured out," Sharon said. "Your only religion is exhibitionism. I swear, the next time we have a plan that relies on a diversion—a contained, sensible diversion—that can be *my* job."

"Sure!" Kango spun the ship on its axis to scoot past a planet-eater tentacle, then veered sharply to the left to avoid a spread of Obliteron missiles. "Because you're such a genius at strategy, and that's how we ended up with a mindless ultimate weapon on board!"

"I'll have you know, I am quite mindful," Horace protested. "And there are mere minutes before my devastation wave is launched from the galactic core. Once it begins, it will sweep the entire galaxy in no time at all!"

"Hey, I did my best," Sharon said to Kango. "It's not as if it was my idea to—" She stopped, because Jara was staring at her. "What?"

"You're doing it again," Jara said. "You're acting as though each of you is the Vastness to the other. I wish I knew how you *do* that. I'm going to die soon, too, and even with the Vastness close at hand, I'll die alone, and for no real reason. You are everything!"

"Listen, Jara," Sharon said, ignoring her nausea as Kango did a series of barrel rolls to avoid explosions that came close enough to rattle her teeth. "Listen. The Vastness is only everything because it's incredibly limited. It can't even see all the things it's not. It's like a giant stupid ignorant blob of . . . wait. Wait a minute!"

"What?" Kango said. "Did you think of something super super clever?"

"Maybe," Sharon said, praying to Hall and Oates that she was right. She ran over and pulled the stolen synchrotrix out of the strongbox, then started wiring it into Horace's core as fast as she could. "Remember what you told me was special about this device?"

"The fact that it's worth a lot of chits?" Kango pulled the *Spicy Meatball*'s nose up so fast that Sharon nearly did a backflip, though she kept one hand on Horace. "It's got a nice color scheme? It has the ability to neutralize . . . oh. Oh!"

"You are everything!" Jara said.

The planet-eater had finally gotten past all of the attack ships that had tried vainly to slow it down. Now it had reached the Vastness, opening the vast gnashing maw at the heart of its starfish-like body to try and devour the mega planetoid. The planet-killer embraced the Vastness with its many limbs.

Sharon gripped Jara's shoulders so hard her knuckles were white. "Tell the Vastness we've got the ultimate weapon, right here on our ship. We can help the Vastness to become completely unstoppable. And the Vastness really will be everything, in an even better way than before."

Jara looked like she was about to cry. "You want me to lie to the Vastness."

"No," Sharon said. "Yes. Sort of. Not really. It's the only way."

"I'm just moments away from a glorious consummation," Horace said. "It's at times like this that I feel like composing a sonnet."

"Jara," Sharon hissed. "Now!"

"I'm trying," Jara said, shutting her eyes and concentrating. "The Vastness doesn't really listen. It just talks. I'm sending the message as hard as I can."

"Now! Please!"

The Vastness reached out with a beam of energy, trying to seize the *Spicy*

Meatball. Sharon rushed to the rear air lock with Horace, which was cobbled together with the synchrotrix. She tossed them out, and the Vastness's energy field captured them, pulling them through one of the Vastness's slavering eyemouths inside its guts.

They were inside the Vastness's own atmosphere, close enough to hear its eyemouths shouting through their countless razor-sharp teeth. "I am everything! Now I have this ultimate weapon, my power will be absolute. I will be all things, and every living being will shout my praises. I am—"

Sharon watched through the air lock as the Vastness vanished from space.

In the space where the Vastness had been, a bright purple and green fissure was opened up. The crack in spacetime was huge enough to let Sharon see through it, as the Vastness was drawn toward the supermassive black hole at the core of the galaxy.

"You are everything," Jara said, sorrowfully, standing next to Sharon.

And then the Vastness was no longer visible. But in its place was a huge distortion, enveloping the black hole at the core of the galaxy.

"The biggest Embarrassment the galaxy has ever seen," Kango breathed from the flight deck.

And then the purple and green fissure closed, leaving a badly injured planet-eater, several thousand confused Joybreaker-class starships, and the *Spicy Meatball.*

"We did it," Kango said, seeming semi-permeable with astonishment.

"The Vastness followed Horace's program and ended up at the galactic core," Sharon said. "And then it Embarrassed itself."

"I just killed my god." Jara looked as though she was too shocked even for tears.

"Look at it this way," Sharon said. "You told the truth. Mostly. The Vastness is everywhere and everything now, in a way. It always will be with you, and it can never be defeated. You can worship the Vastness forever."

"I don't know." Jara tried saying "You are everything," but it wasn't the same when it came in response to nothing.

"Well, meanwhile," Kango said. "We lost the synchrotrix that we were counting on to pay our bills. We lost the super-weapon, too. So we're even more broke than we were before. Unless we can convince Mandre Lewis that we just saved the galaxy."

"We'll figure something out," Sharon said, then turned back toward Jara. "But what are you going to do? There's a huge fleet of ships out there, full of your fellow acolytes, and they desperately need some direction. Plus this star system is rich in resources and technology, and it just had all its planetary defenses wrecked. You could go back to Salubrious, with all your people, and become a countess for real."

"Maybe," Jara said. "Or maybe I could go with you guys? I feel like I have a lot to learn from you two. I'm not sure I'm ready to explain what happened, to the other acolytes."

"Sure. How do you feel about helping to open a restaurant? Do you know how to make a tablecloth?" Kango threw the *Spicy Meatball* headlong into an escape course, before anybody could try to blame them for all the property damage. Behind them, the ruins of Salubrious IV sparkled with the dying light of countless fires as the tributary ships of the Vastness began, hesitantly and confusedly, to make planetfall.

Sometimes you get crushed by a fear so all-encompassing, the only thing you can do is write it down and share it with the world. Back in January 2017, I couldn't sleep. We were a couple weeks away from the inauguration of our forty-fifth president, and I was having nightmares and panic attacks about surviving as a trans person in this new era. I decided to channel all my anxiety, rage, and nausea into a story that would give voice to my worst fears about my body becoming illegal—I couldn't work on anything else until I finished writing.

"Don't Press Charges and I Won't Sue" was both super easy and incredibly difficult to write. I put everything into this story: all the tenderness, all the sadness, all the silliness and defiance, all the *fury*. The line that sticks in my head is "Who even was I, if I let this happen to me?" This story is about fighting back and holding on to yourself at all costs—and here's a good place to mention that this story should come with a content warning, particularly for trans/nb people and anyone triggered by medical horror.

DON'T PRESS CHARGES AND I WON'T SUE

1

The intake process begins with dismantling her personal space, one mantle at a time. Her shoes, left by the side of the road where the Go Team plucked her out of them. Her purse and satchel, her computer containing all of her artwork and her manifestos, thrown into a metal garbage can at a rest area on the highway, miles away. That purse, which she swung to and fro on the sidewalks to clear a path, like a southern grandma, now has food waste piled on it, and eventually will be chewed to shreds by raccoons. At some point, the intake personnel fold her, like a folding chair that turns into an almost two-dimensional object, and they stuff her into a kennel, in spite of all her attempts to resist. Later she receives her first injection and loses any power to struggle, and some time after, control over her excretory functions. By the time they cut her clothes off, a layer of muck coats the backs of her thighs. They clean her and dress her in something that is not clothing, and they shave part of her head. At some point, Rachel glimpses a power drill, like a handyman's, but she's anesthetized and does not feel where it goes.

Rachel has a whole library of ways to get through this, none of which works at all. She spent a couple years meditating, did a whole course on trauma and self-preservation, and had an elaborate theory about how to carve out a space in your mind that *they* cannot touch, whatever *they* are doing to you. She remembers the things she used to tell everyone else in the support group, in the Safe Space, about not being alone even when you have become isolated by outside circumstances. But in the end, Rachel's only coping mechanism is dissociation, which only arises from total animal panic. She's not even Rachel anymore, she's just a screaming blubbering mess, with a tiny kernel of her mind left, trapped a few feet above her body, in a process that is not at all like yogic flying.

Eventually, though, the intake is concluded, and Rachel is left staring up at a Styrofoam ceiling with a pattern of cracks that looks like a giant spider or an angry demon face descending toward her. She's aware of being numb from extreme cold, in addition to the other ways in which she is numb, and the air conditioner keeps blurting into life with an aggravated whine. A stereo system plays a CD by that white rock-rap artist who turned out to be an especially trifling racist. The staff keep walking past her and talking about her in the third person, while misrepresenting basic facts about her, such as her name and her personal pronoun. Occasionally they adjust something about her position or drug regimen, without speaking to her or looking at her face. She does not quite have enough motor control to scream or make any sound other than a kind of low ululation. She realizes at some point that someone has made a tiny hole in the base of her skull, where she now feels a mild ache.

Before you feel too sorry for Rachel, however, you should be aware that she's a person who holds a great many controversial views. For example, she once claimed to disapprove of hot chocolate, because she believes that chocolate is better at room temperature, or better yet as a component of ice cream or some other frozen dessert. In addition, Rachel considers ZZ Top an underappreciated music group, supports karaoke only in an alcohol-free environment, dislikes puppies, enjoys brussels sprouts, and rides a bicycle with no helmet. She claims to prefer the *Star Wars* prequels to the Disney *Star Wars* films. Is Rachel a contrarian, a freethinker, or just kind of an asshole? If you could ask her, she would reply that opinions are a utility in and of themselves. That is, the holding of opinions is a worthwhile exercise per se, and the greater the diversity of opinions in the world, the more robust our collective ability to argue.

Also! Rachel once got a gas station attendant nearly fired for behavior that, a year or two later, she finally conceded might have been an honest misunderstanding. She's the kind of person who sends food back for not being quite what she ordered—and on at least two occasions, she did this and then returned to that same restaurant a week or two later, as if she had been happy after all. Rachel is the kind of person who calls herself an artist, despite never having received a grant from a granting institution, or any kind of formal gallery show, and many people wouldn't even consider her collages and relief maps of imaginary places to be proper art. You would probably call Rachel a Goth.

Besides dissociation—which is wearing off as the panic subsides—the one defense mechanism that remains for Rachel is carrying on an imaginary conversation with Dev, the person with whom she spoke every day for so long, and to whom she always imagined speaking, whenever they were apart. Dev's voice in Rachel's head would have been a refuge not long ago, but now all Rachel can imagine Dev saying is *Why did you leave me? Why, when I needed you most?* Rachel does not have a good answer to that question, which is why she never tried to answer it when she had the chance.

Thinking about Dev, about lost chances, is too much. At that moment, Rachel realizes she has enough muscle control to lift her head and look directly in front of her. There, standing at an observation window, she sees her childhood best friend, Jeffrey.

2

Ask Jeffrey why he's been working at Love and Dignity for Everyone for the past few years and he'll say, first and foremost, student loans. Plus, in recent years, child support, and his mother's ever-increasing medical bills. Life is crammed full of things that you have to pay for after the fact, and the word "plan" in "payment plan" is a cruel mockery because nobody ever really sets out to plunge into chronic debt. But also Jeffrey wants to believe in the mission of Love and Dignity for Everyone: to repair the world's most broken people.

Jeffrey often rereads the mission statement on the wall of the employee lounge as he sips his morning Keurig, so he can carry Mr. Randall's words with him for the rest of the day. Society depends on mutual respect, Mr. Randall says. You respect yourself and therefore I respect you, and vice versa. When people won't respect themselves, we have no choice but to intervene, or society unravels. Role-rejecting and aberrant behavior, ipso facto, is a sign of a lack of self-respect. Indeed, a cry for help. The logic always snaps back into airtight shape inside Jeffrey's mind.

Of course Jeffrey recognizes Rachel the moment he sees her wheeled into the treatment room, even after all this time and so many changes, because he's been Facebook-stalking her for years (usually after a couple of whiskey sours). He saw when she changed her name and her gender marker, and noticed when her hairstyle changed and when her face suddenly had a more feminine shape. There was the kitten she adopted that later ran away, and the thorny tattoo that says STAY ALIVE. Jeffrey read all her oversharing status updates about the pain of hair removal and the side effects of various pills. And then, of course, the crowning surgery. Jeffrey lived through this process vicariously, in real time, and saw no resemblance to a butterfly in a cocoon, or any other cute metaphor. The gender change looked more like landscaping: building embankments out of raw dirt, heaving big rocks to change the course of rivers, and uprooting plants, stem by stem. Dirty bruising work. Why a person would feel the need to do this to themselves, Jeffrey could never know.

At first, Jeffrey pretends not to know the latest subject, or to have any feelings one way or the other, as the Accu-Probe goes into the back of her head. This is not the right moment to have a sudden conflict. Due to some recent personnel issues, Jeffrey is stuck wearing a project manager hat along with his engineer hat—which, sadly, is not a cool pinstriped train-engineer hat of the sort that he and Rachel used to fantasize about wearing for work when they were kids. As a project manager, he has to worry endlessly about weird details such as getting enough coolant into the cadaver storage area and making sure that Jamil has the green shakes that he says activate his brain. As a government–industry joint venture under Section 1774(b)(8) of the

Mental Health Restoration Act (relating to the care and normalization of at-risk individuals), Love and Dignity for Everyone has to meet certain benchmarks of effectiveness, and must involve the community in a meaningful role. Jeffrey is trying to keep twenty fresh cadavers in transplant-ready condition, and clearing the decks for more live subjects, who are coming down the pike at an ever-snowballing rate. The situation resembles one of those poultry processing plants where they keep speeding up the conveyor belt until the person grappling with each chicken ends up losing a few fingers.

Jeffrey runs from the cadaver freezer to the observation room to the main conference room for another community engagement session, around and around, until his Fitbit applauds. Five different Slack channels flare at once with people wanting to ask Jeffrey process questions, and he's lost count of all his unanswered DMs. Everyone agrees on the goal—returning healthy, well-adjusted individuals to society without any trace of dysphoria, dysmorphia, dystonia, or any other *dys*-words—but nobody can agree on the fine details or how exactly to measure ideal outcomes beyond those statutory benchmarks. Who even is the person who comes out the other end of the Love and Dignity for Everyone process? What does it even mean to be a unique individual, in an age when your fingerprints and retina scans have long since been stolen by Ecuadorian hackers? It's all too easy to get sucked into metaphysical flusterclucks about identity and the soul and what makes you you.

Jeffrey's near-daily migraine is already in full flower by the time he sees Rachel wheeled in and he can't bring himself to look. She's looking at him. She's looking right at him. Even with all the other changes, her eyes are the same, and he can't just stand here. She's putting him in an impossible position, at the worst moment.

Someone has programmed Slack so that when anyone types "alrighty then," a borderline-obscene gif of two girls wearing clown makeup appears. Jeffrey is the only person who ever types "alrighty then," and he can't train himself to stop doing it. And, of course, he hasn't been able to figure out who programmed the gif to appear.

Self-respect is the key to mutual respect. Jeffrey avoids making eye contact with that window or anyone beyond it. His head still feels too heavy with pain for a normal body to support, but also he's increasingly aware of a core-deep anxiety shading into nausea.

3

Jeffrey and Rachel had a group, from the tail end of elementary school through to the first year of high school, called the Sock Society. They all lived in the same cul-de-sac, bounded by a canola field on one side and the big interstate on the other. The origins of the Sock Society's name are lost to history, but may arise from the fact that Jeffrey's mom never liked kids to wear shoes inside the house and Jeffrey's house had the best game consoles and a 4K TV with surround sound. These kids wore out countless pairs of tires on their dirt bikes, conquered the extra DLC levels in *Halls of Valor*, and built snow forts that gleamed. They stayed up all night watching forbidden horror movies on an old laptop under a blanket, on sleepovers, while guzzling off-brand soda. They whispered, late at night, of their fantasies and barely-hinted-at anxieties, although there were some things Rachel would not share because she was not ready to speak of them and Jeffrey would not have been able to hear if she had. They repeated jokes they didn't one hundred percent understand, and kind of enjoyed the queasy awareness of being out of their depth. Later, the members of the Sock Society (who changed their ranks over time, with the exception of the core members, Rachel and Jeffrey) became adept at stuffing gym socks with blasting caps and small incendiaries and fashioning the socks themselves into rudimentary fuses before placing them in lawn ornaments, small receptacles for gardening tools, and—in one incident that nobody discussed afterward—Mrs. Hooper's scooter.

When Jeffrey's mother was drunk, which was often, she would say she wished Rachel was her son, because Rachel was such a smart boy—quick on the uptake, so charming with the rapid-fire puns, handsome, and respectful. Like Young Elvis. Instead of Jeffrey, who was honestly a little shit.

Jeffrey couldn't wait to get over the wall of adolescence, into the garden of manhood. Every dusting of fuzz on his chin, every pungent whiff from his armpits, seemed to him the starting gun. He became obsessed with finding porn via that old laptop, and he was an artist at coming up with fresh new search terms every time he and Rachel hung out. Rachel got used to innocent terms such as "cream pie" turning out to be mean something gross and animalistic, in much the same way that a horror movie turned human bodies into slippery meat.

Then one time Jeffrey pulled up some transsexual porn, because what the hell. Rachel found herself watching a slender Latin girl with a shy smile slowly peel out of a silk robe to step into a scene with a muscular bald man. The girl was wearing nothing but bright silver shoes and her body was all smooth angles and tapering limbs, and the one token of her transgender status looked tiny, both inconsequential and of a piece with the rest of her femininity. She tiptoed across the frame like a ballerina. Like a cartoon deer.

Watching this, Rachel quivered, until Jeffrey thought she must be grossed out, but deep down Rachel was having a feeling of recognition. Like: that's me. Like: I am possible.

Years later, in her twenties, Rachel had a group of girlfriends (some trans, some cis), and she started calling this feminist gang the Sock Society, because they made a big thing of wearing colorful socks with weird and sometimes profane patterns. Rachel mostly didn't think about the fact that she had repurposed the Sock Society sobriquet for another group, except to tell herself that she was reclaiming an ugly part of her past. Rachel is someone who obsesses about random issues but also claims to avoid introspection at all costs—in fact, she once proposed an art show called *The Unexamined Life Is the Only Way to Have Fun.*

4

Rachel has soiled herself again. A woman in avocado-colored scrubs snaps on blue gloves with theatrical weariness before sponging Rachel's still-unfeeling body. The things I have to deal with, says the red-faced woman, whose name is Lucy. People like you always make people like me clean up after you, because you never think the rules apply to you, the same as literally everyone else. And then look where we end up, and I'm here cleaning your mess.

Rachel tries to protest that none of this is her doing, but her tongue is a slug that's been bathed in salt.

There's always some excuse, Lucy says as she scrubs. Life is not complicated, it's actually very simple. Men are men, and women are women, and everyone has a role to play. It's selfish to think that you can just force everyone else in the world to start carving out exceptions, just so you can play at being something you're not. You will never understand what it really means to be female, the joy and the endless discomfort, because you were not born into it.

Rachel feels frozen solid. Ice crystals permeate her body, the way they would frozen dirt. This woman is touching between her legs, without looking her in the face. She cannot bear to breathe. She keeps trying to get Jeffrey's attention, but he always looks away. As if he'd rather not witness what's going to happen to her.

Lucy and a man in scrubs wheel in something gauzy and white, like a cloud on a gurney. They bustle around, unwrapping and cleaning and prepping, and they mutter numbers and codes to each other, like E-drop 2347, as if there are a lot of parameters to keep straight here. The sound of all that quiet professionalism soothes Rachel in spite of herself, like she's at the dentist.

At some point they step away from the thing they've unwrapped and prepped, and Rachel turns her head just enough to see a dead man on a metal shelf.

Her first thought is that he's weirdly good looking, despite his slight decomposition. He has a snub nose and thin lips, a clipped jaw, good muscle definition, a cyanotic penis that flops against one thigh, and sandy pubic hair. Whatever (whoever) killed this man left his body in good condition, and he was roughly Rachel's age. This man could have been a model, or maybe a pro wrestler, and Rachel feels sad that he somehow died so early, with his best years ahead.

Rachel tries to scream. She feels Lucy and the other one connecting her to the dead man's body and hears a rattling garbage disposal sound. The dead man twitches, and meanwhile Rachel can't struggle or make a sound. She feels weaker than before, and some part of her insists this must be because she lost an argument at some point. Back in the Safe Space, they had talked about all the friends of friends who had gone to ground, and the internet rumors. How would you know if you were in danger? Rachel had said that was a dumb question, because danger never left.

The dead man smiles: not a large rictus, like in a horror movie, but a tiny shift in his features, like a contented sleeper. His eyes haven't moved or appeared to look at anything. Lucy clucks and adjusts a thing, and the kitchen-garbage noise grinds louder for a moment.

We're going to get you sorted out, Lucy says to the dead man. You are going to be so happy. She turns and leans over Rachel to check something, and her breath smells like sour corn chips.

You are violating my civil rights by keeping me here, Rachel says. A sudden victory, except that then she hears herself and it's wrong. Her voice comes out of the wrong mouth, is not even her own voice. The dead man has spoken, not her, and he didn't say that thing about civil rights. Instead, he said, Hey, excuse me, how long am I going to be kept here? As if this was a mild inconvenience that was keeping him from his business. The voice sounded rough, flinty, like a bad sore throat, but also commanding. The voice of a surgeon, or an airline pilot. You would stop whatever you were doing and listen, if you heard that voice.

Rachel lets out an involuntary cry of panic, which comes out of the dead man's mouth as a low groan. She tries again to say, This is not medicine. This is a human rights violation. It comes out of the dead man's mouth as, I don't mean to be a jerk. I just have things to do, you know. Sorry if I'm causing any trouble.

That's quite all right, Mr. Billings, Lucy says. You're making tremendous progress, and we're so pleased. You'll be released into the community soon, and the community will be so happy to see you.

The thought of ever trying to speak again fills Rachel with a whole ocean voyage's worth of nausea, but she can't even make herself retch.

5

Jeffrey has wondered for years, what if he could talk to his oldest friend, man to man, about the things that had happened when they were on the cusp of adolescence—not just the girl, but the whole deal. Mrs. Hooper's scooter, even. And maybe, at last, he will. A lot depends on how well the process goes. Sometimes the cadaver gets almost all of the subject's memories and personality, just with a better outlook on his or her proper gender. There is, however, a huge variability in bandwidth because we're dealing with human beings, and especially with weird neurological stuff that we barely understand. We're trying to thread wet spaghetti through a grease trap, a dozen pieces at a time. Even with the proprietary cocktail, it's hardly an exact science.

The engineer part of Jeffrey just wants to keep the machines from making whatever noise that was earlier, the awful grinding sound. But the project manager part of Jeffrey is obsessing about all of the extraneous factors outside his control. What if they get a surprise inspection from the Secretary, or even worse that Deputy Assistant Secretary, with the eye? Jeffrey is not supposed to be a front-facing part of this operation, but Mr. Randall says we all do things that are outside our comfort zones, and really, that's the only way your comfort zone can ever expand. In addition, Jeffrey is late for another stakeholder meeting, with the woman from Mothers Raising Well-Adjusted Children and the three bald men from Grassroots Rising, who will tear Jeffrey a new orifice. There are still too many maladjusted individuals out there, in the world, trying to use public washrooms and putting our children at risk. Some children, too, keep insisting that they aren't boys or girls, because they saw some ex-athlete prancing on television. Twenty cadavers in the freezer might as well be nothing in the face of all this. The three bald men will take turns spit-shouting, using words such as psychosexual, and Jeffrey has fantasized about sneaking bourbon into his coffee so he can drink whenever that word comes up. He's pretty sure they don't know what psychosexual even means, except that it's psycho and it's sexual. After a stakeholder meeting, Jeffrey always retreats to the single-stall men's room to shout at his own schmutzy reflection. Fuck you, you fucking fuck fucker. Don't tell me I'm not doing my job.

Self-respect is the key to mutual respect.

Rachel keeps looking straight at Jeffrey through the observation window, and she's somehow kept control over her vision long after her speech centers went over. He keeps waiting for her to lose the eyes. Her gaze goes right into him, and his stomach gets the feeling that usually comes after two or three whiskey sours and no dinner.

More than ever, Jeffrey wishes the observation room had a one-way mirror instead of regular glass. Why would they skimp on that? What's the point of having an observation room where you are also being observed at the same time? It defeats the entire purpose.

Jeffrey gets tired of hiding from his own window and skips out the side door. He climbs two stories of cement stairs to emerge in the executive wing, near the conference suite where he's supposed to be meeting with the stakeholders right now. He finds an oaken door with that quote from Albert Einstein about imagination, which everybody always has, and knocks on it. After a few breaths, a deep voice tells Jeffrey to come in, and then he's sitting opposite an older man with square shoulders and a perfect old-fashioned newscaster head.

Mr. Randall, Jeffrey says, I'm afraid I have a conflict with regards to the latest subject and I must ask to be recused.

Is that a fact? Mr. Randall furrows his entire face for a moment, then magically all the wrinkles disappear again. He smiles and shakes his head. I feel you, Jeffrey, I really do. That blows chunks. Unfortunately, as you know, we are short-staffed right now, and our work is of a nature that only a few people have the skills and moral virtue to complete it.

But, Jeffrey says. The new subject, he's someone I grew up with, and there are certain . . . I mean, I made promises when we were little, and it feels in some ways like I'm breaking those promises, even as I try my best to help him. I actually feel physically ill, like drunk in my stomach but sober in my brain, when I look at him.

Jeffrey, Mr. Randall says, Jeffrey, *Jeffrey*. Listen to me. Sit still and listen. Pull yourself together. We are the watchers on the battlements, at the edge of social collapse, like in that show with the ice zombies, where winter is always tomorrow. You know that show? They had an important message, that sometimes we have to put our own personal feelings aside for the greater good. Remember the fat kid? He had to learn to be a team player. I loved that show. So here we are, standing against the darkness that threatens to consume everything we admire. No time for divided hearts.

I know that we're doing something important here, and that he'll thank me later, Jeffrey says. It's just hard right now.

If it were easy to do the right thing, Randall says, then everyone would do it.

6

Sherri was a transfer student in tenth grade who came right in and joined the computer club but also tried out for the volleyball team and the a cappella chorus. She had dark hair in tight braids and a wiry body that flexed in the moment before she leapt to spike the ball, making Rachel's heart rise with her. Rachel sat courtside and watched Sherri practice while she was supposed to be doing sudden-death sprints.

Jeffrey stared at Sherri, too: listened to her sing Janelle Monáe in a light contralto while she waited for the bus, and gazed at her across the room during computer club. He imagined going up to her and just introducing himself, but his heart was too weak. He could more easily imagine saying the dumbest thing, or actually fainting, than carrying on a smooth conversation with Sherri. He obsessed for ages, until he finally confessed to his friends (Rachel was long since out of the picture by this time) and they started goading him, actually physically shoving him, to speak to Sherri.

Jeffrey slid up to her and said his name, and something inane about music, and then Sherri just stared at him for a long time before saying, I gotta get the bus. Jeffrey watched her walk away, then turned to his watching friends and mimed a finger gun blowing his brains out.

A few days later, Sherri was playing hooky at that one bakery café in town that everyone said was run by lesbians or drug addicts or maybe just old hippies, nursing a chai latte, and she found herself sitting with Rachel, who was also ditching some activity. Neither of them wanted to talk to anyone, they'd come here to be alone. But Rachel felt hope rise up inside her at the proximity of her wildfire crush, and she finally hoisted her bag as if she might just leave the café. Mind if I sit with you a minute, she asked, and Sherri shrugged yes. So Rachel perched on the embroidered tasseled pillow on the bench next to Sherri and stared at her Algebra II book.

They saw each other at that café every few days, or sometimes just once a week, and they just started sitting together on purpose, without talking to each other much. After a couple months of this, Sherri looked at the time on her phone and said, My mom's out of town. I'll buy you dinner. Rachel kept her shriek of joy on the inside and just nodded.

At dinner—a family pasta place nearby—Sherri looked down at her colorful paper napkin and whispered, I think I don't like boys. I mean, to date, or whatever. I don't hate boys or anything, just not interested that way. You understand.

Rachel stared at Sherri, even after she looked up, so they were making eye contact. In just as low a whisper, Rachel replied, I'm pretty sure I'm not a boy.

This was the first time Rachel ever said the name Rachel aloud, at least with regard to herself.

Sherri didn't laugh or get up or run away. She just stared back, then nodded. She reached onto the red checkerboard vinyl tablecloth with an open palm, for Rachel to insert her palm into if she so chose.

The first time Jeffrey saw Rachel and Sherri holding hands, he looked at them like his soul had come out in bruises.

7

We won't keep you here too long, Mr. Billings, the male attendant says, glancing at Rachel but mostly looking at the mouth that had spoken. You're doing very well. Really, you're an exemplary subject. You should be so proud.

There are so many things that Rachel wants to say. Like: Please just let me go, I have a life. I have an art show coming up in a coffee shop, I can't miss it. You don't have the right. I deserve to live my own life. I have people who used to love me. I'll give you everything I own. I won't press charges if you don't sue. This is no kind of therapy. On and on. But she can't trust that corpse voice. She hyperventilates and gags on her own spit. So sore she's hamstrung.

Every time her eyes get washed out, she's terrified this is it, her last sight. She knows from what Lucy and the other one have said that if her vision switches over to the dead man's, that's the final stage and she's gone.

The man is still talking. We have a form signed by your primary care physician, Dr. Wallace, stating that this treatment is both urgent and medically indicated, as well as an assessment by our in-house psychologist, Dr. Yukizawa. He holds up two pieces of paper, with the looping scrawls of two different doctors that she's never even heard of. She's been seeing Dr. Cummings for years, since before her transition. She makes a huge effort to shake her head and is shocked by how weak she feels.

You are so fortunate to be one of the first to receive this treatment, the man says. Early indications are that subjects experience a profound improvement across seven different measures of quality of life and social integration. Their OGATH scores are generally high, especially in the red levels. Rejection is basically unheard of. You won't believe how good you'll feel once you're over the adjustment period, he says. If the research goes well, the potential benefits to society are limited only by the cadaver pipeline.

Rachel's upcoming art show, in a tiny coffee shop, is called *Against Curation*. There's a lengthy manifesto, which Rachel planned to print out and mount onto foam or cardboard, claiming that the act of curating is inimical to art or artistry. The only person who can create a proper context for a given piece of art is the artist herself, and arranging someone else's art is an act of violence. Bear in mind that the history of museums is intrinsically tied up with imperialism and colonialism, and the curatorial gaze is historically white and male. But even the most enlightened postcolonial curator is a pirate. Anthologies, mix tapes, it's all the same. Rachel had a long response prepared, in case anybody accused her of just being annoyed that no real gallery would display her work.

Rachel can't help noting the irony of writing a tirade about the curator's bloody scalpel, only to end up with a hole in her literal head.

When the man has left her alone, Rachel begins screaming Jeffrey's name in the dead man's voice. Just the name, nothing that the corpse could twist. She still can't bear to hear that deep timbre, the sick damaged throat, speaking for her, but she can feel her life essence slipping away. Every time she looks over at the dead man, he has more color in his skin and his arms and legs are moving, like a restless sleeper. His face even looks, in some hard-to-define way, more like Rachel's.

Jeffrey! The words come out in a hoarse growl. Jeffrey! Come here!

Rachel wants to believe she's already defeated this trap, because she has lived her life without a single codicil, and whatever they do, they can't retroactively change the person she has been for her entire adulthood. But that doesn't feel like enough. She wants the kind of victory where she gets to actually walk out of here.

8

Jeffrey feels a horrible twist in his neck. This is all unfair, because he already informed Mr. Randall of his conflict and yet he's still here, having to behave professionally while the subject is putting him in the dead center of attention.

Seriously, the subject will not stop bellowing his name, even with a throat that's basically raw membrane at this point. You're not supposed to initiate communication with the subject without submitting an Interlocution Permission form through the proper channels, but the subject is putting him into an impossible position.

Jeffrey, she keeps shouting. And then: Jeffrey, talk to me!

People are lobbing questions in Slack, and of course Jeffrey types the wrong thing and the softcore clown porn comes up. Ha ha, I fell for it again, he types. There's a problem with one of the latest cadavers, a cause-of-death question, and Mr. Randall says the Deputy Assistant Secretary might be in town later.

Jeffrey's mother was a Nobel Prize winner for her work with people who had lost the ability to distinguish between weapons and musical instruments, a condition that frequently leads to maiming or worse. Jeffrey's earliest memories involve his mother flying off to serve as an expert witness in the trials of murderers who claimed they had thought their assault rifles were banjos, or mandolins. Many of these people were faking it, but Jeffrey's mom was usually hired by the defense, not the prosecution. Every time she returned from one of these trips, she would fling her Nobel medal out her bathroom window and then stay up half the night searching the bushes for it, becoming increasingly drunk. One morning, Jeffrey found her passed out below her bedroom window and believed for a moment that she had fallen two stories to her death. This was, she explained to him later, a different sort of misunderstanding than mistaking a gun for a guitar: a reverse-Oedipal misapprehension. These days Jeffrey's mom requires assistance to dress, to shower, and to transit from her bed to a chair and back, and nobody can get Medicare, Medicaid, or any secondary insurance to pay for this. To save money, Jeffrey has moved back in with his mother, which means he gets to hear her ask at least once a week what happened to Rachel, who was such a nice boy.

Jeffrey can't find his headphones to drown out his name, which the cadaver is shouting so loud that foam comes out of one corner of his mouth. Frances and another engineer both complain on Slack about the noise, which they can hear from down the hall. OMG creepy, Frances types. Make it stop make it stop.

I can't, Jeffrey types back. I can't ok. I don't have the right paperwork.

Maybe tomorrow, Rachel will wake up fully inhabiting her male body. She'll look down at her strong forearms, threaded with veins, and she'll smile and thank Jeffrey. Maybe she'll nod at him, by way of a tiny salute, and say, You did it, buddy. You brought me back.

But right now, the cadaver keeps shouting, and Jeffrey realizes he's covering his ears with his fists and is doubled over.

Rachel apparently decides that Jeffrey's name alone isn't working. The cadaver pauses and then blurts, I would really love to hang with you. Hey! I appreciate everything you've done to set things right. *Jeffrey!* You really shouldn't have gone to so much trouble for me.

Somehow, these statements have an edge, like Jeffrey can easily hear the

behind her grows louder. Then she pushes through the door and runs up the square roundabout of stairs. Behind her, she hears Lucy the nurse shout at her to come back, because she's still convalescing, this is a delicate time.

Rachel feels a little more of her strength fade every time the dead man's hand lurches forward. Something irreplaceable leaves her. She pushes open the dense metal door marked EXIT and nearly faints with sudden day-blindness.

The woods around Love and Dignity for Everyone are dense with moss and underbrush, and Rachel's bare feet keep sliding off tree roots. I can't stop, Rachel pleads with herself, I can't stop or my whole life was for nothing. Who even was I, if I let this happen to me. The nearly naked dead man crashes through branches that Rachel has ducked under. She throws the knife and hears a satisfying grunt, but he doesn't even pause. Rachel knows that anybody who sees both her and the cadaver will choose to help the cadaver. There's no way to explain her situation in the dead man's voice. She vows to stay off roads and avoid talking to people. This is her life now.

Up ahead, she sees a fast-running stream, and she wonders how the corpse will take to water. The stream looks like the one she and Jeffrey used to play in, when they would catch crayfish hiding under rocks. The crayfish looked just like tiny lobsters, and they would twist around trying to pinch you as you gripped their midsections. Rachel sloshes in the water and doesn't hear the man's breath in her ear for a moment. Up ahead, the current leads to a steep waterfall that's so white in the noon sunlight, it appears to stand still. She remembers staring into a bucket full of crayfish, debating whether to boil them alive or let them all go. All at once, she has a vivid recollection of herself and Jeffrey both holding the full bucket and turning it sideways, until all the crayfish sloshed back into the river. The crayfish fled for their lives, their eyes seeming to protrude with alarm, and Rachel held on to an empty bucket with Jeffrey, feeling an inexplicable sense of relief. We are such wusses, Jeffrey said, and they both laughed. She remembers the sight of the last crayfish rushing out of view—as if this time, maybe the trick would work and nobody would think to look under this particular rock. She reaches the waterfall, seizes a breath, and jumps with both feet at once.

Bookstores are my favorite places to hang out. Browsing through shelves and shelf-talkers never fails to cheer me up, even when the world is bleak AF—everything about a bookshop lets you know that you're in a place where stories are celebrated, and you can never run out of discoveries. So when Victor LaValle and John Joseph Adams asked me to contribute to *A People's Future of the United States*, an anthology of stories set in a future USA, I knew I wanted to write about a bookseller struggling to hold things together.

"The Bookstore at the End of America" came just a few months after I wrote "Don't Press Charges," and it's another story that grapples with political nightmares—in this case, the slow dissolution of the United States into two countries that despise each other. But this story ended up being a lot less scary, because I can't write about bookstores without nurturing a spark of hope in the midst of hopelessness.

Heads up: this story contains racism, violence, and implied transphobia.

THE BOOKSTORE AT THE END OF AMERICA

A bookshop on a hill. Two front doors, two walkways lined with blank slates and grass, two identical signs welcoming customers to the First and Last Page, and a great blue building in the middle, shaped like an old-fashioned barn with a slanted tiled roof and generous rain gutters. Nobody knew how many books were inside that building, not even Molly, the owner. But if you couldn't find it there, they probably hadn't written it down yet.

The two walkways led to two identical front doors, with straw welcome mats, blue plank floors, and the scent of lilacs and old bindings—but then you'd see a completely different store, depending which side you entered. With two cash registers, for two separate kinds of money.

If you entered from the California side, you'd see a wall hanging: women of all ages, shapes, and origins holding hands and dancing. You'd notice the display of the latest books from a variety of small presses that clung to life in Colorado Springs and Santa Fe, from literature and poetry to cultural studies. The shelves closest to the door on the California side included a decent amount of women's and queer studies, but also a strong selection of classic literature, going back to Virginia Woolf and Zora Neale Hurston. Plus some brand-new paperbacks.

If you came in through the American front door, the basic layout would be pretty similar, except for the big painting of the nearby Rocky Mountains, though you might notice more books on religion, and some history books with a somewhat more conservative approach. The literary books skewed a bit more toward Faulkner, Thoreau, and Hemingway, not to mention Ayn Rand, and you might find more books of essays about self-reliance and strong families, along with another selection of low-cost paperbacks: thrillers and war novels, including brand-new releases from the big printing plant in Gatlinburg. Romance novels, too.

Go through either front door and keep walking, and you'd find yourself in a maze of shelves, with a plethora of nooks and a bevy of side rooms. Here a cavern of science fiction and fantasy, there a deep alcove of theater books— and a huge annex of history and sociology, including a whole wall devoted to explaining the origins of the Great Sundering. Of course, some people did make it all the way from one front door to the other, past the overfed snake shape of the hallways and the giant central reading room, with a plain red carpet and two beat-down couches in it. But the design of the store encouraged you to stay inside your own reality.

The exact border between America and California, which elsewhere featured watchtowers and roadblocks, YOU ARE NOW LEAVING / YOU ARE NOW ENTERING signs, and terrible overpriced souvenir stands, was denoted in the First and Last Page by a tall bookcase of self-help titles about coping with divorce.

People came hundreds of miles in either direction, via hydroelectric cars, solarcycles, mecha-horses, and tour buses, to get some book they couldn't live without. You could get electronic books via the Share, of course, but they might be plagued with crowdsourced editing, user-targeted content, random annotations, and sometimes just plain garbage. You might be reading the Federalist Papers on your Gidget and come across a paragraph about rights versus duties that wasn't there before—or for that matter, a few pages relating to hair cream, because you'd been searching on hair cream yesterday. Not to mention, the same book might read completely differently in California than in America. You could only rely on ink and paper (or, for newer books, Peip0r) for consistency, not to mention the whole sensory experience of smelling and touching volumes, turning their pages, bowing their spines.

Everybody needs books, Molly figured. No matter where they live, how they love, what they believe, whom they want to kill. We all want books. The moment you start thinking of books as some exclusive club, or the loving of books as a high distinction, then you're a bad bookseller.

Books are the best way to discover what people thought before you were born. And an author is just someone who tried their utmost to make sense of their own mess, and maybe their failure contains a few seeds to help you with yours.

Sometimes people asked Molly why she didn't just simplify it down to one entrance. Force the people from America to talk to the Californians, and vice versa—maybe expose one side or the other to some books that might challenge their worldview just a little. Molly always replied that she had a business to run, and if she managed to keep everyone reading, then that was enough. At the very least, Molly's arrangement kept this the most peaceful outpost on the border, without people gathering on one side to scream at the people on the other.

Some of those screaming people were old enough to have grown up in the United States of America, but they acted as though these two lands had always been enemies.

Whichever entrance of the bookstore you went through, the first thing you'd notice was probably Phoebe. Rake thin, coltish, rambunctious, right on the edge of becoming, she ran light enough on her bare feet to avoid ever rattling a single bookcase or dislodging a single volume. You heard Phoebe's laughter before her footsteps. Molly's daughter wore denim overalls and cheap linen blouses most days, or sometimes a floor-length skirt or lacy-hemmed dress, plus plastic bangles and necklaces. She hadn't gotten her ears pierced yet.

People from both sides of the line loved Phoebe, who was a joyful shriek that you only heard from a long way away, a breath of gladness running through the flower beds.

Molly used to pester Phoebe about getting outdoors to breathe some fresh air—because that seemed like something moms were supposed to say and Molly was paranoid about being a Bad Mother, since she was basically married to a bookstore, albeit one containing a large section of parenting books.

But she was secretly glad when Phoebe disobeyed her and stayed inside, end-lessly reading. Molly hoped Phoebe would always stay shy, that mother and daughter would hunker inside the First and Last Page, side-eyeing the world through thin linen curtains when they weren't reading together.

Then Phoebe had turned fourteen, and suddenly she was out all the time and Molly didn't see her for hours. Around that time, Phoebe had unex-pectedly grown pretty and lanky, her neck long enough to let her auburn ponytail swing as she ran around with the other kids who lived in the tangle of tree-lined streets on the America side of the line, plus a few kids who snuck across from California. Nobody seriously patrolled this part of the border, and there was one craggy rock pile, like an echo of the looming Rocky Mountains, that you could just scramble over and cross from one country to the other, if you knew the right path.

Phoebe and her gang of kids, ranging from twelve to fifteen, would go trampling the tall grass near the border on a "treasure hunt," or set up an "ambush fort" in the rocks. Phoebe occasionally caught sight of Molly and turned to wave, before running up the dusty hillside toward Zadie and Mark, who had just snuck over from California with canvas backpacks full of random games and junk. Sometimes Phoebe led an entire brigade of kids into the store, pouring cups of water or Molly's home-brewed ginger beer for everyone, and they would all pause and say "Hello, Ms. Carlton," before running outside again.

Mostly, the kids were just a raucous chorus as they chased each other with pea-guns. There were times when they stayed in the most overgrown area of trees and bracken way after sundown, until Molly was just about to message the other local parents via her Gidget, and then she'd glimpse a few specks of light emerging from the claws and twisted limbs. Molly always asked Phoebe what they did in that tiny stand of vegetation, which barely qualified as "the woods," and Phoebe always said "Nothing." They just hung out. Molly imagined those kids under the moonlight, blotted by heavy leaves, and they could be doing anything: drinking, taking drugs, playing kiss-and-tell games.

Even if Molly had wanted to keep tabs on her daughter, she couldn't leave the bookstore unattended. The bi-national design of the store required at least two people working at all times, one per register, and most of the peo-ple Molly hired only lasted a month or two and then had to run home be-cause their families were worried about all the latest hints of another war on the horizon. Every day, another batch of propaganda bubbled up on Molly's Gidget, from both sides, claiming that one country was a crushing theocracy or the other was a godless meat grinder. Meanwhile, you heard rumblings about both countries searching for the last precious dregs of water—sometimes actual rumblings, as California sent swarms of robots deep underground. Everybody was holding their breath.

Molly was working the front counter on the California side, trying as usual not to show any reaction to the people with weird tattoos or glowing silver threads flowing into their skulls. Everyone knew how eager Californians were to hack their own bodies and brains, from programmable birth control to brain implants that connected them to the Anoth Complex. Molly smiled, made small talk, recommended books based on her uncanny memory for what everybody had been buying—in short, she treated everyone like a customer, even the folks who noticed Molly's crucifix and clicked their tongues because obviously she'd been brainwashed into her faith.

A regular customer named Sander came in, looking for a rare book from the last days of the United States, about sustainable farming and animal consciousness, by a woman named Hope Dorrance. For some reason, nobody had ever uploaded this book of essays to the Share. Molly looked in the fancy computer and saw that they had one copy, but when Molly led Sander back to the shelf where it was supposed to be, the book was missing.

Sander stared at the space where *Souls on the Land* ought to be, and their pale, round face was full of lines. They had a single tattoo of a butterfly clad in gleaming armor, and the wires rained from the shaved back of their skull. They were some kind of engineer for the Anoth Complex.

"Huh," Molly said. "So, this is where it ought to be, but I better check if maybe we sold it over on the, uh, other side and somehow didn't log the sale." Sander nodded and followed Molly until they arrived in America. There, Molly squeezed past Mitch, who was working the register, and dug through a dozen scraps of paper until she found one. "Oh. Yeah. Well, darn."

They had sold their only copy of *Souls on the Land* to one of their most faithful customers on the America side: a gray-haired woman named Teri Wallace, who went to Molly's church. Teri was in the store right now, searching for a cookbook. Mitch had just seen her go past. Unfortunately, Teri hated Californians even more than most Americans did. And Sander was the sort of Californian that Teri especially did not appreciate.

"So it looks like we sold it a while back and we just didn't update our inventory, which, uh, does happen," Molly said.

"In essence, this was false advertising." Sander drew upward, with the usual Californian sense of affront the moment anything wasn't perfectly efficient. "You told me that the book was available, when in fact you should have known it wasn't."

Molly had already decided not to tell Sander who had bought the Hope Dorrance, but Teri came back clutching a book of killer salads just as Sander was in mid-rant about the ethics of retail communication. Sander happened to mention *Souls on the Land*, and Teri's ears pricked up.

"Oh, I just bought that book," Teri said.

Sander spun around, smiling, and said, "Oh. Pleased to meet you. I'm afraid that book you bought is one that had been promised to me. I don't suppose we could work out some kind of arrangement? Perhaps some system of needs-based allocation, because my need for this book is extremely great." Sander was already falling into the hyper-rational, insistent language of a Californian faced with a problem.

"Sorry," Teri said. "I bought it. I own it now. It's mine."

"But," Sander said. "There are many ways we could . . . I mean, you could loan it to me, and I could digitize it and return it to you in good condition."

"I don't want it in good condition. I want it in the condition it's in now."

"But—"

Molly could see this conversation was about three exchanges away from full-blown unpleasantries. Teri was going to insult Sander, either directly or by getting their pronoun wrong. Sander was going to call Teri stupid, either by implication or outright. Molly could see an easy solution: she could give Teri a bribe, a free book or blanket discount, in exchange for letting Sander borrow the Hope Dorrance so they could digitize it using special page-turning robots. But this wasn't going to be solved with reason. Not right now, anyway, with the two of them snarling at each other.

So Molly put on her biggest smile and said, "Sander. I just remembered, I had something extra special set aside for you, back in the psychology/philosophy annex. I've been meaning to give it to you, and it slipped my mind until just now. Come on, I'll show you." She tugged gently at Sander's arm and hustled them back into the warren of bookshelves. Sander kept grumbling about Teri's irrational selfishness, until they had left America.

Molly had no idea what the special book she'd been saving for Sander actually was—but she figured by the time they got through the Straits of Romance and all the switchbacks of biography, she'd think of something.

Phoebe was having a love triangle. Molly became aware of this in stages, by noticing how all the other kids were together, and by overhearing snippets of conversation (despite her best efforts not to eavesdrop).

Jonathan Brinkfort, the son of the minister at Molly's church, had started hanging around Phoebe with a hangdog expression like he'd lost one of those kiss-and-dare games and it had left him with gambling debts. Jon was a tall, quiet boy with a handsome square face, who mediated every tiny dispute among the neighborhood kids with a slow gravitas, but Molly had never before seen him lost for words. She had been hand-selling airship adventure books to Jon since he was little.

And then there was Zadie Kagwa, whose dad was a second-generation immigrant from Uganda with a taste for very old science fiction. Zadie had a fresh tattoo on one shoulder, of a dandelion with seedlings fanning out into the wind, and one string of fiber-optic pearls coming out of her locs. Zadie's own taste in books roamed from science and math to radical politics to girls-at-horse-camp novels. Zadie whispered to Phoebe and brought tiny presents from California, like these weird candies with chili peppers in them.

Molly could just imagine the conversations she'd hear in church if her daughter got into an unnatural relationship with a girl—from *California* no less—instead of dating a nice American boy who happened to be Canon Brinkfort's son.

But Phoebe didn't seem to be inclined to choose one or the other. She accepted Jon's stammered compliments with the same shy smile she greeted Zadie's gifts with.

Molly took Phoebe on a day trip into California, where they got their passports stamped with a one-day entry permit, and they climbed into Molly's old three-wheel Dancer. They drove past wind farms and military installations, past signs for the latest Anoth cloud-brain schemes, until they stopped at a place that sold milkshakes so thick you lost the skin on the sides of your mouth just trying to unclog the straw.

Phoebe was in silent mode, hugging herself and cocooning inside her big polyfiber jacket when she wasn't slurping her milkshake. Molly tried to make conversation, talking about who had been buying what sort of books lately and what you could figure out about international relations from Sharon

Wong's sudden interest in bird-watching. Phoebe just shrugged, like maybe Molly should just read the news instead. As if Molly hadn't tried making sense of the news already.

Then Phoebe started telling Molly about some fantasy novel. Seven princesses have powers of growth and decay, but some of the princesses can only use their growth powers if the other princesses are using their decay powers. Whoever grows a hedge tall enough to keep out the army of gnome-trolls will become the heir to the Blue Throne, but the princesses don't even realize at first that their powers are all different, like they grow different kinds of things. There are a bunch of princes and court ladies who are all in love with different princesses, but nobody can be with the person they want to be with.

This novel sounded more and more complicated, and Molly didn't remember ever seeing it in her store, until she realized: Phoebe wasn't describing a book she had read. This was a book that Phoebe was writing, somewhere, on one of the old computers that Molly had left in some storage space. Molly hadn't even known Phoebe was a writer.

"How does it end?" Molly said.

"I don't know." Phoebe poked at the last soup of her milkshake. "I guess they have to use their powers together to build the hedge they're supposed to build, instead of competing. The hard part is gonna be all the princesses ending up with the right person. And, uh, making sure nobody feels left out, or like they couldn't find their place in this kingdom."

Molly nodded, and then tried to think of how to respond to what she was pretty sure her daughter was actually talking about. "Well, you know that nobody has to ever hurry to find out who they're supposed to love, or where they're going to fit in. Those things sometimes take time, and it's okay not to know the answers right away. You know?"

"Yeah, I guess." Phoebe pushed her empty glass away and looked out the window. Molly waited for her to say something else, but eventually realized the conversation had ended. Teenagers.

Molly had opened the First and Last Page when Phoebe was still a baby, back when the border had felt more porous. Both governments were trying to create a Special Trade Zone, and you could get a special transnational business license. Everyone had seemed overjoyed to have a bookstore within driving distance, and Molly had lost count of how many people thanked her just for being here. A lot of her used books had come from estate sales, but there had been a surprising flood of donations, too.

Molly had wanted Phoebe to be within easy reach of California if America ever started seriously following through on its threats to enforce all of its broadly written laws against immorality. But more than that, Phoebe deserved to be surrounded by all the stories, and every type of person, and all of the ways of looking at life. Plus, it had seemed like a shrewd business move to be in two countries at once, a way to double the store's potential market.

For a while, the border had also played host to a bar, a burger joint, and a clothing store, and Molly had barely noticed when those places had closed, one by one. The First and Last Page was different, she'd figured, because nobody ever gets drunk on books and starts a brawl.

Matthew limped into the American entrance during a lull in business, and Molly took in his torn pants leg and dirty hands, plus the dried-out salt trails along his brown face. She had seen plenty others in similar condition, and didn't even blink. She didn't even need to see the brand on Matthew's neck, which looked like a pair of broken wings and declared him to be a bonded peon and the responsibility of the Greater Appalachian Penal Authority and the Glad Corporation. She just nodded and helped him inside the store before anyone else noticed or started asking too many questions.

"I'm looking for a self-help book," Matthew said, which was what a lot of them said. Someone, somewhere, had told them this was a code phrase that would let Molly know what they needed. In fact, there was no code phrase, nor was one needed.

The border between America and California was unguarded in thousands of other places besides Molly's store, including that big rocky hill that Zadie and the other California kids climbed over when they came to play with the American kids. There was just too much empty space to waste time patrolling, much less putting up fences or sensors. You couldn't eat lunch in California without twenty computers checking your identity, anyway. Matthew and the others chose to cross through Molly's store because books meant civilization, or maybe the store's name seemed to promise a kind of safe passage: the first page leading gracefully to the last.

Molly did what she always did with these refugees. She helped Matthew find the quickest route from romance to philosophy to history, and then on to California. She gave him some clean clothes out of a donation box, which she always told people was going to a shelter somewhere, and what information she had about resources and contacts. She let him clean up as much as he could, in the restroom.

Matthew was still limping as he made his way through the store in his brand-new corduroys and baggy argyle sweater. Molly offered to have a look at his leg, but he shook his head. "Old injury." She dug in the first aid kit and gave him a bottle of painkillers. Matthew kept looking around in all directions, as if there could be hidden cameras (there weren't), and he took a jerky step back when Molly told him to hold on a moment, when he was already in California.

"What? Is something wrong? What's wrong?"

"Nothing. Nothing's wrong. Just thinking." Molly always gave refugees a free book, something to keep them company on whatever journey they had ahead. She didn't want to just choose at random, so she gazed at Matthew for a moment in the dim amber light from the wall sconces in the history section. "What sort of books do you like? Besides self-help, I mean."

"I don't have any money, I'm sorry," Matthew said, but Molly waved it off.

"You don't need any. I just wanted to give you something to take with you."

Phoebe came up just then and saw at a glance what was going on. "Hey, Mom. Hi, I'm Phoebe."

"This is Matthew," Molly said. "I wanted to give him a book to take with him."

"They didn't exactly let us have books," Matthew said. "There was a small library, but library use was a privilege, and you needed more than 'good behavior.' For that kind of privilege, you would need to . . ." He glanced at Phoebe, because whatever he'd been about to say wasn't suitable for a child's ears. "They did let us read the Bible, and I practically memorized some parts of it."

Molly and Phoebe looked at each other while Matthew fidgeted, and then Phoebe said, "Father Brown mysteries."

"Are you sure?" Molly said.

Phoebe nodded. She ran, fast as a deer, and came back with a tiny paperback of G .K. Chesterton that would fit in the pockets of the donated corduroys. "I used to love this book," she told Matthew. "It's about God, and religion, but it's really just a great bunch of detective stories, where the key always turns out to be making sense of people."

Matthew kept thanking Molly and Phoebe in a kind of guttural undertone, like a compulsive cough, until they waved it off. When they got to the California storefront, they kept Matthew out of sight until they were sure the coast was clear, then they hustled him out and showed him the clearest path, which followed the main road but stayed under cover. He waved once as he sprinted across the blunt strip of gravel parking lot, but other than that, he didn't look back.

The president of California wished the president of America a good spring solstice instead of "Happy Easter," and the president of America called a news conference to discuss this unforgivable insult. America's secretary of morality, Wallace Dawson, called California's gay attorney general an offensive term. California moved some troops up to the border and performed some "routine exercises," so close that Molly could hear the cackle of guns shooting blanks all night. (She hoped they were blanks.) America sent some fighter craft and UAVs along the border, sundering the air. California's swarms of water-divining robots had managed to tap the huge deposits located deep inside the rocky mantle, but both America and California claimed that this water was located under their respective territories.

Molly's Gidget kept flaring up with "news" that was laced with propaganda, as if the people in charge on both sides were trying to get everyone fired up. The American media kept running stories about a pregnant woman in New Sacramento who lost her baby because her family planning implant had a buggy firmware update, plus graphic stories about urban gang violence, drugs, prostitution, and so on. California's media outlets, meanwhile, worked overtime to remind people about the teenage rape victims in America who were locked up and straitjacketed to make sure they gave birth, and the peaceful protesters who were gassed and beaten by police.

Almost every day lately, Americans came in looking for a couple books that Molly didn't have. Molly had decided to go ahead and stock *Why We Stand*, a book-length manifesto about individualism and Christian values that stopped just short of accusing Californians of bestiality and cannibalism. But *Why We Stand* was unavailable, because they'd gone back for another print run. Meanwhile, though, Molly outright refused to sell *Our People*, a book that included offensive caricatures of the Black and Brown people who mostly clustered in the dense cities out West, like New Sacramento, plus "scientific" theories about their relative intelligence.

People kept coming in and asking for *Our People*, and at this point Molly was pretty sure they knew she didn't have it and were just trying to make a point.

"It's just, some folks feel as though you think you're better than the rest of us," said Norma Verlaine, whose blonde, loudmouthed daughter Samantha was part of Phoebe's friend group. "The way you try to play both sides against the middle, perching here in your fancy chair, deciding what's fit to read and what's not fit to read. You're literally sitting in judgment over us."

"I'm not judging anyone," Molly said. "Norma, I live here too. I go to Holy Fire every Sunday, same as you. I'm not judging."

"You say that. But then you refuse to sell *Our People*."

"Yes, because that book is racist."

Norma turned to Reggie Watts, who had two kids in Phoebe's little gang: Tobias and Suz. "Did you hear that, Reggie? She just called me a racist."

"I didn't call you anything. I was talking about a book."

"Can't separate books from people," said Reggie, who worked at the big power plant thirty miles east. He furrowed his huge brow and stooped a little as he spoke. "And you can't separate people from the places they come from."

"Time may come, you have to choose a country once and for all," Norma said. Then she and Reggie walked out while the glow of righteousness still clung.

Molly felt something go all the way through her. Like the cartoon "bookworm" chewing through a book, from when Molly was a child. There was a worm drilling a neat round hole in Molly, rendering some portion of her illegible.

Molly was just going through some sales slips, because ever since that dustup with Sander and Teri she was paranoid about American sales not getting recorded in the computer, when the earthquake began. A few books fell on the floor as the ground shuddered, but most of the books were packed too tight to dislodge right away. The grinding, screeching sound from the vibrations underground made Molly's ears throb. When she could get her balance back, she looked at her Gidget, and at first she saw no information. Then there was a news alert: California had laid claim to the water deposits deep underground, and was proceeding to extract them as quickly as possible. America was calling this an act of war.

Phoebe was out with her friends as usual. Molly sent a message on her

Gidget, and then went outside to yell Phoebe's name into the wind. The crushing sound underground kept going, but either Molly had gotten used to it or it was moving away from here.

"Phoebe?"

Molly walked the two-lane roads, glancing every couple minutes at her Gidget to see if Phoebe had replied yet. She told herself that she wouldn't freak out if she could find her daughter before the sun went down, and then the sun did go down and she had to invent a new deadline for panic.

Something huge and powerful opened its mouth and roared nearby, and Molly swayed on her feet. The hot breath of a large carnivore blew against her face while her ears filled with sound. She realized after a moment that three Stalker-class aircraft had flown very low overhead, in stealth mode, so you could hear and feel—but not see—them.

"Phoebe?" Molly called out, as she reached the end of the long main street with the one grocery store and the diner. "Phoebe, are you out here?" The street led to a big field of corn on one side and to the diversion road leading to the freeway on the other. The corn rustled from the aftershakes of the flyover. Out on the road, Molly heard wheels tearing at loose dirt and tiny rocks and saw the slash of headlights in motion.

"Mom!" Phoebe came running down the hill from the tiny forest area, followed by Jon Brinkfort, Zadie Kagwa, and a few other kids. "Thank god you're okay."

Molly started to say that Phoebe should get everyone inside the bookstore, because the reading room was the closest thing to a bomb shelter for miles.

But a new round of flashes and earsplitting noises erupted, and then Molly looked past the edge of town and saw a phalanx of shadows, three times as tall as the tallest building, moving forward.

Molly had never seen a mecha before, but she recognized these metal giants, with the bulky actuators on their legs and rocket launchers on their arms. They looked like a crude caricature of bodybuilders, pumped up inside their titanium alloy casings. The two viewports on their heads, along with the slash of red paint, gave them the appearance of scowling down at all the people underfoot. Covered with armaments all over their absurdly huge bodies, they were heading into town on their way to the border.

"Everybody into the bookstore!" Phoebe yelled. Zadie Kagwa was messaging her father on some fancy tablet, and other kids were trying to contact their parents too, but then everyone hustled inside the First and Last Page.

. . .

People came looking for their kids, or for a place to shelter from the fighting. Some people had been browsing in the store when the hostilities broke out, or had been driving nearby. Molly let everyone in, until the American mechas were actually engaging a squadron of California centurions, which were almost exactly identical to the other metal giants except that their onboard systems were connected to the Anoth Complex. Both sides fired their rocket launchers, releasing bright orange trails that turned everything the same shade of amber. Molly watched as an American mecha lunged forward with its huge metal fist and connected with the side of a centurion, sending shards of metal spraying out like the dandelion seeds on Zadie's tattoo.

Then Molly got inside and sealed up the reading room with a satisfying *clunk*. "I paid my contractor extra," she told all the people who crouched inside. "These walls are like a bank vault. This is the safest place for you all to be." There was a toilet just outside the solid metal door and down the hall, with a somewhat higher risk of getting blown up while you peed.

Alongside Molly and Phoebe, there were a dozen people stuck in the reading room. There were Zadie and her father, Jay; Norma Verlaine and her daughter Samantha; Reggie Watts and his two kids; Jon Brinkfort; Sander, the engineer who'd come looking for *Souls on the Land*; Teri, the woman who actually owned *Souls on the Land*; Marcy, a twelve-year-old kid from California; and Marcy's mother, Petrice.

They all sat in this two-meter by three-meter room with two couches that could hold five people between them, plus bookshelves from floor to ceiling. Every time someone started to relax, there was another quake, and the sounds grew louder and more ferocious. Nobody could get a signal on any of their devices or implants, either because of the reinforced walls or because someone was actively jamming communications. The room jerked back and forth, and the books quivered but did not fall out of their sconces.

Molly looked over at Jay Kagwa, sitting with his arm around his daughter, and had a sudden flash of remembering a time, several years ago, when Phoebe had campaigned for Molly to go out on a date with Jay. Phoebe and Zadie were already friends, though neither of them was interested in romance yet, and Phoebe had decided that the stout, well-built architect would be a good match for her mother. Partly based on the wry smiles the two of them always exchanged when they compared notes about being single parents of rambunctious daughters. Plus both Molly and Phoebe were American citizens, and it wouldn't hurt to have dual citizenship. But Molly never had time for romance. Now, of course, Zadie was still giving sidelong glances to Phoebe, who had never chosen between Zadie and Jon, and probably never would.

Jay had finished hugging his daughter, and also yelling at her for getting herself stuck in the middle of all this, and all the other parents, including Molly, had had a good scowl at their own kids as well. "I wish we were safe at home," Jay Kagwa told his daughter in a whisper, "instead of being trapped here with these people."

"What exactly do you mean by 'these people'?" Norma Verlaine demanded from the other end of the room.

Another tremor, more raucous noise.

"Leave it, Norma," said Reggie. "I'm sure he didn't mean anything by it."

"No, I want to know," Norma said. "What makes us 'these people' when we're just trying to live our lives and raise our kids? And meanwhile, your country decided that everything from abortion to unnatural sexual relationships to cutting open people's brains and shoving in a bunch of nanotech garbage was A-OK. So I think the real question is, Why do I have to put up with people like you?"

"I've seen firsthand what your country does to people like me," Jay Kagwa said in a quiet voice.

"As if Californians aren't stealing children from America, at a rapidly increasing rate, to turn into sex slaves or prostitutes. I have to keep one eye on my Samantha here all the time."

"*Mom*," Samantha said, and that one syllable meant everything from "Please stop embarrassing me in front of my friends" to "You can't protect me forever."

"We're not stealing children," said Sander. "That was a ridiculous, made-up story."

"You steal everything. You're stealing our water right now," said Teri. "You don't believe that anything is sacred, so it's all up for grabs as far as you're concerned."

"We're not the ones who put half a million people into labor camps," said Petrice, a quiet, green-haired older woman who mostly bought books about gardening and Italian history.

"Oh no, not at all, California just turns millions of people into cybernetic slaves of the Anoth Complex," said Reggie. "That's much more humane."

"Hey, everybody just calm down," Molly said.

"Says the woman who tries to serve two masters," Norma said, rounding on Molly and poking her finger.

The other six adults in the room kept shouting at each other until the tiny reading room seemed almost as loud as the battle outside. The room shook, the children huddled together, and the adults just raised their voices to be heard over the nearly constant percussion. Everybody knew the dispute was purely about water rights, but months of terrifying stories had trained them to think of it instead as a righteous war over sacred principles. Our children, our freedom. Everyone shrieked at one another, and Molly fell into the corner near a stack of theology, covering her ears and looking across the room at Phoebe, who was crouched with Jon and Zadie. Phoebe's nostrils flared, and she stiffened as if she were about to run a long sprint, but all of her attention was focused on comforting her two friends. Molly felt flushed with a sharper version of her old fear that she'd been a Bad Mother.

Then Phoebe stood up and yelled, *"Everybody stop!"*

Everybody stopped yelling. Some shining miracle. They all stopped and turned to look at Phoebe, who was holding hands with both Jon and Zadie. Even with the racket outside, this room suddenly felt eerily, almost ceremonially, quiet.

"You should be ashamed," Phoebe said. "We're all scared and tired and hungry, and we're probably stuck here all night, and you're acting like babies. This is not a place for yelling. It's a bookstore. It's a place for quiet browsing and reading, and if you can't be quiet, you're going to have to leave. I don't care what you think you know about each other. You can darn well be polite, because . . . because . . ." Phoebe turned to Zadie and Jon, and then gazed at her mom. "Because we're about to start the first meeting of our book club."

Book club? Everybody looked at each other in confusion, like they'd skipped a track.

Molly stood up and clapped her hands. "That's right. Book club meeting in ten minutes. Attendance is mandatory."

The noise from outside wasn't just louder than ever, but more bifurcated. One channel of noise came from directly underneath their feet, as if some desperate struggle for control over the water reserves was happening deep under the Earth's crust, between teams of robots or tunneling war machines, and the very notion of solid ground seemed obsolete. Over their heads, a struggle between aircraft, or metal titans, or perhaps a sky full of whirring autonomous craft, which were slinging fire back and forth until the sky turned red. Trapped inside this room, with no information other than words on brittle spines, everybody found themselves inventing horrors out of every stray noise.

Molly and Phoebe huddled in the corner, trying to figure out a book that everyone in the room would be familiar enough with, but that they could have a real conversation about. Molly had actually hosted a few book clubs at the store over the years, and at least a few of the people now sheltering in the reading room had attended, but she couldn't remember what any of those clubs had read. Molly kept pushing for this one literary coming-of-age book that had made a splash around the time of the Sundering, or maybe some good old Jane Austen, but Phoebe vetoed both of those ideas.

"We need to distract them"—Phoebe jerked her thumb at the mass of people in the reading room behind them—"not bore them to death."

In the end, the first and maybe only book selection of the Great International Book Club had to be *Million in One*, a fantasy adventure about a teenage boy named Norman who rescues a million souls that an evil wizard has trapped in a globe, and accidentally absorbs them into his own body. So Norman has a million souls in one body and they give him magical powers, but he can also feel all of their unfinished business, their longing to be free. And Norman has to fight the wizard, who wants all those souls back, plus Norman's. This book was supposed to be for teenagers, but Molly knew for a fact that every single adult had read it as well, on both sides of the border.

"Well, of course, the premise suffers from huge inconsistencies," Sander complained. "It's established early on that souls can be stored and transferred, and yet Norman can't simply unload his extra souls into the nearest vessel."

"They explained that in book two." Zadie only rolled her eyes a little. "The souls are locked inside Norman. Plus the wizard would get them if he put them anywhere else."

"What I don't get is why his so-called teacher, Maxine, doesn't just tell him the whole story about the Pendragon Exchange right away," Reggie said.

"Um, excuse me. No spoilers," Jon muttered. "Not everybody has read book five already."

"Can we talk about the themes of the book instead of just nitpicking?" Teri crossed her arms. "Like, the whole notion that Norman can contain all these multitudes but still just be Norman is fascinating to me."

"It's a kind of Cartesian dualism on speed," Jay Kagwa offered.

"Well, sort of. I mean, if you read Descartes, he says—"

"The real point is that the wizard wants to control all those souls, but—"

"Can we just talk about the singing ax? What even was that?"

They argued peacefully until around three in the morning, when everyone finally wore themselves out. The sky and the ground still rumbled occasionally, but either everyone had gotten used to it or the most violent shatterings were over. Molly looked around at the dozen or so people slowly falling asleep, leaning on each other, all around the room, and felt a desperate protectiveness. Not just for the people, because of course she didn't want any harm to come to any of them, or even for this building that she'd given the better part of her adult life to sustaining, but for something more abstract and confusing. What were the chances that the First and Last Page could continue to exist much longer, especially with one foot in either country? How would they even know if tonight was just another skirmish or the beginning of a proper war, something that could carry on for months and reduce both countries to fine ash?

Phoebe left Jon and Zadie behind and came over to sit with her mother, with her mouth still twisted upward in satisfaction. Phoebe was clutching a book in one hand, and Molly didn't recognize the gold-embossed cover at first, but then she saw the spine. This was a small hardcover of fairy tales, illustrated with watercolors, that Molly had given to her daughter for her twelfth birthday and had never seen again. She'd assumed Phoebe had glanced at it for an hour and tossed it somewhere. Phoebe leaned against her mother, half reading and half gazing at the pictures, the blue streaks of sky and dark swipes of castles and mountains, until she fell asleep on Molly's shoulder. Phoebe looked younger in her sleep, and Molly looked down at her until she, too, dozed off and the entire bookstore was at rest. Every once in a while, the roaring and convulsions of the battle woke Molly, but then at last they subsided and all Molly heard was the slow, sustained breathing of people inside a cocoon of books.

One thing has brought me not just solace but actual delight, during the ugliest of times: the flourishing of the trans/non-binary community. I've seen more and more people transitioning and coming out—and where there used to be just a handful of us writing speculative fiction, there are now many incredible voices. (Just check out the Transcendent series of anthologies, or *Meanwhile, Elsewhere.*) There's never been a better moment for speculative fiction about gender-nonconforming people, and I've felt so privileged to be able to add a few droplets to this wave.

Meanwhile, I'm also a huge admirer of Bikes in Space, a series of anthologies of "feminist bicycle science fiction." So when editor Lydia Rogue asked me to contribute to a special trans/nb-focused edition, I jumped at the chance. "The Visitmothers" was ridiculously fun to write, and I was working on it at the exact same time as a short She-Hulk story I wrote for Marvel Comics. I think a little bit of She-Hulk's fierceness spilled over into this tale.

THE VISITMOTHERS

Cait walks her creaky old five-speed bicycle up the fumbly narrow path on the steep grade of Toothache Hill. At the top she says the nonsense words you're supposed to say, somewhere between a prayer and a petition and an invocation, that will make the Visitmothers show up. Nothing happens. (Except the wind gets stronger and colder, and two middle-aged people give up on foraging for stray Pokémon and trudge down into the curvy, crinkly streets of the city.) Cait hugs herself and fidgets and says the whole thing again, trying not to shiver or bite into the words.

The sun goes down. Cait fumbles in the old knapsack bungee-corded to the back of the bicycle for her hoodie, which is fuzzy on the inside and almost reaches bathrobe levels of comfort despite being so old that the logo on the breast is illegible. A smattering of stars shows through the city light pollution, and yet the moon glows so bright it almost throbs, with its surface visible in crisp detail.

The bike wobbles in the wind, so Cait leans it more carefully against a rock. This Raleigh Chopper has been Cait's constant accompaniment ever since her sixteenth birthday, and she's used to seeing the world from atop its seat. She has decorated its spokes with rainbow colors, and streamers come out of its handlebars, and the seat is covered with a leopard-print fabric.

Cait is going to have a scary ride home on these streets. City darkness, but still . . . darkness. She should leave right now, but she's come all this way, memorized the words, psyched herself up. She doesn't want to go home with nothing. Not because of her iron willpower or determination or whatever, but because she cannot imagine what she will do if this doesn't work. She doesn't have any backup plan.

So she sits on the crest of Toothache Hill, checking the time on her phone constantly, until she risks draining the battery. She sings the entire *Purple Rain* album to herself from memory. The shouts of drunk people fill the streets, then die down. The wind gets colder.

Finally, somewhere between one and two in the morning, a darkness gathers at the top of Toothache Hill. Not the dark of night, but more like a blindfold made of velvet. Cait's heart amps up. The Visitmothers have arrived at last.

It's just like everybody says, in the stories Cait has heard late at night after too many drinks at the Too Queer Karaoke Night, or in certain message board chats. Four Visitmothers descend from the sky, but also seem to glide sideways, as if they were on a conveyor belt coming from someplace off to the side of the hill. They each flex five wings (or perhaps they're legs, or beaks, or something else) from their slender concave bodies, and sometimes the folds and creases on their bodies appear like faces. Pareidolia, probably.

You brought us to visit you, says the Visitmother closest to Cait. *You want us to visit change upon you, to answer a question, or to predict. Those are the three visitations that humans desire. Which?*

The Visitmothers have been appearing for a couple years now, and they've taught a few people the words that would invite them to high-up, isolated places. They only answer the occasional invitation, and you have to be very careful what you ask them—or what you ask them *for.* They're fairies. Or aliens. Or alien fairies. Nobody really knows. But they know secrets, and their predictions come true. If you go with them, they will change you according to your desires. You have ask with precision, because they sometimes misunderstand the speech of humans.

Cait hesitates. Now that it's real, she can't even make a sound. Then she gathers her breath and blurts out words that she didn't practice nearly as much as that invocation. "I want to be changed. I feel so alone. I can't afford facial feminization surgery or any of the other things I need, and I never have anybody around who sees me for my true self. I want to be re-shaped. Transformed. Give me wings and lasers. Give me extra knowledge, or understanding, or cleverness. Make me so beautiful that people have to catch their breath."

Then Cait just shakes her head, and speaks from her heart. "The real truth is, I just don't want to be alone anymore. That's all I really want. Everything else is just . . . just a means to an end." Speaking the truth feels too heavy to brace against, but a moment later, she feels light and kind of empty. And cold, again.

The Visitmothers seem to discuss among themselves for a moment. *As you ask, it shall be done,* the one in front says. Wings/legs/beaks flexing and bobbing.

And then . . . the Visitmothers gently take hold of Cait's wobbly old Raleigh five-speed and pull it inside their black velvet interspace. The knapsack tumbles onto the rocky grass.

A moment later, the Visitmothers and Cait's bicycle are gone.

Cait is left alone on the top of Toothache Hill, cursing herself and the Visitmothers. Mostly herself, though. She worked so hard, she prepared, she coached herself, she studied other people's accounts of their own visits, and . . . she screwed up. They didn't understand. She spoke from her heart, she's sure about that, but not clear enough. She had one chance to make everything different. Now she's as alone as she ever was—except that now she's lost the one thing that always kept her company.

Long walk home. Cold gross streets, sloping upward and downward. Cait starts to wheeze, which gets in the way of blaming herself in a trudgy undertone.

When Cait gets home, she can't sleep for crying. At least tomorrow is Sunday, so she doesn't have to go to work. She sits on her futon and hugs herself and keeps pouring hot water on the same orange spice tea bag over and over, until it just tastes like slightly bitter hot water. She glances at the mirror and remembers the three people who told her she was beautiful in the past month: Luke, Clarissa, Boz. She wishes she could believe them.

She wishes she didn't feel so alone.

Cait finally sets down the lukewarm mug and falls asleep. Her dreams suck, but she doesn't remember them.

She's awoken by a tapping on her apartment door—not like a person knocking but like a backbeat, pounding over and over at slightly syncopated intervals. She goes to the door and doesn't see anything through the fish-eye. She's about to go back to bed, but the tapping keeps going.

At last, Cait, opens her door. And . . . it's her bike. Sort of.

Her bike has wings. And lasers. It's so beautiful, she can't even breathe for a moment. Once she can breathe, she can't see, because tears are stinging her eyes. She tries to speak, and can't.

Her bicycle speaks, instead. "Hey, I'm back," it says. "I'm still the same bicycle that carried you everywhere, your whole adult life. Except now, I can fly. Oh, and I understand the deep workings of the world. Thank you for doing this for me. I have all these thoughts going through my head, it's amazing. Yesterday I didn't even have any thoughts at all, or a head for that matter. There's so much I want to tell you about, but it'll take the rest of our lives to explain all of it. For now, I just want to feel your strong legs moving my pedals again."

So Cait climbs on her bike, still pouring tears, and the two of them race down the stairs of her apartment building, half rolling and half flying. Once they get outside, the bike flaps its wings—she's going to have to find out what pronoun the bike prefers—and they take to the air.

A moment later, they're soaring over the rooftops as the city wakes up underneath them. They race away from the city, over the river and the mountains and the irregular polygons of farmland. The whole time, Cait's bicycle is whispering to her: things from her childhood that never made sense to her before, the hiding places of love letters people wrote a hundred years ago.

"You need a name," Cait says. "What do you want to be called?"

"I'm so new. I've only had words for a short time. Can you choose a name for now? I can always change it later."

Cait thinks for a moment and then decides her bicycle will be called Brave.

"The most important thing you need to remember always," says Brave, "is that I can see you for your true self, and I'll always remind you. And I promise you'll never be alone again."

They fly so far and so fast that the sun keeps rising, over and over.

ACKNOWLEDGMENTS

I can't possibly list everybody who helped shape these stories, let alone everyone who shaped me as a short fiction writer—that would be a whole book in itself. So I apologize to everyone I've left out of this note.

Patrick Nielsen Hayden deserves special thanks and appreciation. He somehow plucked one of my stories out of the slush pile at Tor.com and published several others, essentially putting an end to my long era of toiling in obscurity. And this book wouldn't exist if Patrick hadn't been willing to take a chance on that riskiest of ventures, a single-author story collection. I also owe a huge debt to Miriam Weinberg, Irene Gallo, Sanaa Ali-Virani, Molly McGhee, Jessica Katz, Emily Goldman, and many other people at Tor and Tor.com. Thanks also to the copyeditor of this book, Todd Manza.

My agent, Russ Galen, championed the idea of a honking big book of my stories, and somehow convinced everyone else that it would work. Russ also encouraged me to showcase the full range of my writing here, rather than playing it safe and sticking to stories that had appeared in "year's best" SF anthologies. My foreign-rights agent, Heather Baror-Shapiro, has helped these stories find a new lease on life in many countries and languages. And Nate Miller, my manager, has been relentless in showing the stories in this book to Hollywood folks, leading to some conversations that made me see these works in a whole new way.

Bill Schafer at Subterranean Press generously allowed me to include "Rock Manning Goes for Broke" in this book after it had already appeared as a gorgeous standalone signed hardcover (which is still available!).

I'm absurdly grateful to LeVar Burton for featuring "As Good as New" in a special live version of *LeVar Burton Reads*, and for being such a gracious and reassuring host.

And I owe a huge debt to the editors who published these stories, including (deep breath): Patrick Nielsen Hayden, Miriam Weinberg, John Joseph Adams, Sheila Williams, Elizabeth McKenzie, Catherine Segurson, Kelly Link, Gavin Grant, Victor LaValle, Daniel H. Wilson, Hugh Howey, Junot

Diaz, Eileen Gunn, Lynn M. Thomas, Michael Damian Thomas, Gravity Goldberg, Ken Keegan, Rusty Morrison, Jonathan Strahan, Laura Cogan, Oscar Villalon, Bill Schafer, and Lydia Rogue.

Gordon Dahlquist answered my playwriting questions for "As Good as New." Dr. Dave Goldberg helped me invent time travel for "The Time Travel Club." Elsa Sjunneson-Henry sensitivity-read "Rock Manning Goes for Broke." Many people gave me feedback on "Don't Press Charges and I Won't Sue," including Liz Henry, Danny Lavery, Anna Dickinson, Miki Habryn, Gwen Smith, and Coda Gardner. Claire Light gave me indispensable critiques of many of my stories. Also, I was lucky enough to be an instructor at Clarion West, where I'm one hundred percent sure I learned way more than any of my students did. I belonged to a few writing groups that helped me get less horrendous at short fiction, including the Revisionaries of Raleigh and the LexiCats.

As I mentioned in the introduction, I would never have survived my early years of sending stories into the void without D. G. K. Goldberg, who taught me so much and showed me how to turn a bizarre story seed into a whole bed of strange flowers. I miss her every day.

And finally, my partner, Annalee Newitz, has supported and heartened me throughout all my years of ill-advised writings. They've read early drafts of more of my stories than I can count, but also our conversations and collaborations over the years have opened my mind and helped me to think about storytelling and imagination in whole new ways. My faith in human nature and our ability to survive endless cycles of ruin comes in large part from being exposed to Annalee's panoramic vision.